AMERICAN FICTION

AMERICAN FICTION

volume 11

editor Kristen J. Tsetsi

assistant editors Bayard Godsave · Bruce Pratt

finalist judge Clint McCown

The publication of *American Fiction*, Vol. 11 is made possible by the generous
support of the Jerome Foundation and other contributors to New Rivers Press.

New Rivers Press is a nonprofit literary press
associated with Minnesota State University Moorhead.

Wayne Gudmundson, Director
Alan Davis, Senior Editor
Donna Carlson, Suzzanne Kelley, Managing Editors
Thom Tammaro, Poetry Editor
Kevin Carollo, MVP Poetry Coordinator
Liz Severn, MVP Fiction Coordinator
Publishing Interns: Samantha Jones, Nancy Swan, Sean Templeton, Amber Olds
American Fiction, Vol. 11 Book Team: Caitlin Fox, Allison Hesford, Jenny Hilleren,
      Samantha Jones, Derrick Paulson
Editorial Interns: Heather Ehrichs Angell, Melissa Barnes, Devin Berglund,Noah Bicknell,
      LeAnn Bjerken, Caitlin Fox, Allison Hesford, Jenny Hilleren, Nazrin Jahangirova,
      Samantha Jones, Tiegen Kosiak, Julia Larson, Andrew Olson, Derrick Paulson
Design Interns: Heather Donarski, Morgan Hoyt, Bryan Murphy, Mandee Nyhus
Allen Sheets, Art Director
Fran Zimmerman, Business Manager

Printed in the United States of America

New Rivers Press
c/o MSUM
1104 7th Avenue South
Moorhead, MN 56563
www.newriverspress.com

contents

introduction
Clint McCown

introduction

As creative writing programs have proliferated over the past three decades, the Chicken Littles of the world have warned us that the literary sky is falling. The fear, often voiced with academic certainty, has been that graduates of these programs are being homogenized into a bland similarity, that we are now producing generations of writers who know only how to write a "workshop story."

As if there were such a thing.

In any case, the doomsayers can relax. This collection provides ample proof that American writers are in no danger of homogenization, that no watering-down process has diluted the literary scene. I have no idea which of these writers may have come through training programs, which of them may teach in such programs, and which of them may never have had a workshop in their lives. Whatever route these individual writers took, the end product is what matters, and these stories all testify to the diversity and depth of artistry alive in our culture, each story a robust affirmation of the good health of contemporary fiction. The range in style, tone, form, subject matter, and world view is striking. Every writer here represented is a strong and distinctive talent.

That, of course, has made the task of judging these works extremely difficult, perhaps even arbitrary. While it may be simple to select the best apple from a barrel of apples, the process is more daunting when one is faced with comparing a first-rate apple to a first-rate orange, and a first-rate pomegranate, and a first-rate kumquat. Taste invariably enters into the decision.

For me, the best stories are those which appeal to both the head and the heart. I most appreciate fiction that provokes me to feel for a character's dilemma and to think about what that dilemma might say about us all. Many stories succeed in one of these tasks; few succeed in both.

I also look for originality, plausibility within the invented universe, and a seamless creation of the fabric of reality on the moment-by-moment, microcosmic level. I look for a sustaining pace and the building up of momentum.

The story which for me best satisfies these demands is Andrew C. Gottlieb's "Stickmen." Gottlieb created a funny and moving portrait of a college student whose father is dying, and who distracts himself from this central tragedy by submitting fake resumes to job recruiters and bluffing his way through interviews. His penchant for doodling stick figures to express his moods and feelings serves as the perfect objective correlative in this tale of a young man reluctant to leave his childhood behind. The characters are fleshed out convincingly, the relationships are real and often poignant, and at times the language rises to a natural poeticism. Gottlieb is a writer of keen insight and depth.

Not far behind is "Voyeuse" by Cary Groner. I was struck by the originality of this tale in which a wife buys a camera-equipped helmet for her bicycle-riding husband so she can share the experience of his cross-country treks. Through the camera, she witnesses his fatal accident, and during a long emotional recovery period, she discovers that a stranger has found the helmet and is wearing it around town. The widow becomes obsessed with following the daily routines of this stranger through the Web-linked minicam. This is a fine portrait of grief and recovery.

My third choice was "Souvenirs" by Aimee Loiselle, an engaging first-person account with an unreliable narrator. The story revolves around a wife's attempt to pull herself and her war-veteran husband together enough to make a good impression in family court so they can retain custody of their children. Both parents are emotional train wrecks with serious prescription drug dependencies—brought on by a cascade of misfortune starting with the husband's being wounded in Iraq. This is a riveting account of a family caught in a downward spiral, made all the more powerful by the narrator's complete inability to recognize that anything is seriously wrong.

Among the many other stories deserving of accolades, three stand out. "Twenty Tales of Natural Disaster" by Helen Phillips is a formal experiment that gives us twenty vignettes loosely tied to destructive natural forces. The creative and poetic leaps in this collage were impressive. "Piano" by Terry Roueche generates a quiet power as tensions build between two estranged brothers as they clean out their dead mother's house. Caught between the two is the girlfriend who wishes to shift her allegiance between brothers. This is an insightful examination of stunted love and the legacy of parental abuse. And finally, "Section" by Gregory Williams offers a convincing behind-the-scenes look at a maternity ward as an anesthesiologist struggles to cope with his fear that his own wife might give birth to a Down's Syndrome child. This is a story about the boundaries of love, and how terrifying it can be to face up to our own emotional shortcomings.

Exceptional stories, all. Each one gropes its way forward through undiscovered country, and we are the beneficiaries of the explorations. There are surprises, epiphanies, and moments of unlooked for rebirth.

Fiction, as a body, is a chimera, made of many incongruous parts, and no collection can represent it fully. If there is a gap in this volume, it is in the realm of comic surrealism. The formal experiments of the last fifty years have been fruitful, opening the way for new types of fabulism, genre hybrids, and metafictive departures. So while I'm impressed by the breadth of this anthology, I do note the absence of those more playful strains.

Still, the writers assembled in this collection have much to say. That they have been drawn together into this single volume is no accident; each belongs in this showcase, and each has a singular and engaging view of the world.

stickmen
Andrew C. Gottlieb

stickmen

My father was dying, and everyone seemed to feel as if I should have been acting differently: grief-stricken, depressed, crushed by paralyzing emotions. Like Cassidy Brandon, who lived down the hall in my college dorm. She was the worst. She got all touchy, petting at me, staring with narrowed eyes, asking, How are you? as if I had something to confess. As if only she knew me. My roommate, Dale Jarrett, stayed the same—always aloof and calm—and I liked being around him, away from everything insistent and rude. I liked to draw. I went by Jimmy. My father was on morphine.

It was mid-October—the month our family doctor, Herb Victory, said my father only had a few weeks—when Dale came up with the idea of trying to sleep with the college recruiters. "We'll call it Operation Job Seek," he said. Tuesday night. In the dorm room, watching television, planning for the career fair. I had tests; Dale had schemes. "No. Not exciting enough."

"Operation Position Seek?" I said. "Positions. In bed."

"I see," Dale said, in a flat voice that told me he disapproved. He reached for his dictionary; I dropped the subject. I had notes to read, but I doodled Waiting Stickman—sitting, arms holding head—on the weathered face of my social psych text.

My name's Jeremy Remler, though I used Jimmy because Jeremy seems so, you know. October was cold, already deep into autumn, and walking to class I watched other students move with intention across the quad. My junior year, a psychology major, and I felt like I'd accomplished zero. Did every student move so quickly? Was it the cold? Or did they all know something I didn't? Our college was close to my home town in Oregon. I thought I was enjoying myself. The school was large enough—maybe eight thousand students—that there was always something going on, but it was efficient and anonymous in the way of government offices: generic, brown, often lonely.

My father had been sick for as long as I could remember, so, honestly, the news wasn't a surprise. Degenerative. A nerve disorder. I never named the disease anymore; you'd have heard of it. It got you eventually. My memories of him consisted mainly of his daily failures and gradual loss of mobility. When I was three, he walked with a cane; by the time I was four, he needed crutches; at five, this little battery-powered cart; at eleven, an electric wheelchair that took chunks out of the walls and trim when he misjudged direction. He scarred the house and left my mother screaming for renovations. I could patch and sand drywall better than some contractors.

Now he was bedridden, lying on his back at home, blankets tucked over his thin legs, his arranged arms. He watched a lot of television, my mother caring for him as best she could. He sipped cranberry juice for his bladder, and ate soft foods like tuna to avoid choking. He had pills to take. Stool softeners. Like that. There were many unpleasantries. He moved his head, looking left and right, pushing his jaw in and out, biting at his upper lip with his teeth. He puckered his lips and moved them in a slow circle. He did more with his head than I did with my whole body some days.

I was late for class but didn't change my pace. No matter what I was doing, he was there, staring at the ceiling, each moment like the last. The morphine slowed him down. Often, I bit my tongue until it bled; the pain stopped me from sneezing or falling asleep in class.

The career fair scared me: it'd be a pasture of well-dressed recruiters pressed into smart suits and with practiced smiles. "A company sends their babes to recruit, right?" Dale said, eyes flashing. "Easy. Recruiters collect resumes. The best get an interview the next day. We submit as many resumes as we can to the cutest recruiters. We get the interview. We seduce them." We borrowed resumes from smart kids, kids with grad school offers, kids practically haloed by a golden aura promising a bright future. We scanned the best resumes and printed fresh copies with made-up names and generic e-mail accounts. "They're not forged," said Dale. "They're borrowed. Improved."

I had my feet on my desk. Dale was driven, tapping a pencil against his lip. There was a knock and Cassidy stuck her head in the door, then walked in, angled a hip, glanced around. She said, "You two are demented. Like you're gonna have any luck."

"Ladies don't have problems getting dates," Dale said.

She reflected. "You're an idiot. You can't fake what's on those resumes. You're not that smart."

"Don't confuse lethargy with ignorance." Dale was unperturbed.

My father hadn't had a resume in fifteen years. People like me had a lot in their life: keys, cars, pens, cell phones, notebooks. Stuff we assumed everyone else needs. But for others, it was just noise. When I was twelve, my father showed me a chart. A graph with years on the horizontal axis, and my father's value to the company on the vertical axis. The line was a simple bell curve. It ascended for a good number of years, then crested, descended. "This is why I'm taking disability," he told me. "You understand?" He didn't need a resume. A few years after that, he didn't need utensils.

Cassidy came over, knelt beside me, and put her hand on my knee. "Jimmy, how are you?"

"I'm good, Cass." I held up the resume. "I need a translator." They were indecipherable. Chemistry, physics, computer science—all letters and acronyms. C++, HTML, ASP, XML. On the resumes we weren't going to use, I drew Stunned Stickman. Standing, leaning, stars and lines circling his head. Truthfully, I was no fine artist. I liked pushing a pencil, the slow line that went where I directed.

"Are you sure you're okay?"

I emptied my face. "I'm okay."

She gave me a long look. "I'm going to dinner." She stood up and headed for the door. "You can't have my resume."

After she left, Dale said, "Like a history resume would get us laid. She likes you, Jim."

It wasn't that I didn't want to believe him, but that it's hard to feel close to people who always suggest they know more about your feelings than you do. Cass was like a blanket that's too hot: no matter how much you want it, you push it away.

I sat at my father's bed, watching television. My second visit this week, and Dale compromised: he'd drop off my resumes at the fair. I didn't care. My father liked sitcom reruns and animal shows; he hated commercials. I wish I could claim we'd had a good relationship, but I knew it was mediocre, and anything approaching intimacy became uncomfortable. With his poor lung capacity and diminished memory, any old stories or sage advice were punctuated by long pauses I found disheartening.

His voice was thin and raspy. "Did I tell you the one about this guy? The car he can't sell? Got a hundred and fifty thousand miles. Stupid joke."

"Yeah," I said. "So he turns the odometer back." I told him the joke a week ago.

My father turned his head on the pillow, squinting an eye at me. "Right. So when his friends ask him why he hasn't sold his car, he says." He paused, inhaled. "Why would I sell a car with only twenty-five thousand miles?"

We sat in silence while he caught his breath. The television flashed at us.

"Where's your mother?"

"I don't know." I didn't. "Out there? Knitting?" Out there was the rest of the house, the rooms my father hadn't seen in years, the places to which my mother retreated. She was a big craft person: sewing, knitting, making things we smiled over.

"What are you doing at school?"

"The usual," I said. "Making a resume." I wanted to impress, I really did.

On the tube: commercials. Pick-up trucks morphed before us, fancy computer tricks those brainy computer science students would do in their future. Probably make a million dollars. I had a vision of Shifting-form Stickman and glanced around for a pencil.

"Stupid commercial," my father said.

It made me weary, his judgments. Stupid this, stupid that. Animal shows he couldn't judge. Who could judge a shiny-eyed, whitetail doe trying to survive in the forest, all quick hooves and striped tail flashing high, a warning?

"I had a dream last night that I could run."

"You did?"

"I have those." He cleared his throat. "I tell you this joke? Stupid joke. This guy. Got a car he can't sell." He tried to see my face again, neck muscles taut, grinning like a kid who thinks the Tooth Fairy's coming.

I said, "No, Pop, how's it go?"

"Hundred and fifty thousand miles on this car. So he turns the odometer back."

Dale watched the e-mail accounts. A couple messages came that evening. Interviews lined up. That fast.

"Easy," Dale said. "Got one with Electramed Technologies. Sounds fancy-pants."

"They want me too," I said.

"She was a hottie. Big green eyes. I wanted to lick her face."

"You're a perv."

"Don't judge love. You're a chemical engineer for them. The dupe's in the pile."

"I can do that," I said, doubting. I felt my inner self veering from Dale, and that confused me.

The e-mails read like party invites. *Dear Fake-name-on-resume, Hi! My name's recruiter-name with important-sounding-company-name. We'd like to interview you. You're scheduled for...*and so on. I'd skip classes to go. The rest? Wear a disguise, tie a tie, find the right resume, tell a story to attractive, professional, older women.

I was thinking sleep when my mother called. She was crying, and there were silences where I pictured her sitting on the couch, knees to chest, knitting in lap, pressing a damp tissue against her lips as if she'd be okay if she held it all in. Then her voice would come back, wavering for a few more sentences.

"I'm sorry to bother," she said. "I wish you were still here."

"I'm okay, Mom."

"Things he says sometimes. Never in front of you. Can you come home? Tonight he got angry. I want you to get help for yourself, Jeremy. See somebody. A counselor. I think it's important."

Dale tiptoed out, giving a salute as he closed the door.

"He accused me of trying to kill him. After all these years." She paused. "Dr. Victory says it's normal. Dementia." She sniffled. "I worry about you."

I'd like to say I knew how to handle these situations, that I knew how to comfort my own mother, her darting voice on the line, but I failed at this sort of thing. I wanted her to stop telling me what I needed, and it bothered me to think of my father taking his bitterness out on her. My mother's stories made me feel like an invader in my father's life, privy to his private pleasures and tortures. But the walls to those places had long come down. My father was the only one who thought he still had privacy. Imagine that.

"Those damn jokes," she said.

I pictured Running Stickman: one leg forward, one leg behind. Determined, leaning. "I don't think he means it, Mom," I said. "I'm not sure he can mean it."

I had no interviews scheduled Monday, but I skipped behavioral psychology anyway and went to the gym. I didn't feel like working out, but there I could look active, so I changed into shorts and a t-shirt and wandered the weight room. I sat against the padded wall, hugging my shoulders with my hands, watching other people strain and breathe and prance. My father once told me that in college he could hold a 35-pound weight at arm's length for sixty seconds. Amazing.

Across the floor, on the lat machine, I saw this girl from my social class. I forgot her name. She noticed me, so I waved, got up, and went over to the dumbbells. I picked up two 35-pounders and thrust them up, out to my sides. What a joke. I could barely get them halfway, and after about ten seconds my shoulders started to shake, muscles failing. I tried to drop them slowly; she'd stopped looking anyway. Who was I to show off? I felt like a peacock with its tail plucked. I wondered if my father had lied a little to impress me, but even if it was forty-five seconds, I'd be impressed. Now he calls for a channel change. One day you're lifting, the next you're lifted.

I stopped at the first aid office. There was always a nursing major on duty.

"Can I get a bag of ice?" I asked.

"What's wrong? Gotta log injuries." She had blonde, bobbed hair, concerned eyes, a tanned nose, and was reading a dog-eared novel that, like all my books, had USED COPY taped all over it.

"I think I pulled a hamstring," I said. "I'm fine, really. Wanna get some ice on it."

She walked to the ice machine, scooped a clatter of cubes into a plastic bag, and knotted it. "Here you go. Come back if you need."

"Thanks," I said. "That a good book?"

"No," she said. "It's okay."

In the locker room, I threw out the ice and stood at the urinal. A scoring pencil lay on the porcelain, so while I went, I drew Searching Stickman on the wall. One hand on waist, one hand shading eyes. Then I drew a bubble, and in the bubble I wrote, "I saw Debbie Stitz. Have you?" I put the pencil in my left hand, and in shaggy letters I wrote, "I've seen the whole family Stitz." In block letters with my right hand I wrote, "Don't write on walls."

That night in the dorm, I tried to read, but I couldn't get the coming interviews out of my head. I bit down on my tongue; it helped me clear my thinking. Dale tinkered with his desk clock. I tried to convince myself I wasn't nervous. I liked people. People I didn't know. That's why I'd chosen psychology. People and their problems. For instance: we read this case study of a teenager, the only one to escape alive as his family's house goes up in flames. His parents and siblings burned to death. Kid suffered massive amnesia. Over the next days and weeks he could not recall ever having a family. I found this kind of thing fascinating. The human brain. The favors it did for you.

"What if they catch on?" I said. "Recruiters. They should be smart. People smart."

Dale gave the clock a shake.

I kept talking. "I think I could tell if someone was lying to me."

Our door opened; Cass stuck her head in the room. "Jimmy, come study with me? I need help on this essay." She flashed me cute eyes and a pleading smile. "Please?"

"Sure. In a minute, okay?" I didn't know why she thought I was smart. It was an exercise that promised frustration for both.

"I'll be in my room."

Dale looked at me. "Good luck, professor. Relax, will you? You've got interviews tomorrow. Charm 'em. I don't know, curse occasionally. Make it up as you go."

I actually put on a tie for my first interview, a mid-morning effort with a company called Wellspring Financial. My brilliant resume made me sound like a Rockefeller. On the way there, I forgot my fake name. I glanced as I sat down: William Walters. "Alliteration makes you sound wise," Dale had said. I was relieved at having nothing to lose but felt tense about lying.

The recruiter started right in. "I'm Brenda. My card. Wellspring is interviewing for assistant director of marketing for our on-line brokerage. I'll ask you some questions, and we'll get back to you within..." She kept talking, and I tried to nod in the right places.

Dale had been right. Brenda was a few years older than me and attractive, with short, brown hair framing a vibrant, perfect face with large eyes that made contact. I tried to imagine her a few years earlier: had she struggled? Asked friends how they were? How *are* you? Listened to crying parents? It didn't seem likely. I tried to see her golden aura, then imagined her thrashing away the night in a dark dance club so loud talk was impossible.

She peered at the resume. "William. Tell me what you like about marketing. You have excellent experience." Her smile seemed perpetual.

"Marketing," I said. "Marketing." My mouth was dry. I tried to make this important, but I felt like I was giving up. Brenda was all ears. My mother seemed to think I needed a psychiatrist; maybe this was how it felt. I had nothing to lose. Dive in, I thought. "Well, I have this idea about how it's not important what's really going on, but only what you make others think. Marketing, right? Say you've got your five-year-old girl at home, watching television. She sees a commercial for a new doll, a doll she wants to love and to love her. Well, it's a piece of plastic, and it's crap manufacturing, but you can't tell the truth to the girl no matter how bad you want to. It'll break her heart. So that means in thirty seconds you play pretty music, show happy people playing with the doll, and tell a big fake story about the doll's life. The doll is your friend. That girl believes in that. Which makes it all real. She'll find love in that piece of plastic."

Brenda was listening to me, eyes narrowed.

My words made me feel like a marketer. How hard could it be? I tried to see if saying *crap* had impressed her. I studied psychology. It had to be easier than selling life to a dying person.

"You asked her out for a beer?" Dale asked.

We were in the cafeteria with some folks from the hall. Cass cut her chicken into disciplined bites. Paulie Stockman sat beside me, a kid who never went to class, had unwashed hair, and wore basketball shorts all winter; next to him sat Zeke Lawrence, a theatre major sixty pounds overweight and proud of it, convinced he'd be next in line for the fat skit on Saturday Night Live. There were these girls I didn't know.

"So what'd she say?" Cassidy demanded. I could tell my answer would calm or anger her, depending.

"No." I replied. "I mean, she asked me where I saw myself in five years."

Zeke chuckled. "In bed with you, sugar. That's what you should've said."

"You bet," Dale said. "We got potential here. Big potential for the Penetration Promotion Project."

Cass made a face.

"That's what you're calling it?" Paulie asked.

Zeke poked the air with his fork as if he planned to stab his own words. "You know what I'd do?" His left cheek bulged with meatloaf. "They asked me a question? I'd lean over with a dead-serious face and rip a big brappin' fart."

I thought about coming clean, confessing, explaining there was no way in hell I was picking up recruiters, let alone asking anyone out. The truth was, when Brenda had asked me about the future, I said nothing. My hands shook. I sat in the chair and looked at her, realizing as she stood up to usher me out that I had no idea what I saw in my future, that I hadn't imagined much of one at all.

After dinner, I walked alone along the river, a slow-flowing carpet of brown water that bordered one side of the campus, a half-moat. The air had a muddy, polluted smell to it, cooler and stagnant as the winter seeped in, and the empty soccer fields along the banks looked as barren as the few tattered weeping willows slouching at the shore. Sometimes kids read here, relaxing, but that evening there was no one but me; I sat on a rock right at the shore and watched the water slide by.

I'd heard stories of my father fishing, though I'd never seen him do it. This river, though, he'd never see, and I thought again about how I marked my places like that. Places you'll go your father would never see. We've got this river here, Pop. You'd like it. I'd told him that a million times. I could hear his response: *Did I tell you the one about...?*

Some kids even vacation with their parents. Two weeks in Europe. My mother had visited the college. She'd seen the river. For Pop: no river, no sky, no grass. No airline tickets. No last-minute change of travel. No last-minute change. I felt the ridges of my right molar with my tongue. I slapped the water with the toe of my shoe.

My mother had called me right after Doc Victory told her the truth. She was quiet but not crying then, always business-like when passing crucial information. "It could be any day," she said. "You need to be ready."

"Okay," I said.

"Are you all right?"

I never knew with my mother on the phone. I worried she might tell me what to do next, how to feel, an attack I had to fend off. With my father, it was like, is this the last time? The last conversation? It made his words seem critical and wounding.

In the past, out here at the river, I'd cried, like out of nowhere, and I'd let it happen and thought to myself, Wow, that's what sad feels like, and I'd wondered who I could tell that to.

"Mr. Lewis, what attracts you about Hammond Laboratories?"

"I'm Len. Call me Len." I felt more prepared for this recruiter, an efficient-looking blonde woman, the kind of achiever with poise that screamed ambition. She sat straight up; her eyebrows had clean edges. I'd thought of things to say, but in the end I didn't get the chance.

"What brings you in, Leonard?"

"You did. I mean, you called me."

"We're improving the drug delivery process, our springboard to the top-tier of major pharmaceuticals. As you know from your research, we're targeting specific molecular delivery in tumors. So we can starve or otherwise compromise a tumor's effectiveness. Without injuring or killing other cells in the body like standard chemo. You know, one area gets sick, everything suffers."

"Sure, of course."

"Let me tell you a little more about what we're looking for in a candidate."

In the dorm, Dale and I compared notes; my heart wasn't in it.

"She talked the entire time," I said. "Like she already knew I was a good scientist. I wanted to say stuff but I got cut off. Look, it was dumb."

The phone rang, and Dale picked it up. "Hello?" Then: "Hi, Mrs. Remler. Hold on."

I paused, taking the phone. "Hi, Mom."

"Hi, Jeremy. Bad time?"

"No, it's fine."

She sounded cheery. "Dale's a nice young man. Bring him home for dinner sometime? I'm in the bedroom on the cordless. Say hi to your father?"

There was a pause, then muffled voices, and I pictured her holding the phone to his ear, telling him it was me.

"Hello," he said, barely there, his voice a whisper.

I hated the brittle hiss of him trying to produce words. "Hey, Pop, how's it going?" I tried to sound upbeat, praying I'd be able to understand what he said.

"Pretty good." There was a long pause. "I had this dream last night," he began, and then there was silence.

"Pop?" I asked. "What'd you dream?"

My mother came on. "I'm sorry, honey. He's too tired. Thanks for trying."

After I hung up, Dale said, "So check it out, I didn't tell you yet. I have a date with the recruiter from Pride of Oregon Bank. Well, it's an S&L"

"What do you mean you have a date?" I said.

"We're going out for wings. Beer. She likes me. We're going to make it work."

"Do you like her?" I asked.

"Sure," he said.

"How did you do that?" I asked.

"I guess it's natural. By the way, Cass called earlier."

I knocked, and when Cass opened her door, I said, "Hey. Whatcha doing?"

"Come in," she said. She had one of the few singles in the dorm, a lucky lottery pick.

"Get your essay back?" I sat on her bed, a puffy thing, with a pink comforter and stuffed-animal zoo.

"Nah. Want some fruit?" She locked her door, went to her desk, picked up a cereal bowl, came over, and sat down.

"What kind?"

"Mango and strawberries."

"That's peach," I said. "Peaches."

"It's mango, dork."

We sat there eating the fruit, swapping the spoon. She said, "Forgive me for saying, but you guys aren't gonna score with the recruiters."

I nodded. "I know," I said. She hadn't expected me to say that. I didn't want to talk about Dale, so I didn't mention his date. I was glad to hang out but wanted to avoid her analysis of me, her telling me the way I should think. I'd want to leave. She didn't say much at all. "I think I have to go home again this weekend," I finally said.

"I'm sorry, Jimbo. That must be so hard."

"It's okay." I ate another strawberry.

She put her hand on my arm and asked: "Do you have good memories of him?"

I shrugged. She looked attentive, eyes focused, her mouth in a frown. "One thing I remember is when I was a kid. Like five. He used to drive me out to the playground, but his cart didn't go on grass, so he'd park the car and sit in it and watch from the parking lot while I played in the sandbox. I'd scoop sand, wave, yell for him to watch me and stuff."

"He could drive?"

"His arms were okay then."

Her hand was still on my arm, and her eyes got teary. I said, "One time I fell from the top rung of the jungle gym. I fell on my ass and twisted my ankle. It didn't hurt too bad, but I starting bawling. You know, screaming. I was bruised and dirty. Kids. I was fine, but insulted from falling in the sandbox. He started waving at me from the car. I didn't want to get up. I watched him open the car door. He lifted his legs out one by one and set his feet on to the pavement. I think he was going to get his scooter out, but then he stopped and waved again to call me over. He must have been tired."

Cass said, "It must have been hard for him to sit there, watching you play alone."

"Yeah. I didn't think I was missing anything, though." I knew that's what made the memory special for me. You have to admire a man who could do that every day, who could sit there missing out and knowing it.

Cassidy didn't say anything else; instead she kissed me, kind of leaning in, and so I kissed her back, and soon she put down the fruit bowl, pushing me up on the bed. Then we fooled around pretty hard, and her teeth banged mine a few times, like she was trying to eat me, or at least leave a mark. She took her clothes off pretty fast, with a desperation that was exciting, and so soon we were naked and fumbling.

I wanted to turn out the light, but she didn't seem to care, so when her eyes were closed I looked at her body. To see a woman's body in the light is a privilege. She had these nice round breasts with brown nipples, and I could have stared at them for hours, but I didn't want her to think I was weird.

We lay there for a long time. Eventually she fell asleep, but I was wide awake. Her nose started to whistle, and then she seemed like normal clumsy Cass, and seeing her naked was intimate and embarrassing, so I got up to quietly leave. I realized if she woke up, she'd expect me to say certain things, and I didn't want to have to make any decision about that. On my way out, I was going to draw a Stickman on her blotter, but instead I wrote, "Thank you for sharing your fruit with me."

When I was ten, I got plantar warts on the bottom of both feet. My mother was sick, so my father drove me to the clinic to get them removed. I was used to doing things alone by then, so going in was easy—my father in his chair, waiting in the lobby doing crosswords in his pocket book—but I was scared of the procedure. I felt as if I were going to war in a far-off country. As the doctor prepared the anesthetic, he said, "Don't worry, champ. You won't feel it while it's happening. It'll hurt later, but I'll give you something to take." He used an electric needle to burn everything away, leaving my feet sore though perhaps wart-free.

Afterward, my feet bandaged, my unlaced sneakers in hand, we sat in the car. My father had a gallon of apple cider. We drank it right from the jug, something my mother forbade. He said, "We don't need glasses do we?" He said, "I'm sorry about your feet. They'll heal, though. They will. Take another swig."

He made me feel grown-up, sitting there chugging, and I wanted to live up to everything he'd ever expect of me. I tried to sip from the heavy jug without spilling it down my chin. My father didn't seem to care about spills, which made me like him more, and I felt I understood something important about what it means to be a man.

As we drove home, I took my father's pencil and drew my first stickman in his crossword puzzle book. Drinking Stickman. Standing, jug tilted up. It probably wasn't that good, but I remember considering it an impressive and original doodle. Now I know there are a million different Stickmen.

Someday I'll tattoo them all over my body, and then when people like Cass assault me with hard questions, like how do I feel, all I'll have to do is point.

A couple days later, I skipped my social lecture and sat with Dale and Zeke outside the student union eating subs and drinking Mountain Dew.

Zeke said, "She took you back to her place? You dog."

"We watched a movie," Dale said. He seemed serious, trying to tell us about the recruiter without acting giddy. "When I got a beer from the kitchen, I turned the lights out. I think she was impressed. It was slick."

Across the quad, a crowd stood protesting what looked to be animal trapping, waving signs and marching, hoping to spread awareness and guilt. One sign read: BAN TRAPS, and another said, YES ON 251. One girl held this graphic poster that showed a dirtied swan fighting to get free, wings outspread in a lunge, remnants of one leg torn and bloodied in a sprung trap.

"So did you do her?" Zeke asked.

"Naw." Dale shrugged. "She let me feel her tits, and I thought she was getting into it 'cause I almost had her shirt off, but then all of a sudden she was like, *You have to leave.*"

"She kicked you out," I said.

"I don't care. I don't. That's not the point."

"My what?" I pressed the receiver against my ear. We lived in the same dorm, but everyone talked by telephone.

"Can I get your schedule?" Cass was chewing gum—I could hear the rubbery crack.

"What for?"

"You know, just to have."

"Have for what?"

"So I know where you are. During the day, you know? I think about you sometimes when you're not around, in case you didn't know."

"I guess," I said. "I don't know if it's reliable." I tried to gauge how much I liked Cassidy, hoping to get a better sense of what to say.

"You're not going to your classes, are you."

"Of course I am. Duh."

"So what's on Monday?"

"I don't know, Cass. It's not in front of me right now."

"Mr. Jerk-off, what are your best programming languages?"

"Sorry?" I was tired, had been exhausted all day, but my head lifted, certain I hadn't misheard.

"Let's see? Is this the right resume?"

I glanced at my designated name. Jay Jerkov. "That's me. Call me Jay." I made a mental note to kill Dale.

"Okay, well, Jay, your best languages?"

"Let's see." I tried to look thoughtful.

"How many lines of C++ would you say you wrote for your largest program?"

"How many lines? Tough question." I had no idea what she was talking about, but it didn't matter. I'd thought about what to say to Dale. I'm not into it anymore. You go, okay? I'm tired of lying to these people. Great, you got a date. I knew it might be a bad sign, an indicator of the failure of my imagination, or my optimism, or something, but I couldn't help it. I couldn't adopt his smug indifference. I think I knew then the difference between Dale and me was that he could imagine virtually anything—and revel in it—no matter how foolish or unreal it seemed. I liked to draw the Stickmen; Dale liked to be them. I couldn't hold that against him; actually, I envied him the freedom. But I wouldn't rely on his judgment again.

"Jay? Lines of code?"

"Code?"

"Mr. Jerkov, is it me? Or is it you?"

I prepped myself for what to say to Dale. I was walking back from the library. I sensed an ending, and I started simply: I'm not doing anymore interviews. This is stupid. Don't tell me it's not. I pictured Dale laughing at me, thinking I took everything too seriously. In my head I got mad. That date you had is nothing. She was laughing at you the whole time. You don't take anything seriously because nothing bad has ever happened to you. You're lucky, Dale, that's all. You're not calm and cool, you just never had to care about anything. Better cross your fingers you don't ever have a real problem, because you won't know how to handle it. The more I rehearsed, the worse I felt. I'd probably just sound crazy.

Dale didn't even hear me walk in. So much for my entrance. His back was to the door, hunched over his desk, on the phone. His fingers were in his hair, and there were broken pencils on the floor. I paused, ready to leave. I had a feeling.

He said, "You don't understand, I love you."

I backed out, pulling the door closed, staring through the crack.

Dale said, "What do you mean you can't see me?" There was agony in his words, and I knew he was crying. It's something you can hear in a man's voice, even if you can't see their face.

"Don't hang up," he said. "What do I do now?"

I closed the door and went up to see if Cass was in her room.

I sat next to my father's bed, and watched the nurse squeeze a droplet full of liquid morphine under his tongue. His lower lip cupped the plastic dropper; I thought he would drool. The television was on low, Discovery Channel droning on about a new series, *Wild Animal Survival*. I knew my father was in pain, even though he faked it pretty well.

"This guy walks into a bar," he began, after he'd swallowed, and I nodded and smiled and tried to appreciate the joke. If he wanted to enjoy it, who was I to stop him? If he'd wanted a cigarette, I would have lit it for him.

This was the last time I would see him, but I didn't know it then. The next day, his heart was going to stop while I was in the library checking e-mail. There was a last time for everything, and if you were privileged enough to know ahead of schedule, you were a lucky person. If you were like most people, you might as well keep on telling jokes.

My mother came in and stood at the end of his bed. "Some juice? A bite to eat?"

Dad shook his head, slowly, ignoring her. He hadn't eaten in three days. "How about a martini?" he asked, grinning.

The television said, "Stay with us as polar bears try to survive in the beautiful yet brutal winter landscape of the Hudson Bay."

What I couldn't tell anyone was how much I was ready for my father to die. It was my secret. People would think I was crazy. When I was thirteen, I stole liquor from the dining room, fingers of rum or vodka I was sure my parents—light drinkers—wouldn't miss. I drank late at night in the dark downstairs of my mother's craft room, lighting a few candles, listening to music, reveling in my rule breaking. I mixed the booze with warm soda. One night, I got clumsy, and I tripped over the power cable of the table lamp. The lamp shot from the table to the floor, knocking over three candles that tumbled into a pile of lace my mother was saving. As I watched, the small flames lengthened and spread fast as spilled water. I'm not dumb; I yelled. By the time my mother and I had the fire out—bare minutes later—the lace was a smoking pile of burnt fiber, and the wall behind it was a smudge of black, the fingerprint of near-disaster. In many ways, my family had considered themselves lucky. My parents harbored a serious fear of fire. In the event of a true blaze—the house fully involved—it would have been impossible to get my father from bed, to his chair, to the safety of the outdoors. I was lucky to avoid the burden that would have come with such a disaster.

After the accident, he didn't talk to me for days. When he did, he was calm. "Put your sneakers on. We're going outside."

I followed his wheelchair down the porch ramp, obedient and humbled by my careless and stupid behavior, and we went out into the street, quiet with the emptiness of a suburban evening. He rolled to the middle of the pavement and stopped, then pointed to where the street marker stood, maybe two hundred yards away, the green sign glinting under a streetlamp like a target.

"Go," he said. "Sprint. Fast as you can."

"Why?" I asked.

"I said sprint." He meant business. His face told me that if he could have, he'd have stood up and clobbered me. It was terrible to see that in his eyes. "Sprint to that goddamn sign as fast as you can. Touch it. Sprint back. I want fast."

I turned, breaking into a sloppy, embarrassed run, then a sprint that had me at the sign in maybe half a minute. I prayed the neighbors weren't at the windows. I felt the cold metal in my fingers, and I turned, pushing the ground away from me as I ran back, feet slapping the road. I had to do this right.

Back at his chair, I put my hands on my knees, breathing fast and deep, my lungs already tight from the effort.

He said, "Why'd you stop?" He was glaring. "Do it again," he said. "Faster this time."

I kept it up, running long enough to make my lungs burn, my thighs ache, my eyes run, and my throat heave.

Eventually I squatted a few feet from his chair. "Let me stop a second," I pleaded, sucking for air.

He said, "One day you're going to look around, wondering what to do and how to do it. You're going to try to measure yourself in this world. You'll try to avoid dumb things, and you're going to wonder why I didn't tell you how. Truth is, I got nothing to tell you. Look at me. I'm walking backwards. But you can feel this. I know that. So you sprint again. Until you've sprinted out all that stupidity. You'll remember this."

I ran a long time. I puked beside the sign, leaning on the pole while my knees gave out and my throat made wheezing noises. I was sweaty and exhausted. Above me the streetlights sparkled and spread into vague white stars. I stared at my father in his chair in the distance, a broken king sitting in his shadowy throne in the center of the road, and I knew he was waiting for me to run back to him again, so I held on and inhaled all I could, trying desperately to catch my breath, so I could recover, even a little.

My father died, and a heavy tether between us was cut, dropping away like a wet rope freed from my waist. Cass and I dated for a while, then broke up. Dale got a good job after college working as a press agent for a local mayor's office. Cass became a recruiter. Funny, that.

It wasn't that I'd wanted my father to die because he'd been mean, or heartless, or because I hated him. None of that. I just couldn't take another minute of his life. His life was the longest, slowest death I'd ever witnessed. We were two men fumbling our way, together, separately.

Maybe I should have taken art classes, become a real painter, a fine artist who could really draw. But I shy from imitations. I stopped doodling, because I finally understood what it was to me, those pictures, and I lost interest. My mother gave up knitting and took up cooking. I have an old sweater that I still wear, and I try all her experiments.

My life is a path of broken slates. I try to act genuinely. I'll tell you the truth, even if it hurts us both. My father was right about many things. I can walk across deserts barefoot. Go days without water. My feet are made of steel, and my heart beats on in its closet like a pounding fist.

voyeuse
Cary Groner

voyeuse

My sister, Jen, complains that I no longer return her calls. "I know it's fresh and you're still hurting," began her latest voice-mail, "but I can't do anything for you if you don't call me back." She made a half-joking reference to an intervention of some kind.

Jen had admired my husband, Brian, for his brains and his twisted sense of humor and his weird Olympian stamina. He and I met cycling, but I could never do the kind of rides he did with his hard-core friends, Sam and Nolen and Brenda the Amazon (who got her nickname not because of her size—she was actually quite petite—but because she was so tough she would have survived the Donner Party, at least if she hadn't been a vegetarian).

I'd start out riding with this leggy crew but after a couple of hours I always peeled off and headed home, which made me feel wimpy and left out, so that when Brian finally rolled in later in the afternoon I was sometimes still irritable. I'd never been particularly athletic and my body did its best to make this plain at every opportunity. Some weeks, exercising meant subsisting largely on ibuprofen.

Brian didn't care, though, because we were compatible in most other ways. And when his birthday was coming up, I had a brainstorm: I surprised him with a new helmet I'd had fitted with a web-linked minicam.

"So I can still see all the cool places you go and I won't be so cranky when you get back," I said. He liked it, and that evening when we went to bed he came out of the bathroom naked, wearing just sunglasses and the helmet. I laughed so hard I thought I'd crack a rib.

"Afraid I'll get too rough?" I asked.

"For posterity," he said, with a sort of endearing evil grin. "Be a sport."

But I made him take it off. He looked like an extraterrestrial with an erection, and there was no way I was going to watch a video of myself in the throes of passion, jiggling and shrieking and fattened by a wide-angle lens.

When I had time, though, I'd check in and watch him zoom down Mt. Diablo or cruise the beautiful, hilly back roads between Petaluma and the sea. The picture was sharp and clear, though I was never quite sure if the whole thing made me feel less left out or more so. It was like receiving a gift I couldn't afford to buy for myself, thrilling but also slightly humiliating.

The good part was that on weekends and some afternoons, I'd get a virtual tour of the region I called home from someone who knew the roads better than I did and who thought it extremely sweet of me to be interested. It was sweet of me, though over time I admittedly became distracted by Brenda, because if I noticed he was riding behind her and the camera was pointed at her little butt too long we would have words when he got home.

"I was drafting," he'd say, and I'd smile my knowing smile and say, "Uh-huh." I think sometimes he was afraid he'd created a monster, because once he and Brenda took a lunch break in a field and he turned the camera off. We had words about that, too.

"Why would you want me to drain the batteries giving you a worm's-eye view of a bunch of grass for half an hour?" he protested.

"It's the symbolic act of turning off the camera while you're out in a meadow with a beautiful chick," I said.

"The road was fifty feet down the hill," he said. "There were cars. You think we were going to have sex?"

"It's the symbolic act—" I said again, but he huffed in frustration and headed for the shower. Later, of course, I apologized, and he told me to forget it. He had a tendency to shoulder the blame when we disagreed, and when he decided to make it up to me he was good at it. I sometimes provoked him more than I should have, because of this. It made me feel wretched, but it was also perversely satisfying, because I could see him look inward, scan the possible responses, and choose kindness, after which I felt especially lucky to have him.

One Thursday afternoon when he was out by himself, I surfed through the site as he was nearing an intersection I didn't recognize. I watched for half a minute or so, but cityscapes bored me and I was about to click out and get back to work when a great blue mass suddenly filled the frame and the whole picture went sideways. I saw what appeared to be a truck tire rolling toward the lens, then the camera skittering away from it at the last instant. The squiggly image was replaced by a white screen, then a black one.

Over the next half-hour I tore the house to shreds because I had no idea where he was and his cell was turned off. All I could do was wait, and there was no way to wait for news like that without destroying things, so I destroyed everything I could. When the call came my floor was covered with broken glass and pottery shards, one of which pushed through the sole of my slipper and gashed my foot as I was reaching for the phone. By the time I returned the receiver to its cradle the hardwood was smeared with blood.

After that, there were disorienting events, all of which seemed encased in some kind of chill fog that dulled the light and turned my body inward with cold. There was that first part, with the phone and the laceration and the sudden loss of breath. There was the trip to the police station, where I met the man who had driven the truck; witnesses said it was not his fault. There was the part that included calls to Brian's mother and his brother and my sisters. There was the cremation, the gathering, the ceremony, the scattering of ashes. Some rudimentary sentient portion of me managed to be present through all of this, to acknowledge the good wishes and sympathies of friends and family even though much of the time—for all I understood—people might as well have been speaking to me in Swahili.

Then things changed, and for a while I was infused with a preternatural endurance and grace unlike any I'd known in my life, the kind of stamina I'd always envied in Brian—it was as if he'd willed it to me. I felt wild and strong, tiger-like, capable of anything. I arranged a leave of absence with my editor. I handled the life insurance company. I bought a new car, because now I would have no one to call if my ancient Corolla died again. I laid in enough groceries to survive a naval blockade. My sisters, who helped with some of this, regarded me with what I took to be awestruck admiration, their gazes darting from my face to each others' eyes and then back to me. One of them gave me a book by Elizabeth Kubler-Ross, apparently unaware that when finally faced with her own demise, poor Elizabeth had renounced her tidy theories and plummeted into blackest nihilism as surely as a terrified rabbit dives down its hole.

After a couple of weeks, though, everyone had to go back to their own lives and all that heroic energy drained from my belly as palpably as if I'd been slit open. I lay down on the couch and stayed there—with brief adjournments to the kitchen or the bathroom—for an indeterminate period that might have been days or weeks. Whatever part of my mind had whispered to me to prepare for siege proved prescient. Sometimes the television was on and sometimes it was off, and I had no memory of doing anything about it, although apparently I had. I couldn't go to bed, because the bed was our bed, and every time I lay down on it I felt as if I'd betrayed him. I slept on the couch and sometimes awakened on the floor with a headache and swollen sinuses and no memory of the transition. I tried to read, which had always been my solace, but now I opened books or magazines to find pages full of incomprehensible hieroglyphics. I stopped brushing and flossing and my mouth acquired a bitter, rusty taste. My mother and my sisters called sporadically, as did two or three friends, but they always had much more to say than I did, so eventually I just let the voice mail answer. They left long, complicated messages that I listened to, erased, and forgot.

Our house was a Berkeley bungalow, two small bedrooms, kitchen in the back where it was quiet, nice blue-and-white tile. Earthquake braces under the floors. An abundance of light that had been the main reason we bought the place and that now seemed so oppressive I kept the blinds shut most of the day. I walked up and down the one straight stretch, from the front door through the living room into the dining room and then to the kitchen. I did a half-turn and went back to the front door, now lidded with a shade like a closed eye, then pivoted again and returned to the rear of the house. It seemed an exceptionally long journey; it took courage to complete it and my bare feet became as calloused as a dancer's. I ate occasionally, but for some reason I needed far less food than I was accustomed to. I reflected with satisfaction that this meant my stores would last even longer.

One morning I felt an urge to visit the website, for it was the last place I'd seen Brian alive. I expected to find some sort of oblivion there, I suppose, a small degree of closure. To my surprise I saw not a black screen but a view of a Berkeley street, Solano Avenue near Andronico's market. The cam moved forward at about ten miles an hour and I realized that somehow, miraculously, the helmet had survived the crash. It had not been crushed by the truck as Brian's skull had been, but had flown off at the last second, which would explain my impression that Brian slid away from the truck tire. He hadn't, but the helmet had.

This didn't surprise me because I was always nagging him to fasten the thing on. He didn't like the chin strap because it rubbed his Adam's apple, he said, and so a lot of times he'd let the straps out and ride with it buckled very loosely, which was idiotic for reasons that were now more obvious than ever. In these situations, of course, you're denied the gloat. When you warn someone you love not to do something and they get killed doing it, you don't get to say "I told you so" to them or anyone else.

So after the paramedics had loaded Brian into the ambulance and the cops had hauled away the twisted frame and figure-eighted wheels of his beautiful orange Colnago, someone had found the helmet, presumably parked by a storm drain at the intersection, and thought, *Cool.* Someone who apparently didn't have a helmet before or didn't have one this good. They probably noticed the camera, but it wouldn't matter because they'd have no idea what the URL was and sooner or later the batteries would die.

But I felt as if I were getting a broadcast from a parallel universe, one in which Brian still breathed and stood up to sprint his bike through a yellow light, which apparently was how he met his end. (If you believed the truck driver, the light was red, but I didn't). The driver had apologized to me at the station, but I was in no shape to offer forgiveness and anything he said would have seemed ludicrously inadequate, anyway. He was a fat Teamster with a mustache and a Raiders cap. It seemed bizarre to me then that someone as fit as my husband could have been laid low by this beer-swilling moose. The guy would be obese until the day he died, and Brian was so thin now the wind could pick him up particle by particle and carry him all the way to the sea. Was that right?

———

The next day I was ready. The new owner of the helmet turned on the camera only when he was riding, which would save the batteries but didn't change the fact that he'd have no way of telling anyone where to watch his adventures. Why was he doing this? Maybe he figured someone was watching, and of course he was correct, because from then on I tried never to be out of earshot of the computer. I set up a tone prompt to let me know when the camera came on, and when it did I dropped whatever I was doing and sprinted to my desk.

I was looking for a routine, of course, because I wanted to know who'd usurped my husband's crown. I had my fantasies: I would learn his M.O., track him down, stop him at an intersection. "Nice helmet, where'd you get it?" I'd say, then add, "Oh, by the way, you shouldn't use a helmet that's been in a crash because it might be damaged." He'd ask me how I knew it had been in a crash, and I'd deliver the news that he was a grave robber, a scumbag, and that I wanted Brian's headgear back. He would, of course, be suitably abashed and return it immediately. He wouldn't turn out to be a bad sort, after all, just an opportunist like the rest of us, a guy who didn't like to see perfectly good equipment go to waste. In this same vein, a little later he would ask me out. Naturally, I would decline.

But whoever had the helmet didn't seem to have any routine at all; he moved through the city aimlessly, a sleepwalker on wheels. This lack of purpose was unnerving and bolstered my suspicion that he was impoverished or homeless. By contrast, Brian's legendary rides had taken me to parts of the Bay area I hadn't known existed, brought me astonishing vistas of the North Bay from Crockett or the West Bay from San Rafael or the Pacific itself from narrow roads that draped the shoulders of Mt. Tam like black sashes. The new guy, whom I decided to call Nairb—the opposite of Brian—was, by comparison, a sad sack. I wondered if eventually I'd have to figure out some way to drive him from his doldrums. There was now, for me, no greater crime than having a body and failing to use it well. Anyone committing this offense should have the body taken away and given to someone else. I understood this might involve resurrecting the dead, but that struck me as a workable goal, something reasonable people could negotiate.

One evening, when the sun was setting and the sky turned, I tentatively opened my blinds and let a little soft light into the house. This much, I discovered, I could stand. It would ease in quickly and quietly, like an orange cat coming home to be fed. I had one of those enormous chest freezers that serial killers use to store the dismembered corpses of their victims, but mine was full of food. I defrosted a pizza and ate, but it tasted like the cardboard disk it sat on in the box. I turned on the TV and saw motivated people striving for clear objectives, which made me feel even more alien to the world than I already did, so I quickly turned it off again.

This is what they call existence, I realized, and I wasn't sure how I was going to get through it, all those ghastly years the actuaries said lay ahead of me. I felt as if I had to walk through a long line of boxcars on an empty freight train at a siding somewhere, each with a year stenciled on its side in spray paint, until I reached the last one and stepped off the back into bright air so thin sunlight would ignite it like gasoline vapor and everything left of me would finally burn away.

An hour later, when it grew dark, I opened the blinds all the way, for when it was bright outside I wanted darkness within, and when night fell I wanted my house so full of light it spilled out and overpowered the sky.

———

I watched Nairb wander through Berkeley and North Oakland, occasionally making it to El Cerrito. He frequented health food stores and parks, but he always turned the camera on after he left home and turned it off before he returned, so I couldn't get much of a bearing on where he lived. Still, I reflected, there must have been something he wanted the person watching to see. It was an act of faith; for all he knew, the video might be disappearing unobserved into the ether, the equivalent of shouting from a mountaintop and wondering if anyone could hear the echo. What was he trying to communicate about his life?

I began to look more closely for patterns. My best guess was that he resided somewhere above Shattuck, between Rose and University, which meant he was either camped in a park (possibly the Rose Garden), or had money, because houses and apartments up there were expensive. Either scenario would explain his lifestyle, for in the Bay Area you can afford to be idle only if you are very poor or very rich.

He frequented Berkeley Natural Grocery and Andronico's, which supported the notion of a certain amount of wealth. But why would a wealthy person salvage a dinged-up bicycle helmet from the gutter? Occasionally he would look down while he was on the bike, and I could see jeans, which meant he wasn't an athlete, that he was using it strictly for transportation, which suggested poverty. He usually took the helmet off before he went into the store, so I accepted that as intermission and used the opportunity to pee or get a snack. Once, though, he left it on (forgetfully? provocatively?) and I saw hands reaching out for oranges, apples, peaches, and beautiful Anjou pears. I couldn't tell much about the hands because of the distortion from the lens, but I could see that they weren't hairy, which I found comforting. Hairy hands made me think of truck drivers or dentists, and I wasn't feeling that great about either one given the state of my husband and my teeth. A couple of minutes later I caught a glimpse of him reflected in the glass door of the freezer section. I sat up straight in my chair but the image was too dim to tell much. He wore a gray Cal Bears sweatshirt and seemed compactly built, with long, frizzy hair, which meant he looked like ten million other Berkeley guys. The image was there for a second, a shimmery ghost, then gone.

The next day Nairb went down to the waterfront, to the dog park, where he met a friend, a young woman with a chocolate Lab. They hugged, then he took off the helmet and set it on what must have been a picnic table. I couldn't tell if he wanted me to watch them or not, because the camera was aimed about halfway between them and the bay. On the left I got a view of the water, and other dogs, and seagulls. On the right the woman would occasionally dart into the frame chasing a Frisbee, then turn and throw it back, but Nairb never appeared. I assumed this was deliberate, though whether out of shyness or fear or some other obscure protective instinct I couldn't tell. After a while, the helmet got lifted up and put back on his head, though all he did was sit on the grass with her and smoke something hand-rolled, a cigarette or a joint. It was weird, seeing it come toward the monitor and then disappear down below the field of view, the way a real joint would have if I'd been there in person to share it.

Why put on a helmet to smoke a joint? Was he worried he'd get so stoned he'd fall over? I wondered if he had a droll sense of humor I'd failed to appreciate. In my mind, I retraced his steps over the previous days to see if there were clues I'd missed, but I couldn't put anything together. The friend looked to be in her early twenties, and she was attractive with thick dark hair that almost matched her dog. But from what I could tell, there wasn't any physical affection between her and Nairb beyond the initial hug.

It was only about three o'clock and I had the feeling he might hang out a while. It would be easy to get in the car and drive down; I could be there in fifteen minutes. I got up from the computer, picked up my keys, and went out the front door, but then it hit me that this was the first time I'd done this in weeks. I was shaking; I crept down the front steps, measuring my breath, and put my fingers on the warm dusty metal of the car, my new blue Prius, and then I bleeped the alarm and opened the door. I sat in the car a while, smelling the vinyl chloride that told me it was new but also slightly carcinogenic—a curious mix of prosperity and risk. I felt flushed and jittery, thinking about what I would say to the guy, because the original plan of confronting him had become impossible now that I knew he liked fruit and had a friend with a dog. With his new reality came the conviction that when I met him I would have no idea what to say. So I sat in the car, then I got out again and went back inside.

That evening my sister called again, and when I saw who it was I finally made myself pick up the phone.

"You were a half-hour away from me coming over there with the police," she said, by way of greeting. "Mom lost it this morning; we'd started to think you were dead."

"Hi Jen," I said quietly.

"Why don't you call anyone back? Do you just not give a shit?"

"Of course I do."

There was a pause; I heard her breathing. "I'm sorry," she said. "I didn't mean to sound like that. But we really were getting freaked. Are you okay?"

I spoke slowly. I'd said almost nothing in weeks, and I was hoarse. "I'm all right. I'm just busy."

Another pause. "With what?" she asked. I understood; I was allowed to be neglectful and worry everyone if I was in despair, but busyness was no excuse.

"You'd think it was crazy."

She laughed, then, but less mirthfully than I would have liked. "Diana, we know you're crazy," she said. "We just want to be sure you're *alive*. Do you shop? Do you have any food? Is there something I can get for you?"

I had to think about it, and as I was thinking I glanced out the window and saw that the light was just about right for my daily opening of the blinds. I put the phone down and went to pull the string. Dust filled the air as the slats slid up, sounding like a hundred tiny horses clopping down cobblestones, and I began to sneeze. But outside, oh, it was perfect. That pinkish orange I loved, the clouds overhead bruising beautifully at their edges. I stood watching for a few moments, then heard an odd whistling behind me. When I went to investigate, I realized the phone was still sitting on the table. Jen was whistling into it the way you'd whistle for a dog. I picked it up.

"Sorry—" I began.

"Jesus Christ, Diana, what was that?"

"I had to sneeze."

"For three minutes?"

Had it been that long? I couldn't imagine so much time had passed. "Apparently," I said. "Sorry."

"Okay, look, I've got to get off the train in a sec," she said. "Tell me you're not going to starve or hurt yourself somehow."

"I'm not going to starve or hurt myself," I said. I was a little surprised to hear it.

"Dave and I want to come over this weekend. Would that be okay?"

"I suppose," I said. "If you really want to."

"We should have come a month ago, but we've both been traveling and Lucy's had the flu. And we thought maybe we should just give you your space."

"It's okay," I said. Lucy was seven, a reed of a girl with skin like parchment and a blue vein in her forehead. My precious niece. It occurred to me that in the Middle Ages she was one of the multitudes who would have died in childhood. "Is she better?" I asked.

"Yeah, finally," Jen said. "I'm at the station—I've got to go."

I was already calculating before the receiver reached the cradle. How long did I have before they got here? Five days? The house was a quarter-inch deep in dust. The kitchen counters and table were stacked with dirty dishes and encrusted pots. A family of mice had left their droppings everywhere. The place held enough newspapers and magazines to fill the reading room of a library, and they looked as if they'd been dropped by a plane, along with a small explosive charge to scatter them. I felt so exhausted looking at it that I had to go back to the couch and lie down.

Tuesday morning my editor called and pointed out politely that I'd been expected back at work the previous day. I'd had no idea, though I assumed I'd agreed to some such arrangement in the distant past of the previous month. He asked if I needed more time and I told him there couldn't possibly be enough time, and if he wouldn't mind I'd appreciate it if he'd file the papers for unemployment so I'd have some money coming in, now that I'd spent or given away most of what I had. He said he would. He was sorry to lose me; he said if I ever wanted to work for him again, even just to freelance, I should call. He said he'd never had anyone as good at writing "Gen Z," our teen advice column, and I had to think hard to remember that that had, in fact, been part of my job, that he wasn't kidding me. He said to let him know if there was anything I needed because he was fond of me and, to tell the truth, also a trifle concerned. I laughed then, which seemed to startle him. I don't know why it struck me as so funny, but it was like someone saying they were a trifle concerned about the Titanic. He didn't have anything to add so I thanked him and hung up.

I didn't have much time. I began to send telepathic messages to Nairb. Nothing sinister, but more like morale-boosters or gentle improvement hints, the kinds of things your friends are too polite to tell you, that you need a nagging mother or a good wife to hear. Get off the dope, get off your butt, get more exercise. Splurge on some riding shorts, air out those legs—it's probably getting funky in there.

When he stubbornly continued his boring life I put more energy into it. On Wednesday night I lit candles to focus my mind and really beamed those affirmations out, right through my monitor and into the camera so they'd filter down into his brain. I didn't really expect it to work, of course, but Friday, about the time I'd begun to buff the varnish off the floor with my pacing, Nairb came through and rode the long grade up Spruce to Tilden Park. A little initiative, I thought, a little gumption, hallelujah! He found his way onto Wildcat Canyon Road, which wound its way back into the hills, and the wind was blowing the eucalyptus and the fog was just cresting the hill, and it was wonderful, the kind of beauty Brian used to send me all the time, so thrilling I nearly wept.

Nairb meandered around up there for a long time and then worked his way over to Skyline, which he took south along the ridge before descending via Claremont, a warm-up ride for Brian but a worthy, heroic circuit for my slacker friend. I felt so glad for him. I got up and sashayed around the living room, not quite dancing, but more like kicking up clouds of dust. I knew there was no way I could clean the house by the time Jen and Dave got there; I'd have to trade my broom for a bulldozer and the mice would quickly spoil it all anyway. It might suffocate me, but there was Nairb, at least, out in the world breathing deeply.

Later, as I was getting ready to sleep, I heard the tone from my computer and went to see. A sign, hand-lettered on a piece of printer paper, had been placed in front of the camera. It said: Peet's, Vine Street, tomorrow, 10:00.

There was no way for me to answer, I realized, other than to go.

My back was aching from the couch so I decided to return to our bed and sleep on the sheets Brian had used on his last night on Earth. The cotton felt smooth and cool, very old, as if it had been woven in Egypt and laid on the bed centuries ago. I found the sensation comforting.

As I drifted off I thought of him, of when we were first married and had argued so much it surprised us. When we'd lived together before the marriage, everything had gone well. But as soon as we were back from the honeymoon Brian became stiff, somehow, less spontaneous and funny. At first I thought it had to do with his job, because he worked in disaster planning at Public Health and everyone was worried about avian flu. He'd told me that from what they knew, there could easily be a mortality rate of eighty or ninety percent, which meant two hundred and fifty million Americans dead, five billion worldwide, the end of agriculture and trade and government, the end of civilization.

I found this alarming, obviously, but it turned out it wasn't what was bothering him. This was typical of Brian.

"I don't know," he said, when I'd finally cornered him. "It just feels like, since the wedding, I can hardly take a breath. Like you own me, or at least we sort of own each other."

"Bondage, but not the fun kind," I said, doing my best.

"Something like that." He didn't smile, though, so I knew the situation was serious. I put my arms around him.

"For me it feels safe and for you it feels scary," I said. "We've switched roles for once."

We found a therapist. She listened and nodded and then told Brian he was equating commitment and death. This wasn't all that uncommon, as it turned out, but as I thought about it in retrospect, lying there alone in our bed that night, it did seem funny. Among other things, she suggested that one night a week we have some wine and make love, to break the tension until we got through this.

"We're paying her ninety-five dollars an hour to tell us to screw?" I said on the way home, though it wasn't actually bad advice since we'd all but stopped.

Brian smiled. "Make love," he corrected me.

This had always struck me as the silliest of euphemisms, as if all that piston action somehow manufactured an emotional commodity. I preferred "have sex" or, if I was in the right mood, "fuck," which was at least onomatopoeic.

Once Brian understood his issues, though, he began to relax. But what really makes love, I learned after that, is death. The longing grows in your heart like a crystal blade until it wounds you, opens you up, and all that feeling flows out because it has nowhere else to go.

———

Peet's was crowded, but no one in the place remotely fit the image I'd formed of him. I was hurt, stood-up and alone, but I figured I might as well get something hot to drink. The place was crammed with people and smelled of coffee and hair gel, of fresh dough and sugar, a miasma of scents. Voices pitched up and down, presumably comprehensible to those who spoke and those who listened. I felt nervous, as if I were surrounded by hostile people in a foreign country, and then I remembered: this was the land of the living.

I bought my coffee and turned, thinking I'd go outside to the bench, but then I saw the helmet on a small round table in the corner, to the right of the door, by the bay window. It had been behind me as I walked in. Sitting at the table was a girl of about eighteen who definitely had the hair I'd seen in that spectral reflection in the freezer glass. She wore a simple cotton top, and although she was possibly a little overweight for her age, she carried it well and looked healthy, with strong arms and a reasonably narrow waist. The hair was a thing unto itself, a sort of electrified golden fleece, and her eyes were the color of the bay when the sun is out, a turbid blue-gray. As I stood there two separate guys, passing by on the sidewalk outside, saw her and practically twisted their heads off their necks gawking as they walked by. She ignored these admirers, if she even registered their existence, and sipped from her mug.

I made my way to the table and realized as I drew near that my hands were trembling so much the coffee was sloshing over the side of my cup. When I finally arrived, after a journey that seemed to include mountain ranges, I had no idea what to say, and she just looked up at me, inquisitively, as if she couldn't imagine why I was there. I asked if she minded if I joined her and she said it depended.

"On?"

"Did you get a sign?" she asked.

"A hand-printed one, I think."

She smiled, then, seeming relieved but also, for some reason, perplexed. I put down my cup and sat. She glanced at my hands; I was lacing and unlacing my fingers, so I picked up my coffee and sipped. It steadied me, strangely enough, perhaps for the same reason they give uppers to hyperactive children.

I set down the cup. "I'm Diana," I said.

"Chaste goddess of the hunt," she said lightly. "Trish."

"Pleased to meet you." I had another swallow and felt the warmth slide down my gullet and light a little lamp in my belly. "I gather you like the classics."

She lifted her mug and I realized she was jittery too, which only seemed fair given how much older I was.

She nodded at the helmet. "Yours?" she asked.

"My husband's."

"He lost it?"

"He was in an accident. We've been wondering what became of it."

She looked a little shocked and asked if he was okay.

"He's fine," I said, startled by the words even as they came out. A minor adjustment, I realized, so she wouldn't be upset or repelled. I saw how automatically we do this kind of thing when our minds are working well. For me it was going to be like re-learning everything after a stroke, if I could do it at all. "You shouldn't use a helmet that's been in a crash, you know; it isn't safe."

"I thought someone should wear it a while," she said. "I didn't know why, but since I found it, I figured it fell to me."

She was, I sensed, lying about something. We'd just met and we were both lying, for God's sake.

"You've been watching my webcasts?" she asked. There was anxiety behind the question but I didn't know what it meant. I knew it was best to put her at ease, not to let on how obsessed I'd become.

"I check in when I have time," I said. "Why did you want to meet?"

She shrugged. "I was curious if anyone was really out there. Why did you want to meet me?"

It should have been obvious she'd return this volley, but for some reason I'd failed to anticipate it. I stammered a little and finally managed some further disingenuous patter about curiosity. What I really wanted was to pick up the helmet and hold it over my face, partly to hide myself from her and from the room, but more to smell the inside of it. It would smell like Brian's sweat, and Brian's head-sweat had always carried a slightly different quality, sweeter and less pungent, like a baby's. But of course I quickly realized that by now the helmet would smell of Trish, not of Brian, and I disliked this implied intimacy—between him and her, between her and me.

I asked her about herself. She'd just finished at Berkeley High and was going to UC Santa Barbara in the fall. She lived at home with her parents, but they were traveling for the summer and she was bored.

"They didn't take you with them?" I asked.

"I didn't want to go," she replied, and although she said it politely, I could tell she found the question astonishingly clueless. What eighteen-year-old wanted to go on vacation with her parents? What planet was I living on?

I got the feeling, though, that Trish didn't have a lot of friends. She was bright and seemed shy, rarely a formula for success in high school, as I remembered too well. "It's a difficult time for you right now, I'll bet," I said.

She didn't react with the relieved appreciation I expected. "Who are you, Miss Gen Z?" she asked, a little sharply.

I cringed. "I'm sorry," I said. "It's a reflex; as a matter of fact, I am Miss Gen Z. Or at least, I was."

To my surprise, she seemed genuinely impressed by this, which I found amusing, especially given my faux pas about the vacation.

"No way," she said.

"Afraid so."

"I used to love your column, especially when you talked about sex. It wasn't the usual politically correct B.S."

"Used to?"

She blushed. "Sorry. It just seems like it's kind of gone downhill for the past few weeks."

I was a little glad to hear it, I had to admit. "Someone else has been writing it," I explained. "I decided to take some time off."

She considered this. "I guess that's good," she said. "I think that kind of thing is really important." It was hard not to laugh, she said this so sincerely.

I asked her what she planned to study. She looked a little sheepish and said she was interested in mythology and evolutionary biology.

"I haven't figured out how I'm going to put them together yet."

"Carl Jung, Joseph Campbell, Stephen Jay Gould," I said. "Get them all together in a room and start them talking and you've got a thesis."

"Too bad they don't have the technology for a conference-call séance," she said.

I smiled and said I knew several people who felt the same way. We fell quiet again, but it was a more companionable silence this time.

"How come only you came?" she asked, finally. "Your husband doesn't like coffee?"

"He had to work," I said.

"On Saturday? That's harsh."

"Life can be that way," I said, but I wasn't comfortable talking about myself, at least not yet. "Are you looking forward to school?"

"I'm not worried about the academic part," she said. "It's the rest…"

I wasn't sure how much to ask. "You don't have a boyfriend?"

She exhaled. "Nothing serious, yet. It's like showing up at college without knowing how to read."

I laughed, then, but I was so out of practice I sounded like a whinnying mare. A couple of people turned to look but Trish didn't seem to notice.

"You'll be fine," I said. "You're going to get plenty of attention down there, trust me."

She grinned in a sort of loopy, self-deprecating way, as if this were a radical idea that had never crossed her mind. It struck me that she was maybe one of those girls who grow so used to male attention that it just becomes part of the background radiation, unnoticeable until you're in your thirties, when it diminishes and begins to peter out.

"It's like when you live in a noisy city and then drive to the desert and get out of the car, and the sudden quiet leaves your ears ringing," I said, and then realized I'd just finished my thought aloud, even though she'd have no idea what I was talking about. She looked at me, puzzled but apparently not fazed. I remembered how much credit I used to give adults when I was younger, figuring that if I couldn't follow what they said it was my fault. This ludicrous superstition had apparently, and mercifully, persisted.

I wanted to be her age again, with Brian ahead of me, with everything ahead. I wasn't old, I knew that, but I wasn't young, either, and I was beginning to realize that the balance point straddles a precipice on both sides, one I couldn't go back to, one into which I had already begun to fall.

"Do you like being married?" Trish asked. "I mean, I figure an advice columnist must know how to have a good relationship, right?"

I sipped my coffee. My marriage had been fairly ordinary, I knew, but I'd begun to refashion it, in retrospect, as better than it was. I'd somehow gotten the idea that if I relinquished something flawless it made me a nobler person, and if I couldn't at least be noble, what could I be? What else was there?

"We had a good time together," I said.

"Had?"

But I couldn't say anything more. She eyed me with what I took to be sympathy and I could see she'd drawn the obvious conclusion: like half the other people she knew, even the advice columnist was divorced. I just nodded and let her keep that idea.

"Do you want a scone or something?" she asked.

I smiled, remembering a time when pastry was sufficient to address a great deal of life's troubles. She looked away from me, briefly scanned the room with her eyes, and it dawned on me that she'd been hoping to find a guy here today, the handsome young dude who'd lost his helmet and had been secretly falling in love with her ever since. That's what she'd been lying about; she knew perfectly well why she'd kept up the video stream, but she was polite enough to hide her disappointment when I'd shown up instead of him. I could be so incredibly dense sometimes.

I touched the minicam with my fingertips. "How much life you figure is in those batteries?" I asked.

She shrugged. "I replaced them once," she said. "I guess I should give this back to you."

"It's okay," I said. It struck me as funny that we'd both come here expecting to meet men, though for different reasons. I opened my wallet and took out the last of my money, which came to thirty-seven dollars, and put in on the table in front of her. "Toss the helmet and get a new one," I said.

She pushed the money back toward me. "I can afford it," she said. "Thanks, though. You're a sweet person."

And hearing those words, for reasons I couldn't comprehend any better than the din of living voices surrounding us, I felt a cool relief descend, almost as if I'd been absolved of something. Of what, I didn't know, nor did it really seem to matter.

I stood, wished her well, and began to gather my things.

souvenirs
Aimee Loiselle

souvenirs

I only took one pill the morning me and Victor had to go to family court. I don't know what Victor was taking. He was still fighting the infections in his ankle. He had a lot of pain. I never really knew what he was taking when. At that point, he had more pills than me. But we needed to look good that day, so I made Victor wear his nice jacket and the red army pin, and I wore my nice pants with the new shirt I bought at Fashion Bug. It was kinda silky and plain white, like the women wear in offices.

Me and Victor had to sit outside the courtroom with my brother and his wife even though they were trying to take our kids away. I pretended to read the notices on the wall and whispered a few things to Victor about the courthouse or whatever. We didn't have a lawyer yet. It was just a preliminary hearing to decide whether there should even be a custody hearing. But seeing my brother Darren made me so sick to my stomach I almost couldn't stand being in the same waiting area, him thinking he was so high and mighty after everything Victor had gone through. Darren knew how hard it was.

Darren had seen all our troubles right from the beginning. He'd shoveled the driveway and cut the grass while Victor was in Iraq, and he and Monica had babysat at least once a month to give me a night off. And they'd bought extra presents for the kids—like those sweatshirts from Maine where Darren went ice fishing. And Darren drove me all the way to Logan for my flight to Washington the day Victor was admitted to Walter Reed. Victor had been in Germany for three weeks and kept mostly unconscious because of his leg. The doctors were hoping they could save it, not have to cut any of it off. Darren and Monica watched the kids for me that first week, until I got a motel room near the hospital. So Chantel and Colin could be with us for the weeks of Victor's inpatient and outpatient care.

Darren picked us up from Logan, too, when we all flew home from Washington. He even brought the dog because Victor wanted to see his boy Jake—Victor was the one who'd wanted that dog in the first place. Darren acted like he was so happy we were back, like we could trust him with anything. Chantel ran across the baggage area shouting *Uncle Darren*, her skinny legs moving as hard as they could, her wispy hair caught in the air. Darren hugged each one of us, which he didn't do all the time. He especially held on to Chantel and Colin. And Monica had sent along a bag of groceries because she knew I couldn't go shopping and leave Victor with the kids. Colin was only seventeen months, and he needed to be picked up and have his diaper changed, and Victor couldn't do those things yet.

That first night at the house started out so great. I made pork chops with corn and macaroni and cheese. There were cupcakes for dessert. Victor sat with Chantel and played Connect Four while I cooked. At dinner he ate two plates and helped Colin finish his vegetables. It was the closest to normal we had been in a while. There was only one weird moment because Victor used to clear the table and do the dishes. But I grabbed the plates and took them to the sink, and he grabbed his crutches and went to the couch. We didn't say a word because we just knew.

Me and Victor even had sex that night. It was the first time since he got back that we could try without the kids in the room. I still had to be on top and everything, but it was easier since I wasn't worried about waking them up—I never liked the idea of Chantel looking over from the motel bed or Colin from his playpen to see me wrestling on their father.

Then we both fell asleep, together in our own room for the first time in months with Jake laying at our feet. But Victor yelled in the middle of the night, just like he did at Walter Reed and just like at the motel.

He yelled the same words every time. *Kill 'em.*

Jake jumped off the bed and barked like a crazy dog. He didn't mean anything by it. He was just a plain brown mutt with scruffy fur. But Victor threw our covers in the air, he dropped out of bed and crouched on the floor. I was afraid and embarrassed and confused.

Colin started crying in the next room. "It's okay everybody," I said softly and walked toward the door. "Ssshh. Jake. Quiet. Quiet, it's okay. I gotta get the baby."

I kissed Colin's fingers and fixed the blanket, rubbing his belly until he dozed off. When I got back, Victor was sitting on the bed and the dog's neck was under his left foot. It scared me even though Victor wasn't pushing real hard—he'd never raised a hand to Jake in four years.

"Damn dog," he grumbled. His voice wasn't angry, but it wasn't calm either. Victor had lost weight in Iraq and there was a little loose skin over the top of his boxers. "Thinks he's got something to guard in here, why the fuck doesn't he go watch the door?"

There was nothing to say. I curled my hand around Jake's collar and whispered as I led him to the kitchen. He laid down and I scratched his chest until he sprawled on his side, pressing his paw against my arm. The dog couldn't sleep in our room anymore, that was all. Just because he was happy to have Victor home didn't mean it wasn't an adjustment. Victor had been gone for over a year.

I stood and stared out the window. Early spring frogs were peeping. The outline of the swing set was visible against the purple-black sky—a single ring dangled from the cross bar. An "O" on a foot of nylon rope. My nephew had snapped the other one, and I'd told the kids their dad would fix it as soon as he got home. That was before the mortar rounds hit inside the base, before Victor got pinned under the metal trailer.

I listened to the house. Jake was rubbing his chin against a paw. Colin whimpered and Victor was quiet. I thought about getting a cigarette and watching whatever was on Nick at Nite, but I went back to bed.

Victor was laying on his side, his face gray against the white pillow. Before sitting on the edge of the bed, I pulled the hem of my XL tee-shirt and tucked it under my butt. I wasn't used to Victor seeing me yet, and I hadn't lost all the weight from Colin. The pounds weren't coming off like they had with Chantel six years earlier. I was twenty when I had her though, and working at Denny's every night.

I hoped Victor was falling back to sleep. He took medicine for the pain and other problems. A shattered ankle, infections, fractures in his fibula and tibia. A metal rod and screws. He took sleeping pills too. Like the ones I used to take before I had Chantel—before she turned four months and I went to AA to stop the pills and booze.

I sat staring at the mess on my dresser. A pile of paperwork and manila envelopes, hand lotion, a dented Iraqi army canteen that was in Victor's stuff when it arrived at the hospital. I felt an urge to look in his travel bag. To see what he was taking. But I didn't.

"Lana, I can't sleep now that the goddamn dog woke me up," Victor said. "I need another Ambien."

"The doctors said you shouldn't take that much," I answered.

"They want you off it little—"
"Just get the fuckin' pill," he said.

I didn't start taking any pills until a few weeks later. And it wasn't like before, because I wasn't taking speed and I wasn't drinking and I wasn't going to the bars. I just took one Ambien because I really needed to sleep. It happened at about two in the morning, after Victor yelled again. The same as usual, loud and deep. Jake didn't bark, just like the kids didn't cry anymore. I heard every rustle of the sheet when Victor rolled onto his side. His crew cut showed his face so clear and plain. I could see his stubble and the hard line of his temple. I almost cried because he was right there but looked kinda hollow or something.

The window was open and the fan was on, but the room felt hot. I got out of bed to get a drink of water, and as soon as Jake heard my feet, he hummed with excitement. I could see him in the kitchen, wriggling his whole butt. The hall from the bedroom was short. Just a few yards. The house was a little ranch—three bedrooms, a bathroom, living room, kitchen. There was a breezeway between the house and the one-car garage, and the basement had a washing machine. I'd strung a clothesline from one corner to the other so I wouldn't have to go to the laundromat. Victor had joined the National Guard to have the money for that mortgage, after we saved enough for the down payment. He wanted a house for the kids. And he liked the idea of helping during a blackout or whatever.

I sat on the couch and lit a cigarette. Jake climbed into the recliner, which he wasn't supposed to do. Victor hated finding dog hair on his pants, and I thought it was gross when the kids had it all over them, but I didn't tell Jake to get down. He avoided my eyes and wound himself into a ball, his head hanging over the front of the chair. I smoked my cigarette and thought about what I would drink if I could have a drink. A rum and Coke.

Sitting in the dark, listening to the rumble of traffic on Grafton Road, I felt tired but not sleepy. I just wanted a good night's rest, a blank mind without any dates or lists or prices. But I finished two cigarettes and set the ashtray on top of the refrigerator before going to the bathroom closet for Victor's travel bag. I shook one Ambien into my hand. Popped it in my mouth and bent over the faucet.

The sleep was dark and steady. When Colin woke me up the next morning, I didn't even remember getting in bed. He was pulling on my arm, his brown eyes peeking over the mattress. "Mama, mama. Mama."

"What. What is it? What, Colin?" I asked, running my hand over his dark curls. He got them from me, along with his small ears and big eyelashes. He smelled like butter and cinnamon.

"See it," Colin answered and pointed to the kitchen.

"You up Lana?" Victor called. "I got the kids dressed. Fed 'em, too. You must be tired, with everything."

Colin waddled and crawled out of the room. I stretched my arms and legs and I felt ready for the whole day. All the plates and diapers and sippy cups of generic apple juice and cans of green beans from the Veterans' Food Pantry. Everything.

But I had to start the Adderall after Victor got another infection in his ankle, after I went to see a doctor about my exhaustion. The doctor did one of those surveys and wrote out the prescription with one refill. He said to take it for a while, so I could concentrate and get everything done during the worst of the crisis—Victor had been admitted to UMass Medical and doctors at Walter Reed wanted to see him again. He needed another operation. I called my mom and asked if she could take the kids while I went to Washington for a few days.

"You're not staying with him the whole time?" she asked.

"No, Mom," I said. "Victor might be there a while and we don't have the money for a motel. The kids don't wanna go through that again, anyway." I didn't even want to make the trip. I hated the brown Super 8 Motel and the army doctors and the bright nurse's stations and the lonely worry in plain ugly rooms. But I packed Victor's duffel bag with his clothes and toothpaste. And I packed my own small bag, hiding the Adderall in a tampon box. I didn't want Victor to worry—I knew he'd make a big deal about it just because Adderall's considered an amphetamine. I already had my own Ambien prescription from my new gynecologist, for my problems with sleep and PMS. I stuffed each bottle with tissue so they wouldn't make noise.

My mom watched Chantel and Colin for three nights, but she called Darren to take them during the weekend. Her friends had invited her to Foxwoods, and she liked to sit at the slot machines and get half-price drinks and see free shows in the Atrium. She brought back casino baseball hats for the kids. And my father didn't babysit without my mom. He went to the Knights of Columbus to watch sports and news with his buddies.

When Darren picked me up at the train station in Worcester, he didn't bring the kids and he was asking all kindsa questions. I should've known then that he and Monica were gonna try to take them. He kept staring at my eyes, talking about what a handful Colin was, asking if I was doing okay. I wondered whether Victor had said something about me sleeping late sometimes—which pissed me off, because he'd been sneaking to the liquor store but I hadn't mentioned that to anybody. I didn't stay long at Darren and Monica's. I called the kids and told them to say goodbye to their cousins and get in the car.

When Victor called a couple days later, Chantel and Colin were watching television so I could clip coupons and have a cup of coffee. He said the doctors liked the way his ankle looked and he might be able to fly home in three or four days.

"Are they sure?" I asked. It seemed too soon. He'd had so many infections and another operation. Draining and more screws in his leg.

"They told me it looks good," Victor said. "I wanna get outta here anyway."

"But are they sure? Maybe you need some special therapy or something. They haven't even had you there two weeks."

"The doctors know what they're doin'," he said. "How're Chantel and Colin?"

"They're good," I said. "We're having dinner with Darren and Monica, then the kids can all play and wear themselves out. By the way, you aren't sayin' anything to Darren about me, are you?" I asked.

"No," Victor said. "No, what're you talkin' about? I might've said something about picking Colin outta the crib once or twice, but that's it."

"Why are you telling him that?" I asked. "You know how my brother is with me."

I made an appointment with a counselor after Victor got back, because the situation around the house became such a mess. Victor couldn't get off the couch for at least a month—so neither of us could get a job, and our food stamps were cut because veteran benefits with disability were higher than the regular army pay, and I was taking care of three people all the time, and we didn't have enough money for the mortgage. I had to call Darren to borrow three hundred dollars for September.

The counselor sent me to a psychiatrist, because she was nervous about my anxiety and the fact I couldn't stop crying when I was at her office. The psychiatrist gave me a prescription for Xanax—and I really needed it too, with everything I had to deal with.

So I was taking Ambien for sleep and Adderall for concentration and Xanax for anxiety just like the doctors told me, and I got everything done. There was just one morning when Colin screamed, and Victor fell in the hall and knocked down a basket of dried flowers and scared Chantel. By the time I reached the room, Colin was standing in his crib with tears and boogers all over his face and Chantel was crying.

"Lana. I been tryin' to help, but I can't get Colin outta the crib every morning. I mean look at this," Victor said. "I can't do goddamn shit around here. I can't even get to my son without fallin' on my ass for chrissake."

My eyes felt dry and scratchy, my head lopsided. But I lifted Colin from the crib and pressed Chantel's head against my thigh. "Don't worry about it. You just slipped, that's all. You aren't a hundred percent yet. It was a little accident."

Jake wandered into the room and licked Chantel's tears. She wriggled her face into my leg and swatted the dog.

"Hey, don't hit the dog," Victor shouted. "He was just tryin' to be nice. If you don't want him to lick you, what d'you do?"

"Victor, give her a break. She's upset," I said.

"I don't want her hittin' the dog. What d'you say?"

"No. Sit down," Chantel answered with a sniffle. "No Jake. Sit down."

"That's right. See," Victor said to me. "She knows what to do, even when she's upset."

"Okay," I sighed. "Let's go. Chantel let's go, I gotta get your brother dressed. You look pretty today. Did you pick those clothes out all by yourself—just like a big girl?"

Three weeks later the physical therapist in Worcester asked if I could come to Victor's next appointment. "I'm always there," I answered. "I give him a ride and stay with the kids in the waiting room."

"Yes, of course. That's... I'm sorry," he said. "I meant that you'll need to come into the treatment area, so I was hoping you could find someone to watch your children."

The physical therapist sat us down next to an examination table in one of the small rooms and said Victor would need to get total bed rest for another four weeks. Victor cussed under his breath, but he also sighed and sank into his chair like he was relieved.

I felt sure Victor had told the physical therapist something about me sleeping late, about me not being at the house every night. Heat flooded into my face. "Is something wrong?" I asked. "Is something worse with his leg?"

"No, no. Victor isn't critical, but we aren't seeing the progress we'd expect with his type of injury," the therapist answered.

"Well, if that's what you say he needs... " I shrugged and put out my hands. "I'm just worried about that...about progress. Because Victor isn't on his feet much now." I paused. "I mean, we know he isn't supposed to."

The therapist glanced at Victor, but Victor was staring into his lap. It could've been that he felt shitty because he wasn't getting any better and he couldn't go back to his HVAC job. But I was sure it was because he had complained about taking care of the kids. I felt bad—even though they are his kids too. And I was upset, because Victor kept driving to the liquor store when I wasn't around. I didn't wanna get him in trouble, though, so I didn't talk about that. I just said, "That means he isn't supposed to be driving, right?" to let Victor know what I was thinking.

When we got home, I made sure Victor had his pillow and the remote. Then I let Jake out and brought Victor a bowl of corn chips. He asked if we had any beer.

I looked in the refrigerator. "A couple."

"Can you call Darren and ask him to bring a six pack when he drops off the kids?"

I got the phone from the charging stand and threw it on his lap. "Here. You call him. I gotta start dinner." I couldn't help it. Victor was drinking too much, every night.

"Don't use that tone," Victor said. "I didn't ask for this shit. And my leg'd be a lot better if I wasn't gettin' the kids ready every morning. I might be a cripple, but I ain't fuckin' blind. I saw the empty Ambien bottle that you wrapped in a paper towel and threw in the trash. I can tell when you take whatever—"

"I'm not the one poppin' ten different pills every day," I called from the kitchen as I unwrapped a family pack of cube steak. "Who knows what the hell you're takin'. After all that, I'm surprised you're still awake to drink every night."

"I'm tryin' to get better, Lana," he hollered. "I gotta take those pills for my infection. You don't know what the hell you're talkin' about. And if I wanna have a fuckin' beer, I'm a grown man. I can have a fuckin' beer."

I kept quiet. Pinned my mouth shut. Victor was my husband, and I didn't really know about Iraq. We just had to get through it. "We're going through a rough patch, that's all. It's just... a rough patch."

Darren still didn't say anything about the kids when he was helping us with some stuff around the house, after we finally got the partial payment from that wounded warrior insurance. We couldn't get the full amount since Victor had been hurt before December 2005 and supposedly it wasn't in combat. He was unloading a convoy when the mortars hit. But we did get thirty-six thousand dollars. So we could pay off our credit cards and replace the broken shower door and buy Christmas presents and get a big-boy bed for Colin.

On the day Darren dropped off Colin's new bed, the first fuzzy snowflakes were drifting from the sky. We shook the melting bits from our hair as we carried the boxed parts in from Darren's truck.

"This is a little big for him," Darren said. "You'll have to be careful."

I glared at him for saying it again in front of Victor. "Yeah, but Colin's two now and he's gettin' heavy. I need a break from all that lifting. He'll be fine."

"Well, I'll go'n get it set up," Darren said and headed toward Colin's room.

"Thanks," Victor called from the couch. "As soon as this leg is better, I owe you."

"Don't worry," Darren said and smiled. "I got plenty-a work."

Chantel put down her crayons at the kitchen table and ran to the picture window. "Snow!" she gasped. "It's snowing."

"A little bit," Victor said. He looked at Chantel and pinched his eyes closed with his fingers. When he opened them, they were red and milky at the same time. "It's about time—beginning of January for chrissake."

I called Colin to look at the snow and the dog followed. Jake wagged his tail and stood next to Chantel, who was dancing and waving her hands in the air and patting his back.

I circled the coffee table and sat by Victor. I wanted to know that we were gonna be okay, we could handle a life of army forms and insurance papers and medical offices. We could go on, breaking a little each time. And that what I was doing made a difference in it all.

"I'm gonna fill out an application next week," Victor said. "For the telephone survey job at Holy Cross. Matt said it pays twelve dollars an hour."

"That's good." I nodded. "That's good for now." His skin smelled salty, with a hint of aftershave.

Victor wrapped his arm around me, and I leaned into his ribs. I imagined him and Chantel on a snow tube—me at the top of the hill in a red parka, Colin bundled on a sled. When I looked up, I saw Victor's leg in a brace on the coffee table, and Chantel shaking her hips in front of the dog, and Colin dragging a crayon across the window. I let my face drop to Victor's chest and he pressed his lips against my hair.

Darren left that afternoon and acted like everything was normal. Maybe he and Monica hadn't thought about taking us to family court yet. But a few days later he stomped in yelling my name like he was sure everything was falling apart.

"Lana! Lana! What the hell is goin' on here?"

I woke up and looked at the clock. It was almost eleven. I didn't know where Victor was. If he was in the house or not. "Just a minute," I called. But Darren stormed into my bedroom with Colin on his hip.

"What're you doin' in bed Lana?" he asked. "Your son is cryin' in his dirty wet diaper and your seven-year-old daughter is trying to feed him cereal to make him stop. Didn't you hear?"

"I told you to wait a minute," I cried. "I was just laying down for a second."

"Bullshit," Darren said. "You haven't been outta bed for hours. Why else would Chantel call the house upset, saying that Colin's crying and Daddy isn't home and Mommy's sleeping."

"I was right here," I snapped as I pulled on my robe. "What the hell do you know?"

"I know a helluva lot from living with Mom," he said. "Remember we weren't gonna be like her."

"Gimme my son and get outta my house," I yelled, taking Colin and walking toward the living room. "Don't you dare talk to me like that after all I been through, the infections and everything else. I'm nothing like Mom. You and Monica got your jobs, you both work. So don't come in my house with an attitude. Just get out." I pointed to the door.

"I'm not leaving, Lana. Not until I find the pills. What is it this time?"

I put Colin on the floor and ran after Darren. He yanked the bathroom closet open. "Get out," I said. "Get out. Get outta my house."

"I don't know why I even bother. You hide everything," he said. But he rushed into the kitchen and dumped my purse on the table. Jake was huddled in the corner by the dishwasher. "What's this?" Darren asked holding up a travel-size shampoo bottle. "You carry shampoo in your purse?" He unscrewed the cap and spilled the pills on the counter. "These sleeping pills or amphetamines or… or is it OxyContin again?"

"I wasn't getting any sleep, I had some anxiety." I snatched the bottle from his hand. "The doctors said it was okay."

"You tell these doctors how much you're really takin'?" Darren asked. "Where's Victor?"

"I don't know. He leaves and doesn't tell me where he's going." I stuffed everything back into my purse. "You don't care about that though. Everything's my fault."

"That's great. The two of you. You can't do this, Lana. Not with Victor the way he is."

"I told you to get out," I yelled. "Just get out. And don't worry, we won't call you for anything anymore."

Me and Victor got the summons for family court the next week. I told Victor he better stop complaining about my pills—because if I had to go for treatment, then he was going too. I told him we'd lose the kids, and the court would make us both stay in rehab, and we wouldn't get Chantel and Colin back for months. We'd have social workers and piss tests and supervised visits. They'd make him get off the Ambien and most of his pain pills.

So Victor put on his nice jacket and I put on my new shirt, and I only took one Xanax with my coffee. We told the judge Victor had been in the basement checking the water heater when Darren came to the house that day. It was just that Chantel didn't know, and Victor couldn't hear Colin crying, and I was in bed with a sore throat after taking NyQuil. The judge asked us all types of questions, but me and Victor told the same story. There was no way I was gonna lose my kids. I love them. I'm a good mother—I took care of Chantel and Colin the whole time Victor was gone, and all those weeks in the motel when they got sick of cartoons and Happy Meals, and the long afternoons with Victor drunk on the couch. I did everything. I wasn't gonna let Darren take them.

But of course Darren had to mention the time Victor got in an accident, the time I asked Darren to go to the police station so I wouldn't have to load the kids in the car. The police told him that Victor couldn't remember what had happened, but they'd found him on a side street in town at seven o'clock that night. He'd driven into some mailboxes and gotten out of the car and started walking. When the cops learned he was a vet, they'd taken him to the station and called me without filing any paperwork.

The judge asked Darren if the children were in the car or involved in any way, and he had to say no. So the judge refused to pass the case onto a custody hearing. He said there were no grounds for consideration. But he did assign a social worker to the case. Darren's face got all serious and white, and Monica was crying. "Thank you, your honor," Victor said as he stood with his metal crutches. The tall kind with round arm braces.

We caught up to Darren and Monica at the elevator. "Don't you ever do this to me again," I said. I didn't care a bit about the other people standing around in the big gray hallway. "Chantel and Colin are my babies. They belong with me."

"Not when you're using, they don't," Darren whispered. He kept staring at the elevator numbers. Monica had on these new summer shoes with cork heels. She looked pretty. "Stop making a scene."

Victor grabbed my elbow. "Come on Lana. Not here."

Darren put his arm on Monica's shoulder as they stepped into the elevator. "Let's go," he said. And when the doors closed, I almost cried. I couldn't believe they could be like that, so perfect and everything, and just leave me standing there.

My mom eventually called to say Monica was throwing a big barbecue for the Fourth of July because Darren had fireworks from New York. My mom had asked them if we were welcome, and Darren said it was okay, that we should bring Chantel and Colin around three o'clock. He and Monica really wanted to see them, and there were matching flag tee-shirts for all the kids to wear.

A social worker did make an appointment to visit the house. I cleaned everything and dressed the kids in their Easter outfits, even though Chantel's dress didn't fit right anymore. The social worker was a short lady, a few years older than me. Victor followed us on his crutches until he had to give his leg a rest. I made sure he had mints in his pocket. The lady didn't seem too concerned. She didn't make any more appointments. I'm sure she had other families to worry about—the news is full of babies getting burned or shaken or left in cars. And me and Victor don't do anything like that.

twenty tales of natural disaster
Helen Phillips

twenty tales of natural disaster

1. Flood

The old family farm is going to drown. They've built a dam downriver. The cow dung meadow will be flooded, the disintegrating tractor and the dandelions. You can't think of anything to do but throw an enormous party.

Your mother. Your father. Your two sisters. Your brother. Your one remaining grandmother. Your one remaining grandfather. Your step-grandmother. Your four aunts and three uncles. Your eleven cousins. The greats and the seconds. All your teachers, most loved and most hated. The wide-eyed kids you knew in school. The girl who got the lead in the play. The boy you loved until he got cruel. Your cross-country coach. The narrow-eyed kids you knew in college. The professor who recalls you. Your old one-night stands. Your old landlords. That sympathetic waitress. The sweetheart at the post office. The bus driver who always sneezes. The Brazilian girl you met in Fargo. The baby you babysat who's in fifth grade now. Your editor who got fired from the newspaper for being clever. Your parents' boisterous friends who remember when you were born. The deformed man who once stared at you on a hot subway platform. Your Mormon neighbors. Bob Dylan. The person you want to marry. Hopefully even the ghosts will show up: your great-grandparents who bought this farm, your boss at the candy store who was knifed to death while making the midnight fudge, your sister's ex-boyfriend who died in a crash, Pablo Neruda. Everyone! That's all you want. Everyone!

You just want them all to be there, drinking beer, drinking cheap red wine, eating cakes and cookies, lingering in the light cast by the torches in the woods, you want to look up at the soft black sky with its mournful stars and then look down to see everyone standing around the bonfire, starting to dance around the bonfire, jubilant, playing their guitars and banjos, playing their harmonicas and tambourines, as the river begins to rise, water coming like snakes through the tall grasses and the blackberry brambles, the river rising, rising.

2. Flood

The floodwaters are rising. First, we notice starfish in the subway (initially mistaken for the handprints of homeless men smeared on the tile); we notice sea cucumbers on the tracks (initially mistaken for the discarded produce of tired old Russian ladies). We are charmed by the appearance of these oceanic creatures (indeed, we give them credit for their gumption, to end up here) until we realize what their appearance reveals . . . And in the park we come upon a lone white duck with wild, filthy feathers; he marches along the shore of the lake, waiting for the water to come to him. This duck—he scares us. He's a brave, crazy fellow, and delighted that the floodwaters are rising; he'd kill us if he could. A handful of tiny birds take flight from a chokecherry bush. It is impossible to decipher their feelings about the floodwaters. They are so stupid and beautiful, always following one another in perfect formation, moving up and down in the air like black pearls strung on an invisible net.

Oh—darling—watch those metaphors, you're getting ornate, you're starting to use metaphors from the sea, do you even know what a black pearl is, because I don't. You wouldn't be talking about black pearls if you didn't know, somewhere deep inside, that the floodwaters truly are rising.

We go to the grocery store, where we These fragments I have shored don't know what to buy we try These fragments I have shored against to think logically but fail so we These fragments I have shored against my grab tofu Oreos cinnamon bananas birthday These fragments I have shored against my ruins candles chicken who keeps saying that anyway someone keeps saying something I keep hearing it—

Please—darling—you've got to focus, and stay calm. The floodwaters are rising. Didn't you see the tree that got struck by lightning? Didn't you see how the top fell to the bottom, and how all the leaves and red berries that were once out of reach are now on the ground?

3. Flood

Tonight an old man came in and asked for honey mead. That's not a request we get much nowadays, and I kept a close eye on him. His beard was outrageously long. I couldn't see the end of it from where I stood behind the bar. It had things, twigs and leaves, stuck so far into it that I wondered if they hadn't been intentionally woven among the strands. His hair, too, was chaotic. A bird could've built a nice home there. *Walt Whitman times a hundred*, I thought to myself.

This old man was not like our other patrons. He didn't glance in the direction of the pool tables, and he was oblivious to even our prettiest girl. With each cup of honey mead, he crumpled further into himself. Eventually I noticed that his beard was soggy. I leaned over the bar in a manner that has been known to make old guys tell their stories.

"I didn't get them all," he said.

"What all?"

"Madam." He looked at me for the first time. His eyes were golden, no kidding. "There were small elephants. Beautiful little elephants the size of your goats." I nodded. "Madam, there were mice the size of rhinos and rhinos the size of houses. Fire-breathing lizards with gentle dispositions. Crocodiles three times larger than any you've ever seen. Squirrels as ferocious as bears. Turtles as big as cars. Ten-foot birds that weighed eight hundred pounds. Dragonflies that flew fifty miles per hour. Miniature deer. Bright pink cats. Vicious mountain sheep. Mules with wings. Parakeets with silver feathers."

I stroked his wobbling hand. His beard was getting downright wet. I hung on to his finger. I've seen a lot of sad, crazy old men. But this guy, he was different. He was not crazy, and he had every reason in this godforsaken universe to be sad.

"The rain kept coming," he said. "It became difficult to gather them two by two." I was stricken by the length and filth of his nails. "At times," he said, "impossible."

4. Flood

So often that spring, my parents were worried. They woke early and looked at the falling rain. It rained and rained. The days were warm and wet. It was the kind of weather that makes worms and crocuses rise. Mom groaned. Dad kept saying, "The basement better not flood, then we'd have a goddamn problem on our hands." I almost laughed whenever Dad said goddamn.

"How deep will the water be?" I asked.

"That's not the way it works," Mom said. "It seeps, that's how it works."

"It's not going to be deep and it's not going to seep," Dad said, "because it's not going to flood at all."

"Deep and seep!" I said. "That rhymes. You're a poet and you didn't even know it."

But my parents weren't listening. They were looking at the rain.

A flooded house! It sounded wonderful, like a swimming pool; I pictured myself swimming around, gazing at all the familiar objects preserved and undisturbed in the blue chlorinated clarity.

I wanted the house to flood, oh, how I wanted it to flood!

I'd use my nascent swimming skills to propel myself into the kitchen. I'd look at the table beneath me: half a grapefruit and a toothed spoon. Mom's food. In the living room, I'd float past the underwater books, Dad's old leather books, stroking them with my tiptoes. The bathroom would be funny, the toilet far below, its water joined to the floodwater, and the bathtub submerged. In my bedroom, the dolls would be transformed into mermaids; they'd stare up at me, a green cast to their hair. Perhaps the sun would break through, glowing in the window, and I'd do a water somersault. Next my parents' bedroom, the large maroon pillows still puffy as ever, and then the guestroom, which was now my dad's bedroom.

The basement did flood, and that made the septic system flood, and there was old poop all over the carpet, and my parents had to clean it up, and they were not happy, not happy at all.

5. Lightning

This is what happened: Your mother was sitting on the porch. It was August. The night of light. Everyone hung candles in silk globes on the gingerbread roofs of their cottages. Small kids ran around burning themselves with sparklers. Big kids shared one cigarette, an orange pinprick beyond the pond.

The cottages blazed from the inside too, lamps in the living rooms illuminating the gingersnaps. Great-great-grandmothers' crystal bowls hosted radiant gumdrops. The punch glowed with its own pink light. A group of gay boys wandered among the cottages, singing cheerful songs from a lighter era.

The oldest man in the world had been honored that night. They let him light the first candle, and then let him sit in his rocking chair where he sat for ten hours every day. He had things to tell people, yes he did, yessir, but the light had stolen his voice.

My darling, you who were not there, it wasn't difficult to be happy then. So much less difficult than usual. I found one of the darkest places, beside the lilac bush, and lingered there to catch the last of the light before it was swallowed up by the thick fragrant black of the woods.

Your mother sat on the porch with two other old women. They all had red skin and flowery dresses. They looked as though they could answer any question in the world. I could think of a hundred I wanted to ask. But then the gay boys came by. More punch had to be made, and the seventh batch of gingersnaps pulled from the oven.

It was just then—as your mother held up the bowl of gumdrops for the gay boys, as the littlest kid discovered my hiding spot, as the older kids returned chewing gum—that lightning struck. Drawn by the many sources of light illuminating the cottages that night, it came down, trying to match our brightness with its brightness, it struck the roof of your mother's cottage, my darling, and everything everything everything began to burn.

6. Wind

At times, we wake happy, or at least as happy as one could ever hope to be in this world. Spring has come to the darkest city. Even the streets, which glimmered icily at us all winter, have taken on a hot moist smell. Girls stalk sidewalks in slutty dresses. Teenagers get desirous on stoops. Purple clusters of flowers emerge like warts from the bark of trees. We could float a hundred miles on these vibrant sidewalks! Pointing, we recall the names of flowers. It becomes truly hot, girls crave ice, ice-cream trucks sing faraway songs, sweat manifests itself as a glow in the darkening light; we are all glowing. So this is it. This is what we've been waiting for. The wind sways the tops of trees like a dream. Everything is dreamed, purple warts, lolling teenagers, half-naked girls, light darkening. The wind strokes tits and asses, wants to be a part of this, wants so much to be a part of this—

—grows violent, picks up dirt, throws it in our eyes, yanks bags from hands, yanks tulips from lawns, a tornado, a real tornado, the sky yellow, the sky ill, we crouch on the pavement, branches fall from trees, crack and crash, half-naked girls buried under thousands of leaves, something bloody appears on the sidewalk, something bloody rushes past, we cannot see, the teenagers have vanished, we rattle the doors of neighbors who grinned so brightly at us two minutes ago, we cry out, no one unbolts a door, what did we do to deserve this? Is it just that we were happy? Is it just that we had finally arrived at a time better than the time before? Why didn't you warn us, why didn't you instruct us to build a ship and load it two by two? We would have done it, if you'd told us, or at least we would have tried. The wind scrapes our eyes, our lungs fill with dust, a car lifts off the street and swirls above our heads.

7. Wind

Yet again I find myself obliged to defend myself. I didn't realize what would happen! I swear that when I put my old clothes out on the sidewalk it was a soft, sweet morning. I was desperate to have them claimed by strangers and enter other homes where they could become more fully themselves.

When the wind picked up I was on the telephone, telling him things such as "Sometimes I'm like a screaming woman in a locked room" and "Sometimes I'm like a woman wearing a muzzle." Hanging up, I observed huge trees swaying as though they were saplings. It was then that I recalled my clothes. Rushing outside into swirling yellow pollen, I sneezed nine times and my eyes took on a yellow hue. I saw what I'd feared: twisted, floppy, yellow with pollen, my clothes lay in the street, shipwrecked sailors clinging to an inhospitable shore. They looked familiar, of course, but also strange, like an ex you haven't seen in half a decade. Perhaps that's why I left them—yes, I'll admit it, I left them strewn there. Who knew what would become of them? Nobody would want them now, that was certain; yet I did not reclaim them.

Forgive me.

My mother, stricken suddenly with the urge to contact each of her children, called from across the continent. A knot in her stomach, she claimed, convinced her that something awful had happened. This, from the woman who taught me to say things such as "Sometimes I'm like a screaming woman." I assured her that nothing awful had happened. Hanging up, I was filled with regret; I should have told her the truth. But the truth comes in several forms, and none seem quite appropriate: (a) "This morning I felt like my arm was stretched across his body, but in fact it was lying numbly asleep upon my own torso," (b) "It's terribly windy here; the tops of the trees may soon fall," (c) "All of my old clothes are sprawled out there in the street."

8. Snow

We were young. We cooked dinner. The yams failed. We went upstairs. It was catastrophic. We were unhappy. You were uncertain. We came downstairs. We went out. The subway broke. We walked far. We got cheerful. The night shimmered. The night trembled. The snow came. We forgot ourselves. Boots eluded us. Mittens eluded us. Our hands froze. Taxicabs honked mournfully. They wanted us. We ignored them. I was laughing. You were yelling. You made snowballs. I was crying. You bought donuts. They were hot. We held them. Our hands warmed. The snow spun. We were ecstatic. Where was home? We didn't know. We couldn't remember.

The sidewalks vanished. We were scared. It was midnight. We imagined toothbrushes. We imagined beds. We imagined pajamas. Everything was imagined. Snow speared everything. We got cold. Our stomachs shivered. Our eyelashes failed. Our eyes ached. Nobody was out. We were out. I said no. You said yes. I said yes. You said no. We doubted ourselves. A swan screamed. A woman screamed. Where were we? I saw wolves. You saw elephants. We couldn't agree. You saw unicorns. I saw dragons. It was dark. It was white. You were hungry. I was starving. Candles wavered distantly. Somewhere was warm. Trees hosted squirrels. Pinecones fell down. Cars passed indifferently. Policemen were blind. Twenty-four-hour diners closed. Nobody knew us. Airplanes passed above. The earth creaked. The ocean pressed. We heard everything. We held hands. Park benches vanished. Streetlamps fizzled out. Nothing could melt. We let go. Winter had desires. We couldn't interfere. We were inadequate. Our yams failed. No compass appeared. We guessed west. We walked invisibly. Brick homes appeared. Brick homes disappeared. I followed you. You trailed me. We were blind. We were stupid. Our footprints vanished. We couldn't retrace. This was it. We lost hope. We carried on. Sparrows whistled joyfully. Were they idiots? We pitied them. We craved peppermint. We imagined sunlight. Our door appeared. It was red. Who has keys? I have keys. Open it, please. Joy overcame us. Yes. We ate yams.

9. Drought

This must be the time of year when baby birds fail, for I have seen them plastered to the sidewalk. From a distance they look like brown crumpled leaves, and you wonder how autumn snuck into spring, but then, when you're right on top of them, you see the agony of bent legs and soft bones and black fuzz and incomplete wings stuck to pavement. What oblivious passersby have stepped on the dead birds, pressing them flat? Have you ever done it, or have I?

The doctor says women who feel a lack when they don't menstruate are irrational. That's exactly what we're trying to do here, she says, make ourselves infertile for the time being. Right? She tells me that once, and only once, she knew a girl who lost her period and never got it back. I wonder if I am that girl. I never minded being reminded that there was a red world inside. And yet.

Springtime was born to strive; it strives against the exhaust of trucks, against gynecologists in air-conditioned rooms, against broken lawn chairs stranded in the city park. The sun rises red and violent across the still water of the lake where seven swans glide eerily. I have come upon yellow swamp irises growing in the park. I know a place where an enormous tree fell in lightning, its solar system of leaves crashing down.

When I was a little girl they told me half of my daughter already existed, in a sac inside of me, for girls are born with all the eggs they'll ever have. I was told my daughter would wait there until the proper moment, and then would emerge. New science suggests this model is not accurate. Yet I think of my daughter, fidgeting, impatient, already a teenager but still inside of me, waiting, waiting. I wish I trusted the world more. I wish the deserts of the earth would stop spreading. I wish my daughter were here among us already, because I am no longer certain of anything.

10. Drought

Our parents say *Get ready, it's time to go to the ruin*. The what? *The ruin*. The ruin? *The womb of civilization*. The what?

Getting ready consists of rubbing our bodies with red mud. This mud dries on our skin and we look like aliens. Our parents lead us through a cactus graveyard. Cactus skeletons are sharp and black. We long for a living cactus. The sun dislikes the fact that we have protected our skin with dirt. It attempts to penetrate us, and sometimes it succeeds. The trail goes straight up among stunted and indifferent junipers. We are weary. Our parents are not. We try to take refuge in the smoky smell of sagebrush. We are thirsty. Water is not permitted. The earth is yellow, dry, red, dry, orange, dry, and dry. We wonder if the ancient peoples were more beloved than we. Our parents abandon the trail. Following them, we step over the bones of prairie dogs and swallows.

Our parents stop, and sigh. They have joyous expressions on their faces. We look around. Everything is the same. Dirt and sage. *What is it?* we say. *What is it?* we demand. *The ruin*, they say. *Where?* we say. *Right there*, they say. *I don't see anything*, we say. *Oh*, they say, *did we forget to mention that the ruin is imaginary? Imaginary!* we say. They say: *Don't you love the tidy little houses? Don't the girls look beautiful fetching water in their dresses made of feathers? Aren't the young men beautiful too?*

Mom, we say. *Dad*. This is such a goddamn disappointment.

We pull out our forbidden water bottles. We drink, and wash ourselves until the dirt turns back to mud. We put on American sun-block and sunglasses. We tell our parents we're leaving. They do not respond. They do not follow us.

We do not know it yet, but someday we will bring our children here. We will say *Get ready, it's time to go to the ruin*. We will come again; we will not be disappointed.

11. Extinction

Our bodies have no memory of the seasons. If they did, we'd never stay in the same place; if the cruelty of February and the cruelty of August could play simultaneously over our skin, we would go mad. We'd leave our homes, board southbound buses, wouldn't stop until we reached eternal *primavera*. Thankfully, our bodies are forgetful. They enjoy the strange shocking brightness of spring and fall, then talk themselves into staying for another season.

We go to the primeval park where our prehistoric ancestors can be seen. The path leads down into a canyon. The blackberries are so big they make us laugh. Also, we're laughing because we're frightened, and nervous. What will they be like, these ancestors of ours? Won't they wish to attack, and won't they win? Reeds thick as thumbs grow everywhere. Then we spot one, squatting beside a shallow stream, its hand—yes, opposable thumbs!—outstretched to grab a frog. Its limbs are thicker and shorter than ours. It has a hump on its back. Its hair is stringy. We feel little affiliation with it. Only as much as might be felt with a cow. Its face is more like the face of a dog than like one of our faces. Suddenly, it becomes aware of us. Or perhaps, like any non-human creature, it has been aware of us all along, our hiking boots grinding deafeningly into the reeds, and has just now chosen to acknowledge us. We can tell, when it looks at us, that the latter is true. It looks at us with such compassion! We become shy, and retreat.

One thing we cannot forget, even years later, is the skin of that creature. It was a warm, dark golden color, thick and smooth, durable as plastic—skin capable of remembering the seasons, skin that could simultaneously bear February and August. That body was not forgetful. Those eyes absorbed in minute detail each of our scared, amazed faces. Guiltily, we wonder why we won, and why we have covered the entire globe with our discontent.

12. Extinction

In the American Museum of Natural History, in the year 20—, we come upon the Hall of the North American Environment, but between ourselves we call it the Hall of Nostalgia for Things We Have Never Seen. There are, for instance, dioramas the size of shoeboxes; each portrays one of the four seasons, but none of these scenes are familiar. When was autumn a mule pulling a cart through orange leaves down a dirt road alongside a stone wall past fields yellow with wheat beneath a pure blue sky under branches dragged downward by apples, the cart itself loaded with wicker baskets of apples? Oh, darling diorama-maker. Don't you know we've never tasted freshly picked apples? When was winter a frozen lake, a group of children with ice-skates, a farmhouse releasing smoke into a white sky, heaps of snow tenderly covering the barn and the hills? Was spring ever really this green, I ask you, you diorama-maker, you who painted this optimistic lavender sky, you who conceive of slender white birches, you who still believe in daffodils and in the grass? And wouldn't everyone have died of joy at the height of this summer you've brought us? Oh, yes we can hear the crickets, my dear diorama-making friend, we can smell the hot smell of skin warmed by the sun and we can smell the dark smell of algae in a pond encrusted with lily pads, we can, we can, we can feel the long marks left by the extravagant grass on our bare legs. Radiant dragonflies, mating, skim the water. Raspberries on the bush ripen before our eyes. Oh, oh.

You should not have brought all this to mind.

Because now, you see, aching, we leave the Hall of the North American Environment. We become aware, once again, of the air-conditioning chilling our blood. Unlike the good farmer and the good farmer's wife, we do not stay near each other for warmth. No; we pass through the great synthetic doors and into the glimmering steel city without touching.

13. Drought

"Isn't it *beautiful*?" they say proudly, gazing out over the landscape. Politely, I nod, though it looks like a wasteland to me. I want to ask them, "How long has it been since it even rained here?" They say, "The horizon seems *so far* away. Isn't that amazing!" Their enthusiasm is touching, childish. Imitating them, I put my hand to my heart in a gesture of awe. Unfortunately, though, I'm not awed by all these empty fields. I stare instead at a single black tree cowering under the enormous sky. I'd like to sit beneath that tree and make it feel useful once again so it would produce extravagant leaves. "*Gosh!*" they say cheerily, to fill the silence. "*Gosh!*" I reply. The empty granaries are lined up tidily like the toys of a foolish, anxious child. I don't tell them that these dry streambeds show up in my dreams; I fly unsteadily above white dust where water ought to run, imagining a trickle of dirty water, followed by a torrent, followed by fishes, brown speckled gold, green algae flowing like a girl's hair, a boat made from a leaf, someone dozing, someone whispering *Come here!*

But moreover I see the ragtag armies of the future marching dangerously across these plains, chanting cruel songs in languages that bear no relation to the languages of this era. They're always thirsty. They wear garments made from the pelts of animals that do not yet exist. They smear black blood on their skin to protect it from the evil sun. Their women lay eggs rather than gestating, and their fetuses emerge slimy, weary, already starving. It's enough to make one shiver.

Misunderstanding me, as usual, they smile when they note the shiver passing through me. Surely I am reacting to the sunbeams that have just cut through the clouds, glorious sunbeams now stretching across the plains, illuminating the fields. "Don't those sunbeams look like they're made out of *matter* rather than light?" they say. "Maybe there really *is* something divine watching over this planet."

14. Drought

Buy This Sea SALT! Born From The Warm Waters Of The Mediterranean Sea, Each Crystal Contains The Energy Of The Sun. Our SALT Is Collected By Hand, Then Prepared In An Ancient And Secret Phoenician Tradition. This SALT Will Help You. A Man And Woman Sit At A Table, Nothing Between Them But A Small Bowl Of SALT. They've Just Eaten An Avocado With SALT, Or A Tomato With SALT. They Smile. He Reaches For Her And Knocks Over The SALT. They Each Take A Pinch And (Admiring The Large Crystals) Throw It Over Their Shoulders. No Bad Luck Descends On Them Ever! But You're Still Wondering About The Aforementioned Secret Phoenician Tradition! What A Curious Little Monkey You Are, Dear SALT-Buyer! You're Picturing A Black-Haired Woman In A White Dress, Stomping Around In An Enormous Wooden Vat of SALT. You Are So Imaginative! But That Is, Obviously, An Image Stolen From The Little You Know About The Making Of Wine. The Making Of SALT Does Not Involve The Legs Of Mediterranean Women. However, Rest Assured That Our Phoenician Tradition Is Even More Charming. Enough Said. Shake This Box Until The SALT Sounds Like Rain. (Yes, Standing Right There In The Aisle Of The Supermarket. You Really Must Do Things Like This More Often. Have A Bit Of Fun In Life.) In This Drought-Ridden Time, Humans Need To Hear The Sound Of Rain. Now You Can Keep That Sound In Your Very Own Kitchen! You're Dancing, Aren't You, To The Rhythm Of The SALT? You Still Have A Certain Youthful Enthusiasm. It's Beautiful To Sea. Oops. "See," Not "Sea." But "Sea" Brings Us Back To Sea SALT. This SALT Will Save You. Sample One Crystal, Though If The Supermarket Gives You Trouble Don't Blame Us. Isn't It Satisfying, The Gem-Like Shape Of The Crystal In The Palm Of The Hand? And The SALTiness As You Crush It Between Your Molars. You Don't Need To Say It. We Know You

Feel Better Now Than You've Been Feeling. Buy This Sea SALT!

15. Drought

At the baths, naked women attempt to wash away their unhappiness in six stages: dry sauna, wet sauna, hot pool, cold pool, high shower, low shower. "Cucumber salves inner wounds." Always thirsty, they drink cucumber water in huge, vulgar gulps, and still they are thirsty. "Sea salt removes outer layers." They grind sea salt into their skin. "Twig tea cleanses intestines." As the hot liquid moves through them, they lie back, let their eyes drain and become empty. My sister goes to the baths to transform herself. There are many legs here, slightly ugly, slightly lovely. The steam sauna is a beautiful and dangerous place. Mythological creatures appear out of the mist, transforming into old women with fat encircling their wrists, into young women with bones like jewelry. If only my sister were small enough that I could hold her in my palm. She'd sit cross-legged on my lifelines, telling jokes. One woman instructs another: This is what you do with cucumbers. This is how you plunge into the cold pool. This is how you wash your innards. This is where you rub peppermint oil so your thoughts become cool, clear, empty. A confession: I'm terrified by something inside my sister's refrigerator. I've seen a bowl of flawless fruit decay until it became a gray apocalypse. If my sister were three inches tall I'd take her away. I wouldn't let her open that refrigerator ever again. In a large house as lovely as a dessert, my sister walks down the hallway, enters the kitchen. A metal bowl filled with beautiful plastic oranges. No spider-web and no strand of hair would ever dare mar this house. She opens a glass door. Outside, two lounge chairs. Trees and sunlight billow around her. I hear rumors of a man who can cut houses cleanly in half with a chainsaw. Tomorrow, she'll go to the baths. My sister wears that same nervous, grinning expression she wore when she forgot her lines in the kindergarten play. What has happened to us? What has happened?

16. Drought

The last farmer in the world hears things to which we are deaf. Hears snowflakes hitting cow-dung. Hears the moist, taut sound of chickens laying eggs. Hears the bones of small mammals snapping in the forest. Hears blades of grass slumping in drought. Hears his own innards going about their business. Hears his brain moving toward thoughts like a large, slow piece of machinery. Hears cells dividing in the womb of a horse, and hears the filly plopping into life some months later. Hears pollen hitting his eye and hears himself blinking.

He also hears his invisible wife rolling the piecrust, sprinkling flour, rolling the piecrust, sprinkling flour. Hears the joint between her femur and her pelvis popping when they do what they do at bedtime. Hears cells dividing in her womb, hears his invisible sons and daughters being put together bit by bit until they have lungs, eyelids, ears. When they sleep, he hears the noises made by the monsters in their dreams. When they go to school, he hears their brains learning numbers, a sound like many faucets dripping irregularly. At night, he lies awake, listening to his invisible family digest cornbread, butter, green beans, milk, bacon, blueberry pie. It is a symphony, and he grins. He doesn't know the word symphony.

As the farmhouse is demolished, certain items can be seen in the wreckage. A chair. A cup. A table. The windows splinter first, then the shingles, the walls, the floorboards. The kitchen goes first, then the living room. The upstairs bedrooms cave in. A mattress. A coffee can. A fork. A milk bottle. A white slipper. A lampshade. You wonder why the farmer left these objects behind? You wonder why he is not here to watch it happen?

Already the last farmer in the world lives alone on the thirty-ninth floor of a skyscraper. The yellow taxicabs in the streets below bring to mind crickets. He wants to know how anyone can sleep what with the uproar of water and sewage moving through the pipes.

17. Warming
used to be snow here, everything white and firm and ice; then mud came peeking through, and, mesmerized by the novelty, we surrounded it, exclaiming *So this must be spring!* for we'd only read about spring; aware of how humans are supposed to feel about spring, we waited eagerly for something green to appear, but instead the mud spread; we retreated to our homes, shamefully longing for snow; later, we noticed our floorboards becoming unstable beneath our feet, and rushing outside we saw that all the houses were sinking into the mud—but sinking very gradually, and our lives continue rather normally, with only minor inconveniences: we yank our mailboxes up from the mud every morning, trade our delicate snow-boots for mail-order galoshes, hurry after our babies whenever they sneak outside (we find them floundering and gurgling, delighted, sinking, mud wedged between their rolls of fat); meanwhile, the wrought-iron lampposts lining our streets (pet project of the Beautification Committee) become unmoored and crash down, their frosted glass globes shattering, leaving shards in the mud; the playground sinks quicker than anything, but the monkey bars

remain, now only an inch high, and our resourceful children create games that involve hopping across the metal bars; the graveyard disappears; in the library the books are slimy with mud; and then comes one particularly discouraging moment: a Flexible Flyer sled, capable of making sleek sounds upon fresh snow, appears in a sinking public trashcan, its runners thick with mud, as dead as a sled can be; we try to go forth, we do!; leading their daughters down the aisle, wishing desperately to distract them from the mud on their lacy trains, fathers whisper *Seeing a bride is like seeing a unicorn*; grooms carry brides over reinforced thresholds, but even adding extra concrete to the foundation can't prevent the inevitable; still, newlyweds lie in bed and drink coffee and paint walls, pretending they're starting a stable life together. Eventually, though, it becomes impossible to ignore the fact that everything shall vanish, and we recall that there

18. Fire
When the subway fire begins, we keep our cool, as we've been trained. We don't remove our sunglasses. We don't take deep breaths in an attempt to figure out the source of the smoke. We stand on the subway platform, breathing shallowly, pretending we're merely smelling urine and old gum, chatting among ourselves, avoiding the topic of the fire that's raging somewhere nearby. We don't think about how many stairs stand between us and the outside. We don't entertain the possibility of claustrophobia. If there were a problem, the firemen would be here. If there were a problem, announcements would blare over the loudspeakers. There are no firemen and no announcements: ergo, we keep our cool. This is the logic in which this city has trained us. Disregard the smoke stinging your eyes, disregard the flicker of orange down the tunnel, disregard your claustrophobic heart. Don't sweat on your lovely fabrics.

But. What if one cannot control oneself? One rushes up the first flight of stairs, screaming, embarrassing oneself a thousand times over yet screaming, shrieking even, and others joining, following behind, letting their beautiful sandals fall off their feet, tearing their delicate garments, clawing one another up the second flight, the third, thousands moving upward, stampeding, sunglasses clattering to cement, up and up, arriving wild-eyed and sweaty on the street, panting in the glorious heat of the earth, trees, breeze, ice-cream truck—and then, shamefully, returning to the subway station, back into the intestines of the city, where trains are running normally and no firemen have appeared, where the smell of smoke has dissipated and no flames can be seen.

Anticipating this trajectory, we stay right where we are, cool as cucumbers on the subway platform, wet-eyed and trembling behind our indifferent sunglasses, feeling a small sense of terrible failure, not unlike the sense of failure felt upon using the air-conditioner for the first time each season, or upon seeing four turtles lining a concrete log in the city park, joyously stretching their silly chins up to the sun.

19. Fire

Now that everything's on fire and there's no water anywhere, the violinist is the firemen's only hope. As he plays, his violin produces water. Using the smallest screws, they attach their hose to his instrument. Radiant orange flames stretch up fifteen feet, twenty. Tchaikovsky. Water starts to emerge from the hose. A drip. Then a stream, a torrent. The firemen attack the fire.

It's unclear to everyone whether the violinist is a guest or a prisoner. He's permitted to sleep four hours each night, in a protective concrete tomb in the graveyard. He's gotta sleep, the firemen agree. While he sleeps the fire gains ground. The firemen begin to feel hopeless. They wake him and give him a PowerBar—such a precious resource now, but remember how they used to inhale them during high-school football season? But hell. Who wants to remember. The smell of tackles ripping up a damp field. Grass and fog. Their sons will never know. There are no autumn football fields (wood-smoke, apples) in the skyscrapers to which families have retreated, claustrophobic but alive. Safe. The firemen get angry, thinking these thoughts, and perhaps are somewhat rough leading the violinist back toward the fire. The fire is red and yellow and green and orange and blue and purple and white. Like bonfires in the woods after the games. Their future wives clinging to them. *Look at those colors!* the girls whispered, their skin hot and coppery.

The violinist has also been remembering. His parents, his friends, etc., the memories anyone would have. Nobody notices the slight slowing of his miraculous fingers. Violin lessons in a room that smelled of mothballs and raisins. Then, eventually, her. Hands hovering above piano keys. How dear she was. Sometimes crying for no reason. Sometimes flinging herself into his arms. Rolling dough into perfect spheres to make gingersnaps. Mournfully rubbing her uterus. Standing in the yard with a teacup as the fire approached. That's all.

The violinist drops his violin and walks away. *Hey!* the firemen shout. *Come back! Stop! Hey! You!*

20. Apocalypse

The first sign of the impending apocalypse is that people start smoking cigarettes in the subway. Before, cops with gleaming badges would have materialized. But now? Everyone smokes, for we know our lives will be short no matter what. Subway cars fill with the delicate fog of cigarette smoke. It swirls overhead, makes us lightheaded, reminds us of those faraway days when cigarettes were legal in bars and smoke was a magic substance through which you could view dark, fascinating scenes—a woman leaning against a wall, drinking a golden liquid.

When the heart of the apocalypse beats right above us, we grab cartons of cigarettes and carry them underground. The subway is the final stronghold in the shattering city. We bring tuxedos and party dresses and booze and crystal and heirloom jewelry. When we get hungry, we eat beans out of cans, but we don't get hungry much. We get drunk. We get smoky. There are, of course, moments of repulsion—issues concerning, for instance, the disposal of human waste.

But moreover: knowing we shall die, we're desperate for joy. We measure time by the number of dresses the women go through. "I've been partying for seven dresses," they report. We'll run out of cigarettes someday, yes, and booze, and even dresses, but our amassed resources are quite astonishing. The unreliable subway lights force us to rely on candles—how romantic we all look in the tremulous flame—but then sometimes the electricity flashes on, and we all cheer, drink deeply, throw glasses on the floor, divine tinkle of shattering crystal. Somebody turns up the battery-powered music and we're the best people in the world, carefree, mystically enshrouded in cigarette smoke, our voices rich as money. It's dark down here, and warm, like the nightclubs we've always dreamed of.

When we emerge, old, pale, sick, the world is all tar and steam. We scream promises to the mustard sky: if we find one single blade of grass, we will redeem ourselves, we will change our life, we will change our life.

piano

Terry Roueche

piano

Carol was in the kitchen cleaning out the cabinets. I could hear her packing, the muffled, clanging together of what was left—the pots, pans, utensils, glasses she was placing in the boxes. My half-brother, Tom, had left to take a last truckload of clothing to the Goodwill, boxes Carol had set aside. Carol and Tom had been going out together a couple of years and she had been a friend of my mother's.

I didn't know my brother and he was all that was left of my family. Coming home, I thought at first we'd try to use the time to learn something about one another, but Tom made it clear he couldn't have cared less. I hadn't seen him in almost sixteen years, since he was ten. The truth was, if he had walked beside me down a street I might not have recognized him. I saw nothing of our mother in him, just his father. And that was someone I wanted to forget.

Tom had sold most of her furniture, what was worth anything; the rest we hauled out to the street for the city to pick up. Someone was coming by about buying the house. They thought the house—a small, wood-framed bungalow my father built—would make good rental property. I wasn't expecting anything. Whatever Tom got for the house, or from selling the furniture, was none of my business. I didn't feel entitled.

I first met Carol the morning I came back, three days before the funeral. That was the day before my mother died. My mother wasn't old. She was a diabetic and went into a coma. She didn't wake up. We never spoke. I don't know what had happened with her life, just that she had stopped looking after herself, had maybe given up. I would never know. I tried to talk to Tom, but I got nothing from him. Maybe that was fair. I had abandoned them. All I knew was what her doctor told me in the hallway at the hospital, that if she wouldn't take care of herself there was nothing anyone could have done.

The morning I came back Carol was at the hospital. She was wearing jeans without a belt, a long sleeve, faded flannel shirt tucked in with the cuffs rolled up to her elbows. She was tall and thin and her dark auburn hair was gathered loosely in a ponytail that jumped about with her quick movements. I guessed she was in her late twenties or early thirties. Carol brought flowers and she was putting them in a vase for my mother. She was animated and talking to my mother when I came into the room, though my mother couldn't have heard her. For a moment, until Carol saw me, I had stood at the door watching her. I startled her when she turned and saw me, catching her off guard. Carol took her hair out from the ponytail and she combed it out with her fingers. I told her who I was and we talked for a few minutes before she had to leave for work. I liked Carol right off. She was easy to be with. She was sweet. Watching her setting the flowers in the vase, she was tender.

I thought it was good of her, checking in on how my mother was doing. I hadn't. If I found anything coming home, it was knowing I had forsaken my mother, a regret I deserved, that then couldn't be reconciled. I'd let the time slip away, and I was sorry about that. But maybe I just didn't care enough, and I had found plenty of things to blame for my life.

The day after the funeral I let Carol take me around town, to see how things had changed since I left. We spent most of the day together and went out to eat that night. Tom was working and couldn't get off so it was the two of us and maybe that was wrong.

I'd lived in Florida the past three years, but since leaving home I'd lived all over the country. I had never stayed long at any one place, passing through here and there with no roots, leaving nothing to connect me with any past. Carol wanted to know about places I'd been. California, Oregon, Arizona, New York, Ohio—other places I'd drifted through. I had worked the last few years on construction jobs around Miami. I felt things begin to stir in me I hadn't felt in a long time, feelings so distant and so long forgotten I didn't want to trust to recognize them as my own, as having once been a part of me. I didn't know if it was being with Carol, or wanting to face my past without the guilt, wanting to remember it as good, finding a warmth despite whatever ugly truth I might have lived.

"You never settled long anywhere?" she asked.

"No. I'm still trying to figure things out," I said. "Still looking, I guess."

"That sounds like me," she said. "Looking for something."

"You think one day you'll find it and from then on it's going to be all right,"

I said. But was that the truth? If she had asked what I was looking for, I don't think I could have told her.

"I think sometimes about leaving here," she said.

"I don't know if leaving's any good. Look at me," I said. "I drift and I've got nothing to show for my life."

"You've never had anyone you wanted to be with?" she asked.

"I wasn't anywhere long enough to find that."

I knew the sooner I slipped away the better, come and go like I'd always done. There had been women that came into my life, but without any expectations from them. I picked women like that and I had assumed they were with me for the same empty reasons. When they were gone, I never thought about them again.

"You have to let people in. You can't be afraid to open your heart," she said. "It hurts more to be alone."

I had her take us to a park where I had played as a kid. It hadn't changed. It was nearly dark and we walked along a pond and found a bench. There was a small island in the middle with ducks. There had been ducks in the pond when I was growing up. We had thrown rocks at them as kids.

"What is it with you and Tom?" Carol asked.

"We never knew one another," I said. "I don't know what I expected. I show up."

"She was your mother. He should understand that."

"Tom was a kid when I left. Maybe he feels I abandoned them. I don't blame him."

Taking off came with a price for me, the regrets. I had to have hurt my mother leaving, leaving her with the problems I couldn't take. And if I'd stayed, what difference could I have made in her or Tom's life? Could I have made it any better? Tom's father was no good. When he drank, it was bad. When he drank, he got mean. He hit me and and he hit my mother and Tom.

Late one night he came in. He dragged us out of our beds, me by the foot. I lifted myself off the floor. Tom and my mother were behind me. I saw I was big enough and old enough to try and stand up to him. He came at me and I hit back, hard and mean. I hurt him and the next day, when he was sober, he threw me out. That was fine. I got away. I left. Then once I was gone, I couldn't make myself go back to it. When I learned he left them, I didn't go home.

For a long time I blamed my mother for Tom's father. My mother wouldn't leave him. I didn't make it easy on her. I was a kid then trying to live in a world where choices have to be this or that. Me or him. The blame went to my father too, but all he had done was die in an accident when I was nine.

"I tried to be with her the last couple of months when I could," she said. "Tom didn't know what to do. There was no one else. It was hard. I'm not blaming you for not being here."

"I know you're not."

"Your mother and I got to be friends. She taught me a lot of things, about gardening, flowers. She was a smart woman in her way. I took her to church. She liked singing hymns."

"I didn't know that," I said.

"She had a pretty voice. There was the preacher, but your mother didn't like him. When she got sick she didn't like the things he told her, how she was going to God, Jesus was calling her home. All that."

"I don't know," I said. "I didn't know her really. I don't remember much. I left when I was seventeen. Tom's father and I didn't get along."

"Tom won't talk about him," she said.

"He wasn't a good man," I said.

All I knew was Tom's father had left seven or eight years ago and went to Oregon, for all I knew he was still a drunk. By the time Tom's father had left them, I had been gone long enough. Staying away was easy. Time had worn the rough bark of blame smooth, into indifference. I kept pushing my feelings down to forget. I was good at doing that.

"I've been to a couple of places," she said and took a few steps up to the water's edge. Her back was to me. I didn't say anything. I wanted to let her talk. "I think about things all the time," she added. "Crazy things. All kinds of things. I don't know where it comes from."

I knew she wanted me to understand her, that she was stumbling for a way to tell me something. Another thing I was good at doing was blocking people from reaching me. I'd learned to see what was coming and step aside, but with Carol I didn't.

"I live here and work," she said. "I like my job. It's like there're things I want to do and I don't know enough to begin. I'm not stupid."

"I don't think you are," I said.

"I don't know what it is I want, I just want it." She picked up a stick and tossed it into the water. "I went to Atlanta one time."

"Did you like going there?" I asked.

"I rode down with a girlfriend because she had a job interview. I just went along with her. We had a good time. We spent the night." She turned to me. "I'm very musical. I like playing the piano," she said.

She picked a coffee cup up off the ground and took it to the trash bin near the bench. Carol was standing a few feet away. She pulled her hair back from her face and held it, twisting it up off her neck. She left her arms crossed over the top of her head holding her hair.

"Can you play anything?" she asked.

"Me? No."

"Nothing?" she asked.

"No."

"Your mother played the piano," she said.

"I don't remember."

"She loved playing. She played all the time."

"I don't remember."

"I can show you how if you want. I can teach you a song your mother taught me."

"How? I can't play. And if I did, where's a piano?"

She sat beside me and covered my hands slowly in hers. I did nothing. She took them away but came back, covering my hands again with hers.

"Pretend this is the keyboard," she said. "Keep your hands under mine. Follow my fingers." She spoke softly.

"I have no idea what we're doing."

"Pretend. That's all. Move with me."

Carol began humming, something spiritual. A hymn I remembered even though I'd never been religious. I knew I went to church when my father was alive, but that was so long ago I remembered little, if anything. Maybe Easter and the three of us coming out of the house past my mother's flowers, and my mother in a blue patterned dress. We were happy. But I can't, and will never, know if that was real or just imagined, the memory waking and forgotten like from a dream.

I let my hands move with Carol's, my fingers dip with her fingers, pressing imaginary keys. At first her hands moved too fast, so she slowed until I could keep up. She hummed. Then I was humming with her as it grew darker around us. The street lights were on so it wasn't black. There was light.

"What's your favorite thing to eat?" she asked, but she kept humming. Then she picked up the pace and I was keeping up with her.

"What?"

"I eat anything."

She started humming a song from a movie I knew. Her fingers moved too fast so I just watched and listen to her hum and pantomime playing.

"What do you like to eat?" she asked me again.

"Probably the same things you like," I said and wished I hadn't.

She hummed a country song and made the music with her fingers, then she stopped abruptly.

She stood, bowed playfully. I clapped.

"Thank you, thank you, thank you," she said.

"I'd like to hear you really play."

"Would you?"

"Yes."

"I don't have a piano," she said. "I'm trying to save up to buy one maybe some day."

"What happened to Leonard's? Are they still downtown?" I asked. Leonard's was a music store.

"Same place," she said. "Still there."

"Then we'll go there." I said. "We'll tell them we're looking for a piano. You can play there."

"I'm not really that good," she said.

"I don't care. I want to hear you play."

She came back to the bench and kicked at my shoes. "I guess we ought to go," she said. "It's late. Tom'll be looking for me."

"All right, but we'll go tomorrow to Leonard's and I can listen to you play."

"I got to work tomorrow."

"Then the next day," I said, but I didn't mean it.

"Maybe."

"We're making a date," I said.

"We'll see," she said.

I stood. "Does Tom play anything?"

"No." That was all she said.

"What does he like to do?" I asked. I was wondering what she saw in Tom. I doubted I was the first person that had questioned that, then again it was none of my business.

"He's got his friends. They're all right. They're his friends. We both like to dance. There's a crowd of us that goes out dancing sometimes. He doesn't drink. Not a drop. He works a lot. He does all right where he works. He's got one friend and they do electrical work on the side together. He's good at fixing things. His friends, anything that goes wrong, they call Tom and he helps them."

"That's nice that people look to him for help."

"Things changed with Tom and me. Then your mother got sick and she needed me."

We were walking, and we were close to one another, taking our time.

My hand brushed across Carol's and that was like grazing across fire.

"What are you going to do now?" she asked.

"Go back to Florida," I said.

"Would you really take me to Leonard's?" she asked.

"If I'm still around."

"When are you going?" she asked.

I felt she was reading my mind, that I saw myself already leaving and all forgotten.

"Two or three days," I said.

We walked back to her car and she asked if there was any other place I wanted to see, but I told her there wasn't. Near her car there were some wild flowers. We stopped and she knelt to pick a flower. I knelt beside her and took the flower and placed it in her hair and wished I hadn't.

"I'm looking too," she said.

We were both still kneeling.

"One day I was going to run by to see if your mother needed anything from the store. She was sitting out on the front steps. I sat with her and she reached for my hand. She didn't want me to see, but she'd been crying. I could see her heart was hurting."

Carol picked another flower.

"She told me you need someone to show you how to love. If you don't grow up with it, all you know is how to hurt. She said she could never see how to fix that."

Carol's eyes were wet. She wiped her face and took the flower out of her hair and held it.

"Tom's a good man. I kept thinking things could change with us. But he never had anyone to show him. All he ever learned was how to be cold. There's a way I want to feel. I can't find it in Tom. I can't make Tom see. No one ever showed him so he could learn. I think that broke your mother's heart."

"What was it like for you growing up?" I asked.

"Not much different."

"I'm sorry."

"I don't know how to find it and I've got to. I'm not going to be scared to look anymore."

She dropped the flowers and we left then. We were out late and Tom was mad about that. He'd been out looking for her. He didn't say anything to me, but later Carol told me he lit into her that night about where we had gone. She told him we had just gone to eat, rode around town a little and that was all. I didn't see her for two days while Tom and I finished cleaning out the house. I didn't ask and Tom said nothing about Carol. Tom didn't owe me an explanation. Tom didn't want me around. I was going to stay no longer than a meeting with a lawyer, sign whatever there was away to Tom.

———

Carol brought out beers from the kitchen when Tom left, taking the last load of clothing to the Goodwill. She wanted to talk, but I found a reason to be someplace else then. When I was alone later I opened the beer and sat on the floor in the front room and lit a cigarette. Carol stopped packing whatever it was in the kitchen and came out. I was going to see the lawyer in the morning. Then leave. Leaving once more was all that was left for me.

"I thought I heard Tom come in."

"No."

"I got another load for the Goodwill," she said. "Boxes in the kitchen to take when he comes back."

"Okay," I said.

She waited for me to say something, but I didn't say anything else to her. I avoided her and told myself just see the lawyer and leave. She stood in the doorway a little longer, then went back to the kitchen to her packing, the clanging of the pots and pans and glasses.

From when my father was alive, I was trying to remember coming into his house, when I was maybe seven or eight and playing shortstop. The memories were unsure, there was no one to ask, and so no one to say it was wrong. I felt the two of us pitching in the front yard, my mother on the steps watching, loving us. It might have been just like that. I wanted to remember how my mother and father had looked, but I couldn't see them. There must be photographs of us, but if there were, Tom had pitched them.

The day before, we found my glove and my bat in a back closet. Tom didn't ask me if I wanted it. It went into a box with everything else either out to the curb or to the Goodwill. I had no reason to keep it.

I tried to imagine the warm, generous smells and how the rooms were furnished from my childhood, to see things coming up to the house from the sidewalk, the flowers my mother must have loved and planted along the front of the house and the walk, baskets hanging along the front porch where there was a swing, and two chairs where my parents sat on summer evenings, if they did. I tried hard to imagine going through the house, to my room, the front room, the kitchen, but there was nothing I could see, nothing I could remember of my father's home. I couldn't remember, just the front porch with the flowers, swing, and two chairs. I couldn't make myself see anything more, so maybe it never was, and the bareness then was no different than when I lived there.

Except for linoleum in the kitchen, the floors were pine and there was the outline where a rug must have been spread for years. I could make out the lighter area on the dingy, beige wall behind what must have been a sofa, or a chair, or a cabinet, or something. I couldn't remember what was what, what had been where. There was nothing, no feelings. I tried to imagine a chair, table, lamp. Nothing. There was a light place on the wall across from where I was sitting, maybe six feet wide and four feet tall. Above it was the space where a mirror, or a large picture, must have hung. Tom had cleaned all the furniture out when she first went into the hospital the last time.

Then Tom pulled up in the truck. I heard the back door swing open and close. Carol went out to meet him. I could hear them talking, but I wasn't listening to what they were saying. It was none of my business.

Tom came in with a bag of hamburgers and some soft drinks. Carol didn't want anything to eat, but wanted a beer. Tom dropped the bag on a box.

"Get something if you want," Tom said.

"All right, thanks." I took a hamburger. I stubbed the cigarette out in an ashtray. I wasn't all that hungry. We didn't talk. Tom found a place to sit. Since all the chairs were gone it was a place on the floor. Carol came in with two beers. One she handed me.

"He didn't come about the house?" Tom asked.

"No," Carol said.

"What's left?" Tom asked.

"What you see here and what's packed up in the kitchen," she said.

"You got it all packed then?" he asked.

"Just about," she said. "Are you still planning on going in to work?"

"I got about an hour still," Tom said. "I got to go call that man about the house. See if he wants it or not."

"What did he say when you talked to him? He was coming for sure?" She was calm.

"He said he'd be here by five."

"It's after five. Maybe you ought to call him," she said.

"I don't have his number with me," Tom said.

"Maybe he just forgot," she said.

"Come on. I'll take you home." Tom said.

"I still got packing to do," she said. "I want to finish cleaning out the cabinets. Finish the kitchen."

"Leave it," Tom said. "Let whoever buys the house worry."

"I want to finish. There're some things I left on the counter. You can look through it if you want.

"What for? Throw it all out," Tom said.

"I'm not. We can take it to the Goodwill. Give it to some church."

"Why don't you go with Tom?" I said. "I can finish packing things, I can take it down to the Goodwill."

"I'll finish. I started it," she said firmly. "Then I need to go over to my sister's tonight."

"What for? What does she want?" Tom said.

"She wants me to come by. I told her I would."

"Come on. I'll take you home," Tom said.

"Can't you give me a lift home?" she asked me. "Take me when I finish up the kitchen."

"I'll drop you off now," Tom said.

"You need to get that man's number and call him about the house," she said. "Let me finish up here. You won't have to come back." She kissed him on the face. "Go on. You're going to be late."

Tom left. He shoved the front door so hard it hit the wall and slammed. I took a cigarette from the pack, then offered one to Carol. She took the cigarette and leaned down for me to light it. She held her hair back out of the way, then, when she bent down for a light, her hair fell across my shoulder. Carol leaned back, letting her shoulders fall against the wall with her hips thrust, arched outward. I still sat on the floor.

"I'll wait. You don't have to. Why don't you catch Tom and go on to your sister's?"

"I just told my sister I might drop by."

"Suit yourself," I said.

She slid down the wall and sat beside me, twisted her hair up off her neck. For a moment it stayed there then began dropping back.

"I need a bath," she said.

She opened a pack of recipes that had come in the mail, went through a few, then put them back into the package and slid it away across the floor.

"Just one of us should wait," I said.

"Go on if you want to go," she said. "Leave."

I didn't move. She used the ashtray and looked at me.

"Tom's not going to be looking for me tonight, thinking I've gone to my sister's."

"Then why'd you tell him that?"

"I just did." There was something on my shirt and she picked it off.

"That's your business."

"You didn't want me to?" she asked.

"Why would I care," I said.

"You leaving tomorrow?" she asked.

"After seeing the lawyer."

I could feel her looking at me. It stung. I thought, *stand and leave.* She wasn't my problem.

"I want you to come to my place." She drew her legs up and wrapped her arms around her legs, letting her head rest on her knees. She looked at me waiting still. I felt it.

"No. That's not a good idea," I said.

"I think you're supposed to teach me something," she said.

"Me? What?"

From somewhere a dog barked. Cars passed down the street. I didn't want to move. When I was seven or eight there must have been an Indian blanket or bedspread, something with tomahawks and arrow heads, something like that over my bed. We had driven to the mountains and I remembered bits of a storefront with a carved black bear rearing up on its hind legs. My mother bought the blanket there for me. I knew I remembered that right.

"Are you hungry?" she asked.

"What?"

"I can cook us something," she said. "I'm a good cook. What would you like?"

I took a long time to think, before I said, "Anything."

"Anything I like?" she said.

"Yes," I said.

She didn't move, her head was still resting on her knees. She was calm and waiting. The light and dark patches on the wall across from where we sat took form. I remembered it was a mirror, I saw it in my mind. It was hung over a black, upright piano. I heard it, saw my mother playing for my father. It was like seeing a ghost. When he died she must have stopped until Carol came.

"What happened to my mother's piano?"

"Tom sold it."

"You didn't want it?" I asked.

"Yes," she said. "I wanted it."

We just sat next to one another and let the night and dark ease into the room. There was no rush. There were things we were both thinking about. I knew they were the same things, because that's how life works and she knew that, too; she knew it before me, since the hospital room and her fussing over the flowers, when she loosened her hair from the ponytail. She was waiting for me to catch up to start.

section
Gregory Williams

section

I was still in scrubs, the weight of thirty-six hours in the hospital anchoring my bones to a chair in the OB nursing station, when a shriek like a Confederate charge—"Ay-yi-yi-yi-yi-yi-yi"—tore through the wall of room 626. It was past 7:00 p.m. Dr. Diaz was in the room, pleading with his patient, Lupe, a seventeen-year-old first-time mother patient, to finally accept an epidural. The anesthesiologist taking over for me wouldn't be up for another thirty minutes. He was finishing a hip fracture downstairs. Nevertheless, I hoped to get home before Maggie put the boys to bed.

I slid to the seat's edge, unwrapped a Tootsie Pop, and set my feet on the counter. The unit secretary pushed away from her computer terminal, turned and glared at me over her reading glasses. "Good gracious, how much longer are we going to have to listen to that?"

Lupe's wail had penetrated wood, plaster, and steel all afternoon, every three minutes. Yet her mother was adamant: "No needle in the back of mí niña." She'd had a friend whose sister's friend had an aunt who was paralyzed after a spinal or some such nonsense. Frankly, I was hoping she'd offer her proxy refusal again. I was spent. As a favor, I'd covered the main operating rooms the night before. Between a lady with a roto-rooter poking through her hand and an old guy with dead bowel who required an epinephrine drip to scrape his blood pressure off the floor, I never shut my eyes. Then, in the morning, I took over OB call.

I had hoped to catch a little sleep in a spare room. That didn't pan out. Just after I showered and put on a fresh set of scrubs, Bonnie, the nurse anesthetist on duty, called me with the first admission of the day. Her name was Elizabeth Renke. She was past due with her fourth child and scheduled for an induction of labor. I stopped by her room before breakfast. The nurse was roaming a hockey-puck-like transducer over Elizabeth's exposed abdomen, searching for the fetal heartbeat. I began my "I'm the anesthesiologist on call" spiel, but Elizabeth halted me with both arms extended like a traffic cop and announced with a smile, "I'm here for the Cadillac treatment. No more natural childbirth, especially since I finally get my girl."

She'd risen early for this. There was some serious care taken in the application of mascara and shadow, and her brunette hair, coiffed in loopy waves past her shoulder, had that Cover-Girl sheen. She gazed up to her husband standing at her side. He wore a white shirt with a pink tie and exuded the fresh-squeezed morning aroma of Old Spice. On the tie, the phrase *It's a Girl!* screamed vertically in italic black from his buckle to his collar. She gripped his hand and they smiled at each other, and if this had been a cartoon, little hearts would have danced from their eyes. Then she looked back at me. "So, I'm ready for that epidural any time."

The nurse located the heartbeat, and the machine's tinny speaker emitted a sound like a wooden mallet striking a coconut 138 times a minute. She cinched the transducer in place with the broad elastic bands and said, "Why don't we get you in labor first."

"Of course," Elizabeth said. "I was just saying, whenever you...I mean whenever he . . . oh, I don't know what I'm saying. I'm just so excited to see little Kaylee."

"Kaylee Ann," her husband added.

They glanced at the display on the monitor, then back to each other and squeezed out a few more bouncy hearts. Elizabeth then shooed her husband off to work, reminding him that her mother would take two of their boys to school and watch the third at home.

I filled her order for a Cadillac epidural at about noon. She panted through the contractions, concluding each one with a full deep breath—a cleansing breath, they call it. By the time I finished charting, she had the phone to her ear, talking to her husband. The nurse pointed to a contraction wave on the monitor. Elizabeth looked at it, then down to her abdomen, then over to me, and chatting away, smiled with a wink and a thumbs-up.

As my shift was ending, Elizabeth was still laboring, but Bonnie said she was close. For the day, though, I'd had eight patients deliver—six labor epidurals and two C-sections—all girls. I'd had busy days on OB before, but not a day when each patient I touched delivered a girl. Eight healthy baby girls.

I sucked on the Tootsie Pop and contemplated this statistical oddity. Since we'd found out Maggie was pregnant again, my mind had been filled with statistics. I couldn't remember ever participating in the live birth of a child who was not healthy. I don't mean a kid that came out blue because the cord prolapsed or the placenta separated, but one with a congenital anomaly— small round ears, a fish mouth, a webbed neck. The kinds of deformities that trigger a second glance at the mall. I'd seen none of that, not during my four years of residency or eight years of private practice. What were the odds? I didn't know, but now eight months into the new millenium I pictured myself on a giant swing, paused at the peak of its arc, waiting to descend.

"Doctor, did you ever call your wife back?" The unit secretary's bark startled me.

"Oh, shit." I dropped my feet to the floor and reached for the phone.

"You know, I just love listening to that British accent of hers. Gives me goose-bumps. How far along did you say she is?"

"I didn't," I said, forming the words around the Tootsie Pop before pulling it out. "Now, please don't tell anyone else." That was futile. When a secret entered the hospital, it spread like a drug-resistant bacteria.

Just then, Diaz emerged from room 626. He looked pregnant himself in the yellow gown that covered his slacks, shirt, and tie. He held a print-out from the fetal heart monitor and pointed out something to Bonnie. While nodding, she pulled a disposable bouffant cap from her top-coat pocket and stretched it over her perm. I had a bad feeling.

Diaz looked up and said, "Section."

The unit secretary cheered. I tomahawked the Tootsie Pop toward the trash. It slipped as it left my hand and sailed high, past her ear, shattering against the wall into a dozen violet candy crystals.

"Jesus, Doctor, no need to take it out on me. I just transcribe the orders, I don't give them."

Without speaking or looking at her, I began to pick the candy shards out of the tiered baskets of forms on her desk. She grabbed my wrist, turned me around, and gave me a shove toward Diaz. "Just go take care of that little screamer."

Diaz waved the tracing at me. "Sorry, bro. Just come look at these decels."

I didn't have to. I could trust my own wife's OB. As I moved past him toward Lupe's room, I tapped on the tracing and said, "It's going to be a girl, you know."

Lupe, a slight young lady, whimpered while her boyfriend, Antonio— his name was inscribed on his shirt's breast pocket below "Sandy's Automotive"—clasped her hands and whispered in her ear. The mother slouched splay-legged in a chair, a washcloth on her head. To Lupe, I explained in a low voice what a spinal anesthetic involved. I paused while she vice-gripped Antonio's hand and thrashed through another contraction utilizing her rebel yell. When she relaxed, Antonio massaged his fingers. There were faint grease stains deep in the cuticles, impossible to get clean in a single scrubbing. I knew from restoring my MG. "Cross them like this," I said. And I showed him how I had crossed my index and middle fingers for Maggie during her labors. "This way it doesn't hurt so much when she squeezes."

While the nurses readied Lupe and the C-section room, I walked down the hall to the doctor's lounge. I had at least ten minutes. The lounge was empty. A high school football game blared on the TV. I found the remote on the couch, hidden under the scattered remnants of the morning newspaper. *Mute, Off, Volume*—nothing worked. I dialed Maggie and while the phone rang I stretched the length of the cord and zeroed the volume at the set. Maggie answered five or six rings past when voice mail usually picked up. "Sorry, luv. I was on with Gabby. Her Mikie has a 103 degree fever. Have you left?" Her voice sounded like she was in a tunnel.

"No, I'm stuck with another C-section. Are you on the toilet?"

"I'm just giving the little buggers a bath. It's been a day, Bill."

I reclined on the couch while she told me how she had used ice-tongs to fish Hot Wheels out of the VCR, which our six- and four-year-olds had used as a parking garage while they built a mini-dirt-track on our coffee table. The VCR was ruined, but between what she vacuumed up and what our toddler had shoveled into his mouth, you'd never know we'd had half a bag of potting soil in the family-room where two loads of clean laundry now lay waiting to be folded. I could hear splashing and squealing while she talked. She broke away and threatened "the lot of you" to an extended stay in the Tower of London. They all cheered.

"Maggie, you called me."

"Yes, would you pop into the mini-market when you're done? Buy some Gatorade and some granola bars, the chewy kind, for Ian's match tomorrow. I'm going to switch weeks with Gabby."

"Maggie, please don't go over there. Who knows what that kid has with all the cats and birds she's got. We don't need you picking up something right now."

"She has two Ragdolls and one African Grey."

"Maggie. Please."

"How was your day? You get any sleep? You sound a bit rough."

"I feel a bit rough. The ladies kept me hopping today."

"Any good girls' names?"

"Maggie, I really don't think that's what we should be doing. Not yet."

She became quiet, except for her breathing. It sounded as if she were cradling the phone to her face. I stepped to the door for a second; the hall was empty.

"Diaz is here. Should I tell him you'll be in for the amnio on Monday?"

She was silent.

"Maggie, if we wait much longer, it will be too late."

"Dr. Diaz said the ultrasound looked fine."

"He also said if we want to know for sure, you need an amnio."

She didn't say anything.

"Listen, we've been over this. Ultrasounds aren't one hundred percent. I showed you the studies."

She cleared her throat. "It's a girl, luv. It's a girl and she's going to be healthy."

"Maggie, you need to think this through, rationally."

"So what's rational?"

"If the amnio shows forty-six chromosomes, we can relax, pick out a name, and look forward to the delivery."

"I could do that tonight, if you'd bloody let me."

"So you're fine with taking care of a Down's child for the rest of your life?

"Oh, that's rational."

"Maggie, all I'm saying is you can't keep ignoring the numbers. Take one hundred women just like you—thirty-nine years old, same blood-test results, same ultrasound—one will have a Down's baby. Sure, only one. But at delivery, if you discover you're that one . . . well, then of course it's way too late:"

"Too late?"

"For an abortion."

I wanted to pull back the word *abortion* as soon as I envisioned it spinning toward her heart. In this my aim was spot on. "I'm not saying we should. But how do you know how you'll feel unless you get the amnio? I mean, for sure."

After a few moments I heard stunted sniffing sounds, and then a little far-away voice saying, "Mommy's crying, Mommy's crying."

"Maggie, listen, I'm exhausted. You know how I get." She didn't say anything and I imagined her sitting on the toilet lid, one delicate hand covering her nose and mouth, her blue eyes gazing at our three little naked boys as they flew their Transformers through the air and plunged them under the water to attack one another.

She spoke softly. "But the handout says one out of two hundred have a miscarriage."

I matched her tone. "It's not even that high. Diaz knows what he's doing."

"This is my last chance, Bill. As you say, what if I'm the one?"

It wasn't that long ago that we had joked about our inability to even conceive a girl. She wondered if I had an X-chromosome in me. Some study her mother sent her claimed that anesthesiologists over in England had boys five to one. Years of breathing trace anesthetic gases, they postulated. The same study flipped the odds in favor of girls for British fighter pilots. Probably the Gs they pulled. We had two choices, she said: she could hop across the pond and shag a UAF pilot in Brighton, or I could henceforth forsake using inhalation anesthetics and spend some time on the *G-Force* ride at the State Fair. In jest I countered that X or Y, I hoped my contribution produced a child with twenty digits equally divided among four limbs, a child who could spell *color* without a *u*. That was my hope.

There was a thud and some crying. "Crap, Luke just fell on his bum."

"Maggie."

She cleared her throat again. "I better go. Don't forget the treats."

———

After the C-section, I wheeled Lupe in her bed back to her dimly lit sixth-floor room. Her eyes were closed and her face cocked to the left over a plastic emesis basin. I slid the chair her mother had been sitting in out of the way, a bouquet of Mylar *It's a Girl!* balloons tied to the backrest now. The chair settled under the window. Lightning flickered on the horizon. Taillights edged east along the road leading to my neighborhood in the distant dark. The last mile, wavy with dips, always elicited weightless giggles from the boys. Maggie would be reading a story to them, no doubt *Where the Wild Things Are*, Ian mouthing the words I'd read to him a hundred times as the boy, Max, sailed "in and out of weeks and almost over a year."

The nurse applied the blood pressure cuff. Lupe opened an eye, and then vomited the last, the absolute last mouthful (I hoped) of a banana-pudding shake she'd stopped for at Sonic on the way to the hospital. Sometimes I didn't know what these ladies were thinking. She spat into the basin. "When can I see my baby?"

"Soon. She's with Antonio in the nursery," the nurse said.

For the ten minutes he had balanced his daughter while she lay on her mother's chest in the C-section room, Antonio kept repeating, "she has your nose, she has your nose." I couldn't confirm that it resembled Lupe's nose, but it was beautiful, and it looked normal, as did baby Angelina's eyes, ears, and hands. When the nurse tested Angelina's Moro reflex, her little arms flung out sideways, as if she had been startled and was reaching for the safety of her mother. Even after hundreds and hundreds of C-sections, witnessing the shared wonder of young parents often tightened my throat. On this night, while watching Angelina's tiny hand grasp Antonio's finger, my throat tightened a little more, and I had to turn away.

The nurse then guided Antonio toward the door. He carried his squinting daughter like she was leaking oil until the nurse showed him how to cradle. As the door closed, he framed his face within the narrowing space, his eyes glistening above his mask, and announced, "She's so beautiful. She has your nose." Everyone in the room had laughed—Dr. Diaz running the fascia, his assistant keeping tension on the suture, the scrub nurse finishing up the instrument count—as the door thudded shut. Even Lupe. She laughed, she cried, she vomited.

My long day was over. I had the weekend off, but as I strode to the dressing room I wasn't in a buoyant Friday mood. Since my call to Maggie, it felt like I had a presentation to prepare for Monday. Then Bonnie stopped me. "Sorry, Doctor. We've got another section." There it was. She knew that was the best way to tell me. Don't ease it in through the skin, the sub-cue, the muscle; just give it to me sharp and true to the bone.

"First call still busy?" I knew the answer, but it was after nine. I had to try.

"He's still in with the hip," she said. "The femur fractured. They're going to be a while. Second call's busy, too."

I dropped my head, closed my eyes, and clenched. I wanted to say, "No thanks. I'm beat. I can't think. I'm going home." But I didn't. I simply said, "Okay."

"It's room 622," she added. "Diaz just checked her. I gave the Reglan and started pre-loading. The C-section room's turning over." Which meant: *You've got some time to suck it up. I'm going downstairs for a quick smoke.*

Of course, Elizabeth Renke was in 622, the only woman in a ten-mile radius still in labor. I continued to the doctor's lounge first. I wanted to call Maggie, let her know I'd gotten nailed again, and that I might have to pick up the treats in the morning. I shouldn't have mentioned this amnio business earlier, especially over the phone.

A *Cheers* rerun was playing now, the volume still off. It was the season Shelly Long hid behind the counter because in real life she was pregnant. I had always thought the writers missed an opportunity: a pseudo-pregnancy, a largely psychiatric phenomenon. It's bizarre, but it happens. Coffee, which never much appealed to me, felt like a necessity now. But someone had left the burner on. The glass pot was ruined. I slumped into the cushioned chair next to the couch.

I knew I wouldn't turn back the covers until after midnight. And no sleeping in. The boys would be up by six watching cartoons, and Ian's soccer game was at eight. We'd cart everyone out to the park with their blankets and bottles and strollers and Gatorade and still forget one or two things. After our third boy, Robbie, I had thought we were done. As much as Maggie wanted to duplicate the photograph she kept at her desk in the bedroom—three-year-old Maggie in a white dress, sitting on a booster chair across from her mother, an elegant setting of flowers, fine china, and cakes between them—we were both creeping toward forty. Our chance of conceiving a Down's baby was increasing exponentially. It was time to count our blessings and move on.

And then one Saturday morning, while I was reading the paper, she pulled a chair close to me. Her hair was wet and combed straight back. She had a sheepish expression. We had made love in the pre-dawn hour before the boys awoke. She put her hand on my wrist and told me that she'd removed her diaphragm in the shower. She said she just wasn't thinking.

"Maggie," I said, "How could you just not be thinking?"

"Oh, you rather assume I did it on purpose. Don't you?"

"I only wish you'd been more careful."

"Look, luv. It only happened this once. I'm sorry."

Diaz ordered a serum triple-screening-test at sixteen weeks. The results indicated she had a one in fifty chance of having a baby with Down Syndrome compared to one in five hundred for the average woman her age. He recommended an amniocentesis. When Maggie balked, he suggested an ultrasound first. Although we were past the time to detect nuchal thickening, everything else looked clean: none of the bad markers like a hole in the heart's septum or a short femur. And there was one final finding that prompted Maggie to say, "It's the best mistake I ever made" —no penis.

But a normal ultrasound can't count chromosomes. It can't tell you if there are forty-seven when there should only be forty-six. Maggie still had a one in a hundred chance. I'd taken care of Down's patients in the OR. I'd seen their problems: the heart defects, the cataracts, periodontal disease. It'd be a life-long struggle. Was that fair to the child? I'd discussed all this with Maggie.

I picked up the phone and dialed home. The line was busy. I tried to turn up the television volume, but then remembered the remote didn't work. I hurled it to the floor. The plastic cover ejected and the batteries scattered into hiding. I phoned again. Still busy. Probably our neighbor Gabby, a perfect name even before her divorce. Why'd Maggie tell her about the ultrasound? It was a short trip from Gabby to her orthopedic surgeon ex-husband to the hospital. I closed my eyes and breathed, two slow breaths, sucking it up before returning to Elizabeth Renke's room.

It had been almost eleven hours since she'd given me the thumbs up. Her dark hair resembled tangled strands of seaweed. Only a trace of mascara remained as black smears under her closed eyes. Her jaw hung limp. Her legs were spread wide, and her hospital gown, soaked with sweat, was pulled up to her waist while the nurse inserted a bladder catheter. Without glancing, I knew poor Elizabeth's perineum would be as swollen as an ape's. She opened her ghastly eyes when the nurse addressed me, offered a weary smile and said, "I'm sorry."

"What do you mean," I said. "Sorry for what?"

"Bonnie said you had to stick around for this."

"Hey, don't say you're sorry. I'd like to know how this story ends."

"I didn't think it'd end this way . . . Fuck, my last one, too."

Darrel straightened in the corner chair. "Honey!"

"Oh, go back to sleep, Darrel. They'll wake you when they're ready."

Darrel faced his palms to me and shook his head. He looked like a referee who had stumbled between two boxers: his hair battered, his white collar unbuttoned, and his pink tie askew. The nurse straightened Elizabeth's legs and pulled the gown to her knees. She groaned.

"They turned off the epidural," she said, "to see if I could push better without it. Two fucking hours. There's no fucking way I'd let them do that again."

"Come on, honey. Hold it together just a little longer," Darrel said.

Her eyes were closed again and she laughed the weak, halting laugh of a woman collapsed in the sand a hundred yards from a water hole. "I'm sorry, Darrel. Hard day at the office?"

Darrel gripped his hands together and hung his head.

"They also turned off the Pitocin," I said. "That will help."

"Yeah, thank God. Kaylee must have a head as big as a watermelon."

"And stubborn like her mother," Darrel added, not looking up.

"Darrel, will you just shut the fuck up? I'm trying to talk to my doctor, here. Why don't you go to the waiting room and tell Mom what's going on? See if she's still got the upper hand with our three little darlings."

As Darrel trudged by me, I grasped his arm and said, "A nurse will show you where to dress." Then I clapped him on the shoulder. "She'll be fine."

All he could muster was an exhalation, released as if through a trap door.

Her behavior wasn't anything I hadn't seen before and in less than an hour she'd probably be closer to her morning dreamy self than whatever the pain and the hormones and the exhaustion had turned her into now.

In the C-section room, Bonnie and I hooked Elizabeth up to the monitors— blood pressure cuff, ECG, and pulse oximeter. I positioned the oxygen cannula under Elizabeth's nose, while Bonnie began dosing the epidural. It would take several minutes for the numbness to set up, so I broke for the lounge. On the TV, an anchorwoman with perfect facial features mouthed the ten o'clock news. I plopped into the chair by the phone, dialed, and it rang on the other end. Neighbor Gabby must have run out of gossip for the evening. When Maggie didn't answer, I hung up before the greeting. I tried her cell phone. It went to voice mail immediately. I tried the land line again. While it was ringing, Darrel walked out of the locker room dressed in scrubs, cap, and shoe covers. He sat on the couch next to me and said, "The nurse told me to wait here." I nodded as my voice on the other end of the line said *please leave a message.*

"Maggie, can you hear me? Pick up. It's . . . ten-oh-five. Do you know where your wife is? I mean, where my wife is. You know what I mean." It pissed me off that she wouldn't pick up, and I thought, well fuck her, she can just lay there and worry about me until I get home. Darrel was staring at me with the same weary indifference that I was trying to hide from Elizabeth and him. So I finished with, "I'm sure you've got a good explanation. You usually do." I smiled and shook my head for Darrel's sake.

After I hung up, I asked, "Have you seen Dr. Diaz?"

Darrel angled his head toward the locker room door. "He's back there."

Diaz came out of the dressing room tying his wedding ring into the bow on his scrub pants, hiking the waist after he was done. "Man, I need a little less belly or a little more butt." He clapped his hands together and said. "Okay, let's do it." Looking at me he continued, "How many girls does this make for you?"

"Ten." Darrel looked puzzled. I said, "All my patients today have had girls. If you want a girl, I seem to have a pink thumb . . . at least today."

Darrell took a deep breath and clasped his hands behind his head. "Anything, Doc. Anything. Just get this baby delivered."

Diaz laughed. "Man, this is the easy part. In sixteen years, when your little girl wants a car for her birthday, that's when it's tough. You know where you'll be when she bats her eyes and says, 'All my friends have new cars'?"

"No."

Diaz held out his little finger. "Wrapped right here."

Darrel dropped his hands to his lap and smiled. The first time I'd seen him smile since morning. His bouncy-hearted dream was back on track and chugging toward a day when he'd hand her the keys and feel rich being wrapped around her perfect little finger.

———

Elizabeth lay on her back, slightly tilted to the left, in a modified crucifix position. A blue drape rose from her chest, secured to IV stands positioned near the extended arm-boards. Her arms had been secured loosely to the boards with Velcro straps, a reminder not to touch her belly during the prep. I released the straps. Diaz, his nurse first-assistant, and the scrub nurse were at the table. They were arranging the last few things: raising the instrument tray over Elizabeth's numb and draped legs, throwing one end of the sterile suction tubing to the circulating nurse, wiping the talc from their gloves with a saline-soaked lap. Diaz said, "Kelly." The nurse snapped a Kelly clamp into his palm. He pinched Elizabeth's skin where he wanted to make the incision and said, "Liz, do you feel that?"

"Feel what?" she asked.

"How about here?" He pinched as far north on her abdomen as was exposed by the rectangular opening in the drape.

"Are you doing something?" she said.

Bonnie headed out the door.

I leaned close to her ear. "He's just testing to see if you're numb." I had already checked her, lightly marching an 18-gauge needle up the middle of her chest until she felt a pin-prick. I straightened up and looked over the drape. "She's good."

Diaz handed the Kelly back. "All right, another miracle by the good doctor. Let's do it. Knife please." He palpated her abdomen with his left hand and accepted the scalpel in his right. Then he stopped and looked up. "Oh, how about the father?"

"He's on the way," I said.

A few moments later, Bonnie opened the door and Darrel walked in. She said, "I'm going to check the board."

I nodded and patted the rolling stool positioned by Elizabeth's head. Darrel took his seat behind the drape. He grasped his wife's outstretched hand in both of his and kissed it through his mask. "This is it," he said.

Elizabeth was the only one in the room who wasn't wearing a mask. She turned her head toward him and gave a weak smile. Darrel plucked a tissue from the box on my anesthesia cart and wiped her eyes. She looked back toward the ceiling, her gaze roaming left and right. "Have they started?"

"We're on our way," I said.

Diaz took less than two minutes from skin down to the uterus. All Elizabeth could know, and Darrel for that matter since he didn't stand, was what could be heard. Instruments snapped smartly in latex gloves. Air hissed through the suction wand until there was the sharp slurping of blood being cleared from the surgical field. Clamps closed with a crisp crunch of their ratchets. Her eyes continued to search.

"What are they doing now?" she said.

Before I could answer, there was a gush of fluid onto the floor.

"What, what was that?"

"This is where it feels like someone is sitting on your chest." I said.

The nurse assistant leaned her face over the drape to Elizabeth. "Sorry about this." And then she pressed her forearm and opposite hand into Elizabeth's upper abdomen and drove all that was inside toward Diaz's hand, which cupped the baby's head. The head popped into the world through the open incision and Elizabeth groaned. "Oh, what was that?"

"That's Kaylee Ann taking a peek. Dr. Diaz is suctioning her mouth."

"Is she okay? I don't hear anything. Is she okay? Is she okay, Darrel?"

"Should I look?" Darrel asked. "Is it okay to look?"

"She's fine," I said.

"Can I stand up?"

"Sure," I said to Darrel. "Go ahead. Stand up."

Darrel stood slowly like he was about to view a forbidden land. He kept hold of his wife's hand, never quite pushing the stool back. "Honey, I see her head."

The nurse assistant leaned over again. "One more push. Sorry."

The baby slid from the womb into Diaz's hands and immediately began to wail.

"I see her, I see her, honey." Darrel pulled his mask down and kissed his wife. She was sobbing now and their tears mixed and I thought to tell him later if the chance arose: *I told you she'd be fine.*

The circulator looked at the clock on the wall. "Ten thirty-six." I nodded and jotted the time on my record.

"All right," Diaz said. "There you go. This one is big."

The nurse began drying the baby with a small blue towel, wiping nature's white packing grease from the face while Diaz clamped and cut the cord.

"Pitocin please," he said. I was injecting the amp of Pit into the IV bag when he then said, "Hey . . . Elizabeth."

Darrel looked over at Diaz.

"What?" she said, wiping her nose with a tissue. "Can I see her? When can I see her?"

"Did you buy a lot of pink baby clothes?"

"Well yeah, I guess."

"I'm afraid he was hiding something from us, my dear."

"What? I don't understand . . . Darrel?"

Diaz faced the baby toward Darrel for a moment, and then handed him off to the nurse by the warmer.

"It's a boy, Lizzy," Darrel said. "Oh my God. It's okay Lizzy, it's a healthy boy." He looked back at Diaz. "He's healthy, right?"

The baby cried and punched the cool air with his arms and legs. I pictured his lungs expanding to full rosy capacity. Diaz was easing the placenta free. "He looks great. I'm betting he tops ten pounds."

"You can go over there if you want," I said. Darrel's look questioned me and I repeated, "Go ahead."

He looked down at Elizabeth. Her eyes were closed, her tears gone. "I'm going to see our son," he said. "Liz?" She jerked her hand away and rested it on her chest. "I'll be right back," he said to her and stepped over to his son.

"Elizabeth," I said. "Are you feeling okay?"

She didn't answer for a few seconds, and then inhaled deeply. "No," she said, her pitch rising on the exhalation.

"Are you feeling any pain?" She didn't answer. "Is that tugging bothering you?"

She opened her eyes and fixed them on the ceiling.

"We've got about twenty, twenty-five minutes to go," I said. "Let me know if you need anything . . . Elizabeth? . . . Elizabeth?"

"I thought the ultrasound said it was a girl." She said this loud enough for Diaz to hear. And then louder, "I thought you fucking said it was a girl."

There was silence—except for the monitors, except for the baby. He cried. We looked at one another, all but Elizabeth, our shocked expressions eventually settling on Dr. Diaz. He stared just past the suture he was tying. His hands were running on muscle memory now.

"Ultrasounds aren't a hundred percent," he said. "We talked about that, Elizabeth. Nothing is one hundred percent."

"I don't care. I don't want a boy. I . . . want . . . my . . . girl."

The ECG monitor seemed to beep louder than I'd ever heard it in the C-section room. I was never so conscious of a mother's heart rate. It was the baby's heart rate we all listened to on obstetrics. And after a baby delivered, after he cried his heart out for his mother, after we knew he was safely on his way in the world, we stopped listening and talked about other things. But now, no one talked about what movies they were going to see this weekend, or their kids' soccer games, or their pregnant wives.

At the warmer, Darrel doted on his son, stroking the back of the boy's tiny hand, while the nurse placed a band around the infant ankle. She patted Darrel's arm, whispering something I couldn't hear. He nodded and forced a smile. The baby was quiet now, wrapped tight in a blanket with a stocking cap warming his pointy head. Darrel approached, carrying his son, and I steadied the stool while he sat. He looked at the solemn sleeping face of the boy. "Honey? We could call him Kyle."

She turned her head away. "I don't want to see it."

He leaned the baby's head onto her shoulder. "Liz, don't be silly."

She yanked her shoulder away. "Darrel! I said I don't want to see it. I want my girl."

"Liz. That's not fair." He said this with a gentle yet firm tone, a tone I'd heard from Maggie.

"You're right," she said. "It's not fair."

Darrel looked up at me, then down to his son, and back to me. His eyes, slanted above his mask, pleaded for an explanation: *How could she act like this? How could she not embrace her child?* But I had never seen this before. I had no rational answer; not as a doctor, or a husband, or a father.

"There's no excuse for this, Liz," he said. "No excuse." And then he followed the nurse out the door, carrying his bewilderment and his son close to his chest.

I sat behind Elizabeth's icy expression, not knowing what to say. Listening was all I could do and what I heard was the ECG machine transducing the beat of her heart into a sound that was sterile and alien. "Elizabeth, do you need anything?" Again, she was quiet. "Let me know if you start to feel queasy . . . Elizabeth? Listen, I can't help you if you don't talk to me." I turned away and ripped the packaging from a bag of saline. I laid the liter bag on my workspace, and then drew an amp of Pitocin into a syringe.

"I don't need your fucking help," she said. "I need my girl." I turned to her. She arched her head back so she could glare at me. "You got one of those back there with all your stuff?"

I didn't answer that.

She lay back down. "I should have just gotten an abortion. Darrel didn't think we could afford a fourth kid anyway."

The tenor of my heart was changing, charged with anger and a kind of fear I'd never felt in an operating room. Its beat was as alien as hers and it leapt into my throat, my ears, the tips of my fingers. The needle shook as I tried to inject the saline bag's port. I stopped and in a voice loud enough to merit a glance from Diaz, said, "You're very lucky, you know."

She arched again to peer at me. "Oh am I?"

I pointed the syringe and needle at her. My hand trembled. "Damn right you are."

"I hear you're the lucky one." She smiled in a smug way, like she was privy to a secret, as if by looking at me upside-down she'd found an angle into my soul. "Yeah, Bonnie told me you're having a girl. Want to switch?"

"Sure, maybe I will!" I said, my voice quaking. "You know, there's a chance she might—!" I choked off the rest. I raised the syringe above my head and plunged the needle into the bag of saline, as if driving it into the heart of a beast.

Elizabeth flinched and then her expression steadied. "She might what?" she said. "Be a boy?"

———

I dropped Elizabeth off in her room, and then spoke briefly with Diaz in the lounge. I apologized for my outburst. He waved it off, saying the whole case was filled with antics he'd never seen before. When he told me he'd ordered a psych consult for her, I thought, *He should have ordered one for me as well.* It was past midnight. I didn't bother to change out of my scrubs, but wadded up my clothes and tossed them into the passenger seat of the MG. I put the top down. A thunderstorm had passed through, and the aroma of desert creosote curled over the windshield as I steered eastward along the wet, empty streets.

At a stop light, the phone rang. Maggie's ID came up. Two hours prior, I would have let it ring. "Luv, that was a bloody long C-section," she said. "You coming home?"

"I had another. Why didn't you answer my call?"

The light turned green.

"You called?" she said. I switched the phone to speaker, rested it on my lap, and powered through the gears. "That must have been while I was outside. You won't believe the night I've had." She sounded across the ocean.

Maggie explained how she was reading *Where the Wild Things Are* to the boys when Gabby phoned. And when she returned to their room, Ian wasn't in bed and he wasn't in the bathroom. She ran out back into the thunderstorm and checked the pool. Thank God he wasn't there, so she shouted for him throughout the house but he didn't answer. She checked the front yard, screaming his name so loudly that the neighbors came out, which must have been when I phoned. Gabby wanted to call the police but Maggie went inside to call me first and when I didn't answer, she knew I was with a patient. That's when she noticed a little tuft of red hair poking out of the clean laundry piled in the middle of the family room.

"He's asleep," she said. "I left him there. You have to see him. I could blister his bum, that little bugger, but he looks so cute."

She finished with what sounded to me like a cleansing breath.

"So, luv, how'd your sections go?"

I could have told her about Elizabeth, how she shunned her baby and I lost my cool. I could have pointed out that Elizabeth's ultrasound was wrong, and then regurgitated the statistics. I was full of statistics. But what was the chance a mother or a father couldn't love their newborn child if she wasn't what they'd hoped for? One out of a hundred? One out of a million? Who was the one? Me? I knew it wouldn't be Maggie. At least we had something that was a hundred percent.

I was silent. The dips in the road were flooded and I was struggling to hold a line.

"Bill, you there?" Maggie called into the night.

I took the phone off speaker, pulling her voice close to my ear.

"I'm here."

"You okay, luv. Is everything okay?"

"I hope," I said. "I hope."

the cherry tree

Sarah Blackman

the cherry tree

Everyone had said there was really a very nice quality to the light that would stream, all year, through the windows in her office. This was before she'd taken the job, before it had even been offered; though, from the beginning of the interview process, she had understood the whole event to be a formality. After all, there weren't very many like her in the country. In the world even, if one were to be frank. She was so specialized. And their needs—their pressing, urgent needs—formed such a tight niche.

In fact, she had not been misled. The light that streamed, all year, through her office windows was thick and nuanced. At times, she even found it a little distracting and swiveled away from the two-way mirror, from her computer screen, to pass her hands in and out of its beams, the noises the children made fading to a disarticulated buzz behind her.

In the lunch hour, her colleagues gathered at habituated times in the spacious room that doubled as a presentation hall when the pharmaceutical representatives came to peddle their wares. The room was designed to defy the idea of institutions. Not through luxe carpeting or banks of white, chocolate-scented orchids, as had been the case at her previous place of employment, but through embracing the very iconography of the institutional soul, thus rendering it a null prophecy. This had been explained to her by the director of the facility on her interview tour. He had used those words, "iconography," "prophecy," though perhaps not in that particular order. She remembered looking then as she did now up at the raw girdered ceiling of the lunchroom, with its loops of dangling, color-coded wires, and then over to the riveted steel conference table and the hammered steel door with its improbable, thick porthole window and feeling not as hungry as she had just been, not as sure as she was, say, that morning, of all the possible directions of her life.

One thing the lunchroom and presentation hall had going for it was an emergency exit door that could be disabled and propped open. The man who had shown her how to do this was named Anthony. He was a laboratory technician in the Research and Development sector and thus of a much lower professional standing than she but also not inclined to "give a hot fuck," as he said, slipping a piece of computer paper between the tiny diode and its sensor and nudging the door open with his hip. "After you," said Anthony and she always went, sliding through the narrow space between the doorframe and his chest, hugging the wall where she could not be seen from any of the south facing windows as she accepted a cigarette from his pack and listened to the paper crackle fitfully against his flame.

Anthony wore his lab coat out of the lab, which was a breach of protocol, and filled its deep pockets with a number of stupid items designed, she suspected, to entertain the children if he ever came across any outside of their dormitories, classrooms, or other assigned areas. He carried around little finger puppets shaped like jungle animals and brightly colored Chinese finger traps and little rubber balls just the right size to fit into a child's palm. Anthony's preoccupation with items designed to keep small hands busy made her suspect he was afraid of the children, at least on a subconscious level, and one day, pressed against the wall on the right side of the door while Anthony pressed against the wall on the left—both tearing up as the spring breeze blew smoke back into their eyes, both ducking involuntarily as a shadow crossed in front of a south-facing window—she asked him about his fear, just brought it up as if it were perfectly approachable, perfectly broachable lunchtime chat. Immediately, she was amazed by herself. On the far side of the security fence, a cherry tree was budding in tightly furled profusion and she concentrated on counting its future bloom. One, she counted. Two. Three. Four. Ten.

"I'll tell you something," said Anthony. "A lot of times, with a woman like you, eventually we will reach the point where there is nothing to it but just to put each other up against the wall." She stopped counting the cherry buds and looked at Anthony. He had a long upper lip and a short, fat underlip. He looked at her and scrubbed his hand back and forth over the hollows of his cheeks as if he had made them with his hand, as if he were still in the process of sculpting himself. "I'll tell you something else," Anthony continued. "When that day happens you are going to like it, a lot, but it won't change anything for you and that's why at the end of your story it's always still you.

No transformation. No like mystic power or secret identity. Just you. You understand what I'm saying?"

She said she thought she did and looked down at anything, happened upon his lab coat pocket. The nubby arm of a tiger finger puppet protruded over the edge of his pocket like it was waving. Or going under.

"Uh-huh," said Anthony. He dropped his cigarette onto the walkway and ground it out. "I don't know if you do. I'm saying I'm going to fuck you. It's as simple as that." Anthony bent down to pick up the Styrofoam box lid he had wedged between the door and the frame as a prop and motioned her in front of him. As she edged by, he reached around her and grabbed her breast, finding the nipple through her blouse and her bra and twisting it hard. She gasped and Dr. Rutgers looked up from his turkey club and waved. That afternoon she stood in a reticulated lozenge of light in her office window and counted all the buds on the cherry tree. One hundred and sixty-two, she determined, though the angle was not clear enough to ensure perfect accuracy.

Some time later, she was pressed against her window and noticed the cherry tree was fully immersed in its own foliage. It looked preoccupied, but, she supposed, so do we all. She, for example, could not recall what its blooms had looked like in the height of its season, whether it had been a good year for the tree or a disappointing one. She considered asking Anthony, but he was working hard. He put his hands on her hips to steady himself and worked harder, hurting her, really digging in. Behind them, on the other side of the two-way mirror, the children were being led in some sort of song. They were getting the words wrong, she suspected on purpose, and laughing about it, laughing and laughing. The children's laughter sounded spiny to her—brittle, harsh with edges—but perhaps it was only this way because of the quality of the light that today was even more than usually resplendent, falling as it did over her breasts and then beyond them, paying attention to all the details.

my yard
Neil Crabtree

my yard

My backyard faces east to Miller Lake, a narrow body of water that runs several long Miami blocks and connects by canals to the Everglades, Snapper Creek, and Biscayne Bay. There's a chain link fence across the back of the yard, right along the top of the seawall, with a gate for fishing, but I've chained the gate and double-tied it to make sure my granddaughter doesn't open it and jump in.

Black and white ducks are on the water below the gate and Aliyah is standing on a chair I've pulled to the fence, throwing them pieces of bread. She's just over three feet tall, so even on a chair, she has to throw the bread up and over. Agile as a monkey, she'll climb the chain links or balance on one arm of the chair to get her head and shoulders higher than the fence top. I have to keep one eye and one hand on her to feel safe. She can find a way to hurt herself no matter what I do. In a room made of foam rubber, she would find a way to get a bruise.

It's February, the dry season, and the lake is down a couple feet. On this bright cool Sunday, fat black ducks and skinny white ibis are marching along the shore's bleached grass to get over to the free food festival. The many ducks sleep in midday—under the big tree in the common field we share with the neighbors on the other side—but will wake and waddle for a handout. The condos across the lake are ugly, two-story beige stucco with barrel tile roofs, and their backyards face us through their crappy little fences and seem small and claustrophobic. The Ghettos of Kendall, I call them. My yard seems bigger than three of theirs. A hundred feet of lake and shore separate us, thank God. They all have dogs that dislike one another and bark constantly, big retrievers and obnoxious little terriers, Chihuahuas and wiener dogs, one or two per yard, so they never stop, until their indifferent owners bring them in.

In the water below us, a peacock bass hovers over a nest in a sandy patch of bottom. We see the colors easily in the clear water, the green, blue and yellow, orange on the fins, three vertical stripes and a black circle in a halo on the caudal fin. The mouth opens and closes as though the fish is exercising its jaws. When we throw bread for the ducks, any that swim over the fish get a bite on the belly. It's funny to watch, the fat greedy duck going for the morsel, the fish tensing, then ZING! A strike! And the surprised duck swimming quickly away. After a while the bigger ducks become wary and stay back. But a mama duck with her three little chicks around her comes waddling along the shore below the seawall, and they dive in for the bread, and POW! The bass hits one of the little ones, who comes shooting out of the water, and walks around in circles cheeping, trying to figure out, *What just happened?*

Aliyah throws the bread in the other direction so they won't get hit again. Then the one-winged ibis comes strutting along. He has both wings but one is completely turned around and useless, like he flew into a car or something. We have been feeding him but the other birds try to take the food right out of his beak. The trick is to separate him from the pack and give him a fighting chance. I throw bread one way, she throws the other. The ibis grabs a big hunk and starts hotfooting it away along the shore, pursued by another healthy ibis who apparently dislikes mixing it up with the white-headed ducks. Meanwhile, the bigger ducks have begun pecking at the baby ducks to keep them from the bread. Aliyah gets mad and gets down to look for a rock to drop on the bullies. A different fish, its body a graceful curve, swims into view and starts eating bread the ducks miss.

It's a Nile perch, or tilapia, as they're called now. They're vegetarians and constantly hungry, and eat all the weeds and other plant life that used to grow in the lake. James W. Hall has a novel where his hero, Thorne, tries to stop an evil madman from dumping tilapia into the Everglades canals and eating all the flora. Apparently, some got away. When the tilapia swims too close, the bass charges and chases it away. A little further out, turtles poke their heads out of the water to see what's going on. Seagulls come join the fun. They swoop down and grab bread chunks that have drifted out away from us, but their real trick is to catch a piece of bread in midair if you throw it high enough. The turtles go after what they miss.

"Why are there only three duckies?" Aliyah asks. Yesterday we were feeding five. Ten were hatched a week ago.

"Some must be sleeping," I tell her.

"No. I think they're dead," she advises me.

We have seen little corpses left after cat attacks. And one day we watched astonished as a Great White Heron flew in and, after standing idle for ten minutes, scooped up a chick in its beak and proceeded to drown it before swallowing the little bird whole and flying away. Mother Nature's a tough old broad.

"Do ducks go to heaven?" she asks. Every other piece of bread she takes a bite, so our birds only get fresh food. She has breadcrumbs around her lips. I wipe them away with my fingers. Against her pale smooth skin, the back of my hand seems as scaly as the hide of some ancient lizard, scaly and scarred and showing little florets of red from blood thinned by heart medicine and daily aspirin. Her eyes are blue like the sky above us, her long brown hair now getting blonde highlights like her mother's. I am in a constant state of wonder with this beautiful small female person. I live with her and her mother and her grandmother, my wife, and the three of them control my life as surely as if I were their indentured servant.

"I think ducks go to heaven," I say.

"And dogs?"

"Dogs too."

Since Aliyah's been here, three different dogs and two cats have run away. One cat got run over and I had to go get it and put the dead body in a garbage bag and we buried it under the banana tree. We let her hamster go out into the Free Range one day as well. Her turtle still lives in the lake. My wife is getting her a Siberian Huskie puppy my son's dog has sired, and I will be guarding it with my life.

"My daddy can feed them in heaven, right?"

Aliyah's father died four months before she was born. She knows him only by stories and by asking questions. At her pre-school, she is not the only kid without a father. Just the only one with a dead one.

"Your daddy feeds all of them every day, because he knows they're your friends."

"Are you going to die soon?"

"Me?"

"You, Papa. You'll be dead when I'm fourteen."

"I hope not."

"When I'm a teenager," she says, not a question, maybe a prediction.

I'm not sure where she got this idea, but I know my own children lost all four grandparents during their teenage years. First my mother-in-law to stomach cancer, then my mother to chronic alcoholism, then my father-in-law to a long series of complications after several strokes. And then my father from adult diabetes which destroyed his immune system after he contracted Hepatitis-C.

My wife had told me Aliyah asked her when she was going to die one day on the way to school. It catches you by surprise, we agreed. You get old enough to be unconcerned about your own passing and then someone reminds you are bound to this life by commitment and obligation. Acceptance of life's end does not mean your heart will not be broken in two when you fade.

"Maybe I'll wait until you're a mommy and have kids of your own."

"Papa. I'm not going to be a mommy."

"Why?"

"I'm going to be a rock star."

"Like Hannah Montana?"

"Oh yeah, baby." She holds an invisible microphone to her mouth. "You got the limo out front," she sings, and shakes her hair like Mylie Cyrus does on the Disney Channel. "Can we play Hannah now?"

"Sure. Go get your stuff."

"Can I wear my costume?"

"Tell Mommy to get it for you."

"You get The Fans."

The Fans are her bigger-sized baby dolls. Each day, we open the side door of the van and arrange the dolls facing the stage Aliyah has made of the small hill in front of the house. Then Hannah Montana performs for them, before jumping in the back of the van for me to rush her to the airport for the next show.

"I love you, Papa," she says, giving me a big hug. For a moment, that is all that is happening in my life, at this place, at this time.

Can I make it another ten years? I wonder. In ten years she'll be about to turn fifteen, a high school girl with a boyfriend, and a clique of girlfriends she's in constant contact with. Her *Quince* party will be coming up. I see a beautiful young lady in a black dress, sitting in the back of another kind of limo. Jesus.

Then the side gate of our wood picket fence opens as I pick her up in my right arm. My brother wheels in a red and white cooler, which I know is full of ice and Budweiser. We are supposed to barbecue at three this afternoon, but Dave's been waiting for a cold one since he woke up this morning. *Cook whenever you damn well please*, he'll tell me.

I'm only here for the beer.

"Uncle Dave!" Aliyah screams in delight.

"Baby Girl!" he screams back. And he reaches for the bag he set beside the gate, and shows her he has brought her a present, as he does every time he comes over. She wiggles free and runs over to see what he's brought her. I look down at the water. Mama duck is escorting the ducklings away from the big ducks swimming in circles waiting for round two. The bass hovers in the clear water over the sandy bottom. The turtles have come closer and float like fat guys at the surface. The one-wing ibis has come back. I throw him the last piece of bread.

the tenant

H.E. Francis

the tenant

He had to collect from the remaining tenants. He was wobbly. His head was in a whirl. He felt along the corridor wall. If he hadn't lived forty years in this building, with his bad eyes he'd never have found his way through the chaos of passages as deep and dark as the questions he had all his life put to himself. Strapped, nobody wanted to spend on big bulbs to light the way. You could break your neck on loose tiles and shaky banisters and a child could fall through where the rungs were missing. A century ago this then-public building had been sold and chopped into a labyrinth of apartments of all sizes. His, on the third floor, seemed a hidden afterthought at a dark, almost hidden turn; a tiny, deep two-room vault with one large window giving onto an interior patio. Always it had been silent in his nook until straight across—alas!—three students from Germany had moved in and lived a perpetual carouse, marring his concentration. Time he had now, no longer tutoring English day-to-day, so at last he was writing his book on tragedy. And he knew tragedy. Forty years in Madrid! He had seen the collective tragedy the Civil War had brought to Spain. In the aftermath he had lived with the people in their poverty, retaliations and repressions by the caudillo, Franco. He had come to love these people. But more—he was one of them. Hadn't his father died fighting for their lost cause: freedom? And hadn't his search for his father brought him to Spain? How does it begin, this darkness? Where does it come from?

His mother would never speak of his father. He sometimes thought—that cast a light on his mother which he did not want to believe—that she had not known who his father was. All his early years he had wanted to know who his father was. Nobody knew what his days in school and out were like, what *bastard* was like, *son-of-a-bitch*, *illegitimate*, *out-of-wedlock*. But she would never speak. Then she was struck down. Her heart had to be operated on. The operation failed. Before she died she broke: "Your father's name is George Lasher," she said. "In 1937 he went to fight in the war in Spain. He never came back."

He had known no man in her life. In later years he thought how she must have suffered the loss and shame, but more how she must have suffered for him, her son. But who was his father? Where was he from? How'd they meet? When? He had tried to imagine then how it had been with her; how, by what chance, they had crossed paths. From nothing he had tried to build the scene of that moment so he could grasp it and hold it as his own, his history, for she had left him none.

All he wanted was to know. It did not seem just that he should live all his life without that knowledge, that he could not like other boys play ball or go fishing or hunting or swimming with this pal, companion, friend, his father, or that he could not say with pride and pleasure to friends and classmates and teachers when he saw him on the street: *There goes my father. That's my father. Hey, Dad.* But what was justice? If you had no father you were crippled. Everybody knew. And on papers where it indicated father? Blank. Bastard. You could drown sometimes in feelings too confused to understand.

When she died, all he had was the name, George Lasher, but finally that at least. He was through the university then and had begun work as assistant manager at the local Woolworth's 5&10 before going back to study for an advanced degree in the humanities. He had no relatives. He had no reason not to pursue his obsession, the one thing he desired—to know something of his father, who he was, what. So he did not hesitate—he sold the house, everything, and went to Spain to find him.

He was young enough to get a cheap student rail ticket to travel thousands of kilometers. Jammed between others on wooden benches in third-class wagons, he learned Spain, learned Spaniards, their bags, bundles, boxes, bread and wine, live chickens jammed under seats and on overhead shelves; and whenever the train stopped at every local station, day or night dozens of hungry disabled *mutilados de guerra*, arms missing, legs, blind, disfigured, dragging, crawling, on crutches, filed through the wagon—filed in terrible silence, and the travelers silent—for what to give? And he learned the language the practical way—in talk, talk, talk. At the beginning he traveled even in dreams, and awake he was so possessed that—how many times!—he imagined a man in the Metro, a man sitting on the plaza, a man in a crowd, waving, called his name; suddenly, he felt he was the child crying *Pa, Pa.* Maybe his father was not dead, was here; he might pass him on any street in any town, city, and not know he'd passed him. At such thoughts he felt a quick song of blood run through him.

He convinced himself that his father willed himself into his dreams and that by insistence he could call his father into being—because surely he existed somewhere in his memory. He knew that was an obsession. He knew too the nature of obsession, that if its object came from outside yourself, once it was alive in you, it presented itself to you no matter what reasoning you used against it (but what was in you that let it?). You came to desire it; you could not not desire it, you knew that it held some truth, something undeniable. At the same time you wanted to exorcize it, but how to exorcize what you did not see, what you carried and did not know how to escape?

How could he prolong the dream until he reached his father and pulled him out of it to keep him alive here? In the dream he tried to run faster, but always his pace and the distance between his father and him remained the same; and when his father turned and he was about to see his face, light struck him awake—Morning!

Now not even memory could trace the complex labyrinth he had gone through over the years, cautious because, as he was a foreigner, the clerks, administrators, Franco's Guardia Civil were cautious—formal, polite, but suspicious—whenever he made inquiries at offices, went through papers in towns, cities, cemeteries, through lists of the International Brigade, the places where they had fought, lists of war dead, foreign volunteers, Communists, Reds, Nationalists—fragmented, blotched, deleted, never complete. He had located witnesses—to no avail. He knew now the places: he had covered the country, had gone to base headquarters at Albacete and at Figueres; he had gone to the sites at Brunete, at Zaragoza, to remote sections of the Guadarrama; he had located veterans of the Abraham Lincoln Battalion who had been through the Battle of Jarama, the siege of Madrid, of Teruel and the Ebro river...until he was so saturated that he felt he had been there. For forty years he had never ceased to follow any lead, had gone even to the location of any legendary tree, cross, stone, mass grave. But nothing— no name, no marker, no bones. Could his mother have been wrong? The man, his father, have lied to her? Perhaps he had never gone to Spain. Though he had not given up the search, in this sequestered corner in a building old and decaying in Madrid, he'd found his life. To survive, with less time free over the years, he'd done little searching. He had to survive even though his father, this phantasm, inhabited his mind, reminded him there were still places he must travel where his father might have been, where his bones might be.

After years of problems with the authorities, bureaucratic paperwork, and years of teaching English, he had decided to become naturalized. Hadn't he spent most of his life here? Wasn't his father, alive or dead, here? For years he had had steady work teaching English in the schools until he had retired on a pension, a pittance, but it gave him joy to be able now to concentrate for long hours and set down his theory of tragedy. Oh, over the years he had written bits of it applied to individual Greek or modern works or groups of tragedies. Some, after the dearth of journals during Franco's rule, had been published in resuscitated journals or new ones that had sprung up after the dictator's death in November of '75. Over the years he had had some correspondence with specialists and some of the great scholars who had gone into exile. He had found that the truest philosophers were humble before any serious thought.

In the *barrio* he had come to be the familiar bearded sage. "Ask *el sabio*," they'd say. When—with his black beret and always a book or satchel—he sometimes sat on a wooden bench on the plaza or under the statue of Tirso, defying the pigeon droppings, this one or that, in good humor or comic disparagement, would call *"Hola,* Cervantes." "How goes it, Unamuno?" "What say, Ortega?"

In the building he was respected. The *inquilinos* would bicker and shout— it would be defective pipes or dampness crumbling the first-floor corridor walls or the Jiménez' dog so noisy all night long or the scandalous carousing of young Marcelino upsetting the whole building. As he served as president of the community, they would end up coming to his door with their appeals to settle this matter or that at the monthly meetings: "Don Eduardo, *por favor...*" Though, in his own eyes, he was neither wise nor practical, but dedicated to order. Amid the arguments and bickering and shouts, in a voice so quiet it would still them, he would utter a possible solution, though these days when he sat down at his desk to concentrate on his own work, there would come the cries and laughter and drunken shouts of those German students living it up in the building facing his rooms. He was appalled that even in winter through his closed window he could hear the raucous chaos they made in the German language with which his beloved philosophers had created their ordered systems.

He came to 3-A and knocked. He almost expected the moans of doña Elvira and the drag of her feet; it was hard to believe she had been carried off to a *residencia geriátrica*. María Sanz had moved in not long after. The apartment was no more than a cubbyhole, a converted storage area at the head of the stairwell on his floor. There was light under the door. It was the supper hour. A short, dark-haired woman opened the door barely wide enough to show her face. There was an instant's rush of hot air filled with the smell of garlic and chorizo and the sizzle of frying.

"Good evening," he said. "I'm the president of the community, Eduardo Grant."

"Ah." She smiled sweetly and said in a voice sweet too, "It's…I haven't the right change. I'll bring the rent to you when…"

"No, no, *señora*. Don't you worry. Anytime. I merely wanted to introduce myself. I'm in 3-E at the farthest turn of the corridor…" He heard a rapping like a spoon against the floor.

She turned her head quickly. "My son, hungry and impatient." She called to him, "*Sí, hijo, sí*" and said, "*Gracias, señor*," and shut the door.

He groped his way back to his rooms and heated the lentils, and after eating sat down at his worktable by the window for a moment before he started work, letting his gaze range over the windows of the buildings facing the interior patio below. He had become so familiar with the activities of the neighbors that, although he had never talked to one from any of those other buildings, he heard their voices, knew who they were, what they worked at, how many were in the family. His was a distant intimacy; he was the unknown invisible member of this enormous family. He saw them through his own reflection in the pane and imagined what they saw, an old man at his books.

But he could not concentrate. Each time he tried to interpret the unfortunate Oedipus—who in his fury had unknowingly killed his own father and then unknowingly married his own mother; who in the course of the action had guessed, no, knew, who he was—he was besieged by memories of his own mother, her secret. Even now those memories caused anguish when he thought of the years of his search, of his failure. Why did he still insist? He could almost not forgive himself for not forgetting. In dreams he had gone through battles, had seen his father die. Awake, he had imagined battles so as to kill his father, end him, end his search; but the imagination was a torment he could not control: out of the dead body rose a living body, but he yearned for a face. But nothing! He would find himself gazing at a wall, book, dish, flower. In moments of despair he thought: *Why live this futility? End it.* And for support he cried out to the myriad dead shadows of writers who had committed suicide. And wasn't Oedipus' gouging out his own eyes a form of suicide? But you did not kill the ghosts in you. Weren't the ghosts of all whom he had ever known alive inside him? Wasn't his father? Wasn't his memory subjected to their will?

The lives you carry erupt in you and displace time.

No, he could not concentrate. His mother haunted. He heard the soft voice, saw the dark hair and dark eyes and that expression so sweet but invulnerable. Was it because of that young woman? María Sanz. Her face he was seeing. He was disturbed. She had stirred something in him. She had held the door so narrow: fear and secret and vulnerable, he thought. And son. He had not seen him, but heard.

The next night, late, he heard quick, energetic little steps along the corridor—new steps. He knew everybody's walk. It was María.

"Ah, forgive me this late hour, don Eduardo. I work late, and it's so far, I take the Metro, i must change twice..."

"*Qué va*! You see my light's on, and who sleeps!" He laughed.

She laughed too. "Such luck! Sleep I don't know. It's run, run, day and night, but who doesn't? It's the law of life, *verdad*? Pardon me, don Eduardo, but I must hurry. Jacinto's waiting. He'll be starved."

"Your receipt!" he cried after her.

"Ah, my useless head." She laughed at herself.

He heard her quick short steps echo down the far corridor.

All week he caught himself listening for those steps on the stairwell and down the three flights mornings when she left, some mornings her voice prodding the boy, hustling him along, and evenings mounting the stairs, a little dynamo, sometimes talking to Jacinto, then the sound of her key; some nights alone, opening the door and calling at once, "Jacinto? Jacinto! *Mamá* is here, *amor mío*." And now and then, rarely, he would hear her come home at midday, briefly, and then scurry off. Six days she worked and a half day on Sundays, then went off with the child for the afternoon. "To the zoo," she told him one day when, sitting on the plaza in the sun, he saw them come out of the Metro, she with her bag and a basket, and hailed them. The boy was a handsome little thing but sagging wearily with a look dark and a scowl like a little old man's. "Look at him, poor Jacinto, half dead. How he loves the animals. He's half animal himself. When we go to the Retiro, I can't keep him from climbing trees. I have to keep an eye out every minute or he'd be in the lagoon."

That made him think of his own childhood by the sea, how he wanted to go into water, and deep, and far; wanted to stay with horseshoe crabs and skates and schools of minnows and explore the dark—he could never go far enough, his lungs drove him back up. Sometimes in dreams he still went down there, but always he woke too soon.

"Say hello to don Eduardo, Jacinto." But his eyes half closed, the boy clung to her leg and buried his face against her.

"Shy, is he!"

"This one? Never! He's just worn out. *Adiós*, don Eduardo."

How neat she was, this María Sanz, and trim. One night he mounted the stairs to collect her monthly rent. "Just a moment," she said. "Come—" He stepped in, startled at how she had transformed the tiny place. The walls were washed white. It looked bigger. He had never seen it so clean, ordered, so homey it invited. The boy was sitting at the table. "Hola!" He smiled a bright smile and his dark eyes shone as bright; and the tabletop and sink and stove and floor bright too. A rose dress hung on a rack and on the narrow bed in the nook a pale green bedspread lay neat. And the clean scent. And the window wide open to the night. She must never stop working, this María Sanz. "Some bean soup, don?" "No, no, thank you. Eat, señora, eat."

One night the García woman from 2-D complained to him that some loose tiles had been torn from the landing and she had stepped in the space and almost fallen. "I'll bring it up at the next meeting." "Well..." She hesitated as if she had more on her mind, but shrugged and left. Some days later Leonora came up from the second floor to complain about noise in the interior patio at night. Everybody heard. You couldn't shut your windows in this heat, could you? "Perhaps since it comes from above your apartment, you might talk to her about it." "No, no, not to that woman." "But, Leonor—" "No, no, don Eduardo, it's your job." And two or three times in the corridors he heard the residents repeat *that woman*, and even the young *marroquí* on the street floor, usually as discreet as any well-behaved immigrant seeking naturalization, strict in his religious views on women, gave the nod at the phrase. At the next junta he mentioned the displaced tiles. The *vecinos* complained of poundings on the third floor. Immediately María Sanz said frankly, "It may be my son. If it is, I'm sorry. I'll see that he doesn't do it again." Her unexpected responsibility silenced but did not satisfy, though they saved their grumblings until after the junta.

Noises there were, troubles between neighbors, momentary nuisances, apartment problems, but María Sanz had no man. It was that—no man—yes. And what remedy for that? That was her life. He pitied her—alone, the neighbors against her. And more and more. And she in a nook too cheap to leave and cheaper hard to find.

The complaint made him dream, sent him back to that town and that other woman long ago who had never for a minute seemed far because she was all he had had then, and he all she had had. His mother had worked at the U.S. Rubber factory and had walked proudly before town with him, her son, silent but never ashamed, silent because she kept her life her own and respected that man he did not know, who was his father, who was in his flesh, in his looks maybe, whom he would never be free of. His mother had never repented but borne that stigma then. He was aware now that what she had suffered on his account he would never know as later on perhaps Jacinto would never know. So when he saw María Sanz, he saw his mother, young, who had taken his hand, who had petted, scolded, trained, encouraged—it was as if María had come to this building to restore her to him, an unexpected presence. So he liked to see María, talk to her, hear her soothing voice; and by a trick of his imagination, whenever he saw her take the boy's hand and go down the stairs, he was that other boy.

María was a country girl from a village in Extremadura, which she loved, but there was no work there and there were circumstances... "—and you cannot change people, especially in small towns. You could die from their hates, don Eduardo. A boy like my Jacinto could die like a melon without water, yes, and who could care?"

Yes, who? he thought, listening to her tell of her town and seeing the longing in her as she talked of green and river and solitude and peace; and then knowing not solitude but isolation because even in a village with green and river and solitude and peace you could die without love you dreamed of and breathed for and waited and watched for.

"My father and mother are there. Good Catholics. They said it's what you must be because there are always the other people. And me not a good one—because pregnant. I should be dead, they said. Oh, I can't condemn them—they think it's wrong, they think they're right, they even went to the priest, prayed with him for solutions. What solution? What did they think the priest could say? Padre Marcelino was trapped too because he was the Church so what could he say but find a husband to give the baby a name. He said he would pray, and again and again told me to. The padre was a good man, kind and tender. I could not blame him; it was his duty to tell me in good conscience because he believed that, he'd sworn to that. But my mother said praying will conceal nothing, praying will not take the shame away, no. Like a thief, they made me feel, but not knowing what I was stealing. So I left, don Eduardo. I didn't tell them. And you'd think I'd had enough of the Church, but it was the sisters here in Madrid who gave me charity and brought Jacinto into the world like a son of the Church itself. He has my name, my father's, because I would not, never, tell the name of Jacinto's father because it was for me love, I couldn't hide that, no; but for him maybe it was just a moment, passion you can't stop. Oh. I don't blame him because I wanted that moment, I had it and I've never regretted it no matter how hard it's been. It's the one moment of my life, and every time I look at Jacinto...Why would I regret it?"

Yes, why? It was as if at last he were hearing his mother telling him the story she had never told him about her moment with his father.

There were days when he passed her apartment and heard sounds. He'd stop in the corridor to listen: scrapings, drags as if by rats, a dog, cat. And then, as if the creature were alerted by his presence, the sounds ceased. When he moved off and halted at the head of the stairs, the sounds began again.

And sometimes whispers, murmurs.

And crying.

He stopped, mute. He heard himself. He saw himself. He, Edward, was behind that door. The illusion was so strong that he doubted the man standing there, weak and dizzy, clutching the banister.

He was not the only one who heard the boy crying. Soon came idle mutterings against "that woman"—of irresponsibility, neglect, abuse. What was going on in her place? And he thought, *What was in others that made them stalk you?*

As casually as he could, he asked María about the boy, how he was, what he did all day, where—?

"But he's here. Three days he's home alone, don Eduardo. Oh, you're kind, you're hiding it, but I know what they say. How can they help it? He's almost five, and alone, three days a week he's alone. Oh, I come home noons when I can, when I'm supposed to be eating, but I'm not supposed to leave work, they want me there cleaning and tending to them every minute to get their money's worth, not like my Monday, Wednesday, and Friday people, who let me take Jacinto to work, he's no trouble, he's good, don Eduardo, and smart. I've trained him don't touch the stove or lean out the window or open the door to anybody. Yes, those days I leave him by himself, but what can I do? I manage—just—with what I earn, and there's no way I could pay anybody to keep him or send him to a *guardería*. And don't think I'm not half crazy all day thinking of Jacinto, what he's doing and what could happen to him. I tell him don't go into the hall, hide if somebody comes, don't open the door ever—because I don't lock the door, don Eduardo, suppose there's a fire or he has an accident and somebody has to get in. You see why it's driving me crazy I can't take him with me all the time?"

He saw tears edge, but she held her head up. "I don't mean to burden you, don, but since you asked... I know you understand. It's not easy. *Perdóneme la molestia.*"

"No, no, María, por favor. What are friends for?"

"You!" She laid her hand on his arm.

Not long after on a night of intense heat, he felt sluggish, weak—his blood pressure, his sedentary work, the reading, the writing he let keep him from exercising. He went dragging his feet from chair to table to bed... And those German students, how they irked! He could not ignore them now that he needed sleep so. One day he could hardly stand, barely made it to the refrigerator and stove and table—and then fell and lay on the floor—hours? he did not know how long—and when he came to, he crawled to the bed and collapsed, his sight hazy and his hearing muffled so he was not sure who was coming and going. Sometimes a face neared and neared and he reached out to touch it but it vanished. Then the haze cleared and he was standing at the edge of the playing field behind the grade school and she was calling him home, calling and calling *it's time for supper.* The kids were playing ball but he was watching the man standing in the shadow of the tree on the other side of the field, and he thought: *That's my father.* And when the man crossed the field toward him and walked straight through the game, his heart was beating so hard he couldn't move, but the man kept coming until he was a dark shadow over him and touched his face—He gasped and opened his eyes: the hand was on his cheek, the face bent close staring at him. "Jacinto!"

His voice was so raucous he startled himself. He bolted from the bed and out. "Jacinto," he called weakly, and slumped, sinking... But a voice, soft, brought him back, and a hand cool. Ma? She was dampening his face, smoothing his hair back. She said, "*Ay de mí,* don Eduardo. Jacinto came crying in and gripped my dress and pulled. Thank God your door's open or who'd know. You should have called out, banged, anything. *Dios mío,* what are we for if useless, eh?" She propped the pillows up behind him. "I'll be right back. Now don't you think of moving."

His eyes roved. His room. Summer sun struck high in the patio, the sky burned blue, the high dormer windows opposite afire and the white walls. Pots and dishes sounded, and voices, the supper hour, yes, but still bright outside. The red tiles of roofs opposite stood sharp. This. His hand rose, he wanted to touch. From down the corridor came voices and steps. Doors. His mind saw doors and doors. You! he thought, always traveling. Why can't you stay? Why do you condemn yourself to a labyrinth with no end?

"Come, don Eduardo—" María sat by the bed. "Some *caldo* you need.

Here. Take." She spooned him the broth. It was delicious. It made a quick hot path. His body quivered. His mouth could not get enough. "Careful, don! *Cuidado!*" She laughed, wiping dribbles from his chin.

That night several times his sleep broke, he opened his eyes stark. The face? Where was that face? He sank, thinking, I'll go back into my dream where I left off. I'll go back to the school yard, I'll wait until he comes, he'll cross the street, he'll... But no school yard came, no children playing, no tree or man, no face. He woke frenzied. How could the face go? His whole self was geared to that dream as if it were trying to tell him something. Years it had tortured him coming closer and closer until at times he'd thought: *Now the man would reveal his face at last and say,* "Seek no more, I'm your father..."

But no—not.

Now early morning and late nights, María brought him food. In a matter of days she had him up, tottering and then solid on his feet; always before leaving came her question, "You took your medicine?"

But the medicine did not cure his dreams. Always the face came; it neared and neared, ghostly. Who? he murmured when it closed in. The face was no longer blank. Under hair as thick as his own, a face materialized clear and staring: Jacinto! He would open his eyes. But Jacinto was not there. What was Jacinto doing in his dreams?

Jacinto.

When the boy did come to his room, María cried, "Jacinto, don't you bother don Eduardo!" He was not dreaming now. He said, "But, María, don't tell him *Don't*. You told him don't go out but he came here and found me—and look—here I am. Who knows what might have happened to me?"

"God sees, don Eduardo."

He did not tell her how he blessed his good fortune. Renewed he felt. He said, "I'll look in on the boy when you're working or you can leave him with me the three days."

"But..." Startled, she flailed. "...your work. How could you..." Her mouth quivered. She bit it still. Her eyes went glossy.

"Oh, I'm a night owl. I think best in the quiet. And you'll be with Jacinto then."

If only those German students would calm down!

As María had to leave for work very early, long before his usual hour, those mornings the boy opened the door and came in and stood by his bed staring at him. He would feign sleep until the boy whispered, "Don Eduardo," and he would open his eyes and growl and grab him and draw him into the bed and Jacinto would squeal with pleasure and play with his beard.

So the days began. Jacinto helped him, "Here," handing him the shirt, a shoe; and then both pitched in, clumsy, to make breakfast and eat, Jacinto's head barely above the tabletop, and together made the bed, and then came pictures in books and "You know some letters? We'll make words," and drawing, and—the best part—Jacinto said, "Now? Can we go down now?"—down the stairs, Jacinto holding his hand, leading him, pulling—"Slow, Jacinto. Wait"—and up Lavapiés to the plaza, where among the old people and dogs and children Jacinto fed and shooed and chased and tried to catch pigeons; and some days to the Casa de Campo and the zoo, Jacinto staring fascinated at giraffes and panthers or laughing and shouting at monkeys; and some days to the Retiro, where he ran into other children and could play and have ice cream and watch the puppet shows and the artists draw pictures in chalk on the pavement and revel in clowns and the feats of the strong men, and then back at three to eat and take the siesta; and before he knew it night and María—"Mamá, we saw snakes this long"—and then Jacinto was gone and he went back to words and silence and dark.

One night he found María desperate—yes, desperate, he could tell—from her silence, her brusque motions at the stove, a frustration.

"And you, what?" he said.

She was reluctant to say, so strong she was, independent, but helpless.

"School. I can't take him—" Because two jobs she had, she worked seven days, cleaning weekdays, kitchen help Sundays at El Gato restaurant.

"And the law says…"

"But María—I can take him."

"No, no, don Eduardo. Too much you do. You are not for that."

He stared. Not for that? All the years he had not thought, *What am I for?* Because all those years—of what?—writing articles and essays for a pittance and for a pittance maintaining the shell of this decaying building with its remaining half dozen tenants, their rents happily frozen by law to the few *reales* they had paid before the Civil War and paid now when they could pay: he knew their losses; he could not—it was not in him—exact immediate payment any more than anyone might have from him with his dearth since his arrival here years after the Civil War, when he had to learn what it was to survive, not long before he came to understand and sympathize with the trials etched in those faces Republican or Nationalist, the faces of this people, this pueblo, this Nación, his now.

Now mornings he took Jacinto's hand and they went down the street to the underground and dropped him off at the *cole*; and at three he returned and waited outside the school with the crowd of mothers, reminding him of his time as a child when his mother used to come for him, flagging, "Edward, here, Edward," himself looking, longing—no papa. Where was his?

He exulted when that flow of unbridled flesh came pouring from the school and Jacinto came running and with joy leaped and latched his arms around his neck and pressed his face against him, crying "Papi, papi!" And he laughed—*me clutched, never before clutched*—seeing in that boy himself, and him the father, but who? He remembered the long ago day in the A&P with his mother when he asked a man, "Are you my father?" and when the man laughed and said no, he went up and down the aisles asking men that until people began to laugh and his mother heard and came after him, so humiliated that she left the buggy of groceries in the aisle and gripped his arm and lugged him out of the store.

Remembering, he stared into his shadow on the walk.

He took Jacinto's hand and they went home.

Soon came the day that he and the renters had expected but dreaded. Warnings they'd had, *avisos* from the Comunidad de Madrid posted on the building: condemned. The ex-owner, Rafael Uribe, came with lament for him and all the inquilinos. The building now belonged to the municipality, so the remaining tenants, some old ones who had been living there since before Franco, were to be evicted. Only María had not been there many years.

He gathered the only ones remaining—old Folledos and his wife, the Robles with their seven children, the nurse Carla, and Mati Fernández and her three brothers. For the last meeting—sad faces, silent, resigned, worse the old ones who had lived in this building all their lives and endured the unspeakable during the war and after. They would not dwell, gave quick hands, embraced, kissed cheeks.

María was upset—so little time to hunt for a place. "Nights I must. All the time I have—nights, late. And you, don Eduardo, what?"

And he?

What?

Too long in this barrio to leave it, while Jacinto was at school he explored, trudging the streets in his district until he found a small place, cheap, in another old building, with light, much light, no dark, overlooking the plaza of Lavapiés.

So in the building the final movings began, strange intermittent rackets, furniture moved down stairways creaking under the weight. He would be the last to leave the building, lock the door and hand over the final rents and the keys.

One night María came home excited, relieved, talkative—because "Saved! Lili—she works with me at El Gato—got me the place next to hers, poor, *pobre*, sí, but all we need—and such luck, easy for me, near a bus stop and the *cole* so I can drop Jacinto off. You see, God listens, don Eduardo."

Now he walked the long corridors, the four floors, this labyrinth of empty apartments dark as caves in day; walked his life, his mind running over the forty years of inquilinos who had peopled his life. Up and down stairs he went, through all the corridors, as if something not yet revealed to him were evading him, as if some memory he had lost might still be recovered intact.

Dead, this building. He had not realized how hard it would be to shed it like a skin he had lived in.

Before moving he decided his beard had to go. He clipped with scissors, soaped what remained, shaved. In the mirror that unburied face—racked by the infinitesimal valleys of time; its life shriveling, only his eyes glittered of life—seemed almost alien to him.

Is this all I will ever know of George Lasher?

When he went to María's door, she was startled an instant. "But, don Eduardo, look at you! Such pink skin. So *anglosajón*. I'd only by your clothes know you. Jacinto, you know who this is?"

"Papi!"

Jacinto clutched his leg.

"You can't fool children," he said.

Two days later Lili's brother came to haul María's possessions in his *camioneta*. After the truck was loaded, once outside, Jacinto said, "Come, Papi."

She said, "On Saturdays or Sundays when no school you must come, don Eduardo. Jacinto will be lost without you."

Saturdays. Sundays.

He knew there would be no Saturdays or Sundays, and no more Jacinto mornings.

But he nodded.

María gripped the basket.

"Don Eduardo...," she murmured. Her shoulders quivered. She did not kiss his cheeks or offer hers. Quick she turned away.

"Papi?"

Confused, Jacinto.

"He doesn't realize yet. Come, Jacinto—"

"Papi!"

"Now, Jacinto."

She drew him into the front seat beside her.

As the camioneta moved off, he gazed after them—hazy his vision —and waved.

He felt he was waving goodbye to himself.

The dirty window of the camioneta blurred Jacinto's face. It stared back at him like a little old man's.

remember guernica
Kate Gale

remember guernica

Vaseline
   When I split open the curtains to my mother's bedroom, I found Vaseline by the bedside table. A small plastic jar with a lid. Took off the lid and smelled it. Not much smell. Just that strange nearly odorless gel. They find it near oil drilling. I check the Vaseline every time I go in there, but they use it very slowly. There always seems to be a fair bit left.

The Writer in the Family
   In a family, somebody has to play each role. I am the clown, the funny man, the fall guy. If someone did wrong, they blame me so fast their head spins. I've been blamed for things that happened while I was asleep, at school, out of the country. I can guarantee you this, if I die, they'll say, *he did it.* Someone will say, *How could he have done it, he's dead!* And someone else will say, *Trust me, he did it with his bare skeletal hands. His skeletal feet ran away and hid in his coffin.* My sister is the angel. My stepdad is like God. Ready to provide loaves and fishes. Angry when you do evil. Not fixing the world. Just watching. My mother is the writer in the family. But she may have messed these things up. She may blame me for things I didn't even know about.

Zuma Beach
   My mother fell in love with a man whose hands shook. She told me about this while we drove to the beach. I asked her about being in love. Nothing I really understand. Because I love them all. I really do. So I asked her. Because it was a perfect beach day. Southern California. One of many

perfect beach days. I asked Mother about love, and she told me about the man who loved her so much that when he walked her around his garden, his hands shook. She thought this was the great love of her life. "Then what?" I ask, and she says, "Well, he came over for dinner and afterward we played Jenga and I realized that his hands just shook like that. He was like an old man. He had shaky hands. So it had nothing to do with me. Or love." The beach sunlight is almost white. I almost can't see the girls who I know are spread out all over it like music you could walk into. All their legs, their high pitched laughter sailing out across the water, the way they reach and reach. For what? You don't know with girls. They're always reaching.

We pull up and I say, "What happened to Jenga man?"

Mother says, "He turned out to be just a man whose hands shook. Not the great love at all."

"Is there a great love?" I ask.

"Yes," she says, "there is. But it's too big to talk about."

"Bigger than the ocean?"

She puts on her sunglasses then. She smiles like she has a secret. We walk down to Zuma beach. Girls everywhere. In the sunlight.

Zuma. Zuma. I say to myself. I may name my first child that. Especially if the child happens here. Anything is possible. I am fifteen.

Zebra Porn

My high school has every conceivable kind of person. There are stoners and metal heads, punk rockers and the endless wannabe rappers. Not too many real rappers. There is no cool group, no popular group. We are many. There are four thousand of us wrapped around the school mascot. The campus security see us as the faceless many, as predators, as trouble. We are the prisoners, they the guards. They are virgins all of them. Their faces very clean, they smell of soap, they walk outside the chain linked fence, eat food that is not slop. They peer in on the packed halls, the throngs at lunch time like birds of prey, eyes hungry and yellow, heads cocked sideways. Reptiles and birds of prey have that sideways look. Campus security too. At food breaks, the rush of humans looks like a circus. The freaks, the Asians, the Armenians, the football players, the tall black girls in their tight jeans, the cheerleaders, crowds of dark-haired girls, so many nationalities piled so close together, you wouldn't know which was which, the Pacific Islanders, the Middle Easterners, the Filipinos, Latinos, and the endless mixed-race students with names like Javier Yan, Osama Covarrubias. My sister and I are in the small minority of Whites, but I will not adapt. I wear my Iron Maiden,

Pink Floyd, Black Sabbath close to me. I walk the talk, I listen to music, I am the street, the sound, the dirt, the hooded head, the low, torn sweatshirt, the sagging pants; I am over six feet and I am every security person's nightmare. I laugh out loud in class. I make the class laugh by just looking at them. I am the cool pants they always wanted to have, the girls waiting for me outside class are their girls.

Campus security were once people in another life. But in this one, they were born little zombies and all their school life, they smelled like zombies, looked like zombies, kissed like zombies, their mouths tasted like zombies. Their girls didn't demand to be on top, didn't scream at the top of their lungs. Their girls were zombiettes. They smelled like powder; they never walked around the house naked. They never used handcuffs for recreational purposes. They cooked scrambled eggs for the zombies and served them with orange juice. Campus security have their orange juice wives and their clicking pens and their mouths tasting like old mint. On weekends, when they're feeling frisky, they watch zebra porn.

After a weekend of zebra porn, one found me. With my hood up. Violation of school rules. Called for a backpack search. As he began the unloading, I knew it was going to be bad. I'd been camping that weekend and I'd taken every conceivable thing to impress my two friends. Spence was about to be sent away to drug rehab for teenagers. He had his hair dyed jet black, he'd sniffed glue, tried jabbing himself with needles. My friend Scott wanted to be Spicoli. Spicoli, stoned since the third grade; he was Scott's hero. Scott claimed to have tried heroin. At fifteen in the San Fernando Valley that takes some doing. Heroin isn't lying around. Heroin! Who was I? I had to go the whole way. I stole/borrowed my father's switchblade and added in a butterfly knife I'd gotten for my birthday. The knives were wicked and would get me some play. But I needed more. I brought two pipes, two lighters, my stash. By the time this zebra porn watcher was unloading my backpack, the stash consisted of 1/3 of a gram of mj. He laid it all out in an orderly way on his desk smacking his orange juice lips. He called in a cop. They began taking pictures, taking notes. They were busy. I was texting. The cop pulled out my journal, a gift from my mother, a fine thing in a green leather case. He sat down at the desk and read it. I texted and began to pray. Not that I believed in prayer, but there wasn't much else to do. The typewriters were marching. I could hear their tiny keys in my ears and under my skin.

Handcuffs

Maybe Mother wouldn't have taken it so badly if they hadn't shoved me against the wall and handcuffed me. She was doing pretty well up 'til then. She'd arrived quietly in a short dress and sandals. She had just gotten back from running and I could tell she was faint as the zombies began showing her the pages they'd typed up. The lists. The pictures. She held on to the desk to balance herself, readjusted her sunglasses. My father is better in situations like this. He isn't afraid. I know the voices that tap inside my mother's head tell her she's going to be beaten, I'm going to be beaten. We're all going to be beaten. My father has never been beaten. He thinks he's going to beat someone. My father couldn't get away from work; my mother was home. And would my father have come? I don't know. He might have let the zombies eat me. He and my stepfather understand the world to be an orderly place in which I need to find my position. I need to learn to walk in line. My mother and I live outside the lines. Her makeup is smudged, and her hair drifts around her shoulders like a cloud. The cop takes her outside, but I hear them.

I read his journal. He is sexually active. This is like clockwork for this boy.

As if my mother doesn't understand.

I know my mother would not have believed the journal even if she'd read it. She and I live in the world of our imaginations. She would have thought I was writing my fantasies. But she would never have read the journal.

You should read this journal, the cop tells her. You must read this. He shows her the rest of the evidence. He speaks slowly as if she is slow. My mother can think circles around this zombie, but I know she is giving him her look, the vacant stare which looks like she is taking in nothing, but means really that she cannot feel herself in the world. That she feels like a cardboard cutout in the wind. She cannot stand. I see her hands moving through air and I wish very much that I had not made her stand here like this. The day is perfect. The California air steams yellow.

At the police station when the cop returns everything that is not deemed evidence, he hands my mother the journal. *Read it,* he tells her. *You'll see what I mean.* He says the words slowly and distinctly. As if my mother may not understand how evil this is. I know for a fact that zombies don't get sex. I've researched their lives and habits enough to know that. They get weekly sex until they turn forty, then monthly until they're fifty, and then their only pleasure is zebra porn and orange juice.

Man Against Zombie

My mother is leaving for another run and I am lying on her bed talking with her while she pulls her hair into a ponytail. She is telling me what to read while she is gone, and I'm trying to concentrate, but I notice something. She rubs Vaseline on her arms and legs.

"What's that for?" I ask. Casual.

"The Vaseline? It's to prevent rub burns from running in the heat."

"Oh."

"What did you think it was for?"

"Sex."

"No. We don't use Vaseline. I don't know. Maybe some people do. I hadn't heard of that."

I had.

"That's why the policeman wanted me to read your journal. He could tell I needed to learn something. But I didn't read it."

"I know. Does life ever go back to normal?"

"It never does." She laces up her shoes carefully.

"What do you do?"

"I don't know what you do. I run."

"Maybe something good will come of all this," I say.

"Yeah, it will. We don't know yet. We won't know 'til later."

"Maybe," I say, "you'll write about this in a story or a poem. The conflict will be man against zombie."

"Or man against himself," she says.

"Who wins?"

"We don't know yet, do we? The story isn't over."

"Does the story, if it's good enough, make it all worth it?"

"No," she says. "Very definitely. Remember Guernica?"

"My life is hardly the Spanish Civil War," I say. And she's just staring at me. I know she needs to go out running to sort her thoughts that are tossing in that blender mind. And I say, "Write it from my point of view."

And she says, "Sure, but remember."

"I will," I say. "I'll remember Guernica." She goes out the door. I hear it close behind her and I start my reading. I'm halfway through *Fight Club* and it's just getting better and better. They never taught this in school.

Shadows and Mirrors

Even if you are a real person there's nothing you can do about a haunting. Once you've been exorcised, all that is left is your ghost self. And what do you do with yourself if you feel you're only haunting the place where your life used to be? You are somebody who lives in music, who can change the music and the song and the lyrics and the clothes. Who can sky dive and play out tunes in your head. Who can run through more comedy skits in an hour than most people can in their whole life.

But you can be cut out of the picture by zombies. You can be left on the hill hanging there alone, even the two thieves you came with still talking, still real. You outside. Even if your mother loves you, she's just one person, and the mirror is broken. You look down into it and what you see is long shadowy shards of yourself. But there's no whole you. And mirrors can't be fixed. The sun is setting off the California coast. Your girlfriend has moved to Arkansas so you don't even have that. You wonder if you cast a shadow any more. If you're invisible. You wonder if your father was right. You have to walk in line before you can break out of line. You wonder if you went way out on the ocean to where the sky touches, if you could become part of the sky. Would you be a seagull then? Or a cloud? Could you soar inland, over the vast landscape until you saw the tiny prison school and from up there, the tiny zombies thumping their chests? From up there, would human beings look ridiculous? You hear the music playing. Next week you're going to a play. You love theatre because in that tiny world somebody is controlling the strings and you get it. You get that the curtain goes up. It goes up and it comes down. That play is over. Another begins. Someone just needs to write the play. You will never attend high school again. You fucked up. Your mother's music is playing. It's the Lisa Germano album. *Geek the Girl*.

They say she got just what she wanted, Lisa sings. And you don't know. Maybe she's right. You can't take a hit any more, so you drink a Diet Coke. You read Palahniuk and you keep Eddie Murphy on in the background. That's what you want. A foreground. A middle ground. A background. The elements of a real story. A real life.

moon tide prayer
Catherine Gentile

moon tide prayer

*et us lower the drawbridge for this little one, for he glistens with hope
and inspires each generation to instill in the next values permeated with
goodwill. So crucial is this responsibility, if we fail in its propagation, we
compromise our hope for the betterment of humanity.*

—Fletcher William Hart's journal entry: July 12, 1930, written upon returning
from Savannah

Torchlight shimmering along the veranda of the Grand Mitreanna outlined
the base of the rambling three-story hotel from the dance pavilion along
its southernmost railing to the crimson-carpeted boardwalk winding around
the bathhouse toward the sign for the whites-only beach. That a black man,
Fletcher William Hart, stood mere yards from the bold letters crying out
against his presence created a sensational attraction. One that bloated the
pocketbook of Mr. Fredrick, the hotel's owner, and gave Fletch a paying job
when there were few to be had. He pulled a rag from his back pocket and
mopped his face from the widow's peak gracing his broad forehead, over
the round of his cheeks, down to the troubles anchoring his lips.

From behind the railing on the veranda, the white patronesses of the
Mitreanna watched with attentive yet discreet Southern interest while Fletch
staged their evening's entertainment. Naked to the waist and perspiring
from hoisting shovel after shovel of damp sand into the forms he'd made
especially for this show, Fletch's muscular body glistened. "We no better
than whores, but what we gonna do?" his wife, Egypt Ann, whimpered
earlier this evening as he prepared to leave for work.

Although he dared not look directly at the women, he could feel them
staring. From the corner of his eye, he saw them lean into one another, point

their gloved hands, and whisper. He guessed at the heartless insinuations they were making through their muffled giggles. His wife was right—their imaginations erased the tableau of a poor man earning a night's wages and replaced it with the spectacle of a lion in the throes of mating. Angry heat shot across his chest, down his arms, and into his fingertips. He raised his shovel high and plunged it deeper than ever before. The women inhaled sharply, as though... the thought was too terrifying to complete.

Mr. Fredrick smiled at one gentleman and called to another as he strode past the women toward Fletch. Fletch had overheard Mr. Fredrick explain to his new assistant, who'd offered to accompany him down to the beach, that his being alone with the nigger is part of the show: "My guests feel safer when they see me with the beast."

Within a short minute, Mr. Fredrick arrived unaccompanied by his assistant or his smile. Fletch moved his equipment out of Mr. Fredrick's way. "Sandy, my boy, you're late. People threatened to leave if you didn't show."

"Yes sir, I is," Fletch answered, hating his po' boy talk more than the circus nickname Mr. Fredrick had slapped on him.

Mr. Fredrick slid his tuxedo jacket aside and planted his thick palm on his hip. "Hotel's full up and tide's coming in fast." As he spoke, his round belly pushed against the black pearl buttons on his pleated white shirt. He returned his gaze to the veranda, where, bathed within auras of golden torchlight, small groups were seated on velvet chairs around linen-draped tables.

Fletch swallowed. Mr. Fredrick was checking the crowd for indications of boredom—the start of a quick game of cards, excessive drinking, women signaling their husbands for the keys to their rooms—any of which could sound the death knell for Fletch's act.

Mr. Fredrick brightened, waved to a gentleman at the far end of the veranda, then looked up at Fletch and scowled. "You've never been late before. What's happening to you, Sandy?"

Fletch respectfully averted his eyes. "I be tryin' my best, sir."

"Make sure tonight's show is better than your best." Mr. Fredrick brushed the sand from his cuffs and marched toward the boardwalk, shouting greetings as he went.

He climbed the staircase to the palm-lined entrance of his hotel. In the center, a glass bowl rested on a table, the top of which rode the backs of two regal lions. He faced the crowd gathered along the railing. "Ladies and gentlemen, tonight we have a first at the Grand Mitreanna—the highest tides in history will wash the shores of the Mitreanna as Sandy the Sandman attempts to build a three-story castle at the edge of the sea. Yes, folks, tonight you will witness the Sandman compete with Mother Nature." Necks craned toward Fletch. Mr. Fredrick stretched his arms wide and the whispering settled. "There's more. My bet says tonight's tide will destroy the Sandman's castle before he finishes it."

Nervous laughter rippled through the guests. Mr. Fredrick grasped a five-dollar bill by its edges, raised it above his wispy hair and turned slowly to his left, then to his right. When the *oohs* and *ahhs* subsided, a tuxedoed waiter took the bill, set it in the bowl, and lifted a silver tray. He held the tray while Mr. Fredrick chose one pen from several, unscrewed the cap and wrote his name in the register and, beside it, his wager. The crowd applauded.

"Ladies and gentleman, the betting has officially opened: Sandy the Sandman versus the moon tide." The waiter offered the tray to the first gentleman to step forward.

Other nights, Mr. Fredrick's familiar attempts to heighten the evening's tension didn't worry Fletch. Tonight, however, as he'd unhitched his old mule from her wagon and hid her in the barn far from the shiny coupes parked like crooked teeth along the avenue, he heard the thrum of dissatisfaction. From the far edge of the veranda, a little boy cried out, "He's here, the Sandman's here."

Ordinarily, Fletch allowed himself plenty of time in which to build a solid base for his castle. But this evening he'd had difficulty pulling himself from his daughter's bedside and feared, with the way Belle was slipping in and out of consciousness, by the time he bought her the medicine she needed, heaven would claim her sweet smile.

Strong and quick, he could make up for being late as long as he removed the distractions vying for his attention. He hurried, tamping sand into the base form, sprinkling salt water over the dry spots, and filling the remaining gaps with moist sand. He tightened his grip on the long handle of the tamping tool and leaned hard, sending the force of his two hundred pounds downward onto the flat wooden square he'd attached for just this purpose. He pressed with all his might and muttered, "Egypt Ann was right. What made me think Dr. Rovner would come to see a black man's child?" Instead, he'd sent a signed *Original Prescription Form for Medicine, F281776* and the address twenty miles away of a pharmacist who would fill it for Fletch, if he arrived while Savannah slept. The city was five hours one way, depending on the liveliness of his old mule. He reminded himself that first he had to earn the money to pay for the medicine Belle needed. He finished squeezing air pockets from the base of his castle and headed past the dunes by the boardwalk to get the forms for the second tier.

Two years earlier he and his brother, Hugh, calculated the dimensions for this castle. They built the forms and tested them on the far side of the Martons Island fishing pier, beyond the skeleton of a grounded ship on the Negroes-only section of the beach. That afternoon, after they'd finished building their three-story castle, Hugh dug a moat down to the water. Gentle waves washed hermit crabs, coquinas, sponges, and feathery seaweed into the moat. Fletch arranged shells into a coat-of-arms and pressed it into the wall of one of the turrets. He planted a small American flag on one side of the driftwood drawbridge and Georgia's flag on the other. They laughed. The seven-foot structure drew the attention of the guests on the Grand Mitreanna side of the pier. Soon, Fletch and Hugh were surrounded by a sea of curious white faces.

Mr. Fredrick bustled through the crowd. "What's going on here?" he demanded, rolling and loosening his shoulders in readiness to defend his patrons from this Negro annoyance. When he saw the castle and took note of his guests' enchanted expressions, he changed his approach. "Ladies and gentlemen ..." he edged closer to Fletch, whose dark skin was sprinkled with sand, "...I'm delighted to announce that I have arranged to hire the Sandman to build his extraordinary fortresses on our side of the beach." The crowd broke into hearty applause. "A dollar says the tide takes the castle away by six o'clock," one ruddy-faced gentleman in a damp bathing costume shouted. "My dollar says six-fifteen," said another. Sandy the Sandman had been born.

Fletch jumped on the lowest rung of his ladder, stepped down and pounded sand around its wooden legs until they stood firm. How he wished someone would do the same for him. Perhaps he'd rediscover the confidence he'd basked in after Dr. Rovner had openly admired the carpentry Fletch had completed in the library of the doctor's new home. Convinced of the good doctor's sincerity, Fletch was certain Dr. Rovner would find a way to see Belle, despite the Jim Crow laws. "Not what white folks are inclined to do." His wife's words chided as he reached for the wooden form for the next tier of his castle. Now the work became dangerous. Once he found his footing on the slick ladder, he would lift a brimming bucket of sand over the edge of the form and empty it without disturbing the lower tier, falling and making a fool of himself. Again.

The taller the castle, the more difficult to build. He and his brother had made several attempts at ungainly castles, all of which collapsed under the weight of the third tier. Finally, Hugh increased the castle's base to a four-by-four square that was a hefty three feet deep. He narrowed the second tier to a three-by-three and added a taller deuce as the third and least stable tier. With torches burning on either side of the moat and flags flying, the finished castle had been impressive indeed.

The misty air temporarily distorted Fletch's vision. At first he thought he recognized the black man running toward him, a jug clutched in one hand and a small sack in the other. Whoever he was, the newcomer handed these items off to Fletch, huffed, "Sandwiches from Mr. Fredrick," and sprinted into the shadows. Ladies in evening dresses and shawls twittered at this Negro marathon. Anxiety, the human version of thunderclaps before a storm, rippled through the crowd. What did they expect him to do, tear into the sack with his teeth? The last he'd eaten was breakfast. Had this been a different crowd and another, less crucial, situation, he'd have reached into that sack and devoured this meal. Instead, he placed it to the side. Mr. Fredrick had never sent him food before, and this made Fletch more wary than ever. He'd learned a lesson from Dr. Rovner; never again would he put a black man's hunger on display.

Just then two young boys came toward him, kicking and chasing a ball. The ball was skittering across the sand when a gust of wind catapulted it toward his half-built castle. The boys froze.

Fletch clutched the bucket of cold wet sand to his chest and continued to climb the ladder, where from the next-to-top rung he could watch the children without being obvious. God forbid anyone were to catch him looking at a white child; the boy's hysterical mother would rile the crowd and create a deadly situation for a nigger. In no time, Jim Crow enforcers, men who'd stored their white robes in the backs of their coupes and on the floorboards of their Model T trucks, would gladly employ him for a different kind of amusement. After all, what would be more entertaining than a moon tide lynching?

The wind teased the blond boy's curls, tossing them this way and that, while the other boy's straight dark hair stood on end. The dark-haired boy spoke a few words to his companion, then nudged him in the ribs. The fair-haired child yanked off his jacket and, with the flair of a circus clown who'd just entered center ring, spun it in the air and released it. He glanced at his friend, took three dramatic breaths, and burst into a run. Sand sprayed from the soles of his small churning feet. Waves exploded on the sand bar.

Fletch checked the high-watermark on the breakwater. The tide was coming in fast. If he worked steadily, he'd finish before the waves flushed his moat and eroded the base of his castle. Like it or not, today he was more caught up in the betting than usual. If he finished ahead of the tide, his take of the purse increased from five to ten percent. If not, his efforts went the other way—out to sea, along with the chances of little Belle recovering, and her mother forgiving him for forgetting who he was.

The little boy ran head down into the wind toward Fletch. His friend had, no doubt, dared him to retrieve his ball before the Sandman captured and buried him, and it, within his castle.

Sand swooshed from Fletch's upturned bucket into the second tier. If he hurried, he could tamp it, fill in the uneven spots, and set up the third tier.

With luck, he would soon plant the flag of the proud state of Georgia in the top turret and the crowd would cheer. Not for him, but for Georgia and themselves. He, Fletcher William Hart, was a mere fly that happened to hatch in their midst. He needed to keep that in mind. He banned all thoughts of his brilliance, of reading and writing at the age of three, and later secretly studying philosophy, history, literature, and mathematics. He touched his back pocket in which he kept the acceptance letter he'd received from Harvard University. There, he'd assured Egypt Ann, the color of a man's skin didn't matter. But all she wanted was for him to fill the prescription he'd tucked inside his ticket to a better life.

Fletch scrambled down the ladder and grabbed the tamping tool. The crowd gasped. Ladies covered their mouths, their eyes widened with horror. A distraught woman—most likely the blond boy's mother—pounded her husband's arm and sent him sprinting toward the boardwalk leading down to the beach. A woman in a flowery dress put her arm around the boy's mother. Little actions had taken on enormous meanings.

Sensing that he appeared to be armed, Fletch set his tamping tool aside. Another ripple rose from the crowd. He rubbed his back, picked up his dinner sack, and sauntered toward the breakwater. The crowd released an audible sigh of relief. His ploy worked.

He made a show of plunging his dark hand into the sack, knowing its rustling could never be heard above the waves crashing and men shouting, urging the boy to give up his trajectory. "Take off your shoes, so you can run," a woman screamed. Even with Fletch chomping on his sandwich, the father closing in on his son, the boy heading toward his father's rescuing arms, the boy's mother grew more hysterical.

The boy, who had by now sensed his mother's concern and became concerned himself, slipped and fell, then scurried to his feet and raced even faster toward his father, far from whatever was terrifying his mother. The father lifted the boy and swung him around while the boy laughed with relief. "Papa, put me down," he said and, wiggling from his father's grip, retrieved his ball and sped toward his sobbing mother. The mother clutched her son to her breast. The crowd's cheering funneled into a raucous obscene roar. By then, the other boy had, at the frantic pleading of his parents, abandoned his friend and returned to the safety of the boardwalk.

So this is how it starts, Fletch thought, angry at the whites for sowing seeds of contamination in yet another generation, angrier with himself for being party to it. That the crowd showed no interest in examining the senselessness of the drama they'd witnessed left him exhausted. Appalled.

He stuffed the remainder of his sandwich into the sack and hurried back to his castle. There was no way, no way in hell, these people would derail the completion of his castle.

But first, Fletch grabbed six empty canning jars with MASON in raised glass letters on each and ran to the boardwalk. The women drew back from the railing. He lined his jars in a row and pressed a sign into the sand behind them. On his way back to his castle, the light-haired boy, who'd been used to fuel their bigotry, read the sign aloud: "Tips gratefully accepted. Thank-you kindly." Perfectly read. Sadly satisfying.

Fletch worked quickly to finish the second tier. Then he lifted the wooden forms for the third and held them in his outstretched arms. The muscles in his shoulders quivered. Tonight they ached more than usual. He moved his head from side to side, trying to release the tightening that made his temples throb. Miraculously, he lowered the forms into the exact position. He filled bucket after bucket of sand and carried each, without slipping, up the ladder. After completing this last tier, he unlatched the hinges and slowly, cautiously, so as to keep the work he'd done intact, removed the forms.

They were too heavy to toss down from the ladder, although he was certainly tempted. Unwilling to chance the damage this might cause, he balanced the forms on his head and eased his way down. After the show, he would store them under the boardwalk, where he always kept them. For now, he piled them beside his five-foot sandwich board sign. He sighed, grateful Egypt Ann worked as a morning maid at the Mitreanna and not at night. Choking on his humiliation when he was alone was one thing; Egypt Ann seeing him alongside the huge black letters—SANDY THE SANDMAN—was another.

He gouged out a moat and poked his torches into the sand, one on each side of the moat. When he lit them, the crowd crooned. Carried on the moon tide wind, a gentle new force billowed over the railing of the veranda. Fearful of misinterpreting it, Fletch hesitated before accepting this admiration, not that it was intended for a black man, or a man born white, but for accomplishment, that of a fellow human being. His eyes blurred as he fashioned turrets and crowned them with the flags that represented them all. From deep within the crowd, a thunderclap startled them all: "Pay up, the nigger's won."

Fletch's stomach muscles contracted. This bitter victory was another reminder that, despite the letter in his back pocket, he would never be one of the select. The little blond-haired boy's mother joined others clamoring after Mr. Fredrick, who was busily reassuring them, he, too, had lost. The boy stepped away from his mother. Without drawing attention to himself, he turned toward Fletch, slipped his small hand into the air and waved.

mauricio fabiano weinstein

Daniel M. Jaffe

mauricio fabiano weinstein

Perhaps Dr. Ricardo Weinstein found out in 1979 like this:

Staring at his neighbor, he narrowed his eyes to slits as if he could shrink her, thereby diminishing her truth. What could she possibly know, this hunched old woman in a tattered gray cloth coat, so foolish as to go out in the middle of cold June drizzle wearing blue socks and bedroom slippers? "You sure it was him?" asked Dr. Weinstein. How could she be relied upon for any sort of truth whatsoever? "You sure it was Mauricio?"

"I wasn't at his bris?" wheezed Estella. "I haven't seen Mauricio nearly every day these last eighteen years?" She coughed into a fist covered in protruding veins reminiscent of ombu tree roots.

"My Mauricio?" he said. "Not possible. Not possible."

"I must sit, Ricardo." She extended a hand.

He reached, gripped her elbow, guided her into his apartment. For twenty-five years he and his wife had been living down the block from Estella, who shared Shabbes dinner at their table once a month, who always brought homemade *empanadas* on Rosh Hashanah. How often had they left little Mauricio in her care while attending a performance at Teatro Cervantes or a concert? Dinner out with friends. A party at the Facultad de Medicina where Ricardo's been teaching forever.

"Water, Ricardo, please water."

He rushed to the kitchen and returned, careful not to spill on the parquet floor.

She guzzled, coughed some more.

Clenching fingers, he sat on the brown leather loveseat opposite. "Details, Estella." He unintentionally tugged so hard on his black mustache that he winced from a pain which, he noticed, blocked out all other feeling.

"Maria was weighing tomatoes for me," said Estella, "from the crate out front of her shop—"

He had to maintain control until he could find a way to tell his wife the truth that Estella was telling him now. Yes, truth.

"—and I glanced down Viamonte," she continued.

Control until he could dash to the police station.

"I saw Mauricio coming, a block away at the corner of Pasteur."

Control until he could find his son. Until his son returned home. Dozens of other sons and daughters in Buenos Aires had not yet returned home, but his would return because this was his son and there was no reason the military would kidnap his son because his son was a good boy who maybe spoke out a little too much about the flaws of dictatorship but he was a good boy. He was his son. That goddamn idiot boy who never learned to keep his fucking mouth shut. Who grew up to be the independent thinker Ricardo had raised him to be. "You're sure it was Mauricio?" He knows the question's pointless, but he's got to ask again. "My Mauricio?"

"My knees, not so good, but my eyes—telescopes. Curly hair, smile so wide you could swim in it. Just as he lifted a hand to wave at me, this black car raced down the street, stopped with a screech. Two men—" Her voice caught. She whispered, "Bendito Mauricio!" Ombu root hands covered her eyes, trembled.

Ricardo echoed her gesture with hands still fairly smooth.

———

Or maybe Dr. Weinstein found out in 1979 through a very different scenario:

Mid-consultation, his telephone rang. Dr. Weinstein's assistant—his wife—was visiting her sister in Rosario. So, Dr. Weinstein lifted his stethoscope from the hairy, half-naked man lying on the consultation table. "Excuse me, Mr. Jaroslavsky." He lifted the receiver. "Yes? I'm in the middle—"

"It's Deborah Finkel, Dr. Weinstein."

His son's girlfriend.

"Deborah, you meant to dial the other phone, the residence. You've dialed my *consultorio* number by mistake. I'm in the middle—"

"It's about Mauricio."

Dr. Ricardo Weinstein noticed a belabored quality in Deborah's breathing. "Deborah?"

She whispered—from necessity or from physical inability to speak louder?—"May I come to your consultorio?"

"Now. Tell me right now." His own breathing quickened and he intentionally tugged so hard on his black mustache that he winced from a pain he knew would block out all other feeling.

"Between classes," she said. "Two men on the street. I yelled and grabbed Mauricio's arm, but they punched me and dragged him away. Dr. Weinstein, it was terrible. They screamed 'terrorist!' and 'subversive Jew!' They shackled him, blindfolded him, kicked him, threw him into the car floor and drove off. What do we do?"

Dr. Weinstein nearly collapsed onto Mr. Jaroslavsky's naked chest.

Or perhaps Dr. Weinstein found out in 1979 this way:

"Deborah," he said into the telephone, "this is Ricardo Weinstein." He tugged so hard on his black mustache—a frequent tic—that he winced from a pain that blocked out all other feeling.

"Dr. Weinstein, it's seven in the morning."

"I apologize. Mauricio didn't come home last night."

"He didn't? But, last night he left before midnight. He was going home to study for an exam. Dr.—?"

Dr. Ricardo Weinstein dropped the receiver, raced out of his apartment and down the block and past the Water Palace. He checked every hospital although he knew Mauricio was not in a hospital. He visited police station number 50, one he'd heard to have been involved in other such neighborhood cases. The police, of course, knew nothing. The army, of course, knew nothing. The navy, *tampoco*, knew nothing. Dr. Weinstein telephoned Jewish patients so wealthy they owned entire buildings in Recoleta, and he begged them to ask their cronies in the police, the army, the navy. "Sure thing, doctor, sure thing." No return phone calls. Not then in 1979, not later in 1980, not in 1981...

However it was that Dr. Weinstein found out in 1979, Matt Klein is learning about all this only now, in 2008:

"I'm Ana's assistant," the young woman says to him in Spanish. "Why do you wish to speak to her?"

Thirty years after high school, Matt feels uncertain that his Spanish is up to this telephone conversation, even though, dictionary in hand, he's been rehearsing in his hotel room. "I'm calling because I have for Señora Ana documents."

"Documents? Which documents?"

"Documents written by a friend. From ago thirty years. About the Jewish *desaparecidos* and international law. Including correspondence from B'nai B'rith."

"These documents were written by a friend of yours?"

"Yes."

"Why didn't your friend bring them?"

"She lives in Los Angeles."

"And you also live in California?"

"No, Boston. Massachusetts."

"You traveled all the way to Buenos Aires for the purpose of delivering your friend's thirty-year-old documents to us at AMIA?"

"No, I on vacation. But since I coming, I offer to bring documents from my friend."

"Who is this friend?"

"She called Judy Frankel and—"

"Why did she write documents about the Jewish desaparecidos?"

"She's a lawyer. Ago many years, she did human rights work."

"She's Jewish?"

"With that name, you need to ask?"

"Be polite, please."

"It was joke."

"Human rights is not a joke. It's our lives."

Matt takes a deep breath. "Judy Frankel an old friend."

"Your girlfriend?"

"She's married with children in California. We old friends. Why do you need to know this?"

"You called me, so I ask the questions."

Matt wants to hang up, but recalls his promise. "Oh, Matt," Judy said on the phone, her voice with a verve he hadn't heard since their younger days, "if only you could deliver the documents to AMIA, I'd feel like my efforts weren't a total waste. What good are those papers doing in my attic?"

He breathes deeply, now says, "Together, my friend Judy and I study in law school. Harvard Law School—" Maybe he can impress a little and end this interrogation. "Ago many years. Judy work on human rights law. International."

"But you did not?"

Wince. "Look, I have documents my friend wrote about Argentinean Jews disappeared by the military dictatorship. If you not want, I return documents to her in the U.S."

"You have these documents with you?"

"Yes."

"Why do you wish to give them to AMIA?"

"AMIA is Buenos Aires Jewish community center."

"Why does your friend wish to give these documents to Ana, in particular?"

"My friend say Ana in charge of archives of AMIA."

"How does your friend know about Ana? How did she obtain this phone number?"

"How I know? Your website maybe. Or maybe Gypsy."

"Another joke?"

Enough! He'd hate to disappoint Judy, but he had his limits. "Never mind. I only try to help my friend. A mistake. I put documents in toilet instead. Goodbye!"

"Hold the line one moment, please."

Matt shakes his head. Has he finally gotten through to this bureaucrat? He toys with the beige telephone cord, looks up from his narrow hotel bed to the window and out at the gray sky. Day after June day: gray. He knew it would be winter in Buenos Aires, but he'd expected a little sunshine here and there.

"Can you come tomorrow at 12:30?" she asks.

"Yes."

"And you will bring the documents?"

"Of course."

"Which hotel are you staying at?"

"The Bauen on Avenida Callao."

"The telephone number in case we must reach you?"

Matt recites it.

"Your room number?"

Matt recites it.

"When you arrive, you will need to show your passport."

"Okay."

"The original, not a photocopy."

"Okay."

"Give me your passport number please."

"Now?"

"Yes."

"One moment." Matt rolls his eyes, sets down the telephone receiver, goes to the desk drawer, returns with his passport, recites the number.

"And the exact spelling of your name. Exact."

Matt recites it. "And your name?" he asks.

"We're on the fourth floor of AMIA. Friday at 12:30."

"Yes. And your name?"

"You'll bring the documents."

"Yes! And your name?"

Dial tone.

He hangs up. Before he can stand from the bed, the telephone rings. He picks up. "Hello?"

"Hello," she says. "Just checking the number you gave."

"And your name?"

Dial tone.

———

Matt's annoyance at the telephone conversation blocks all pleasure from his lunch of empanadas—*verduras* (spinach), *pollo* (chicken), *carne* (beef)—at La Continental across the street from his hotel. He walks down the avenue, stops and examines Congreso, the gray granite edifice structured, he reads in the guidebook, to resemble the U.S. Capitol with its Greco-Roman columns and central dome while bearing Parisian Beaux Arts ornamentation reminiscent of Paris's Opera. Fronted by a central pediment and horse sculpture echoing Berlin's Brandenburg Gate. He agrees with the guidebook that the synthesis of styles results in unusual beauty. He recognizes this intellectually, but doesn't feel it.

Come on, he tells himself, you're in Buenos Aires, for God's sake. Enjoy! One of the main reasons Matt chose to vacation here was to pursue his hobby of wandering foreign cities and enjoying architectural design. This "Paris of South America" is known as a safe and walkable city, rich with early twentieth-century facades.

He slows his pace to a leisurely stroll along Avenida de Mayo which, according to the guidebook, is the grandest in Buenos Aires, comparable to the Champs Elysée. He passes the Madres de Plaza de Mayo building with its bright blue sign—offices of a group of mothers who march in protest every Thursday at 3:30 p.m. Judy told him they've been marching in front of the President's office building, the Casa Rosada, for thirty years, ever since thirty thousand people, arbitrarily labeled terrorists and traitors, were kidnapped, tortured, and murdered by the military dictatorship in power during the late 1970s and early 1980s. That's what Judy's documents are about, the Jewish *desaparecidos*, the Jewish Disappeared. Hmmm…Matt's heading toward the Plaza anyway. It's Thursday and—he checks his watch—two o'clock. Should be interesting. And afterward, he can check out the pedestrian shopping mall on Calle Florida.

He consults the guidebook as he walks past a huge ombu, the quintessential Argentine tree whose above-ground roots protrude and twist from the earth like varicose veins. Along the avenue, he tries to appreciate Palacio Barolo's Dante-esque bronze lobby medallions representing male and female dragons, and the ornate Art Deco Federal Police Headquarters with its faceted-frame windows—how many of those thirty thousand victims passed through its doors? Over there's the Art Nouveau Hotel Chile—round-topped windows and Mideastern-influenced faience ornamental tiling. And there's Matt, sitting on his hotel bed, nervously stumbling through the AMIA interrogation. Who did that secretary think she was, speaking to him that way, putting him on the defensive? Treating him like some criminal?

He stops at the famed Café Tortoni, finds an empty table, orders the guidebook "must" of hot chocolate with three churros. Dunk, munch, sip. The churros are salty, the hot chocolate—gritty. Photos and plaques on the dark-paneled walls, pictures of tango artists and literary celebrities. Matt's heard of Borges, and in preparation for the trip, he even read a couple stories by Cortázar. He especially liked "Axolotol," about a man who stares so long at a salamander in a tank that he transforms into one that's looking out from within the tank.

Matt has half a mind simply not to show up at AMIA tomorrow. But he promised Judy. And he gave that secretary his hotel name and room number—if he doesn't show up, she'll probably send some kind of security after him.

Stepping out of Café Tortoni, Matt zips up his leather jacket—colder than fifteen minutes earlier?—continues down the Avenida to Plaza de Mayo, a broad brick plaza with fountains, grass, palm trees, and the central May Pyramid, a white commemorative column crowned by a statue representing Liberty. Just beyond is the pink Casa Rosada, supposedly painted with bull's blood. What does it say about a country that paints its most famous government building with blood and boasts of the fact?

A dozen people are milling about the plaza, and a couple of elderly women in black cloth coats and white kerchiefs manage a table of books published by the Madres organization. If Matt's Spanish were better, he'd consider buying some.

A souvenir vendor with a car displays lapel pins and knickknacks, but not much else commercial. A sign of respect, he supposes. It's three o'clock. He stands and waits as more people show up, some speaking English or French and carrying cameras. The guidebook says the government is concerned because most of the surviving mothers are in their eighties and nineties, so what will happen to this protest-turned-tourist attraction after they've all died? Maybe the government will have to recruit more mothers, not actual mothers of murdered children, but fake mothers, actresses. Tourists won't know the difference.

A group of school children. Ah, so it's not just a tourist spectacle, after all. What is their teacher telling them? Governmental murder of people in foreign countries is one thing, but the kidnapping and murder of one's own citizens is different. Unlike wines, domestic lives are of much greater value than foreign.

Precisely at three-thirty, a group of ten Madres, all in black cloth coats and white kerchiefs, walk to the center of the plaza. A young man unfurls a blue and white banner stating, *"Distribución de riqueza."* "Distribution of Wealth." Matt gets it—what began as a protest against the kidnapping of their children has evolved into a protest against social injustice of all kinds. The Madres hold the blue banner at waist level and begin to march around the plaza's central column.

Matt spots only one elderly man among the crowd. Just one. Had fathers marched thirty years ago under the dictatorship they'd have been shot instantly, says the guidebook. Mothers took the risk. How guilty, wonders Matt, do the fathers feel for having hidden behind their wives' skirts—out of life-or-death necessity, to be sure—but, still?

The Madres march in silence, circling the central May Pyramid. Slowly, members of the crowd fall in place behind them. A young woman with wavy black hair tugs Matt's elbow, tilts her head toward the marchers. "Is okay," she says in accented English. How does she know he's American? "Is okay," she repeats, and he follows her into the growing crowd.

He feels self-conscious and glances around, but nobody's looking at him, not even the young woman who drew him into the crowd; she drifts out of sight. They all march around the central column. Looking at the white kerchiefed heads up front, Matt wonders who lost a son, who a daughter, which of their children were shot, which were drugged and then dropped from a helicopter into the Río Plata to drown. The Madres themselves will never know. He recalls the High Holiday *unesaneh tokef* prayer he used to recite every year in synagogue, listing different ways we might die during the year—by fire, by water, disease... Was murder by fascists on the list? Maybe if he started attending services again, he'd find the answer. Damn, does participation in a human rights event always bring emotion and guilt to the surface? How does Judy cope?

Matt marches around the column a second time for all these mothers, feels pride at marching, feels shame at taking pride, shame at never having marched before, not here, not back home against the Iraq War, not as a pre-teen against the Vietnam War, not as a toddler with Dr. King. He looks down at the red brick plaza floor, wonders at the white forms painted on the perimeter of the red brick circle, white shapes with little ears, reminiscent of the Playboy Bunny symbol. No, it can't be. No—he realizes: the symbol of a white kerchief around a woman's head. At least a dozen such symbols stenciled onto the circle's perimeter. This public plaza now belongs to the Madres.

Around the column a third time and all emotions give way to pride. The Madres are looking straight ahead, but they must know there's a crowd behind them. They must know that younger people—locals, foreigners—are here to pay their respects and express support. Can his meager, anonymous presence impart a modicum of comfort, offer meaning that their children didn't die completely in vain?

Isn't every death in vain?

Matt notices that there's no chanting. How much more powerful a silent presence than a noisy one. Rocklike. Immovable. Which words could capture their loss?

The police remain at a distance, perhaps to signal clearly that they pose no threat.

After the third time circling the column, the Madres stop, fold the banner. The crowd stands for a moment. No one's ready to leave.

Slowly, they disperse. Matt steps over to the table of books being sold by the Madres and examines the titles. Maybe he can understand something, after all. He picks up two books, *Historia de las Madres de Plaza de Mayo*, which is self-explanatory, and *Nuestros Hijos*, which he automatically understands, *Our Children*. He flips through it. Each page contains the photo of a Disappeared child and key biographical data: birthdate, mother's name and father's, grandparents' names, those of spouses and siblings and children, name of elementary school attended, high school, university, workplace. A web of connections, reverberations. In order to terrorize an entire population, a government need not arrest everyone—just a select, arbitrary few. Five hundred fourteen pages in the book, a mere fraction of those lost. How young each desaparecido looks in the photos, these men and women, boys and girls. It's like flipping through his college yearbook, thinks Matt, or even his high school one.

He knows he won't read every entry, nor is he likely to struggle through the history book. But he must buy them to offer financial support, and to show at least one of these mothers that he's here and notices and will remember. To connect. He hands the books to a Madre standing behind the table, her gray hair tucked neatly beneath a white kerchief, her nose bulbous and slightly misshapen, her cheeks acne-scar mottled. Wire-framed glasses. She tells him the *quarenta y dos peso* price, he hands her a hundred peso note and says, "*No cambio*," No change. She nods a *gracias* and as their eyes meet, Matt purses his lips into a small, I'm-sorry smile, and she nods again, more quickly this time, then averts her eyes...to maintain composure? Matt realizes that he must be approximately the same age her son or daughter would have been.

He steps away from the table, pulls his cell phone from his black backpack and calls his mother in New Jersey. How surprised she is to hear from him all the way from Argentina! Yes, he says, he's just fine. Yes, he's having a wonderful vacation. Yes, he's eating. He's just calling to say he loves her. "Oh, darling..." she replies. He promises to call with details as soon as he returns to the States. Hugs to Dad.

He's no longer in the mood to hunt bargains on sweaters or leather jackets on Calle Florida. He flips through the guidebook index to find the listing for the Templo Libertad. It's a hike up to Plaza Lavalle, but the walk will do him good.

———

"Why do you want to know?" asks the husky synagogue guard in blue jacket and red tie, switching to English in response to Matt's fumbling Spanish request.

"Because I'd like to attend services Friday night."

"You're Jewish?" The guard stares into Matt's eyes.

"Yes." Matt matches his stare.

"What's your congregation in the U.S.?"

"Beth Israel," Matt lies. He's not affiliated with any congregation in Boston, has not been to services in years. But he grew up in a conservative congregation back in New Jersey.

"I see," says the guard, his eyes on Matt's backpack. "Well, you can't bring any bags of any kind."

"Okay."

"And you'll have to wear nice clothes." He raises an eyebrow at Matt's gray sweater, jeans, running shoes.

"Of course."

"And you'll need to bring your passport. The original, not a copy."

"Okay."

"And arrive before 7:30."

"Okay."

"We won't let you in after 7:30."

"Okay."

"And we won't let you out until services are over."

Matt nods, deciding then and there that today's sudden spiritual impulse is not as strong as all that.

———

The next day, in gray tweed jacket and burgundy tie, Matt reaches 633 Pasteur half an hour early. He notices two dark-uniformed guards in front of AMIA, Asociación Mutual Israelita Argentina. He passes by because he doesn't wish to arrive early. He just doesn't want to be late, that's all, so he's scouting the location ahead of time.

He crosses the street and strolls toward Avenida Puerreydón, around what the guidebook describes to be the old Jewish neighborhood, a garment district called "Once." He knows that in Spanish it's pronounced "on-say," but thinks how telling that in English it's "once." Once upon a time Jews lived here. Once upon a time we lived, until we were massacred, exiled, gassed, or burned. "Once," a fairy tale name for a Jewish neighborhood. Grimm's. In 1919, he reads in the guidebook, anti-labor riots turned into a pogrom in this Jewish neighborhood. *La semana trágica.* Tragic Week. Once upon a time.

Matt passes storefront after storefront filled with bolts of cloth in solid colors, floral prints, taffeta, gabardine, linen, corduroy, jersey, some wrapped in plastic, others not. Young men bear bolts of cloth on a shoulder or push yellow metal carts down the narrow streets. Shoe stores, candy stores, Estella dress shop, a produce market named Maria. Display windows of bras and panties, Mama Jacinta kosher *parilla*—grill restaurant—on Tucumán. Super Modelo Kasher, a grocery store two doors down from a men's sweater-shirt-slacks shop.

A group of young teen boys, some in baseball caps, others in colorful knit *yarmulkas.* A few *chasids* in black yarmulkes or *fedoras, peyess* sidelocks and Tzitzit fringes, dangling from beneath shirt tails. A Sephardi kosher bakery. Sidewalks in disrepair, potholes covered with wooden planks, dog dirt here and there beneath orange plastic litter buckets metal-banded to street corner posts. The perpetual sound of car engines, taxis, buses, small trucks...white noise. The smell of exhaust.

For a moment, Matt feels at ease, as if in New York's garment district or Lower East Side.

By 12:25, back to Pasteur and, with passport extended, over to a muscle-necked guard. Matt states his rehearsed announcement about his appointment. Matt has practiced a variety of reactions, depending on how the AMIA guard responds: "I'm Jewish, too. How can you treat me this way?" "I'm just here to help!" "You people don't want the documents, then fine, I'll take them back to the U.S.!"

The guard politely takes Matt's passport, excuses himself, invites Matt to wait just a moment. The guard steps inside, returns, holds the door open for Matt, apologizes that he must search Matt's backpack. He motions Matt through a metal detector, asks him to please stand in front of a black glass window and stare at a red laser light.

With a nod, the guard returns Matt's passport, indicates another door.

Matt walks through to an interior courtyard with various plaques on the walls and a colorful sculpture. The actual building stands beyond the courtyard—the security checkpoint he's just passed through, it turns out, is housed within an outer wall. Structured like a Medieval castle, thinks Matt, but once inside the compound, all is safe.

He enters the building expecting additional security, but there's just an information desk. "Fourth floor," says the young clerk with a smile, gesturing behind her toward the elevators. No security escort? Matt walks past an art exhibit, a cafeteria filled with people. Alone, he takes an elevator and finds the right office.

"Ana will be right with you," says the voice from yesterday's telephone interrogation. Younger than Matt thought, in her twenties although her voice has the authority of a fifty-year-old. She looks away from him to papers on her desk. Just as cold in person.

An elegant woman—maybe in her forties—in green turtleneck, gray slacks and jacket, steps out of an office, extends her hand with manicured nails, and says to Matt in flawless English, "How nice of you to come. Please." She welcomes him inside, offers a chair, shuts her office door, sits behind her desk, and initiates small talk about the cold weather. She inquires as to his reaction to Buenos Aires, and he comments on the beauty of the city's architecture. She remarks that there's much for visitors to do, especially if one likes theater. And he purposely mentions how impressed he was by yesterday's Madres.

"Ah, so you troubled to see them."

"An honor to march with them."

She smiles, folds hands on her desk. Her eyes relax. "My assistant tells me that yesterday you spoke with her in Spanish."

"I tried, but…you know…high school language study."

"Very kind of you to make the effort."

"Well, I am in your country, after all."

She nods just a bit, the way Helen Mirren's Queen Elizabeth nods in pleased acknowledgment of respectful gestures.

Ana continues, "Her questioning was probably quite thorough, even intrusive. You must understand—exactly thirteen years ago, in July 1994, we were bombed."

"Here?"

"AMIA, yes. Eighty-five people were killed. And this only two years after the bombing of the Israeli Embassy. Twenty-two people were murdered then."

"In Buenos Aires?"

"We, too, reacted with shock. The Embassy—understandable as a terrorist's political target. But, AMIA? We're a social services organization, a cultural community center. Why were we targeted? It is only now, so many years later, that the government has begun to investigate with Interpol. Back then, Menem was president. He's of Syrian ancestry, had various relations with the Middle East, so there are speculations, but…" She lifts her hands, palms up, and shrugs. "You may know that the government welcomed Nazis after World War II. We've heard recent news reports of a growing Nazi movement in Bariloche. In Patagonia. So you will understand if my assistant was… zealous on the telephone."

"Of course. I totally understand," Matt says with all sincerity.

"You're very kind. So, I've been taking a great deal of your time. My assistant tells me you've generously brought some documents?"

Matt takes the folder from his backpack—he placed Judy's correspondence with B'nai B'rith on top so as to establish immediate legitimacy—and hands them to Ana, and while she peruses the papers, he talks about Judy, her dedication to Jewish human rights causes. He explains that the documents contain discussions of various international human rights treaties and advice she offered as to the sorts of affidavits B'nai B'rith should gather from the family and friends of Jewish desaparecidos: testimony describing forcible arrest, statements that there had been no trials nor judicial hearings of any kind, declarations from witnesses that victims had been seen in particular prisons, that their torture screams had been heard.

"It's all thirty years old, of course," Matt adds, "and doesn't contain any new information for you. Part of an effort to use legal arguments to exert political pressure on the military leaders. Judy thought you should have these documents for your archives. Evidence that we were trying to help."

Matt reddens after using "we," hopes that Ana doesn't ask about the sorts of human rights causes he fought for while Judy worked on behalf of Argentina's Jews. How could he explain that he chose to spend every minute in law school studying for top grades that would lead to top corporate law firm dollars? He quickly adds, "Judy asked me to apologize that she didn't do more."

"Ah, but she did no less," says Ana, raising a rabbinic index finger. "Her work is of great importance. Please convey our gratitude. And our thanks to you, as well, for taking time from your vacation to deliver these papers to us."

Again Matt reddens, imagining scales of justice weighing vacation interruption versus remembrance of torture victims.

"We have not," says Ana, "as a community come to terms with the issue of the Disappeared. It was only three years ago that we put up a plaque in the courtyard in commemoration. By Sara Brodsky, the mother of a Disappeared. Her son was sixteen when taken for participating in forbidden student council meetings. In high school. During the Dirty War, the Jewish community was not unified as to an appropriate response. Some preferred not to antagonize the authorities further. Afterward, not everyone agreed that we should commemorate the suffering. Perhaps because many of those we lost were not religious or affiliated with institutions here. This reasoning is mere speculation on my part, of course."

"I'm grateful for your openness."

They share a warm smile.

"You know," says Ana, "we have an organization of Families of the Jewish Disappeared. They should see your friend's documents as proof of North American efforts to provide assistance. Might I impose further upon your time? Would you be interested in meeting the president of the organization?"

"Certainly." A knee-jerk response. As Ana flips through her Rolodex, Matt acknowledges the heaviness in his chest, asks himself whether he actually wishes to engage more deeply with the suffering here.

But how can he refuse?

Ana dials, and Matt follows her Spanish, "Dr. Weinstein, there's a North American in my office with documents you should see. About the desaparecidos, yes. May I arrange an appointment?...Yes, he speaks Spanish...with a few imperfections."

She smiles, concludes the telephone conversation, writes down Dr. Weinstein's telephone number. "My assistant will photocopy the documents you've brought so you can give them to Dr. Weinstein." Ana stands. "Again, much gratitude to you and your friend."

Later, downstairs in the courtyard, Matt stops to examine the variety of plaques until he finds the one by Sara Brodsky, who lost her sixteen-year-old son. It's a bronze high-relief entitled "Ellos Están," "They Are Here," depicting the body of a woman as a tree trunk with a knothole in her womb. Her arm-branches reach up in menorah shape. Heads sit on the branches.

Matt exits through the security checkpoint outer wall. He walks around the neighborhood without noticing storefronts or building facades, people or cars. He walks and he walks.

———

"It's near a famous monument," Dr. Weinstein told Matt earlier over the phone, "near the Water Palace."

Passing the Facultad de Medicina, Matt realizes he's heading in the wrong direction, reverses, and winds his way to the corner of Viamonte and Riobamba—yes, the unmistakable, High Victorian structure that houses the water company. Along Viamonte, he gazes at the symmetry of the building's ornamentation, repeated sections of gray shale columns bordering patterns of red and black faience bricks.

He crosses Ayacucho, checks the numbers, finds 2043, buzzes the apartment. Quick intercom hello, long door buzz, elevator ride to the second floor, knock. Dr. Weinstein strikes Matt as "spry," an adjective reserved for thin, energetic old people. Wiry. Shorter than Matt, stoop-shouldered, bags under his eyes, straight gray hair and mustache, Jewish nose right out of Hitler's guidebook. Striped shirt, rust-colored corduroys.

Matt hands Dr. Weinstein the paper-wrapped half kilo of assorted cookies he bought at a nearby bakery.

"¿Qué es eso?" What's this?

"Algo dulce," Matt replies. Something sweet.

"Soy un flaco," says Dr. Weinstein, I'm a skinny guy. He shrugs and takes the small bundle. "This is my *consultorio*," Dr. Weinstein continues in Spanish, "not my apartment. There was a time when it served as both, but then we moved, my wife and I."

Inside the front door, Matt steps past a low bookcase. The top shelf supports a couple of plants and a framed photograph of a curly-haired young man. Small grandfather clock on one wall beside knickknack shelves holding Russian *matryoshka* dolls, a *shofar*, a silver candlestick. A poster of Picasso's Guernica hangs on another wall, a poster of Charlie Chaplin as the Little Tramp on another wall. A computer on a desk, a chair.

The doctor gestures Matt to a brown leather loveseat, then sits on the one opposite. "So," he says, "tell me who you are, why you're here, what you want."

Matt's nervous and doesn't like the feeling. He unzips his backpack, takes out the documents, and repeats in Spanish the rehearsed background explanation that Ana received so graciously, about Matt's friend Judy, her efforts and those of B'nai B'rith to help. During the explanation, Dr. Weinstein coils tighter and tighter into himself, wrapping his arms, strangling his crossed legs, narrowing his dark eyes. His face reddens. Matt hands him the documents, emphasizing the B'nai B'rith letterhead for legitimacy, the signature of the director of B'nai B'rith's Department of Latin American Affairs.

An overwound spring, Dr. Weinstein uncoils, flinging out arms and legs. He screams, "*Hijo de puuu-ta!* This man from B'nai B'rith is an hijo de puuu-ta! Hijo de puuu-ta!"

Dr. Weinstein's spit leaps across to Matt's face, and Matt jerks back, blinks in shock. He understands "son of a bitch!" But he does not understand why the doctor's screaming at him.

"Hijo de puuu-ta! Hijo de puuu-ta! This man did nothing to help! Nothing!" Dr. Weinstein leans so far forward on the edge of the loveseat he nearly topples. "Nothing! B'nai B'rith did nothing! The World Jewish Congress did nothing! The American Jewish Committee did nothing!" He yells while glaring as if to dare Matt to challenge. "*Raptaron a mi hijo*—and North American Jews did nothing! Raptaron a mi hijo!"

"Raptar" is not a Spanish verb Matt has encountered before, meager as his vocabulary is, but the word is clear in context. "Kidnapped." Dr. Weinstein is saying that the local authorities kidnapped his son. "Raptar." Matt thinks of Spielberg's Velociraptor, that vicious, toothy dinosaur in the Jurassic Park movies. He dwells on the thought as a momentary reprieve from the screaming, from the live electric current of this man's thirty year-old pain.

"I didn't know," says Matt, shaking his head. "I thought B'nai B'rith help.

I not know."

Dr. Weinstein sits back on the loveseat, tugs on his mustache with thick-veined hands.

Matt notices that the doctor's zipper is open—a patch of white briefs peeks from within the rust-colored corduroy. Matt focuses on the absurdity. And then his shock-frozen mind thaws, comes alive: how did Dr. Weinstein learn of the kidnapping—did some neighbor witness the abduction and rush to tell him? Or, maybe his son had a girlfriend who tried to stop the kidnapping, and who later called Dr. Weinstein in panic? Or, did Dr. Weinstein grow suspicious and fearful after Mauricio failed to return home one night? The doctor doesn't volunteer a historical scenario, and Matt won't probe the wound further by asking. Speculation will have to suffice. Speculation and imagining . . . Very much the way, Matt senses, that Dr. Weinstein must forever speculate and imagine his son's final, tormented days.

The doctor breathes out several times through his nose. He rocks in place until the redness of his face pales to pink. Then he asks, in a softer voice, "How old are you?"

"Fifty."

"Fifty." Dr. Weinstein nods.

The doctor's son would have been about Matt's age now. Everywhere Matt goes in this city, he's a walking reminder to the elderly of the children they lost.

"Of course you didn't know," says the doctor. "You were too young."

Perhaps I was, thinks Matt. But Judy knew. Judy did something all those years ago. "I marched with the Madres yesterday," Matt says in a feeble attempt to...to...he's not sure what.

Dr. Weinstein nods, and his voice softens further even as he says, "Where did the Argentine military learn their methods? From the United States and your School of the Americas. Kissinger, that so-called Jew, supported the *junta*. Only Jimmy Carter refused to support the murderers."

Was all this true? Matt doesn't know.

Dr. Weinstein traveled to Tel Aviv, he says, to an international gathering of Jewish leaders, including the very man whose signature is on those letters from B'nai B'rith. "He agreed to see me for thirty seconds in the hotel lobby on his way to breakfast. You know Hebrew?"

"A little."

"In the hotel lobby, he patted me on the shoulder, this Jewish leader, and said in Hebrew, '*Savlanut*', patience, and, 'Things will get better.' Better? How would things get better? Raptaron a mi hijo! My Mauricio. That B'nai

B'rith hijo de puta! Patting me on the shoulder. I turned my back on him and bent over for him to kick me in the ass."

"*Lo siento,*" says Matt, concerned that the doctor will object to his presumptuousness in using the Spanish "I'm sorry," which literally means, "I feel it."

The doctor continued, "After the Second World War, Argentina welcomed Nazis. So, when the military kidnapped Jews, they tortured them longer than other desaparecidos, murdered them sooner after arrest."

Matt wonders how Jews could have been tortured longer but killed sooner. He doesn't comment on the seeming contradiction.

"Instead of burning Jews, the Nazis drowned them this time, dropping them into the Río Plata. And North American Jews did nothing!"

"Lo siento."

"And Argentinean Jews—hah! Most Argentinean Jews are middle class—doctors, lawyers, middle class. But who runs Jewish organizations here? The upper class Jews. They don't live in Belgrano like we do now, but in Recoleta with the other rich. Recoleta's like your Beverly Hills."

"Yes, I've been to Avenida Alvear. Hermes, Ralph Lauren."

"So, you understand something." Dr. Weinstein nods. "The upper class Jews socialized with the military leaders. Many fewer of their children were kidnapped. Some, but many fewer. Those rich Jewish leaders refused to rock the boat and make things worse. Worse for whom?!" he screams. "Worse for whom?!"

Dr. Weinstein sits and breathes hard for a moment, tugging on his mustache. "They're rich, sure. Big shot Jews. But my family came over with Baron de Hirsch in the nineteenth century," he says, "the first European Jews to arrive."

As though pedigree adds to the horror. Or entitles exemption. Every group, thinks Matt, has its Mayflower bluebloods.

Dr. Weinstein tugs hard on the corner of his mustache. "What is your work?"

"A lawyer. For corporations."

The doctor nods and stands, goes to the bookcase bearing the framed photograph of the curly-haired young man. From the bottom shelf, he takes out an over-stuffed folder, opens it, sifts through yellowing papers and newspaper clippings. He hands Matt a letter from the U.S. Department of State, March 20, 1981, from an Assistant Secretary for Congressional Relations to Senator Bob Packwood: "Pursuant to your request on behalf of your constituent, our Embassy in Buenos Aires has made repeated inquiries concerning the disappearance of Mauricio Fabiano Weinstein. Unfortunately, Minister of the Interior Horacio Liendo, as well as the Argentine Foreign Ministry's Working Group on Human Rights, has replied that the Government of Argentina has no record of the detention of Mr. Weinstein, nor any information concerning his whereabouts.

"(As an aside, we note that Oscar Camilion, the Argentine Foreign Minister, has acknowledged to Secretary of State Alexander Haig that the regime has recently been compelled to take security measures against revolutionary elements intending to create chaos in the country.)

"Please be assured that we will remain alert to any information that might become available concerning Mr. Weinstein and will notify your office of any significant developments."

"*Eso es mierda,*" says Matt. This is shit.

"Ah, so you're an honest lawyer." Dr. Weinstein's first smile. "Yes. It's shit. They asked the kidnappers for information. This is help? Trusting government officials is like putting *habetzim bashulchan.*"

Matt understands the Hebrew phrase. Trusting leaders is like putting your balls on the table. Or the chopping block.

Dr. Weinstein sets down the folder of papers. "As a lawyer, you know how to write?"

"Of course."

"In Treblinka, they scratched onto walls that writing outlasts us all. So," he says with a raised index finger and in a louder voice, his face so close now to Matt's their noses nearly touch, "since you know how to write, then write! Write! Write! Write science fiction or Kafka. Take this shit letter from your government and write something about it. Write!"

Matt nods.

"Write! Write! Write!"

Matt nods.

"Okay," says the doctor, tugging on his mustache. "So, you got what you came for?"

What he came for? Matt came to give documents to Dr. Weinstein. He came to show a kindness. Why on earth did Ana send Matt to this man? Surely she understood his rage and conviction that North American Jewish organizations did nothing to help. Yes, Matt realizes, that's precisely why she sent him. As living evidence that some groups did, indeed, try to help. But Dr. Weinstein won't be convinced. How could he possibly be?

"Yes," says Matt, "what I came for."

Matt extends his hand, which Dr. Weinstein takes limply.

Matt leaves.

He walks down Viamonte and crosses Ayacucho, again looks up at the ornate Water Palace. How beautiful the repetition of ornamentation patterns, the precision. There's comfort in the repetition somehow. He walks the length of the block, not taking his eyes from the enormous building. At the next corner, Matt turns and continues around the Water Palace, observing the symmetry. How can he possibly write the story of Mauricio Fabiano Weinstein? How can he do justice to the young man's suffering, to that of Dr. Weinstein? How he wishes to tell Judy every detail, to praise her goodness for having devoted herself to such causes, and to thank her for never having made him feel mercenary, selfish, ignorant of the world...all the things he feels right now.

Matt pictures himself in law school in the early 1980s—a full head of hair, bushy brown beard, eyes burning with classroom notions of justice and equity—being picked up in Harvard Square by the CIA because someone overheard him grumbling to Judy against President Reagan. What if? At Judy's emergency phone call, his parents would frantically drive from New Jersey to Boston in the middle of the night, wake each of his friends, plead and grill for leads. They'd scream at local police, race back down the Eastern Seaboard to Washington, storm Congress, picket the White House.

He could just see his mother gathering with the Madres, risking her life, marching every week for thirty years, growing thinner each year, grayer, more stooped, until she, too, transformed into an iconic figure, another old woman in black coat and white kerchief, a talisman of grief, a reminder to tourists and school children, a living cautionary tale. Would all tears have been spent after thirty years? Would the weekly march become—after year ten or fifteen or twenty—mechanical?

Matt completes a circle around the Water Palace and decides to circle it yet again. And again. He feels a need to march, to do something physical, something out in the world, to act visibly in the face of anyone who might choose to notice or question. Even if for just a safe moment, Matt needs to imagine himself a Jewish insider. He needs to become, by walking, part of this place, taking steps on these neighborhood sidewalks while picturing a black car stopping, two men stepping out toward him.

house of nightlights
Christiana Langenberg

house of nightlights

Mabel has a blue one. It is shaped like an aquarium, and if left on long enough the small plastic fish in it begin to swim. Something about the heat of the oval bulb and the liquid inside the rectangle. There are angelfish and goldfish, gouramis and painted tetras, nothing out of the ordinary, save one baby shark that has a fin glued on in reverse. It looks as if it's floating more than swimming and, from its fixed position, waving at every fish that passes by. They bob and nudge each other as they jostle together. Some nights Mabel watches long after bedtime with her one good eye, until the temperature heats up and the fish dive, surface, and gurgle. A sound of contentment, thinks Mabel.

Raoul has one that is a small version of him, or what could be him if he ever sat like that. A boy with his head on his knees, a large sombrero over his face, his arms tight around his shins. The bulb behind the figure illuminates his pant legs, which are orange, and his shirtsleeves, which are green, but does not reach far enough along his body to light up his head, which is, after all, guarded by the sombrero. Raoul thinks the sombrero was added after the boy was complete. There is a seam along the plastic, a bulge where the hat meets the head. Raoul only has one more surgery before he gets to go back to his foster home for good. They are thinking of adopting him, they like him that much. Raoul is a good boy. Waiting to be whole requires much patience.

Nakeeyah's is a tiny lava lamp. The top and bottom are black, the liquid in it is clear. The globules that melt up from the bottom set in motion as red, then retreat into pink. The first one arches toward the top of the lamp, knocks its top and divides into four or five smaller pieces. These begin as spheres, but collide and stretch into capsules with hips. They dance a type of hula and never rejoin the first great glob. Like the islands in Hawaii, Nakeeyah says, as she taps the plastic cover. Volcanoes underwater, until the ocean threw them up.

Vivi's is a cinder block. It is not concrete, but that is the only difference. It is hollow in places, as cement blocks are, but less heavy, of course, and it looks like a sponge when the light shines through. Small as it is, it appears strong and amazing, though it is wise not to hold it, as it is rough to the touch. Vivi has said nothing, not a single word in the three weeks since she came here. Under her nose is a thin dark line where her mouth used to be. Right there is where she is.

There was a bomb on the subway the day her class took a field trip to see an exhibit of Holocaust memorabilia. Only one person died, a custodian at the high school. Vivi was standing next to her deaf mother, looking at the floor, ignoring the rapid taps on her shoulder, giggling, embarrassed that her mother would have been cleaning toilets and wiping *Jason is a dickface* off of bathroom mirrors if she had not asked for the day off. And then there was the scream of light and heat and no sound and no words.

Suelana's looks just like a small mannequin. The bulb is inside the torso. When it lights up, the circulatory system is visible, the blood moves along through the map of veins. The face has no features, just a smooth surface of what could be any girl. The body is the color of flesh. Ms. Houselog painted it with flame-retardant, so Suelana can place miniature wigs on the head and nothing catches fire. Suelana asked Ms. Houselog if there were a way to add a nose to the face, a way to sleep around the corner from the outlet, where the light is less bright, see the shadow, and know what her profile will look like when she gets her new nose. Ms. Houselog says she will look into it. Which means, always, eventually, yes.

Everyone gets one before they get here. Ms. Houselog tells each child it is a sign that everything is going to be all right. When things seem dark, it is just a question of shining the right light. People say Ms. Houselog is "Off," but she says that does not matter. She feels "On" even when she is sleeping.

Raoul tells Vivi that when she gets her lips back, they will remember what to do, that she should not worry about it, she will have things that need to be said. She signs something to him and he gasps. Raoul says just because you understand sign language does not mean you want to.

Raoul says it will be great to turn down the volume on his eyes after his ears are done. Raoul is almost complete, but he is still a boy and does not realize that not long from now, he will not be able to forget the time he wasn't. Since the moment he was born with earlobes but no ears, he has not been able to unhear anything. It seems the things that can be fixed are not always the things that need fixing.

The children first see the nightlights when they unpack in their rooms. They are always in the outlet closest to the bed. Ms. Houselog says it is supposed to be kind of funny that they wake toward the light, but most of the children do not understand this. Still she smiles. She must think some things are funny, because so many are not. Ms. Houselog is good. She is the kind of good you see one day and somehow, on the next, you feel it nesting inside yourself.

Ms. Houselog read Suelana's file after the first few nightmares. She has seen in her mind over and over the moment Suelana ducked and turned her head as her father shot her, her mother Suzette, and her sister Suzanne, before he put the gun to his own head and relieved himself of the contents of his skull. There was a basket of clean laundry in the middle of the living room. Suelana used the towels to try and stop all the bleeding. At first all she could know was that her nose was missing. That was something that did not make sense.

The doctors do not know if Suelana's alopecia is related. Ms. Houselog says you go from a family of four during a *Rugrats* rerun at 7:00 a.m. on a Saturday to orphan by the noontime news, and anything is possible. She thinks there is an Aunt Sue in New Mexico who might be coming after the nose is on. The aunt has daughters of her own about the same age; says this wasn't in her plan, but Ms. Houselog has sent her the before pictures and hopes the after ones are as good. She helps Suelana rub sun block on her scalp in the mornings.

Locks of Love just sent a new wig yesterday. Suelana lets the long strands of hair curtain her face as she walks backwards around the yard against the wind. Ms. Houselog asks, "How does it feel?"

Suelana says, "Like my sister's. Hers was very long, mine was short, but we were the same color. She could hang upside down from the top bunk and if I was sitting on the bottom, we would pretend it was my hair."

Lucio gets the lighthouse. Ms. Houselog said that was easy. It is ceramic and strangely heavy and when it is turned on the bulb on top rotates under the roof. She could have thought of that one in her sleep. Some things are like that. It is important to know the difference, to be struck by the things that are easy when they are.

Lucio nods when Suelana draws an "L" on a piece of paper. He shows her how to make the alphabet in tidy block letters. Lucio wants to be an architect so much it almost pains him. His family is from El Salvador, but he was born here, on the night of summer solstice, while his father and four sisters picked cabbages and his mother was attended by a woman whose own mother had been a midwife in San Salvador. Lucio's father was told he had a son, finally a son with a face like light itself, but then he saw the spinal cord—a snake, not an arrow—an announcement to the world that he had made a son who was not strong.

The midwife's daughter said, no, no, no, she'd seen those kinds of spinal deformities before. She said Lucio's body must have crumpled under the weight of his mind. If Lucio's mother and father could just be strong, if they could wait to see the light of day. But then the placenta would not let go and the blood hurried after the baby until finally Lucio's mother was lighter than air. She was carried away by a simple breeze, like another plastic cabbage bag unwound from a worker's belt.

The woman who delivered Lucio was also a wet nurse and did what she could for a year and a day, and then, well, there were other children claiming breath, and he had become so heavy in the shawl on her back.

Miracola calls, though, once a month. Ms. Houselog accepts the charges.

Nakeeyah wants to play with Vivi, but Vivi won't. Vivi's fifteen and too old to play with six-year-olds. Vivi e-mails this to Ms. Houselog when she is surfing the internet for pictures of celebrities who have had lip surgery. "Who wants to kiss a paper cut?" is what she asks. At lunch she looks, then stares, at Nakeeyah's full, perfect lips, at the way Nakeeyah grasps the plastic handle of the Barbie spoon, her thumb against the tablet of fingers on her right hand. The spoon clatters onto the plate.

They look like Barbie fingers, thinks Vivi. Melted together at Nakeeyah's mother's meth lab on the day of the fire. *Plastic fingers*, she thinks. A hand like its own mitten or spatula or toilet brush. Nakeeyah could use it as a garden spade or ice cream scoop or just to cover her mouth in shock. A hand like that could be useful.

A mouth with no lips is good for nothing. She reaches over Nakeeyah's plate and herds the peas onto the spoon with her finger. Nakeeyah smiles and tilts the peas over the dam of her bottom lip.

Vivi coughs and clears her throat.

Raoul signs, "Why?" and bends his middle finger onto his chest.

Vivi signs back, "I like peas and quiet."

Ms. Houselog tells Keekee to pass the water to Vivi, whose eyes get bigger and the dark line of her mouth curls like a wave.

"Vivi's face is laughing," says Keekee.

Ms. Houselog smiles, too, the littlest bit. She knows Vivi thinks too much laughter is a luxury for those who do not know what isn't funny.

Vivi wipes her eyes, sniffs, holds her nose with her napkin. Her eyes water.

Raoul says, "Too much pepper in the potatoes." He lands a fake sneeze into his elbow.

"Did it burn your mouth?" asks Keekee.

Raoul waits.

Vivi shakes her head and coughs again.

"It's okay," says Ms. Houselog. "Vivi is just giving us the universal symbol for swallowing your pride."

A.J. has one that is simply a large question mark. The round ball at the bottom is the kind of dark blue that is almost black in daylight. The blue gets lighter as it moves up to the right and then around and over to the left, as if it were a blueprint of a light bulb itself.

Once Ms. Houselog showed A.J. a picture of Crater Lake on a cloudy day, taken from the east side of Phantom Rock, where the water looked like bloodstone or granite, something impenetrable. "That lake never freezes, no matter how cold it gets," is what he heard from Ms. Houselog. "There is always a way to the bottom, even if no one can see it."

A.J. understood. He began to worry less about the muck at the bottom that he could not see and the debris floating on top that he could. "You'll get there when you get there," Ms. Houselog told him. "And your smile—my God—it could light the dark."

So he keeps going to the appointments for the prostheses even though Lucio says, "You keep going to Hell, kid, and expecting to find God there. What is it with you?"

A.J. looks at the ground, at the spots where his ankles and feet should be, at the small round depressions his stumps leave on the pitcher's mound. He does not want to—and Ms. Houselog doesn't make him—wear the foam slippers that make it easier for everyone else to look at him. He says, "My legs they are like baseball bats, is that not right? My thighs, see, they are strong, hit home run."

"Kid," says Lucio. He calls everyone kid. "Kid, you don't have feet."

"I travel far," says A.J. "No have walk. I am here." He nods. "Like you." He points at Lucio with one of his crutches.

Lucio looks at him, at his long sinewy arms, blue-black skin and eyes the size of passion fruit. "Hey," says Lucio. "You should pitch."

Ms. Houselog puts swiveling wheels on the Radio-flyer. A.J. looks to his right, then his left, brings the ball to his chest and arches it perfectly over home plate.

Mabel is left-eyed and sees it coming. She hits one into the alley. "Shee-yit!" she says. She is working on losing her accent. She wants to blend. She has been practicing. She can hold her breath now for six minutes straight. Vivi had a stopwatch yesterday at the pool. "That's seventy-six breaths if she's going to be the youngest person ever to swim the freaking English Channel," she e-mailed Ms. Houselog when she got back up to her room. "She can do this, really," Vivi types. "She's a fish trapped in the body of a human. I'll watch her do laps while you take Keekee to OT. You have to let her go back after they move her eye. Even if all she does is try and then come back home."

"Bloody hell!" shouts Mabel after she slides into home.

"Watch your mouth," says Lucio. "No offense, Vivi," he yells back at the house.

"A.J., kid, you're supposed to make it so they can't hit it!" He holds both arms in the air. "Touchdown!"

A.J. smiles his equator smile and the place lights up. Next one is over the plate. Suelana asks, "Was that a ball or a hummingbird? I saw a thing and felt air." Lucio calls it. "Strike!"

Ms. Houselog sits in the shade with her laptop. "Hey batterbatterbatter!" she yells. "I got a swing in my backyard looks better than that!" and she types back to Vivi, "Let's talk about it."

Vivi lowers the shade on her second floor window, turns the volume up on her iPod. Her shadow does the *merengue*.

Vivi writes everyone's name on their napkins and puts them on their plates. She wants to sit by the door. The person who sets and clears the table gets to decide. The person who washes the dishes gets to pick the next day's menu.

The person who dries gets to pick the next table setter.

Ten minutes into dinner, Suelana walks in the back door with a volunteer from the hospital and says, "What smells good?"

Vivi drops her silverware and stares and stares and stares.

"Go ahead," says Suelana. Touch it. I'm going to e-mail *tia* Sue a picture.

"Make it sniff," says Lucio.

"Key-rist," says Mabel. "It's bloody gorgeous."

Raoul has his headphones on. He will not eat. He wants to hear reggaeton or nothing at all. His foster mother brought him back early from his home visit. She is standing on the porch talking to Ms. Houselog because she doesn't want to come in. This place gives her the creeps. She tells Ms. Houselog Raoul's doctor had to reschedule because something came up. "Listen, it may be a while," she says. "Let him stay, please. We're getting a terrific new girl this week and she's half black, too. It would be easier for everyone. We're sort of full up."

"Really," Ms. Houselog says. "Really? You step inside this house and tell them all the world is full up. That there's no room for another eye, ear, mouth, hand, straight-up spine, or footprint." She crosses her arms. "You tell them you need things to be easy."

Nakeeyah, who is supposed to be napping, sits up on the porch swing and smoothes her wild hair with her Barbie hand. "What color is the other half of the new girl?" she asks. Her eyes are tiny road flares.

Raoul's foster mother looks away and checks the screen on her cell phone. "Look," she says, "The new kid's a better fit and she's two, so we'll have her for a while. She doesn't have any problems. Her family's just messed up." She snaps the phone shut and jiggles her car keys like a rattle.

Ms. Houselog hands back the box of cherry cordials and waits for Raoul's foster mother to look up and take it. "You don't know what you're missing," she tells her. She takes Nakeeyah's hand and heads back in. "Pink," she says, and turns Nakeeyah's palm up to show her. "The inside of all of us is pink."

Nakeeyah traces her good hand and then her other on a sheet of construction paper. Mabel said this is how she was taught to draw birds in Wales. "See how the thumb makes the perfect head, the other fingers the feathers? Can somebody help make the feet?"

Ms. Houselog draws feet like forks. She finds it disturbing that all the birds look shocked, their feathers fanned out like crazy jazz dancers.

A.J. says he can help, he knows how to draw feet and smooth feathers. He remembers his feet whole, before they peeled away from his legs, just after he grabbed the guinea and stepped on the landmine.

Nobody can say A.J.'s name. He came here from Sudan. When he says his name it has a hum in it, but the other children cannot make that sound, so when Mabel called him A.J. he did not mind. She said it sounded like an athlete and A.J. believed her since she'd been here the longest.

Vivi says some well-meaning white people wanted to adopt him and save his life to save their own. But their own took up more time than they had imagined, and when they became pregnant, after they had been told they would not, they stepped back. A.J. was so foreign. They thought once he got here, he would be more American, less African, and even though the agency in Darfur told them he had tested negative for HIV, they were not positive it would not show up later. It was a risk they said they could not take, considering their unborn baby was innocent in all of this. They decided A.J.'s needs would be better served with people of his own kind.

Mabel guesses they meant a kid from Wales, one from Appalachia, one from Houston, and others from somewhere in Canada and El Salvador. Is the world not one place? she asks.

Vivi rolls her eyes. "You all need to grow up," she signs.

Raoul says, "Isn't that what we're doing?"

Lucio knows Miracola isn't his real mother, that she continues to work in the fields where he was born, and that she would rather be with him, smoothing his long black hair into a ponytail, as the *sopa de garrobo* simmers on the stove. She sent him a jar for Easter packed in dry ice. Ms. Houselog said he did not have to share all his gifts. Lucio knew what she meant. He ate one bowl on Holy Thursday, another on Good Friday and saved the last for Easter Sunday. The children watched him without a word. Everyone brought their nightlights to plug into the dining room outlets. Keekee could not see candles as holy.

His surgery is on the Wednesday before the Fourth of July. "Independence Day," says Lucio. "It is written in the stars. The first holiday in this country after my birthday."

"Is it morning?" asks Ms. Houselog, "and if so, whose turn is it to set?"

"A.J.'s," says Lucio, "but he's got an ortho appointment at nine and Raoul's going with him." Vivi's hands yelled at him. "That kid's funny. She has a voice and will not talk, and Raoul has no ear but he listens." He smiles at Ms. Houselog. "I'm hungry."

She sits down, sighs, and takes his face in her hands. "Everything you say makes perfect sense," she says. "Especially when you've got those mooneyes shining. C'mon, just give me half your eyelashes, pretty please?"

"Think of the young ladies that haven't met me yet." Lucio's smile expands. "They're going to want all of me."

"I can't argue with that," says Ms. Houselog and shakes her head. "I'll bow my head in shame and squeeze the oranges."

"I'll set," Lucio replies. He rolls his walker to the plates cupboard and starts in.

Suelana walks into the kitchen carrying her nightlight and wearing her new hair. She has small butterfly clips that hold it back from her face. "Is it morning?" she asks. "It's dark. I want bacon and eggs and it's my turn to choose."

"It's morning somewhere," says Ms. Houselog. "And anyway, our night owl is up."

"Can I pack this for my visit with tia Sue?" asks Suelana. She holds out her circulatory system mannequin.

"Of course," says Ms. Houselog. "Your nightlight brought you here and will follow you wherever you go." She yawns and wads her long hair into a bun, grabs a pen from the table and sticks the chignon to her head.

"Cool," says Suelana and lays the nightlight on its back.

"Does it have to be naked?" asks Lucio. "Kid, we have to eat here."

Suelana drapes a napkin over the torso, tucks it into the armpits and under the chin. "There," she says. "It's looking up."

Ms. Houselog takes the children to the Science Center just before dawn. She knows somebody. Three hours before the place opens to the public and it's just the exhibits and these children.

The security guard says, "So they're all missing parts."

Ms. Houselog replies, "Not like you think."

She tells him the basics, not because he asks, but because he needs to know. One night, she and her husband and daughter bought a pizza and a Powerball ticket at the Gas-n-Stop and were two miles from home when a compact pickup t-boned their small car. She'd been driving. She always drove. She liked the idea of being in control.

Four days later, after taking her family off life support, she sat in her kitchen with her brother, trying to plan a double funeral. She had a second cup of coffee halfway to her mouth when he said, "Jesus Christ, Sadie. You won the goddamn lottery," and he showed her the ticket he found at the bottom of her purse. He was looking for gum since he'd just quit smoking. Apparently the winning numbers had been running on the bottom of TV screens all over the city for days. Who knew? Who pays attention? Who ever really wins?

"Um," says the security guard. "I'm not really . . . I don't . . . "

She points at Lucio scooping water out of the hydraulic maze and flinging it at Nakeeyah. She asks the guard, "Is it possible to resist such joy?"

He—Jim—stares at her. "Um," he begins, "we only went out a couple of times in high school."

"Oh, I don't want you," Ms. Houselog says. "No offense. I just thought if you were seeing only what's wrong, then you'd miss what's right. Do I wish my husband and daughter had not died? Of course. Would I be having this moment of clarity if they had lived? Probably not. So. You see the dilemma."

On the drive back to the house, the sun is right at eye level. She holds her palm against her forehead. "I can't see a godforsaken thing," she says. "Hope that's not a problem for anyone."

"Turn off the sun!" shouts Nakeeyah.

"Oh all right then," says Ms. Houselog. "I wasn't going to, but now that you asked." And she turns right and goes to the park at the edge of the woods, finds granola bars and juice boxes in the back of the van, chases the merry-go-round in circles as the sun slides up. Other kids start walking to school and the children of Hope House go home.

Ms. Houselog says the first word, the one before House, is what it's all about. It's why all the children are here. It is why people like me take the bus to get here even for just a few hours a week. I do the laundry. There is a lot of laundry. There are many towels and sheets, and many articles of small clothing. I cannot forget this. I cannot forget my friend Eileen's boy, Harold, who was four and here a few years ago.

It was like any day in a row of others. Eileen went to lie down with Harold after lunch as she always did. "Her nap went to sleep and did not wake up," is what Harold told me later. Harold waited and ate the crackers he found in the cupboard on the first day. He was still waiting on the sixth day, the day the neighbors complained about the smell coming from apartment 2B. Harold was very, very thirsty. Could he remember what happened before his mother took her nap? Eileen, did she cry out?

"No, no, Mama did not cry. A woman at the church said,' Maybe dye and beeties?'" Harold remembered. Yes, there had been a blood test.

I was only gone for one week. I had no idea. A half-sister of my cousin said there was more money up north, and so I had gone to find it but had no luck.

Ms. Houselog had a nightlight for Harold that was shaped like a world. All the countries were shapes of beige, the same beige as the moon that rose on the day we left our country to come here six months before. I came back to Hope House on Harold's first night to see him sleeping in his new bed with his arm around Momo, Ms. Houselog's cat. Momo had six fingers on each hand just like Harold. Ms. Houselog said Momo had a better grasp on things than other cats.

I could not believe it. I put the small bundle of Harold's clothes on the dresser next to his bed. His grey shirt with the elephant on the shoulder I put on top, so he would see it first thing in the morning. I put my hand over all his fingers as I had so many times before. Like this it was difficult to feel that there was anything wrong with him.

Momo stretched and raised his head. Harold slept on like any other tired boy.

"I have no money," I told Ms. Houselog.

"I do," she replied. "If you want to help, really help? I hate to fold laundry. Cannot stand it. You'd be doing me a huge favor if you came in a couple of times a week and did just that."

In this way I kept Harold with me after his father came to take him, into the jungle, into the dark, when only his left hand was finished.

"Coffee trees and chickens do not have mind of fingers," his father answered after Ms. Houselog said, "Please. Think of his future. There is one more surgery next week for the other hand."

"No," said Harold's father. "He not be here. Go back now."

I cannot forget. I am still afraid of that dark.

My daughter, Ophelia, listens. She says there is honor in my fear. She puts my voice, these stories, into a small recorder her teacher has loaned her. She will listen again and weave her words with my voice for her big class project. She will get the same thing as a high school diploma.

She says her schoolmates are bored and sleep when the teacher turns the lights off to show documentaries. She says she told them one day about the children who wait for the rest of their bodies to find them and where they live now. Everyone was quiet. They stared at her.

One boy said, "Do they have a forwarding address? Do they know, can they say, where they are?"

One girl said, "You can't just make shit up for a grade. You're supposed to write a project about something that happened to you."

This is what I mean. I do not speak this language. The children *have* happened to me.

Ophelia says the stories, the children, will happen to her teacher and then that teacher will tell someone else. She says together we have this language. "Tell me the one again," she says, "about when A.J. got his feet, the day he walked Mabel to the gate at the airport and Vivi said—no sorry, yelled—'Go fish, Mabel! We will watch you on the telly!' And Lucio said 'Hey Kid!' And so many children turned to see who was calling their name."

metal and glass
Kristen-Paige Madonia

metal and glass

My mother got her third tattoo on my sixteenth birthday, a small navy hummingbird she had inked above her left shoulder blade, and though she pretended it had something to do with me becoming sixteen and her knowing that one day I would fly away from her, really it had to do with her wanting to screw Bobby Drinko, the tattoo artist who worked in the shop outside of town.

"You again," he said when we entered. He sat in a black plastic chair in the waiting area flipping through a motorcycle magazine, and he looked up at us and smiled. Big teeth, freckles. "It's good to see you, Stella." He put the magazine down on the table and stood as the bell above our heads tinked when the door closed behind us. It was the beginning of July, and he was tan and toned with a line of sweat snaking down his neck. His blonde ponytail hung to his shoulders, and his sharp blue eyes darted about the room while he talked. I remember trying to keep up with those eyes as best as I could.

My mother told me about Bobby Drinko after he gave her the orange and blue fish on her hip six months earlier, but I expected him to be an older scummier version of the man I met that day. I expected him to be as unlikable as the other burn-outs Stella hung around with back then.

"And you brought your kid sister this time." He winked at her, and I rolled my eyes, popped a bubble with my piece of pink Trident, and listened to the hot hiss of the tattoo needle inking skin somewhere inside the shop. It smelled like plastic wrap and cigarettes and the faint scent of sweat that hovers over everything in Virginia during the summer.

The hummingbird was my mother's third tattoo, but it was the first one she decided to get without being boozed, so she was nervous, her hips shifting from left to right inside her tiny white shorts. It took a lot to make her shaky, and I could tell she wanted a beer or a joint or a highball of vodka on the rocks, but I knew she wouldn't cave; she'd go through with it because once she made her mind up there was no going back. It was one of the things I liked and disliked about my mother, a trait I recognized in myself years later.

"Lemon's my kid," she said to Bobby, and she tucked a panel of frizzy bleached hair behind her ear. She'd gotten a perm that summer, and she was still adjusting to the weight of the nest hovering above her shoulders. It was the first and last perm she ever got, but I'll never forget the vast size of her head with her hair frazzled and sprung out around her face.

Bobby Drinko wiped his hands on his jeans and ran his eyes up along the slopes of my shape. "Lemon? How'd you get a name like that?"

And then my mother used the laugh she saved for men she wanted to screw when she wasn't sure they want to screw her back. "Look at her." She nudged me toward him. "Sharp and sour since the day she popped out."

I rolled my eyes. The phrase as predictable as Domino's for dinner on Fridays.

Bobby Drinko sat down behind the cash register and lit a Marlboro Red while my mother leafed through binders of tattoo sketches, the pages slipped into clear plastic protectors that reminded me of elementary school. I could feel Bobby watching me from behind the counter, so I put my hands on my hips and struck a pose, reciprocating.

I lost my virginity earlier that year to a senior at school, and even though we only did it four times before he got suspended for selling pot at a soccer game, I considered myself to be experienced. The first time, the pothead and I tried it regular. The second time, he did me from behind, and the last two times he used his tongue first, so even though I was just getting started, I thought I knew what felt good and what didn't. I had learned enough, at least, to recognize that a guy like Bobby Drinko could teach me all the things I still wanted to learn.

I moved next to his chair and looked at the photos taped onto the wall behind his head: Polaroids of bandana-wearing bikers and blondes with crooked teeth showing off sharply inked dragons and crosses on forearms and ankles. There were tattoos of sports team emblems and Chinese characters, pictures of girls in low-slung jeans with fresh flowers and vines tattooed at the base of their spines. Aerosmith played out a set of cheap speakers mounted on the wall above us, and a fan blew warm air inside from a corner by the window. Bobby leaned over a leather notebook, sketching a tree with long-reaching roots, thin naked branches.

"You go to the race last weekend?" he asked me.

I shook my head, and behind us my mother said "Oh, I think I like this one," to no one in particular.

Stella and I lived in a small city in southern Virginia that had a NASCAR race track built on the outskirts of town. That was our second summer there, but the closest I had come to going to a race was parking with the pothead that spring in a cul-de-sac near enough to the track that we could listen to the buzz of race cars between beers and awkward conversation.

"I must have inked a hundred race fans last weekend. This one guy had me do a foot long car driving up his back. It was pretty cool, really." Bobby nodded to the photos on the wall. "I did a good job."

I looked at him, shrugged, and popped another pink bubble, a gesture that had become my trademark that summer. My mother called the habit white trash, but I decided it was seductive, having read an article in one of Stella's magazines about the importance of drawing attention to your lips when flirting with boys.

"His old man had been a racer, got killed back in '81 in a crash," Bobby said between drags off his cigarette. "That tat was really important to him."

From where I stood I could see the black ink of a design inching up the back of his neck, and I suddenly wished my mom wasn't there so I could reach over and take a drag off his Marlboro. I needed my lips around the tight white tube where his lips had just been.

I started to say something insignificant and predictable like, "That's too bad about the racer," or "How long have you been doing this," but then a woman with bright red hair came out from the back, pushed aside the sheet that separated the waiting area from the tattooing room, and emerged with wet glassy eyes and a square of Saran Wrap taped below her collar bone.

"All good?" Bobby asked as he punched buttons on the register.

"It's a keeper." She smiled.

I looked at her and the way she was looking at Bobby, and I had a quick but detailed vision of the two of them screwing in the back of a white pickup truck. She was on top, bucking back and forth with her palms digging into his chest, leaning on him. His eyes were closed as his body shook beneath her pumping. He might have been enjoying himself, or maybe not, I couldn't decide. I felt my face heating up as I thought of him naked like that, and I looked away from Bobby and the woman before they could see the pink spreading across my cheeks like a rash.

My mother called my name then, and I looked up and winked at Bobby before I turned away from him, practicing a mannerism I'd seen women use on TV.

It took about twenty minutes for Stella to settle on the hummingbird. She handed Bobby the sketch and leaned over the counter where he sat.

"You mind?" she said as she took a smoke from his pack. I thought of her mood swings back when she quit, the nervous way she used to bite her nails. She looked at me when she brought the Marlboro to her lips and inhaled. "See something you like, kiddo?" she asked, and then she followed Bobby Drinko to the customer's chair behind the white sheet.

The other tattoo artist, a man with a thin black braid, finished cleaning his gear while Bobby completed the stencil and poured ink into tiny white paper cups on the stand next to his chair.

"I'm taking lunch," the other guy said, and he pulled off a pair of pale blue surgical gloves and tossed them in the trash can.

And then it was just me, my mom, and Bobby Drinko squished inside the heat of the tattoo room.

That was the third town that we had lived since we left Denny back in Philadelphia, and I liked it best because of the low mountains and the sticky summers and the way our apartment smelled like fresh bread all the time since we lived next to the sub shop near the mall. It was a tough trip to get there with Stella's nervous breakdown, the arrest in New York, and the six months at the Jersey shore with Rocco who ran the pool hall, so I was relieved to be in Virginia, where my mom seemed calmer and the men she dated seemed quieted by the innate laziness of a small town. My best friend Molly-Warner had a car and a fake I.D., and we spent the summer making out with boys from school and smoking cigarettes at the public pool in town. I'd finally found my lady-curves, as Stella called them once, eyeing me under raised eyebrows, and I spent day after day in my bathing suit reading magazines and gossiping with my friends. It was the first time I felt like Stella and I were ready to put Denny and Rocco and those last years behind us, and I hoped that we stayed in town until I finished high school. I was sick of moving boxes and cheap motels and having to make friends every time my mom picked a new place for us to live. Plus she had a good job working in the jewelry department at JC Penney's, and I could tell she liked the cheap rent and the apartment that smelled like bread.

Bobby Drinko was pressing the hummingbird stencil against my mom's skin when she licked her lips and said, "Get me some gum from my purse, Lemon. I need something to put in my mouth."

It was not the first time I watched my mother throw herself at a man. Ever since we left Denny after the black eye, she had been throwing herself at men in each town that we passed through. She was pretty and thin back then with cute tight clothes that got her a lot of attention, and after the breakdown when she and Denny split up, I was glad to see her back on her feet. She was happier when she had a man to play with, which was fine by me; the more distracted she was with her life, the less she bothered to ask about mine. But there was something about Bobby Drinko that made me nervous, something I sensed right away that day at the shop, something controlled and focused, marking. We had been living in Virginia for over a year, and things had finally evened out, but I was constantly afraid she might let her guard down, and I knew it would be someone like Bobby Drinko that would send us moving.

I used to tell my friends my mother was made of metal and glass. Smooth and sturdy on the surface, strong, but there was always that part in danger of shattering, a child-like aspect that never went away. I tiptoed around the threat of another breakdown, Stella bursting into a million pieces, melting down and dragging us out of one city and into a new one. It was this unpredictability that kept me from really trusting my mother. And even now, from trusting men.

She took the gum, stuffed a piece in her mouth, and then settled into the chair where I watched Bobby Drinko ink a perfect permanent hummingbird onto my mother's shoulder blade.

———

The next time I saw Bobby Drinko he was sitting in my living room on a Tuesday afternoon. Molly-Warner and I spent the day at the pool, but we were hot and bored, so we headed to my house because I knew my mom would be at work. Molly-Warner wanted margaritas and I wanted air conditioning, and Bobby Drinko was on the couch watching Crocodile Hunter when we opened the front door.

"What are you doing here?" I said, and Molly-Warner mumbled "he-llo" behind me.

He looked good and cool, his golden arms stretching out from the sleeves of a tight black tee-shirt with the Rolling Stones tongue printed on the front. His hair was loose this time, thick waves hovering above his shoulders. He smiled and checked us out from the couch as I tugged at my striped bikini top, sucked in my stomach.

"Stella gave me the key." He leaned for the remote and turned down the volume.

I tossed my towel on the floor by the door and tried to decide if I liked or didn't like seeing Bobby Drinko in our apartment. My afternoon had just gotten a lot more interesting with him sitting there looking at me that way, which I liked, but I didn't like that he saw my mom, that they were together earlier that day and that she had invited him over.

"We don't have air conditioning in the shop, so I closed early." He leaned back in the chair and put his feet up on the coffee table like he owned it, and I decided that, overall, I did in fact like his presence taking over our apartment like that. "Your mom said I can cool off here."

We moved into the room and I shifted my weight to one foot, put my hand on my hip, and arched my back. I felt good, a little nervous, but having him there made me feel important, him looking at me and me looking back at him. I was glad Molly-Warner was there to see it.

"Who's your friend, Lemon?"

"Molly-Warner," I said, and he nodded.

"You thirsty, Molly?" he said, but she rolled her eyes.

I said, "It's Molly-Warner."

"It's a family thing," she shrugged.

"Whatever you say, Molly-W.," he said. "Now which one of you knows where the liquor is?"

Bobby Drinko taught me and Molly-Warner how to make Tequila Sunrises, and we drank them in the living room while we finished watching the episode of *Steve's Journey to the Red Centre*. The two of us sat on the floor in front of the television screen, and Bobby stayed on the couch, but I could smell him from where I was, the distinct mix of sweat and tequila with the chemical scent of ink from the shop. When the credits finally started rolling Bobby Drinko announced that he needed a cigarette, but I told him Stella didn't let me smoke in the house, which I guessed was true since I had always hid my Camel Lights from her. He shrugged, and Molly-Warner and I followed him when he left the apartment.

The three of us stood outside the sub shop and took turns using Bobby's Zippo to light one of his Marlboro Reds.

"You girls old enough to smoke?" He inhaled deep, and I studied the way his eyes closed when he finally breathed the smoke back out.

"What do you think?" Molly-Warner said as she wiped the sweat from her forehead.

Molly-Warner and I met in chemistry class the year before, and I liked the way she was impressed when I told her I slept with the pothead before he got kicked out of school. She was still a virgin, but there were rumors at school that she gave blow jobs, so she and I were a top pick when the boys looked for girls to screw around with on the weekends. She was my most confident friend even though she was a little bit fat, and she had short spiky hair that made her look tough and unpredictable. Both of her parents worked at the furniture factory in town, and they bought her a used Toyota when she turned sixteen so they wouldn't have to worry about driving her to school. She was my only friend with a car, and I was her only friend that didn't mind talking about what it felt like to have sex.

We lied and told Bobby Drinko we were eighteen, and when he said he was twenty-six, I decided he was too young for my mom anyway, that he probably didn't know she would be thirty-five that September. She had a tendency to let the fact slip through the cracks.

"You girls like living here?" he asked as a woman and her son nudged past us and headed into the sub shop.

I looked at him and tried to decide if he liked living there, but it was too hard to tell since he was wearing sunglasses and watching Church Street in front of us as the cars moved down the road.

"It's okay, I guess," I shrugged.

"It's a shit-hole is what it is," Molly-Warner said, and I wished I could sound as assertive as she did when I talked. It was something she was always telling me I needed to work on.

"Oh yeah?" Bobby eyed her up and down, and I tried to telepathically tell her to suck in her gut. I wanted him to think I was the kind of girl who had interesting thin friends with strong opinions.

"There's nothing to do here, it's the same old shit all the time." She rolled her eyes and flicked her cigarette on the pavement.

"That's kind of what I like about this town," Bobby said.

I wanted to tell him that's exactly how I felt, that that was what made the town my favorite place Stella and I had lived in, but I kept my mouth shut and finished my smoke instead.

We were pretty drunk by the time my mom got home, so my voice was slow and slurry when I tried to explain why Molly-Warner and I were sitting around in our bikini bottoms taking tequila shots and playing strip poker with Bobby Drinko. She said something about us acting like prostitutes, and then she told me to get some clothes on and get in my fucking room. Bobby was on his feet pretty fast considering how many cocktails he'd had by then, grabbing his tee-shirt off the floor and pulling his tennis shoes on as he headed towards the door.

"It's cool, Stella," he said as he dug in his pocket for his keys. "We were just hanging out."

Molly-Warner and I stood in the doorway that connected the kitchen to the living room, and we held hands and smiled as we watched my mom throw her cell phone at Bobby's head.

"Are you insane?" she yelled right before the phone hit the wall.

We stopped smiling then, and I started to feel a little queasy when Molly-Warner began to cry, the tequila sneaking up on me like snakes in my stomach. But I squeezed my friend's hand and whispered "Shhh, it's gonna be fine," and then Bobby called my mom a crazy bitch, and he opened the door and headed down the hallway.

She followed him out and stood at the top of the stairs yelling, "They're only sixteen, you sick fuck," until he was gone. I listened from the apartment and hoped the neighbors weren't home from work yet.

My mom kicked Molly-Warner out, and I sat on the couch as I watched her slam the door and call my friend a dumb slut. Then she turned her eyes to me.

"Are you crazy? Have you lost your mind?" she asked.

Which made me think of her at the Motel 6 during the nervous breakdown, of the way I dragged her out of bed on the third day and dumped her in the shower. It was fast and furious, the meltdown and the depression hanging on her like a debt she couldn't pay off. I was only thirteen, but I watched as my mother lost her mind over Denny, a drunk who treated us like crap, a loser who took all her money.

"Jesus Christ, Lemon. He's twice your age."

I looked at her in the tight black mini-skirt, the low cut tank top and the chunky wedge heels she wore to work. I looked at our tiny apartment, the stacks of dirty dishes taking over the coffee table and the trash spilling out of the bin in the kitchen. And for the first time I realized how embarrassing it was to have a mother who acted like a child, to live in an apartment where two people in the building couldn't take a hot shower at the same time. I decided then that I had outgrown Stella's choices: I wanted a permanent address, a home with enough space for us to unpack all the boxes, a family that made more sense than we did.

"You're the one who gave him the key," I said even though I knew it had nothing to do with me and Molly-Warner getting drunk with the man my mother wanted to screw.

"What does that mean?" She came toward me, looked down at my shaking hands, at my tiny bikini top that I had tied back around my neck, and my jean shorts on the floor next to the couch. She ran her eyes over the empty shot glasses that had left sticky rings along the edge of our second-hand coffee table, at the tequila that had spilled and ruined her stack of *US Weekly* magazines piled on the floor.

"It just means he was here when I got home. He was here because of you." I stared at her. "They always are."

Her face changed right before she slapped me—it was hot and tight and far away, her face like sculpted metal and her eyes like broken glass. It looked just like it did after the fight with Denny.

I brought my hand to my cheek, my skin throbbing, and my eyes watering over. And when she turned away, headed to her bedroom and slammed the door behind her, I knew we would be moving again within the week.

———

The last time I saw Bobby Drinko was the next day back at the tattoo shop. He was ringing up a man with a buzz cut and a square of Saran Wrap taped to his forearm, and I stood outside the window looking in as Bobby handed the guy a credit card receipt.

The customer left, and then Bobby came out, lit a cigarette, and squatted down on the pavement next to me. I didn't say anything for a long time, but then he reached over and hooked his finger under the edge of my silver anklet.

"I hope I didn't get you and your friend in too much trouble," he said.

I remembered the way his skin looked when he took off his shirt the day before, the way the black tattoo on his back reminded me of the Egyptian hieroglyphics I learned about the year before in social studies class.

"Nah, it is no big deal."

He dropped the silver chain but kept his grip on my foot as he rubbed his thumb along the curve of my heel, which made me hot and anxious in a way that none of the boys from school ever had.

"You seem like a good kid. It's too bad." He stopped.

I fidgeted with the button on my ripped jean shorts and imagined how his breath might taste. Like sweat and cigarettes. Tequila and ink maybe.

"It's too bad, what?" I asked.

I thought of the pothead and how I kept my shirt on the first time we did it in his car down at the cul-de-sac. We were rushed and awkward and childish, and it embarrassed me as I stood outside the shop with Bobby Drinko. I imagined it would be better with Bobby, that he would be smarter and less clumsy. He would make me feel grown up, and I would finally understand why Stella wanted to be with men like him.

He ran his hand up my calf and squeezed my leg. "It's too bad about you being so young." He rubbed his thumb along the slope behind my knee. "And me being so old, I guess."

When I followed Bobby Drinko back into the shop and behind the white curtain, I was thinking of my mom across town behind the jewelry counter at JC Penney's, how she was probably planning the move, deciding what we would need to leave behind this time and what we would have space to bring.

And then Bobby sat down in the same chair my mother had sat in a week earlier and pulled me toward him. Behind him I saw myself in the glass mirror above his work counter, me looking down at him as he tugged me to his lap. He tasted different than I expected. . . I had been right about the cigarettes, but there was also something cinnamon and hot like the thick red After Shock liquor Molly-Warner and I drank sometimes at her house. At first his tongue was slower than the pothead's, but it sped up as he shoved his hands under my tee-shirt, his fingers darting back and forth across my skin, pinching.

"Should we lock the door or something?" I asked when I pulled my face away from his.

"I already did," he said right before he reached for the button on my shorts.

———

My mom and I moved to Morgantown, West Virginia, the next weekend. I didn't get a chance to see Molly-Warner or Bobby Drinko again, but I copied down the address of the tattoo shop from the phone book and promised myself that eventually I would find words good enough to write down and send to Bobby from the road on our way to our new town. I lost the address on US-19 somewhere between Oak Hill and Flat Woods.

The day we left, I ran into the pothead at the gas station near the mall. At first he pretended he didn't know me, but when Stella went inside to pay, he came over to the car and leaned down at my window.

"I heard about what you did, Lemon," he said. He smiled and reached inside to graze his fingers across my cheek, but I shook his hand away.

"You fucked that guy down at Atlas Tattoo."

I squinted and looked behind him at my mother who was handing her credit card to the man at the cash register.

"When you turn out like your mom, just remember who taught you first," he said before he laughed and walked away.

Later, when those years in Virginia were far behind us, my clearest memories of that time weren't of Bobby Drinko or Molly-Warner or even the apartment that always smelled like bread. Not really. They were of that kid, the pothead leaning down and breathing on my skin, the way he looked at me as I sat inside the car. In that instant I became a girl worth talking about, a person worth remembering once I moved away.

nearby
Loren McAuley

nearby

I sit in Central Booking in downtown Brooklyn waiting to be arraigned for assault, trying to be inconspicuous, but I am what my friend Margaret sarcastically calls me, a "Bed Stuy matron," so I stick out like a toad on an ice cream cone. I roll my butt on the rock hard bench and chat with "Mama," who is in for drug possession, and the ridiculously dressed working girls who are surprisingly friendly and without malice. The evening wears on, dry peanut butter sandwiches on white bread are passed out with lukewarm containers of milk, the guard shouts out names to go to court, and those called clap and bounce out happily. Roaches pop up and disappear into the cracks of the walls. It is incomprehensible that I am here. So many other times in my life I could have been arrested and wasn't: shoplifting in my teens, drugs in my twenties, later pedestrian tax fraud. Why now? What cosmic reason? I do not cry. I am working on my last nerve, but I do not cry. I close my eyes for a moment and allow myself to think of what happened, the events leading to this, for they are remarkable, and I drift swiftly there like an unmoored boat—almost as good as sleep—to weeks before, when it began.

The smells wafted out of our tenants' apartment downstairs, a mix of spices and meat boiling away, sticky rice simmering. It rolled into the hallway and mingled with the scent that came off my husband James' drum sets assembled in the garden level of our brownstone for easy exit when he had a gig. It was a musty smell, like old skin.

I regretted renting to the couple—Remi and Rene Lewes, pronounced Looz—but it happened when I was out of town on a rare visit to a friend.

James decided it, right on the spot, he said, because the two had an earnest look about them, as many immigrants freshly arrived do, and they had cash in hand, first and last month's rent, which was meaningful to James. It's how they continued to pay their rent for the next three months, crisp bills tucked in a white envelope, the word "Rent" in flowery script on front, slipped under our parlor door, exactly on the thirtieth of the month for the next month coming up.

"Why don't you like them?" James asked that when I pursed my lips at the sounds emanating from the apartment along with the exotic odors, pots clanging together, the whine of foreign music, the murmur of talk. I was embarrassed that he thought I was intolerant, which I wasn't, and I told him that he was imagining things, that I was fine with the couple, why wouldn't I be? He didn't believe it, but already past caring, he moved onto something else.

There were other sounds which eased out of the tall thick doors. The sound of water constantly being run, for they washed their clothes in the tub, even their sheets, wringing it all out and draping them from door knobs and chair backs to dry. And they took baths. I interrupted them once to deliver a letter-size package that arrived crumpled from their country; it looked important so I didn't want to wait. I was surprised to see the two of them in the open doorway, their torsos wrapped in thick towels, Remi's hair up in a silly twist.

"I'm sorry, Claire, we were about to take a bath."

"A bath? Is there something wrong with the shower?"

It was none of my business really, but no one I knew, certainly no one in my family, ever took a bath when there was a shower available.

"I wouldn't know. We don't take showers, you see. We prefer baths."

They thanked me profusely and shut the door and walked back down the narrow hallway to enter the tub, giggling softly as they lowered their bodies into the shared bath water.

And the sex sounds. The first time I heard them I was throwing out trash in the cans lined up near their entrance underneath our stoop. It was early morning on a weekday, they were both off at odd times being in service industries, Remi at a hospital, Rene in a restaurant. I lingered, listening to Remi's high pitched affirmations to whatever Rene was doing, his low soft moans in agreement; no words, just sounds, rhythmic and somewhat reassuring.

They were our first tenants, though we'd lived in our four-story brownstone on Gates Avenue in the Bedford Stuyvesant section of Brooklyn, New York, for over twenty years. Four whole floors for two people and a handful of rescued cats; it had been self-indulgent, irresponsible even, since for years we had needed the rent money. The subject came up, but as we became more financially secure neither one of us pushed it. James enjoyed the space for his drums and the cats liked to play in the empty rooms. I loved the access to the yard, an old cracked sink in the small back extension served as my watering place—pots piled up along the brick wall, bags of soil. It was my private hideaway, where I escaped James and the hopelessness of my office job, even the city for a while. I imagined I was in a country house in Connecticut, widowed or divorced, getting by on a pension and wise investments. I would have more animals than I had now, dogs (James is allergic), some chickens for eggs, perhaps a goat. Neighbors would be considerate of my solitary nature, stopping by for only a moment, or calling first. Maybe a few grown children, moved away, on their own.

James and I never had children. It slipped by us, our first years too rocky to consider it, later, trying unsuccessfully, until I simply became too old. It was a child who started the whole business of renting our garden apartment; one of James' sons from a previous marriage, in from California for a business seminar and visiting, sniffing around our house like he was sizing it up for a sale.

"You know the real estate values in this neighborhood have skyrocketed. This place has proven to be a great investment."

James looked pleased that his son approved of something he did; they had always had a strained relationship.

"It's been a little big for the two of you, hasn't it? Why not rent out the bottom floor? I'm sure you could get at least a grand for it. What? Don't you need the money?"

The last was a dig; the drummer's son who believed his father played around, not working at a "real" job, but James ignored it, lighting up at the word *grand*.

"Really? A thousand bucks a month? You think?" James glanced at me. I had no idea what rentals go for—why would I?—but I knew he was already convinced, a little in awe of what his son believed to be true.

I emerged out of the subway from the C train on Fulton Street and began my ten-block walk home. There was a drizzle and I put up my small umbrella. James would usually pick me up when the weather was bad, but tonight he had a gig and I was on my own. I thought of the night ahead, no dinner to prepare, the TV all mine. Something to look forward to.

The neighborhood has changed. When we first moved here from Boston I was nearly the only white person for blocks around. I didn't know how I would be received; we are a mixed couple and I was prepared for stares and whispers behind my back, but there were none. Our first place was an apartment a few blocks from where we live now, a floor-through with tall windows and long thin rooms. We had nothing but a mattress, so James' larger drums served as makeshift tables; other things we picked up at the thrift store or from dumpsters. I took pride in decorating, sewing curtains from sheets, nailing posters to the walls. When James was away on tour it kept me occupied, took my mind off wondering if he was being faithful to me or not.

As I came to my block people began to wave, the younger ones calling out "Hi Miss Claire!" as I passed. It had taken me a while to get used to; at first I thought it was because I was white and it was embarrassing, but I soon learned it was a respect thing, many of the families coming from the South where elders are referred to in that way. I wondered what our children would have looked like; mixed children were always so beautiful. It was a regret, one that sprung up at odd times.

I got to the house and went to the mailbox to retrieve the mail, a chore I could never get James to do although he was home most days. It was so entrenched a habit I didn't notice the statue directly underneath the tenant's window. It was as big as a boulder and nearly knee high. I stepped back; I didn't know what to make of it. Had they left it here on purpose? Were they throwing it out? I hoped the latter, for it was the ugliest thing I'd ever seen, with a pot belly and squat thighs, a drape around its private parts resembling a large diaper. I grabbed the mail and went up the stoop, glanced back at the large painted lump, and felt violated at the intrusion. What could they be thinking, putting such a thing out in the open, in front of my house for God's sake? My home?

"I don't know how you have a tenant. I know I couldn't."

I called my sister out of a tenuous sense of duty and now I regretted it, for there it was, the Pauline jab, so efficient I often barely noticed until I felt bruised, trod upon.

"They're very good tenants. They don't make any real noise or ask for anything. And they're paying a good rent."

I immediately wished I hadn't said that, for it smacked of financial difficulty, which Pauline had known about in the past and had never believed we'd gotten over. She was very well off, my sister. She had her late husband's life insurance policy and pension, her own salary as a hospital administrator (which was considerable), and of course, the accumulation of years and years of being cheap.

"Well, tell them to move the darn thing, Claire. It is your house."

I got off quickly, agreeing to a weekend visit sometime soon, which would hopefully be put off indefinitely. Through the years our relationship had dwindled to phone calls and the obligatory Christmas visit, but when her husband died suddenly from a savage cancer, I had attempted to reach out. Loneliness or curiosity led Pauline to respond positively, and we endured longer visits, always with the exit date clearly indicated so there was no question of escape. When I hung up, the thud of the phone was huge in the quiet. I heard them downstairs, the rustle of pans, Remi's soft laughter. Then the spices rose, surrounded me, reminded me I wasn't alone.

Winter came, and the snow; Rene took to shoveling the stoop and the tiny brick courtyard in front, the steps to their entrance. I spied on him from the long window on the parlor floor, how he leaned on the shovel—one he had bought himself from Home Depot—and surveyed the job, then made a few more swipes at some errant streaks of white until he was satisfied. He gave off the aura men do when finished with something physical, a task done well, almost a smugness.

"I didn't ask him to shovel."

I said it more to myself than to James, who was reading the part of the Sunday paper delivered on Saturday.

"Hmm?"

James was immersed in an article about a friend who had died recently, a fellow drummer. The funeral service—which James would attend and probably play at—was planned for the following week. They did that at musician's funerals, they played.

"I said I didn't ask him to shovel."

"Who?"

I turned again to the window and watched Rene as he carefully skirted the walls of snow leading to their door. He bent down and gave the statue a quick wipe before he stowed the shovel and went back inside.

"I wonder if they're even married."

James looked up; he'd finished his article.

"Who cares if they are or aren't. We weren't when we first moved here. Remember?"

I glanced at his down-turned head, once more turned to the page. Twelve years of living together, often fitfully. When we finally made it to City Hall, a few friends from work in attendance—I was a full time secretary by then, an assistant—and James' closest musician buddies, it certainly wasn't the over-the-edge-of-happiness event that I'd imagined when I was younger. It had been, if I were truthful, more about the beneficiary name on both our pensions, a what-if-something-happens kind of thing.

"They seem in love," I murmured as the snow began to fall, a miscalculation on Rene's part. He'd have to shovel again. James didn't answer. I was surprised I'd even said such a thing, and I let it go into the quiet warm air of the living room.

I ventured downstairs to the garden level, convinced it was at Rene and Remi's invitation. They'd asked me down a number of times, to taste one of their intensely aromatic meals, to hear a recording by a musician from their home who was imprisoned and smuggled out his compositions, a horn that shrieked up to our parlor floor, a sound not unlike one of my cats stuck in a thorny bush. I'd mentioned it once to Remi, who was on her way out to work—again at an odd hour, nearly midnight—and she'd taken the question as interest, instead of as a hint to turn the volume down.

I got to their doors and knocked, first gently, then more firmly. I still didn't know their erratic schedule. They were hardly ever home on the weekend, which it was, late morning on a Saturday. I knocked several more times and called out their names until I was sure it was all right to open the door a crack and peek inside. It creaked as I did and my heart stopped, but I kept going, all the while calling their names. At least if they popped out I had the appearance of looking for them.

"Rene? Remi?" one last time, high pitched, like an annoyed teacher. I stood in the living room. It was completely still. Even the traffic noise outside seemed muffled. I glanced around, pivoted on my stocking feet. There was a platform with pillows serving as a sofa, a low table on wheels with stacks of plates and cups, bright napkins held with carved wood holders. Strung from the picture frame molding were streams of fabric in rich reds and blues and greens, sprinkled with tiny rhinestones. I walked to the galley kitchen of haphazard cupboards and the small squares of refrigerator, stove, and sink all lined up. It was thick with spices and the cloying scent of different oils, so heavy for a moment I felt I couldn't breathe. As I reached for a glass for some water I spotted the paper on the refrigerator, stuck there by a magnet in the shape of a frog, a note or letter, but no, a poem, written to Remi and signed by Rene. I couldn't help it. I read it. It was out in the open, after all.

There were feeble attempts at rhyme, awkward phrasing, faulty grammar, but I was struck, like a slap, a punch to the chest. It was pure love, word after word, a simple declaration of what Rene felt, his admiration, his need for who she was, what she brought to his life, their connection. I stumbled back and my butt hit the counter and I turned toward the living room, assaulted once more by color, the scents closing my throat. It was no longer my space. It was theirs. I was the intruder, and I half ran to the doors, shut them and returned upstairs.

I found myself in the garden level nearly every day. It became easy to pinpoint their goodbyes at the door, the clank of the heavy wrought iron gate, the turn of the key. It was frightening at first, but then I felt it was all right, I wouldn't get caught, and even if I did, it was my house after all, I heard something odd coming from their apartment, I thought they might have a leak. I was overseeing their property, protecting it.

That day James had a rehearsal, and I'd heard them leave. I entered their apartment and went into the bedroom. It was a small, cave-like room in back, the deep-set windows overlooking the yard. When I stood at the sills my shoulders were ground level since the garden floor was partially underground, and it was a strange perspective seeing the yard in that way, like a woodchuck peering out of its hole. They had a mattress on the floor and I noted it wasn't made, which was odd since the rest of the apartment was so tidy. It must have been because they were always in it when they were home, reading (for there were stacks of books on either side of the bed) or sleeping (for I'd learned both Remi and Rene held two jobs). Or they had sex. Abundant, frequent sex. Love made frantically, desperately, because there was never enough time and they couldn't get enough of each other; they were that in love, that in lust.

I stood at the edge of the bed and fingered the vibrant pink and purple spread flung across the open crumpled space. It was gauzy, hardly for warmth, but they loved color, required it, shocking, ripe, pulsating color. The air was thick and yeasty coming in waves off the wrinkled linens as if Remi and Rene were still there, entangled. I thought of our bed upstairs, the thick box spring and mattress, so high a stool was needed to get into it, the sheets pulled tight under its edges, the expensive quilt we didn't even sleep under. I sat, ran my hands over the moist linens. Did I dare look inside their drawers? I went over to the bureau and pulled open the top one. There was underwear and pantyhose—it must have been Remi's—and a small box filled with costume jewelry; I took out the strings of beads and held them in the light. I'd never seen them on her. She must have waited for those rare times when she could put something on other than a uniform. I imagined her tall thin frame draped in the bright fabric of a dress, for she must have color, and the tiers of beads reflecting the luminosity of her smooth brown skin. She would look beautiful, as would Rene, for they were a stunning couple, effortlessly athletic, sculpted features, brilliant smiles. I put the beads back and searched the drawer. I hit a metal box and I pulled it out and opened it. It was filled with envelopes, obviously letters, one after the other, some from Rene but most from Remi addressed in her lovely handwriting, her name and return address in the top corner. There must have been a hundred or more, and I quickly saw the postmarks as I flipped through them, dates that went back seven years, to 1999, and then I settled on the address under Rene's full name and I read it more than once, thinking I was mistaken. It was an address in Haiti, Penitentier National, Bois Cellblock, Prisoner #1601.

"Se—i—sha Marshall!"
The guard appears at the cell, Fu Manchu fingernails the color of limes tap on a pad with our fates written on it. She has a voice that cuts through flesh, and when one of the working girls, her name is Violet, asks to go to the bathroom down the hall instead of using the cell toilet in plain sight of all who sit waiting, she is summarily screamed at to sit down. "Why didn't you go in the house before you left for your corner? You know better than that! Se—i—sha Mar—shall!"
It's been nearly ten hours since I was arrested in front of my house, half the neighborhood as witness. There's a good possibility I could be here all night. One of the women told me that if I don't get called by midnight then I'll likely not get called until the next day since the judge and the DA go home by twelve-thirty on the dot. If you have a lawyer, or so she told me, then you might get called sooner. If you don't have a lawyer, you're probably screwed.
"Des-i-ree Mon-a-co!"
The girl who had been giving me advice squeals, sashays out of the cell and waves to me over her shoulder. She told me her pimp springs her right away, and I guess she's right. Why can't I have a pimp? James said he would call his friend Todd, who's been in trouble a number of times with the law, to find out what lawyer he used. He yelled this out at me as I was being cuffed and put into the backseat of the patrol car, not yet crying, but angry and spewing out instructions to James about the cats, the plants, the mail, as if I were leaving for a stay at a spa. He followed me to the precinct, and

they let him in the back where they have the holding cells. He handed over several quarters through the bars, which he said the desk sergeant told him I would need, and told me that I should stick them in my socks or my bra to use later at the payphone in Central Booking. I stare now at the payphone being steadily used. Some women cry into the mouthpiece, others yell, their whole lives known in a steady stream of cuss words. I don't call. James will pull through for me; I can feel him working his way through his own disbelief at what happened, then getting on the phone and getting help, almost being boastful that his wife, *yes, Claire!* got arrested. He'll joke with his fellow musicians, most inherently sympathetic with anyone on the outs with the law, and he'll get information, names. I settle in. I have the time, God knows. My back screams with leaning against cinder block, the cold of the cement seeping into my spine. At first I had been all right with all of this, almost cocky about how it didn't bother me all that much, but it's gone on too long, feels like torture now, some sub-human practice.

"Don't be giving me no lip. I'll put you at the bottom of my list for court if you don't watch your mouth!"

The FuManchu guard is nasty, but I try to be generous; it is an awful job. If I didn't have James, I could be in such a job, needing the security, the health insurance, the pension.

"Patrice Watson!"

She will never call my name. I feel it. I see myself sitting here, calcifying on this bench, my back bent to the wall, the women—who are becoming scarier as the night wears on—deciding to eat me instead of the peanut butter sandwiches. What is it like in here at two in the morning? Four in the morning? I don't want to find out. Has James abandoned me here? Totally, finally abandoned me?

I had taken the metal box of letters upstairs. It was a bold move; I couldn't know how often Remi retrieved it from her drawer or if, in fact, she read over those letters every day as I had been doing. I took it anyway, blood rushing in my ears, the box singeing my fingers as I grasped it and ran through their apartment and up the stairs.

I kept it in my underwear drawer as Remi had, tight against its back under flinty layers of panties and old socks. At night in bed I stared at the bureau, at the drawer, and thought it was going to pop open and reveal its contents, scream out to James brushing his teeth at the sink between the two second-floor bedrooms that it was there, it was taken, abducted!

It never happened; he was oblivious, content in his universe.

That morning, I took it out. Everyone scattered, Remi and Rene to one of their collective four jobs, James to an early rehearsal. I had the day off, or rather I'd called in sick, a mental health day, one of three I took every year whether I was particularly mentally ill or not. I was up to the midpoint of letters, three years to be exact, according to the postmarks. Rene's letters were far fewer, I supposed because he was in prison and wasn't allowed to post as often as Remi could. His were the ones I wanted to read, however. They were long and rambling, barely touching on what he was going through because he wouldn't want her to know, but it was there regardless, the words giving off a subterranean heat. *I have been alone for a while. You might not recognize me. I've learned things no one should be taught . . .*

I sat in the worn armchair by the window in my bedroom. The sunlight streamed in tunnels. "My dear love," was how Rene started his letters, old fashioned and proper, which was how Rene was, still. He went on about her, always her, "What do you do in the mornings now that you don't have me to fuss over? Tell me of your day, your evenings . . . Do you go to visit your sister? My Uncle? Do you eat enough?" I put it back when I finished, the cumulative effect of the words a weight, hot and flush. They were so in love, were still so in love, now, downstairs, in their mismatched three-room apartment, with their baskets and odd spices and streams of color everywhere, the bedroom full of books and recordings, their love awash with bodily fluid, permeating the linens below them, wrapping them in safety at last.

I got up. I had to go down. I grabbed the box, thinking I'd return it. I had no right to it, none whatsoever, but I simply had to know, know them.

I grasped the rickety handrail and trod the steep staircase down. I knocked as I always did and called out their names, a silly habit since I knew they were gone. I entered and it was as it always was, tidy, filled with fragrance, bright against the below grade darkness. I went into the bedroom and opened the top bureau drawer. Remi's panties were folded neatly as before, the thick white pantyhose she wore when she worked at the hospital rolled, toes tucked under. I went to put the box in its place against the back but something stopped me. If I did, it would be over, the story. I wouldn't know how it ended. Rene got out, that was obvious. He was here in Brooklyn, free. But surely somewhere in those letters he explained what had happened. I opened the box and reached further back in the pile and pulled out one of Rene's final letters, the postmark nearly seven years from the first. The return address was the same, Penitentier National, and my fingers shook as I unfold it. It was short, as somehow I knew it would be, and my eyes settled on the last two sentences, a mere statement, like an invitation to a party or a plea to write back soon. *All murder charges have been dropped . . . I will be home soon . . . Don't worry, I will make my own way . . .* I read it two, three times, so casually expressed, *All murder charges have been dropped.* It occurred to me that Rene couldn't write of it before, for his correspondence was surely reviewed, as was Remi's to him. She might have been working all those years to get him out, their letters might have been in code. Who knows? It had to be a mistake, a political arrest and conviction, Rene was incapable of such an act. Such a sweet person, always asking if he could do anything, water their plants, shovel their snow, surely he couldn't kill someone. And a murder charge in a place in Haiti was suspect to say the least. Yet, murder. What if I were wrong? What if it were true? I took the box and left the bedroom and the apartment and went to the stairs, grabbed the door knob and twisted hard and the brass egg came off in my hand. It had been loose forever. James should have fixed it long ago, but he ignored me, always ignored me. I turned and went to the entrance under the stoop and reached in my pocket and gratefully felt my keys. I found the right one and thrust it in the security door lock, turned the stubborn lock as quickly as I could, got on the other side and balanced the box in one hand and closed the door while twisting the key to lock it with the other, my fingers barely keeping hold of the door and the box and the key.

"Claire?"

I straightened. The key fell to the ground. I turned. It was Remi and Rene. Remi was leaning on his arm; she looked faint or sick. Rene's clear brown eyes fixed on my face then down to my chest, downward to my two hands, the box held there like a child would hold a cookie stolen from a jar.

"I was just . . . I thought I heard a . . . " My practiced excuses trailed off. They were there, catching me, and Rene straightened, his face blank, stiff. He walked up to me, left Remi—who was oblivious, swaying under the spell of some sickness—and he held out his hand, so smooth and brown it looked like marble, his thin graceful fingers reaching out, almost touching my waist.

"Doesn't that belong to us?"

I believed for a moment that I could hand it over and he'd hide it and not say anything, that it would be an exchange between him and me, something to be forgotten, a misstep, a faux pax. He continued to extend his hand, to stare, to be still, and I slowly brought the box forward, my head reeling with excuses, explanations, none sounding even remotely reasonable, and he took the box and turned to Remi who had slumped against the stoop, wiping at her forehead, damp with sweat.

"My wife is ill. I need to get her to bed." He began to balance the box and Remi much as I had with the door and the key, and I thought I might have been right, he would let it be, when suddenly Remi saw what he was clutching, and she stopped. She'd seen the exchange but none of it had registered. She might have thought I was handing him the mail.

"What was she doing with our box!?" She pushed Rene out of the way and took the box and came up to me, her face puffed with anger, her eyes wild.

"How did you get this? Did you go in our apartment? Through our things?" She shook it in my face, her body wobbled on her heels.

"How could you? How could you do this? How could you read our private letters? Who do you think you are? A spy? The police?"

Rene tried to soothe her, his voice slow and urgent, "Calm down, it doesn't matter," but she was past consoling. I stood not moving, watched her as she cried out to Rene in their language, the neighborhood behind her slowing down, taking notice, smirking, until she began to curse and call out in English at me, "Cheat, sneak, thief . . . " and I felt the need to get out, out of my corner pressed against my house, my home, where I allowed them to live, under false pretenses, the two of them with pasts, with shadows and ill doings, with undisclosed criminal records.

"Well, at least I didn't murder anybody!"

Remi looked struck, and she reached out and grabbed my collar, spewed out sharp words in her language, her breath hot in my face, her spittle stinging my eye. Rene was at her back. His fingers tried to pull her off, his soft voice saying, "No, Remi, she doesn't know, doesn't understand," and I suddenly wanted her away, gone, and I pushed at her shoulders and she stumbled. Her feet caught, her arms flailed, and her mouth was a round "O" as she fell down, her head landing square on the hideous statue they'd placed under their window, her coat flying open revealing what I had thought was a sweater, but was in fact a bulge, a baby bump.

"Claire Johnston!"

I don't move. The woman's elbow next to me thrusts into my side. "They called you, girl. Get up!"

I go out into the narrow dark hallway that leads past the two cells for women, then the two for men. Some cheer as I pass, the women at least. The men look to see if anything interesting is passing by. It's near midnight and police with their shields hanging by metal chains around their necks haul in felons, the noise ear-splitting, shrieks and laughter, a nonstop flow of cursing. There's not a spot left on the benches in the cells, even the floor is crowded, the flimsy plastic coated mats flung down, bodies curled up on them. I cannot believe that I will get out, that it might happen if I see a judge quickly. The new guard—FuManchu is long gone, replaced by a more reasonable female—is nonchalant and business like, her fingernails short and neat. She leads me to an area outside of the courtroom. I'm locked in, another bench against another cement wall, but there's a toilet and no one in sight so I quickly pull down my pants and relieve myself. Lawyers come and go, the Legal Aid attorneys harried and jaded. What am I to tell a lawyer if one shows up for me? If James has hired one? The whole shameful tale, the theft, the discovery, the struggle. It wasn't me, it was someone else, someone possessed.

"Claire Johnston!"

The same guard unlocks the door and motions to follow her, then she instructs me to approach the bench with my hands folded behind, and to not say a word unless the judge speaks to me. I get inside the courtroom and it's a world apart from the jail, cavernous and paneled, everyone suited and full of purpose. I feel small here, ridiculous. A Bed Stuy matron. What would Margaret think of me now? The courtroom guard tells me to approach and I stand, my hands uncomfortably at my back. They say my name and the charges. The assistant district attorney looks up from her enormous pile of folders, for a moment looking as lost as I am, and she says, "All charges have been dropped, your honor." The judge asks her to approach and they have a few words, "They didn't press charges?" and "Yes, we're satisfied, no charges."

"Case dismissed. You're free to go."

I turn. I forget to unfold my hands, but then I unfold them and walk to the tall back doors and go out into the night air. There are vast marble stairs, wide and low, scoops molded in the middle from thousands of feet rushing down them to get away. *Case dismissed, you're free to go.* They hadn't pressed charges. Remi and Rene. They might even have gone to the police station to make sure of it. I could see them doing that, even after the unspeakable invasion I committed, even after what I said—"At least I didn't murder anybody"—the untruth of it of which I have no doubt, yet a weapon to hurl and wound. And why? Because I'd been caught? Embarrassed? I still see Remi clutching the box to her chest as she fell; they're probably packing it right now, along with their fabrics and bowls, their books and music, their tins of spices. So little, barely four cartons when they moved in. They've added to it, though. They were making a home, a nest, for the two of them and their child. They'll pack it tightly, forgiving me as they do. They've been victims before. Forgiveness gives them power, the power of grace. I start to walk home. It's cold this time of night. The air, even in Brooklyn, is clear and crisp. I look up. The sky is rushing with clouds. It might rain, and I don't have an umbrella. I feel the quarters in my sock, but I don't call James.

two natures
Jendi Reiter

two natures

When we came down to breakfast, Mama was burning Uncle Jimmy's birthday card.

"Eew, what's that smell?" Laura Sue squealed, flinging herself into her chair. At the last moment she remembered her manners and settled herself primly with her hands folded on the green-and-white checked tablecloth, anticipating communion with a stack of pancakes. My little sister had been wearing the same blue kerchief every day for the past two weeks of Vacation Bible School in hopes of being cast as Mary in the end-of-term talent show.

"Good morning, Yentl," I greeted her, and she jabbed me with her elbow, making me spill syrup on the tablecloth. I flung my napkin over the spot. We couldn't let Daddy see anything out of place.

Whatever was in the sink, dampened, refused to burn cleanly. Mama snatched up the half-blackened pieces of paper in a tea towel, dropped paper and towel in the trash, and began scrubbing her hands vigorously under steaming water, but not before I recognized the bright blue envelope with the Savannah postmark that I'd taken out of the mailbox the day before. I ran over to the bin. Mothers have eyes in the back of their head, it's said, and so perhaps do wives, able to see what's behind them better than what's ahead.

"Julian Selkirk, get away from there this instant!"

"But it was my card. I didn't even get to open it yet because my birthday's not until next week and you said . . . " I would soon be twelve, too old for strategic whining, but Daddy wasn't downstairs yet and Mama was always a sucker for babies of any age.

Not this time, though. She slapped my hand back. "I told you, don't touch that." Mama didn't know how to hit in a way that really hurt, but I pulled away anyhow. "It's got germs on it. You know what kind."

"But it might have had money in it," I complained. It was a feeble protest and I knew it. Uncle Jimmy was the proprietor of a weird little shop that sold orphaned bits of china and used books alongside the occasional stuffed parrot. He lived with Grandmère Dupuis in a drafty pink-plastered house she called Belle Rêve. My father's company had just won the contract to build a new 25-lot subdivision in Gwinnett County and Mama had sold an article on low-calorie cocktails to *Southern Living*. The cash flow direction was definitely not from Mama's family to ours, notwithstanding the two months last winter when we lived in Grandmère's spare room, which my big brother Carter vigorously pretended didn't happen. Seriously, for the first couple of weeks we were back home, I might say something like "Remember those great French fries we had at the Shrimp Factory?" or "That praise band isn't half so good as the choir at St. Vincent's," and Carter would pull a face and say "We've never been to the Shrimp Factory, dumb-ass," and so on.

Laura Sue looked mournfully at the stack of pancakes, which were turning limp as they cooled. Her hand reached for the plate just as Daddy's footsteps sounded in the hall. "Mama, when are we going to visit Uncle Jimmy?" I asked loudly.

"Hush, we'll talk about that later," she whispered. She pushed an imaginary curl of hair out of her face and smoothed down the front of her rose-printed dress.

"You always say that, but then you never do it," I argued, to distract her. "You've been saying that since he went into the hospital." Out of the corner of my eye, I saw Laura Sue snatch a pancake and stuff it under her loose denim shirt.

"Uncle Jimmy's a faggot," Carter spoke up. He gulped milk out of the cow-shaped creamer so his cup would still look clean. "We saw the video about it in health class."

"Children, watch your language," was all Mama said. She had that pinched, puckered expression on her face like she was shrinking inside, like the house that implodes at the end of *Poltergeist*.

"This guy in the video lost all his hair and he had these big purple sores on him like a leopard," Carter went on.

"Leper, asshole," I said, my voice cracking. And there he was, suddenly. Our Father who art in the kitchen.

How can I describe Daddy? My mind slides away from picturing him as just another object in the room, on a par with Laura Sue's pinched cheeks and unruly auburn curls, the dull silver curves of the coffee pot, Mama's wide blue eyes carefully framed with mascara and foundation over a yellowing bruise, the pink rounds of Canadian bacon cooling in their grease. I see my brother's face, a rough copy of the big man's, with fleshy forehead and small dark eyes. But Carter's shoulders are hunched where Daddy's are straight, his hands, still grimy from yesterday's scrimmage, too large for his china cup, while Daddy knows just how to hold a briefcase, a dollar, a bottle, a woman.

"What did you say?" Mild-mannered this morning, on the surface, an ordinary businessman in his pressed white shirt that by day's end would be stained with sweat and enthusiasm for the big score, so many acres bulldozed and walls raised.

"Nothing, sir," I muttered. Carter opened his mouth to tell on me but reconsidered. He'd deal with me later, if he remembered. Wiry and small for my age, I could no more beat my brother in a fistfight than I could resist provoking him, like the time I told him Daddy had named him after his favorite bluegrass band (which was true) and that the real name on his birth certificate was Mother Maybelle (which was not).

Daddy shouldered his way past us to get a cup of coffee. We all prayed it was still hot. I was tired of this routine. In a few days I would be twelve, five or six more years and I could go to college, or travel the world, like Uncle Jimmy before he got sick, finding treasures in the back rooms of shops in Morocco and Shanghai, where Pastor Steve said the heathens lived. Thinking of Uncle Jimmy made my stomach constrict. This was the last birthday card I would ever get from him, I knew that, and it was nothing but a heap of disinfected ashes in the garbage, underneath the eggshells and coffee grounds, like he would be soon, dead and underground, and nobody was willing to say so.

I felt the heat of Daddy standing behind me. He smelled sober, like aftershave and shoe polish, and I hoped we could keep it together until my birthday. Last summer we'd gone camping, and while the girls drank cocoa in the tent and slapped at mosquitoes, Daddy and Carter and I had played at being Indians in the woods, stalking each other and trying not to make any noise when we stumbled on sharp rocks and walked into branches. That's why our baseball team was called the Braves, Daddy said, because Indian warriors were so brave that they didn't let out a sound even under torture. In the starry blackness of the woods, I had felt their massacred ghosts around us, watching, inaudible, unsuspected.

Outside, a car honked. Darcy Preston's mother was waiting to car-pool us to camp. "Won't you sit down and have some pancakes, Brad?" Mama pleaded to Daddy, calculating that she had about three minutes to get some nutrients into her precious children.

Daddy poured out the rest of his coffee in the sink. "Meeting with the bank at nine," he announced. "Houses don't pay for themselves, y'know." He smiled at his own familiar remark, and we relaxed. Mama glowed as he patted her cheek, the flat of his hand alighting there gently. "Hansons coming for dinner tonight. Wear something decent." And instantly she faded, like a weak winter sunbeam.

Laura Sue and I made a dash for Mrs. Preston's Buick, while Carter hopped on his bike. Having aged out of Bible camp, he was free to play football with his buddies all day. I sat in the front seat while Laura Sue and Darcy pretended to get along in the back. Darcy didn't have to pretend very much because she had long blonde hair and had once been in a pet food commercial with her dog Sal. She still spoke like the cameras were rolling, with that over-enunciated good cheer.

My sister passed me half of her stolen pancake. It was linty but I ate it anyhow. "Mommy, Laura Sue isn't sharing," Darcy complained.

"To them that hath, more shall be given," I retorted. "Bet you don't know which chapter and verse that is."

"What do you want to bet?" she bluffed.

"If you're wrong, you'll cut off all your hair."

"Julian, behave," Mrs. Preston snapped.

"Cutting off your hair is an important spiritual discipline," I argued. "Nuns do it all the time."

Bad move. Mrs. Preston sniffed. I'd forgotten we weren't in Savannah anymore, where Catholics were considered Christian. I had sung a solo in "Laudate Pueri" (probably my last turn as a darling boy soprano) at the Christmas concert at St. Vincent's, while Grandmère dabbed her sparkling eyes with a lavender silk handkerchief. I was too young to know the term "liturgy queen," but I couldn't take my eyes off the gangly red-headed deacon who laid out the gleaming chalice and cruets so gracefully on the altar, like Mama setting the table, a table that would stay the same forever.

When Mama fell down the stairs last Thanksgiving, Daddy had taken us kids out for a steak dinner. To cheer us up, he said. He was so solicitous, his big face flushed with wine, re-folding Laura Sue's napkin every time she ran for the bathroom, letting Carter and me order off the menu like real adults. I pushed my privileges to the limit, to see if we could get away with ordering lobster tails and jumbo onion rings for dinner, and when it came I had no intention of eating any of it. Daddy's good cheer grew over-inflated, dangerously close to bursting, each time he would glance up from his plate and see the three of us sitting still, unable to open our mouths.

The following morning Uncle Jimmy had pulled into our driveway in Grandmère's 1968 turquoise Thunderbird. He said he was taking us to visit Mama in the hospital, but he left Laura Sue and me down in the lobby gift shop for the longest time while he and Carter went up to her room. When they came back, they were pushing Mama in a wheelchair. They pushed her right out the front doors and lifted her into that boat of a car, stretched out on the back seat with her head on my lap and her plaster-encased legs across Laura Sue's knees, and four hours later we were in Savannah.

Our escape was sudden and unendurably slow, all at once. Every curve on the interstate jolted Mama's slumping head, her hair darkened with sweat across her forehead. I was on mascara duty, dabbing her tears away with a tissue between rest stops, holding up the pocket mirror so she could repair the damage when we pulled over for gas. "I can't let your Grandmère see me like this," she moaned, fussing with the sweater Uncle Jimmy had thrown over her hospital gown. Laura Sue hung onto her legs like a drowning person clinging to a spar. Carter got to ride up front and hold the map, which was useless because we already knew where we were going.

I was grateful to Uncle Jimmy for keeping him busy. My brother had been the first to voice what was happening to us, which he did with his usual tact and charm. "If I was going to run away from home, I wouldn't take you with me," he grumbled to me in the parking lot of the Burger King outside Macon. He was stuffing his face with a fruit pie and at that moment I thought I'd never seen such a disgusting sight in my whole life.

"Well then, when we get there, you can just keep on going," I said, and kicked him in the shins. My brother, who had once eaten five raw eggs on a dare without puking, who scored the winning goal in peewee soccer with a bloody hole where his two front teeth used to be, my brother dropped his fruit pie on the asphalt and began to cry.

"I'll come with you," I said. Still the tears streaked his big red face. Because I knew he wouldn't want me to touch him, I scooped up the fruit pie from the pavement.

"Dare you to eat that," he gulped.

I examined the squashed pastry, oozing red jelly dotted with black flecks of gravel. In a way, everything was mashed into everything else, clean and dirty, sense and no sense. Disgusting was just one way to look at it. I flashed back to the time we'd gone camping and Daddy had taught us how to dig a latrine. Now maybe I'd never see him again. I felt like the top of my head was floating away. To stop it, I lifted the fruit pie to my mouth, but Uncle Jimmy intervened.

"Julian, don't be such a savage," he scolded, but with a wry smile. "Get in the car, you two, and try not to set each other on fire for the next fifty miles."

Back in our mobile rescue unit, I watched the back of my uncle's head as he sped calmly down the highway. On past vacations, I'd joined in, somewhat reluctantly, when Carter and Laura Sue made fun of him behind his back, mocking his soft reedy voice, his rooster-like shock of reddish hair, the dusty corduroy blazers he wore in shades of plum and olive green. Did he know? Would it have mattered? Maybe now our lives would be so quiet that we would stop wanting to be bad.

Naturally the arguments started as soon as we settled into Belle Rêve. The three of us, over bed space, lights-out time, whose clothes were on which side of the tiny room. Mama against Grandmère, over what came next. Us against Uncle Jimmy, because we could. Beautiful dream. Grandmère had named the old pink house after the Louisiana plantation that her father lost when his commodity trades went bad. She had been a high-end milliner in the French Quarter before she married a Georgia man. We used her feathered creations to play Zorro, sliding down the long mahogany banister with terrible war cries, glee tempered with anxiety as the holidays passed and we were not sent to school.

At night, fed up with Laura Sue's whimpering and Carter's snoring, the smelly familiarity of us, I would creep halfway downstairs and sit on the landing. *I am a soldier,* I imagined, *sleeping on the hard, cold ground.* The women's voices drifted up from the parlor. Though I couldn't see them, I knew Grandmère was ensconced before the fireplace, drinking Amaretto-laced hot cocoa, perhaps resting one hand on the silver knob of her cane. Mama would be on the sofa, her plain wooden crutches within easy reach. "It's not that simple, Maman. The boys need a man in their life."

"Not that one," Grandmère growled.

"Bradford is a *good* father," Mama pleaded. "He gets carried away with discipline sometimes, but I don't know, maybe that's what children need, to grow up strong and—and *proper.*"

In the dark of the landing, I felt the chill of Grandmère's silence. Widowed early, she had raised her two children alone in this house, excepting the occasional servant.

"Discipline? Your daughter is nine years old and still wets the bed, your older son's a hoodlum, and Julian—well, Julian's the only one who might have potential, if he'd stop sneaking around and say what the devil's on his mind."

My mother choked back a sob. It was wall-to-wall girl tears in the house that night. If she began wetting the bed too, I was going to run away in earnest.

"I'm only trying to do my duty," she protested.

Grandmère spat something in French that translated literally as "pigs' testicles." The grandfather clock ticked heavily in the front hall. I wrapped my arms around myself to keep warm. Now I was no longer a soldier; I was one of the violinists on the Titanic, scraping out "Abide With Me" with deliberate slowness as the icy black waves foamed higher, seductive in their immensity.

"Don't drag the children into this," Grandmère's voice cut through my reverie. "You've always been crazy in love with that man and no mistake."

My mother sighed, or perhaps it was the wind, the whole creaking house conceding the point. "You don't understand. He really loves me. He always makes sure I have the best things. I just need to work harder to keep the house under control, because he has a stressful job and deserves to relax when he comes home."

La-di-dah, boring sitcom excuses. I knew what she wanted from him. We weren't supposed to know such things existed, but Carter had found some wrinkled copies of *Playboy* in their closet and shared one with me in exchange for my Boba Fett action figure, a trade I instantly regretted.

Grandmère was right, as always. Children change nothing. Even on the soap operas we're a hindrance, disappearing at infancy and returning two years later from Swiss boarding school as gorgeous, troubled teens. All through that sparkling December and sodden January, our parents were that age again, Daddy lovesick and reckless, ringing us up at all hours, Mama by turns flustered and coy, smiling as the phone jangled unanswered. My brother grew tired of tearing the place apart and spent his evenings in the basement of the house across the square, playing Space Invaders with the son of a woman who sold postcards at the Confederate Museum. Laura Sue took up needlepoint. I rehearsed with the boys' choir at St. Vincent's after finishing the rather eccentric lessons Grandmère assigned in lieu of school: learning all the country flags in the *Encyclopedia Britannica*, for instance, or memorizing bits of the *Norton Anthology of Modern Poetry*. Father Louis was a large, stoop-shouldered man who smelled of whiskey and Brylcreme. He had droopy basset-hound eyes. His steady mournfulness somehow increased for me the appeal of a priestly vocation.

And then, bones mended, Mama announced that we were going home. Laura Sue cried, as if she hadn't cried just as hard when we left Atlanta. She'd become the darling of Grandmère's sewing circle, who praised her crookedly stitched napkins and fed her lemon bars. Carter swore undying friendship with the postcard woman's son and spoiled his last good shirt pricking their fingers to be Indian blood brothers. And I took pictures of everyone with the new camera Grandmère had given me for Christmas, borrowing madly against my allowance from Mama, who felt guilty enough to buy me film whenever I asked.

Our final night, again unable to sleep, I took up my place on the landing. This time I didn't want to pretend it was anything but itself, the old wooden staircase of Belle Rève, down which Mama would descend into Daddy's arms tomorrow like it was their wedding day, like when you've watched *Gone With the Wind* all the way to the end and you rewind the tape so you can see Tara as it used to be, green and full of laughter.

The front door opened, painting a streak of light across the floor. In the glow of the streetlights I saw Uncle Jimmy, wrapped in his striped scarf and overcoat, and a young man I didn't recognize. They were both bare-headed despite the cold, and the other man's tousled blond curls shone almost as brightly as his fair skin. As I watched, my uncle put his arms around him and touched his mouth to those gently curved lips. They hung together like that, seeming to breathe one another's breath.

My camera's shutter clicked. At the sound, the two men pulled apart. Uncle Jimmy looked up. The shadow across his face might have been regret, or reproach. It was not surprise. The square of light vanished as the door closed behind the golden-haired man. I fled up the stairs, into the deeper darkness, past our room (soon to be ours no longer) and up to the attic. There I pulled the little door shut and leaned against it, panting, under the low eaves. I had done exactly what was expected of me, and that was precious little.

I held my camera away from me, imagining something warm and alive trapped within that nondescript box. The dusty, mildewed air caught in my throat. *You wanted to see, Julian, well, then see.* We were leaving Belle Rève because I hadn't behaved, any more than the others. Carter was the one who broke Grandmère's vase, now lying in shards in a cardboard box up here next to the water-stained dressmaker's dummy, and Laura Sue had spoiled the mattress, it was true, but I could have stopped them, if I knew so much better, if I'd cared. One taste of freedom from Daddy and we all went crazy.

The attic smelled like St. Vincent's, musty and full of interesting secrets. I got the idea into my head that it would all vanish with the sunrise, like Cinderella's dress turning back into sticky cobwebs. Goodbye to the iron-banded trunk, goodbye yellowed stacks of dress patterns, plaster St. Joseph, unshaded lamp. I didn't dare take another picture to remember it by. To see, to see and do nothing, to see what I shouldn't have seen, to break it like a hatching insect's wing, that experiment all schoolchildren ruin.

I rubbed my eyes hard with my fists. My knuckles felt wet. I would *not* cry. Not a sound. My throat was sore with the effort.

Footsteps shook the stairs. I kept my back to the door. In the attic window I saw the reflection of my uncle standing behind me. My shoulders stiffened. I'd never been afraid of him before, silly old Uncle Jimmy with his beaky nose and elbow-patched jacket, but then I'd never given him a reason. Our teasing hadn't scratched his protective coloration, not the way I had, shining a light on that thrilling, unnatural kiss. It was wrong, what he'd done. I would tell him that if he tried to hit me.

But he didn't come any closer. "Are you all right, Julian?" Still I said nothing. "Are you angry?"

This role reversal was so surprising that I nearly turned around. Yes, I decided, I was angry. This place was crazy and everything we'd done here was a waste of time. I clenched my fists.

"I'm sorry we can't keep you here," my uncle said. "It was rather nice, having some life in the old place for a change." He chuckled. Then his voice turned serious. "But Bitsy believes your father deserves another chance, and when the Dupuis women get an idea in their head, there's no prying it out again."

"Mama's stupid," I burst out.

He sighed. "She's in love."

"Then love is stupid."

He came up beside me. I waited for him to try to touch me, but he only stood there, watching the clouds scrub the pale disk of the moon, dim and bright, dim and bright.

"Sometimes," he said, "it's okay to feel stupid. And a lot of other things, too." He offered me his spotted handkerchief.

"I'm not crying."

At this obvious lie, he looked at me sternly for the first time. "You're an unusual person, you know that." It wasn't a question. "You like to understand how things really are. But what are you going to do when you find out?"

"Does Grandmère think what you did with that man was wrong?"

His mouth tightened into a thin line, which he attempted to shape into a smile. "Even your almighty grandmother has to realize you can beat a dog all you want, but it's not going to turn into a cat."

"Does that mean I'll *never* be good?" The tears spilled out.

"Oh, Julian." He sighed again. "You'll be good when you want to be good."

At last I crept into his arms. We sat together on the deep window ledge. The stars glittered in the cold air that blew in through the rattling panes. Eventually I must have fallen asleep, because I woke up on the couch in our room, to the sound of Carter throwing his sneakers into a suitcase, and our life speedily rewound itself to where it had begun.

Now, half a year later, Daddy was fine and Mama was acting fine and I was playing an angel in the Vacation Bible School pageant and the summer sun was shining and Uncle Jimmy was going blind. I had seen that same video they showed Carter's science class; even down South they had to talk about it eventually, if only to teach us about the dangers of blood and needles. This was 1984, so we were also afraid of kissing, sharing a spoon, or sitting on the seat of a bus that had been to San Francisco. And that other thing, of course, that the beautiful boys had done to each other before they began tumbling into the orchestra pit, collapsing behind their barber chairs, taking a spill into the bouquets of roses arrayed in their climate-controlled shops. We had always been afraid of that.

At Atlanta First Baptist summer camp, however, all was bright and cheerful as we rehearsed our assigned parts with much roughhousing and off-key singing and adjusting of bathrobes, with the exception of Laura Sue who had locked herself in the girls' bathroom because her nemesis, Darcy Preston, had beaten her out for the role of Mary. Pastor Steve's young wife was trying to lure her out with Rice Krispie treats, but like the manna in the desert, these were not enough to boost my sister's flagging faith. Laura Sue had always cared the most about being the perfect one, a china ballerina too sweet to smash. Given the stakes, I could see why she was having a Gloria Swanson moment. I could have told her not to bother, though, since Daddy was generally unimpressed with matters religious. It was something women did, like cleaning the oven—necessary, perhaps, but not interesting.

But I was not around to cajole my sister, because I was wrestling with Bill, who had been assigned the role of Jacob. To prolong the scene, and give us time to remember our lines, we threw in a few chokeholds and smashed each other against the turf in a style more reminiscent of Madison Square Garden than Peniel. He was bigger than me and usually landed on top.

Time and again his stout knee bore down on my belly, my face pressed into his sweaty collarbone, our arms gripping and pushing against each other. I let out a winded sigh that stirred his damp black hair. He elbowed my ribs. "Julian—your line!" he whispered.

"Let me go," I mumbled hesitantly, "for the day is breaking."

"I will not let you go unless you bless me!" he shouted.

My mouth opened, empty of words, so close suddenly to his cheerful round face. I felt heat all down my legs, and shivered.

"Ooh, Julian has a boner!" called out one of the girls watching us.

My face flushed red. Shoving a surprised Bill away from me, I pulled myself up. "I don't want to be in this stupid faggot show," I said. Then I ran for the woods, stopping only when the stitch in my side was sharper than the memory of how close I'd been to kissing a boy.

Southerners know all about curses, how they make themselves known by slow inexorable signs, in the dusky complexion of the slave owner's heir, in the fitful sleep of the madwoman's daughter. Signs for which you checked yourself every day, like residents of a fallout shelter, telling yourself that your teeth were no looser, your hair no thinner.

This is not going to happen to you, Julian, I told myself, resting my face against the rough bark of a tree to remind myself that I was still here, among the saved children of Georgia, and not in the lake of fire reserved for communists, idol-worshippers, and homosexuals. When I thought of my uncle in pain like that, I wanted to scream.

"Well, it looks like the Selkirks have called an actors' strike," drawled Pastor Steve, who had come up beside me unnoticed. Through a gap in the trees I saw Darcy swanning around as Mary looking for her runaway boy, while Donny Jenkins warbled "On My Father's Side" to the synagogue elders. I hung my head and stared at the dirt. Penitence was the quickest way to avoid telling adults what you were thinking.

"Did you and Bill have a fight?"

I shrugged, which wasn't exactly lying.

"Would you like to tell me what happened?"

Again I was speechless before Pastor Steve's warm, puppyish energy, and something else beneath it that stirred up even more hopeless, angry yearnings. *Blessed assurance, Jesus is mine.*

"You know, Julian," he said gently, "it's normal for boys your age to have all kinds of confusing feelings. You just need to ask God to help you direct them into channels that are more natural and wholesome." He paused, with an encouraging smile. "Do you understand what I mean?"

I did and I didn't. Who doesn't want to be someone else? That was why my sister was on a hunger strike for the privilege of reciting two lines to a couple of kids with cotton-wool beards. But how to stop what my body was doing was beyond me. *If your right eye offends you, pluck it out.* Sometimes I thought I'd rather be dead than blind, not that God was waiting on my opinion.

"How do I do that?" I asked. My voice sounded alien, cracking into manhood with a few sharp notes, like the stuck keys on Grandmère's piano.

Pastor Steve stroked his beardless chin. I sweated and reminded myself to breathe. Would the rest of my life be like this, suppressing a madness that could be set off by a flash of skin, a smile, a careless touch? I wished I could ask Carter if it was just as bad for him, waking up hot in damp sheets, unable to solve for X because the math teacher was wearing a tight sweater. With my father I could only listen to the sounds from the room next to ours, the creaks and thumps and cries that were sometimes of pleasure. Everyone was stuck in this same stupor, and only God decided when it should stop.

"I've noticed that you spend a lot of time alone," Pastor Steve mused. "Taking pictures."

"I'm going to be a photographer when I grow up." At that time I had dreams of exploring South American jungles for *National Geographic,* facing down pygmies and crocodiles.

"You like taking pictures of pretty girls?"

"Sure, I guess." It was better than talking to them.

"Well, maybe you could take the next step and ask one of them out." Mistaking my confusion at this non sequitur for anxiety, he went on, "Come on, don't be shy. You're twelve now, and you'll be a teenager before you know it. Time to start thinking about these things."

Back at camp, negotiations were still at a standoff. When she saw me, Darcy flicked her long blonde hair over her shoulder and winked in a most un-Marian way. Remembering Pastor Steve's advice, I twitched one side of my mouth up in a smile. She was so excited that Donny, as young Jesus, had to tug on her arm to remind her that she was supposed to be looking for him. Inside me, a fresh restlessness overlaid the old. This new power of being desired—what was I supposed to do with it?

To quote Spider-Man, or maybe Winston Churchill, "With great power comes great responsibility." At the snack break I brought Darcy a frozen orange juice pop and a proposition. "If you swap parts with Laura Sue, I'll take you out to the movies."

She licked the juice pop delicately as a kitten. "I don't know. Are you sure you really want to go out with me?"

"Sure I do. I'll see anything you want, even if it's about horses and Shirley MacLaine crying."

She giggled. "I like you, Julian. You're not like other boys. You say the funniest things."

And so I gave Laura Sue her debut as an actress and Darcy's as a fag hag, sitting beside me in the darkness of the Corona Theatre watching Tom Hanks fall in love with Daryl Hannah in *Splash*. Despite myself, I became entranced, not with Darcy's cool little hand in mine, but with the story. I was sad-eyed, baby-faced Allen, working alongside his fat, lusty brother Freddie in the fruit warehouse, pining for a magic that no ordinary woman seemed to possess. Then I was Madison, golden-haired and innocently nude, a mermaid lost in the two-footed world, learning English from the TVs at Bloomingdale's while dodging the unexpected splash of water that would expose her. I almost couldn't watch how Allen's face changed from infatuation to hurt and disgust when he opened the bathroom door and saw her beautiful guilty face wreathed in steam and that scaly tail arcing out of the tub.

I glanced over at Darcy. Her eyes shone with the big screen's reflected light. She was like me, in love with something we mistook for each other. Believing herself ready to wager it all on that first plunge, until—"I'm in love with a *fish*," Allen laments, unable to face himself, or her.

The next part of the movie was the same as *E.T.*—the escape from the laboratory, the triumph of love over science. Of girls over boys, or boys over men? Back to the ocean she goes. If you love something, set it free. By that standard, no one in our family would ever see each other again.

"People fall in love every day," Allen tells Freddie, his excuse for letting the mermaid leave him behind in his sad, safe life. John Candy, as Freddie: "Well, that's a crock. A lot of people will never be that happy. *I'll* never be that happy!" When a clown yells at you, take it seriously.

So he follows her after all, giving up the last sight of land and the people he knew to become what he was, a man who could breathe underwater, who loved a fish. I trembled, electric with something I had no words for. Fear, possibly—fear that my body wasn't big enough to contain what I felt. Darcy squeezed my hand. If I were ever going to start liking girls, it would have happened then, when she saw the tears on my face and didn't laugh.

But it wouldn't happen. I knew that as I popped a kiss on her strawberry-scented cheek before her beaming mother let me out of their car in front of my house. The Buick's taillights faded into the trees that were darkening with sunset, ripples of crimson flowing into violet and blue. Somewhere up there was heaven, where I would probably not be going, so I had better take a good look at it now.

Through our picture window, I saw my parents at dinner. Mr. Hanson from the bank was there, and his wife with the Nancy Reagan hairdo. The candle flames flickered. Daddy leaned over to his business partner, Mr. Crosby, and said something that made them both guffaw. Mama stood behind them, gripping the soup ladle tightly, so she could serve without spilling a drop. On nights when there was company we were supposed to eat in the kitchen, but I was full of popcorn and the fear of eternal damnation, so I crept quietly past the dining room and into the den, where my brother was breaking several house rules at once by eating Doritos on the white sofa while watching *Charlie's Angels*. Soon he'd be too old to care whether I tore his comic books or messed up the battle formation of his army men. Good for you, Carter, I thought; I hope you find a girl like Farrah Fawcett and she lets you stick your face in her boobs all day.

Up in my room, I was afraid again, as night filled the sky over our quiet suburb. Why couldn't I be like Laura Sue, drinking her milk at the kitchen table, with her ankles crossed under her chair? Then I could find a man to hold me and it would be all right. But what if I picked the wrong one, and he beat me, and for the rest of my life I would have to cry and serve him cocktails? I sank down on my knees and buried my face in the bedspread. "God," I whispered, "make me different." But I said it without any conviction, which was another sin. There was no one else I wanted to be like. No one except Tom Hanks, swimming through the blue paradise where his love belonged. Were mermaids an abomination, like the shellfish in Leviticus? More to the point, they weren't real. I was betting my life on something that didn't exist.

I groped around among the outdated magazines and dirty sneakers in my closet until I found the shoebox of my mementos from Savannah. Carter had the right attitude; I should throw these old things out and not think about last winter anymore. As I lifted the lid, a faint puff of incense sent me back to cold mornings at St. Vincent's, our blended voices squeaking out scales while Father Louis stole a swig from the flask in the pocket of his enormous cassock. There was the stub of the candle I'd carried in the Christmas procession, next to a grinning porcelain monkey from Uncle Jimmy's shop, which had scared me so much that I'd wanted to own it. Underneath those were some cheaply tinted postcards of Jefferson Davis and Robert E. Lee, and my photo of my uncle's kiss.

I held the picture up to the bedside light. Their faces were smooth and young, their eyes were closed. Nothing in the world existed for them, no sickness or punishment, in that moment when their lips met, warm and alive and kind.

I went down the hall to my parents' room, where Mama kept stationery in a white-painted writing desk that she used for her magazine articles. Not knowing the address of Uncle Jimmy's hospital, I addressed the envelope to him at Belle Rève. Grandmère would know what to do.

I took a last look at the photo, to memorize it, and pressed it to my cheek, as I'd seen Laura Sue do with pictures of Corey Hart in *Tiger Beat*, pretending I could feel the golden-haired man's skin against my own. On the back, I wrote "I love you." Then, my heart pounding, I dropped it in the envelope and sealed it up. I was afraid to write my name on it. I thought Uncle Jimmy might prefer it that way. If he was already blind, Grandmère would describe it to him, and he would see that kiss again in the darkness, better than any sight in this world or the next.

two ham theory
Matt Riordan

two ham theory

June. When we pulled up I could see the ham lying there out on my lawn. It was one of those spiral sliced jobs they coat in a corn syrup compound. It was swarming with ants and wasps and there were grass trimmings stuck to all sides of it, from which you could tell that it had arrived there laterally and with some degree of violence. We were in my brother Kenny's old Volvo. He had picked me up from work at the City-County building with the heat going full tilt because he was trying to repair the leaking heater core with a bottle of that stuff you pour into the radiator and circulate. Like automotive cholesterol, it's supposed to skitter down the car's veins and coagulate at any leaks. It wasn't working. Bluish antifreeze water was pooled in the passenger side floor pan so that I had to hold my feet up out of it. I had to be careful to keep Kenny's old dog in the back seat, because dogs love to drink antifreeze and it will kill a dog, especially an old frail dog like his. She sat in the back in the heat waiting for her chance to fall on that antifreeze and lap herself into geriatric dog kidney failure oblivion. I know a lot about this kind of thing because I once ate a fistful of muscle relaxers and chased it with a big bottle of cherry Robitussin. Smoked both kidneys in one shot. Those kidneys saved my life, but it's all they had in them. Now I've got one of Kenny's. And now he's got me.

I was out of the blasting heat and on the lawn before Kenny had the parking brake all the way up. He and his dog joined me by the ham and all of us stood looking at it. I would have kicked it around but I was wearing wingtips and I didn't want to get the bugs and corn syrup on the toe. Several of the spiral slices were missing, so you could see that someone had enjoyed a portion of the ham before it came to rest on my lawn.

We spent a few reflective moments with the ham before the screen door on my neighbor's house banged shut and—in a space of time inadequate to get from her door to where we were standing in any kind of a dignified fashion—she was on us. When I looked up she was also looking at the ham. She is a freckle-faced and angular woman, kind of pointy in spots, but she manages to be attractive anyway. Her drapes are open most of the time but I've never seen her walking around naked, although I often check while drinking my coffee, just in case she slips up and starts masturbating in front of one of her windows. Her name is Meagan.

Together we watched the ham-insect ecosystem rage for a quiet minute. Then Meagan spoke. "That your ham?"

Kenny looked at me. I looked back at him and didn't move. This part was his show. "I think it is," he said. "On our lawn, makes it our ham." He looked down at his dog, which was showing the faintest signs of interest. His dog has a tumor that's roughly the size of a lemon on the back of her neck, but it's not noticeable in the folds of old dog skin that pile up behind her head. The vet said it would be four hundred dollars to remove it, but that if we just left it there it wouldn't hurt her any. Whenever someone pets her for the first time and feels that big lump in her loose flesh you can see their mind snap to and think hard about cancer and hospice and other dark things. Their mouths usually open for a second, just until they can get it back together.

"Happens I'm missing a ham," Meagan said. "Happens I was thawing it on the side deck yesterday and it disappeared."

"Well," said Kenny, "do you recognize this ham as yours?" He and I looked at Meagan. It was easy to do. She was wearing cut-offs and a tee-shirt under a bathrobe. She was skinny like a woman who stepped out of a time machine from 1974. She fished a cigarette out of her robe pocket and lit it with a red Bic lighter, and pretty quick we were all smoking.

"I can't tell," she said. "This ham here has been cooked." She nodded at it.

Kenny poked a crispy part with the toe of his engineer boot. "That's a fact," he said. He wears engineer boots and dark blue Levis and white tee-shirts, like he just missed catching that plane with the Big Bopper. I was seven when my parents brought him home from the hospital. I watched him closely until the gnarled stub of his umbilical cord fell off, just as my mother had said it would, and then I didn't really notice him again until he gave me his kidney. When I was a kid I had two imaginary friends. They were both trees, I think, or maybe logs, and they came from a place where everyone was a log. It must have been a quiet place. Kenny also had an imaginary companion, except his was an imaginary older brother.

Meagan gave the ham a push with her flip-flop. "The ham I left out yesterday was still in the package. I can't tell if this is it."

"You might want to be careful putting your meat out of doors like that," said Kenny. "There's more than a few raccoons around here. Dogs too, of course."

Meagan looked at the dog. "I think it's a two-legged dog I'm looking for." She looked at Kenny and then at me.

"It isn't certain that this is your ham," Kenny said. He looked nervous and shifty. He has a poker face like an extra from a Godzilla movie. Sometimes when startled he bends at the waist and makes a vowel sound that lasts several seconds. "And it would seem more than a little odd that a person would steal your ham, go home and cook it up and eat a little of it, just to bring it back here and toss it up on our lawn."

I had to agree with him that it was odd, and I had said so the moment he had brought the idea to me the day before. He had been in a high state of agitation, though, and he had insisted that I go over and swipe the ham he had spotted on Meagan's side deck while he watched from the safety of my kitchen. I did the thieving, as he had asked, but the deeply weird part, the part that bothered me because it smacked of fetish, the cooking and the lawn placement, that shit he did on his own.

"Somebody trying to make a point maybe," I said.

Meagan snorted. "And just what point might that be? That's just a dirty ham lying there. It is in no way symbolic."

"Some people don't eat ham," I answered. "They believe their God frowns on it, that it's unclean." I said this just to say something because Kenny was looking squirrelly and I didn't want him to blurt out anything incriminating. Our domestic arrangement was complicated enough without revealing to the neighbors that we cannot be trusted not to burgle their cured meats. I did not in fact believe anybody's god had anything to do with the ham on my lawn. That should have been perfectly obvious to Kenny, as he was the one who asked me to go swipe it in the first place, and though our conversation had been intense, there had been no mention of any gods.

"I'm not following you," he said. "Are you suggesting that maybe some people who don't eat ham because of their religious beliefs stole Meagan's ham, and possibly cooked it up and threw it on our lawn? What would be the point of that? Or are you saying that maybe someone thinks we don't eat ham because of our religious beliefs, so they threw it up on our lawn to intimidate us?"

My strategy with Kenny emphasizes peace at the expense of justice. I mostly do as he asks and hope that he loses interest in whatever scheme he has asked me to undertake. Usually he does, but sometimes he doesn't, and on those occasions I end up out on the lawn with him and a ham, or someplace like that.

"I remind you that you all are Lutherans," said Meagan. Meagan does not attend the same church that we do not attend. "And me too. As a rule we eat beaucoup ham."

Kenny snapped off a sharp drag from a cigarette I had paid for. "Yeah. Well, anyway, I think Meagan's missing ham and this ham here are unrelated." He flicked his cigarette butt out into the street in front of my house. "I favor a two ham theory."

After dinner I sat with Kenny in the kitchen waiting on the coffee pot. In my house we drink expensive coffee and we smoke only the finest cigarettes available—Winstons. Those are my priorities, and since Caleb left, I am the sole resident of this house with gainful employ. My decision to spend the lion's share of my discretionary budget on cigarettes and coffee means that we do not feast on pie and ice cream the way we did when our mother was alive. We have, as a result, grown skinnier than our mediocre genes and strict policy of inactivity would otherwise dictate.

Caleb is the youngest. He eats the most, so the austerity measures hit him the hardest. He eventually took up with a girl down in Bedford. He keeps a room in my house, but mostly he stays shacked up with her and has dinner at her folks'. He has gained weight. Caleb was in charge of the cable for the TV. I asked Kenny to take care of it after Caleb left and he agreed, but one day after work I turned on the TV and found nothing but snow, which I watched for a while.

"She's looking good," said Kenny. He pulled open the drawer where we keep the cigarettes and took out a fresh carton. We purchase Winstons in bulk from the Indian reservation in Brown County. He tossed me a pack, a gesture that did nothing to dilute the effect of watching him pluck out yet another fresh pack of cigarettes I had paid for. Kenny smokes at a fever pitch, often leaving multiple butts burning in various ashtrays around the house.

"Who?"

I thought he meant the dog. I was confused because she was not looking good. She had a big tumor and bald patches and each new day she cheated the reaper she looked a little more unlucky to be alive than she did the day before. She also smelled faintly of shit.

"Meagan," said Kenny. "Meagan's looking good."

"Yes. Yes she does look good. And she thaws her meats outside, and in the late afternoon of a weekday she can be found at home in her bathrobe. And I think she suspects we took her ham."

"You think she knows?"

Kenny lit his cigarette from the element in the toaster. We endure a chronic match shortage. Kenny compulsively lights them all as soon as I bring any home and then the house smells of sulfur and he wears Band-Aids on his fingers to cover the blisters where he has burned himself.

"I didn't say she knows," I answered. "I said she suspects. Of course she suspects. She sits alone in her house at night and wonders if some shitbird wino ganked her ham as a crime of opportunity, or if it was the Boo Radley oddball who lives next door."

"Yeah, well, maybe she does know. And maybe she's not exactly Junior League, but you know, we are not without certain eccentricities ourselves."

He gestured with his cigarette hand at the room around him. "We live on store brand frozen okra and corned beef hash from the can, here in the house our mother left us."

Strictly speaking, that wasn't true. My mother's will was quite clear that the house was left to nobody but me. "To my son James," it said, though she and everyone else had always called me Jimmy. Nothing in there about Kenny or Caleb getting the house.

When I didn't respond, Kenny went back to looking out the window at Meagan's house while touching his lips. He was touching them in a way that made you think they had just been installed and he was trying to get a feel for how they might work.

———

When Kenny was fourteen our mother took him to a doctor because, when she asked him, he admitted that he had no friends. She called me at school with that news and I told her not to ask him that anymore. She asked me to talk to him and handed him the phone. I told him to lie the next time Mom asked him anything like that. There was a pause on the phone, and then Kenny asked me why he should lie.

"Because Mom doesn't want to hear any shit about you being friendless and maladjusted. It makes her feel bad. Hell, it makes me feel bad. The truth is, your suffering is more or less your problem and there isn't fuck-all anybody can do to help you anyway, so you may as well keep that shit to yourself and spare everyone else."

"I don't feel bad. I'm fine."

"This isn't about you. Not everything is, you know."

The doctor said he thought Kenny might have some form of mild autism, so Mom threatened to sue his ass and decided Kenny might be diabetic or possibly gay. When those hunches didn't pan out she decided he must be fine after all, and to my knowledge Kenny has never been officially diagnosed with any kind of disorder. He doesn't try to hurt himself or others, but there is no denying that his behavior suggests the need for some sort of custodial arrangement. Since he moved into my house he has tried to trade his car for an ice cream maker he found at a garage sale, and he signed up to buy three thousand dollars of cutlery from a college kid who was selling it door-to-door.

Kenny can spend a week close to catatonic, during which he bathes rarely and under protest. Without warning he just checks out, and then he isn't present in his life to the degree required by the world of waitresses who introduce themselves and credit card companies that call him when he buys something to ask if it's really him. Other times he becomes agitated about something he read in the paper, about seals maybe, or what an iodine deficiency will do to you, and he wakes me up in the middle of the night to discuss it. He has called me at work to say he couldn't be there to pick me up because he'd driven to another state and was on a walking tour of a cement factory. I don't know if he meets the legal requirements for possession of his faculties, but it's fair to say he has developed into a person more or less exclusively to his own tastes.

He handed over his kidney to me without pause or discussion. There is no way to characterize such an act as anything other than generous and courageous, unless you believe the donor to be playing with less than a full deck. It took me by surprise. I didn't mention to the doctors that Kenny might be a little off, and they didn't ask. They were essentially virtuoso technicians, focused on the procedure. There was no legal impediment to him giving away half of his renal system, and us being brothers, no one saw any reason to be suspicious. I was in the room, harnessed to some surprisingly grimy and cheap looking blood straining hardware, when a doctor said to him, smiling, "You haven't asked me if this will hurt."

Kenny looked at him and said, "I had my appendix out and that didn't hurt at all. They gave me a kind of tropical ice cream. I want to say it was mango, but that's not right. Maybe it was papaya, or guanabana." The doctor smiled because he thought Kenny was trying to be macho. The doctor was a transplant surgeon and could appreciate someone being macho.

Because of the sameness of our genes Kenny's kidney slipped right in and went to work without complaint. They just unplugged it from him and plugged it into me, the way you might swap out an oil filter, which is basically what it is. Neither of us suffered much, and shortly after we came home from the hospital Kenny was back living in the same upstairs bedroom he had occupied before he left for Purdue.

Kenny worked in Palo Alto for a year after Purdue, writing code for a video game company. He's supposed to be brilliant at it. He stepped in and wrote the patches on a couple of their games that had been stalled in development for years. One of them was a particularly vicious game called *Whaler*, where the protagonist harpoons various cetaceans. Kenny fixed the problems it had and added a graphic portion where the carcasses could be rendered in huge coal-fired deck cauldrons for extra points. Kenny worked out an electronic sizzling noise that won an award. It was like a dog whistle for teenage boys, whom it drove to shrieks of bloodlust, while repelling everyone else within earshot. *Whaler* went to market in October and finished second in sales for the year. On the success of *Whaler* a Korean electronics conglomerate bought the company.

Kenny's idiosyncrasies were apparently garbled upon translation into Korean. They saw no reason not to give Kenny his own studio and send him off, unsupervised, to write them another blockbuster. He cloistered himself away for five months. When he finally let them in on his project it turned out to be not a video game at all, but a three foot tall robotic doll dressed in paramilitary garb that was supposed to perform unpleasant household chores. Among other tasks, it was supposed to toilet train toddlers. It shouted guttural commands in Spanish and English. Kenny called it Subcomandante Feco. The Koreans thought he was putting them on, or he was on the payroll of the competition. They fired him on the spot and sent people to his house to search for and destroy any prototypes he might have hidden there. He came home to Indiana honestly stunned.

Kenny's return coincided nicely with my need for his kidney, but his personal habits made living with him difficult. He ate Cheerios while on the toilet. He sharpened pencils with a knife, leaving the shavings where they fell, although he apparently had no need for the pencils once sharpened. He blew his nose in the shower. One day the guy who delivers the paper, himself only a half step from whatever welfare they give the hopelessly retarded, told me he saw Kenny smoking. What he said was that he thought someone was giving Kenny cigarettes. He said it like Kenny was a chimp.

I watched him as he watched Meagan's house, and I tried to see where he was headed. Why Kenny does what he does and what it is he wants is a mystery, but his interest in our neighbor was something new. Maybe something healthy.

"Like you asked, I took her ham," I said. I do these things for him because he is my brother, and because I walk the earth with his kidney straining the dregs from my blood. "But I will tell you, again, it would have been simpler to just go ask her to the movies or something. You could have driven her out into the country for a picnic. Taken the dog. Something wholesome. Instead we stole her food."

"I've watched her. The woman does not go to the movies, or bowling, or out to eat, or anything remotely social such that I could find a reasonable avenue of approach. This is the right play, and by the time she realizes my design it will be too late. Rope-a-dope."

Before he gave me his kidney I might have tried to put a stop to this kind of thing. Now I assist. Like Kato, Tanto, Sancho, and other two-syllable men who have misplaced their independent will; I am Jimmy and I steal hams in the service of my brother's convoluted romantic schemes.

That July the sun moved closer to Indiana and we took a fearsome grilling. It brought to flaming intensity a six-month drought. The cornfields outside of town were full of dwarf stalks and tiny ears perfectly sized for happy magic little sharp-toothed elves who were maybe preparing our world for colonization. The black faded from the dirt and it turned a khaki color, and Kenny started spending evenings at Meagan's. As planned, he used the ham disappearance as a pretext to go over there, checking her yard for signs of raccoons. I think he went so far as to suggest a possible trespass by coyotes. She resolved to henceforward thaw all meats indoors, and they moved on to other matters.

By August theft was no longer necessary as we were eating Meagan's hams at her invitation. Meagan bakes an inspired ham, with cloves and brown sugar, and it was usually more than enough for her and the two of us, with a meaty bone left over that she boiled for bean soup. The ham was generally followed by a chess pie, demolished in one sitting once Caleb was back, and pots of hot coffee and many cigarettes. I said nothing, but I felt that no one needed that kind of meal in the middle of the afternoon in August, least of all a room full of heavy smokers, each with a half pot of coffee in them. In the two months after Kenny asked me to steal the first one from her back porch, Meagan's hams became a Sunday routine. We ate at her kitchen table because it was directly in front of the air conditioner.

Caleb came back because the situation with his Bedford woman had deteriorated, in the manner the situations with his women generally do. Caleb evidently tried to get a leg over her sister. He is a man driven by uncomplicated and immediate physical urges. He works until he sweats through his shirt, eats until he groans with discomfort, and heeds the call of his reproductive organs wherever they lead him.

I was with Caleb when he met the Bedford woman. She was our waitress at an Applebee's. She was wearing jewelry in both her eyebrows and her lip. She had ample breasts, which, together with her slightly greasy hair and facial piercings, gave an overall sloppy impression that made me think she was providing trouble-free and happy sex to someone. In straight-ahead fashion, Caleb just asked for her phone number when we left. She gave it to him and smiled, despite the mud on his work boots and the fact that he smelled of sawdust. In short order he was eating pork tenderloin sandwiches at her mother's table and spending his nights examining her for other piercings. In a month he was commuting from her rented limestone bungalow to the construction sites where he worked as a carpenter.

It is widely held that all the men in Bedford beat their wives and that the children are encouraged to play with firearms. Meagan is an EMT, and like all the county emergency services personnel she dreads the Bedford calls. "It's hilljack Blade Runner down there," she would say. "White trash Somalia. At night the fires from exploding meth labs light up the sky."

At Caleb's first ham dinner Meagan told him he was lucky to have shaken off Bedford and its women without disfiguring injury. "First call I took down there was a kid who got shot by another kid. So far, routine, right? Except the kids were both under twelve, and the weapon wasn't a pistola, it was a bow and arrow."

Meagan uses words, like pistola, that are not age or gender appropriate. Sometimes she sounds like a retired machinist you just met while drinking at an American Legion post.

"The first kid, the eleven-year-old shooter, he gets on the bus with his dad's compound bow in a hockey bag. The second kid, all of eight, he's the principal's son. When they get off the bus the second kid runs screaming for the school door while the first kid drops to one knee and draws a bead. Put the arrow right though the other kid's upper thigh. The shooter still had the little archery glove on when I got there. He was in the back of a police car waving at his friends. Way fucked up down there. Strange rangers, every last fucking one of them."

When we started eating her hams I learned that Meagan kept odd hours and that she was handy around the house. She moved in a way that didn't suggest doubt, and she sometimes wore things on her belt, like cell phones or sunglasses in their case. Caleb suspects she is a lesbian who has been forced by her circumstances to settle for men. A plight to which he is uncharacteristically sympathetic. "Tough break for her," he said, "but I'm not sure I give enough of a shit to mount a rescue mission, like my-lesbian fell-down-a-well sort of thing. Besides, getting some is doing Kenny heaps of good."

Meagan and Kenny did not touch one another in my presence, and he said nothing about his progress, but he spent time in her house after dark, and he didn't ask me to steal anything else from her.

One afternoon in September Kenny did not pick me up from work. I called several times but he didn't answer. I was forced to take the city bus, which is otherwise patronized only by illegal immigrants and the infirm. When I got home Kenny wasn't there. He was next door at Meagan's, and he explained that he had lost his car keys, probably forever. I asked him what he was going to do about his car sitting in my driveway, but he hadn't thought about it.

At Sunday ham dinner that week, Kenny fished a pack of cigarettes from his pocket. We smoke during the actual meal proper, while others are still eating. This is a treasured privilege that may be exercised only when among the most devout smokers. The pack he retrieved wasn't the familiar red and white of the Winston pack. They were some kind of hippie all natural organic cigarettes, and they were lights. I detest lights. I had not purchased them. I ate Meagan's scalloped potatoes and listened while the two of them asked Caleb if he could build them a sauna in the backyard. My backyard.

On a weekday morning in October I sat at the kitchen table with coffee and the paper, preparing for my workday as a dispatcher for the public works road crews. My office is on the first floor of the City-County Building, which is a large squat building built by the WPA. I have two multi-line telephones on my desk that ring with complaints of potholes, dead deer, and in the winter, snow. Mostly, it's as fiendishly boring as you would imagine, but in emergency conditions I use a radio to direct the plows, which is oddly thrilling. The radio sits on a credenza behind my desk. The radio is an old model, made entirely of steel, and a cable runs from the back of it out through a hole in the window frame to an antenna tower on the roof. The microphone is on a short stand that has a transmit button on the base. On those nights when blizzards sweep over Indiana I sit at my desk with a thermos of coffee and direct the plows. There is a battery back-up system for the radio so that even if the power goes I can sit in the dark and talk to the drivers through the worst of it. On those nights I waive the office smoking ban, though I have no power to do so. The cops and public works guys who wander in on those nights seem to appreciate it, and no one complains. Together we smoke and drink coffee and pull through until the snow stops, and then we hand the building back to the probation officers and the registrar of deeds.

I was thinking about that radio as I drank my coffee and watched the sliding glass door that separated Meagan's kitchen from the side porch that faces my house. Without prelude she bounced, smiling, into view and her robe flew open. Finally she was naked. But there was Kenny, right behind her, also more or less bouncing. Similarly, without benefit of undergarments. She turned around and knelt on the linoleum and began, unmistakably, fellating him. It was a sight that reached out and snatched off my eyelids.

On the Saturday before Christmas, Caleb was reading the paper and drinking coffee in the kitchen when I walked in. He has warned me about my coffee consumption and told me to treat my kidney carefully, because, brother or not, he isn't sure he'd part with his if I needed another since by that point I'd have already blown through three of them this side of thirty-five. There was smoke coming from the little stack on the sauna. Caleb looked up at me and put down the paper. "It's maybe six degrees out, and the motherfucker went by me wearing nothing but a balaclava and a pair of New Balance."

They had taken to sitting in there naked and then coming out and rolling in the snow. Like they were Swedes. They had rolled in all the snow immediately adjacent to the sauna and were forced to run farther afield to find snow unpolluted by man or dog. I had warned Kenny about this, about running naked in the yard in daylight and about the neighbors. He replied that he was running naked in the yard with the neighbors and that I needn't worry.

———

When I talked to mom's lawyer, he said it was legal. Stupid, but legal. He said that a peppercorn can serve as adequate consideration, so a used Volvo with a leaking heater core will do. Of course, I couldn't put "kidney" on the fucking forms. The house is Kenny's. It comes with a sauna.

I don't know if Meagan knows about the ham, knows this whole part of her life is the part where she is the victim of a strange trick, perpetrated by my strange brother. She gave me a lot of knowing looks though, so I wanted to tell her, but I didn't. I believe this proves that I am a good person after all. They invited Caleb to stay on. I wouldn't, but I wasn't asked. The movers took a van full of my stuff and then there was nothing left of me in the house. I bought a fresh set of keys for the Volvo and a carton of Winstons for the drive to Milwaukee. It is a long drive, and it snakes through some unpleasant real estate, especially around Gary, where the air smells like burning tires. In Milwaukee there is a new job directing more plows, and the promise of frequent heavy snow.

Meagan and Kenny and the dog stood on the porch as I put the last of my laundry in the Volvo. It was fresh from the dryer and smelled nice. When I got in I honked goodbye, but Kenny was gone. Then he came out of the house at a jog and cleared all the porch steps in a bound. There was something in his hand and he was smiling. It was a bottle of the radiator leak repair stuff. He handed it to me through the window. The liquid was black and kind of chunky, and it looked like the primary ingredient was some kind of industrial ash. "It's for the leak in the heater core," he said. Then he started back to the porch and Meagan. After a stride or two he turned back and the look on his face had changed. I had no idea what he was about to say, or what was about to happen, so everything was exactly the way it had always been. He looked at his dog, and then he looked back at me.

"Don't drink it," he said.

children of ike
Fred Setterberg

children of ike

Folks in our town talked about the war only as it faded from recollection. Aiming to piece together what had actually happened, we spent Saturday nights at the Alameda Drive-In, absorbing the lessons of Mister Roberts and Teahouse of the August Moon. When it finally arrived in the suburbs, my father praised the Rodgers and Hammerstein version of history: South Pacific featuring Mitzi Gaynor in PanOVision. Dad spoke pointedly of Rossano Brazzi's rich tenor voice as though it somehow modified the atrocities at Tarawa and cut short the bloodshed in Guam.

My Uncle Win, a navy veteran of both Pearl Harbor and the Solomon Islands, complained always about Hollywood's omissions.

In the movies, Win pointed out, nobody ever got sick. But in the South Pacific—not the musical, but the actual theatre of operations—Win had contracted malaria, dengue fever, and whenever possible, the clap. In the movies, bullets passed through shoulders, hands, or the fleshy part of a thigh. Win assured me that hot flying metal was just as likely to tear the meat off the arm or shatter the bones or lodge in the intestines or snap the spine or strip the skin from the face and leave the skull glaring back, naked and white.

"Body parts," Win explained in a hoarse and confidential whisper as we stood in line at the snack bar, waiting out the twenty-five-minute intermission between Hell Is for Heroes and The Wackiest Ship in the Army. "Body parts is what they always leave out." Win's half-dollar skidded across the glass counter and landed on the Ben Franklin side. We scraped up two sacks of popcorn, each stamped in red and black newsprint with the terrifying faces of cartoon clowns. "Pieces of men," hissed my uncle, purchasing a twelve-ounce paper cup of Pabst Blue Ribbon drawn from a cold keg underneath the counter. He slowly lifted the cup to his mouth, denying himself its pleasure by quarter-inches, and then he splashed down a mouthful. Pabst Blue Ribbon smelled to me like the night's stale cigarettes and Wednesday morning's fresh white bread straight off the Langendorf truck. "They're scattered here and there," said Win. "My sweet Jesus Christ, you wanted to puke—did you ever, Little Slick." He stroked my head with the same firm, soothing touch he usually reserved for Joe Louis, his dachshund. "Bodies piled up like firewood. Everybody's afraid, that's the plain God's truth. Everybody's afraid, all the time."

After the war, my uncle read more deeply into the events that his own participation had originally obscured. He picked up William Shirer's *Rise and Fall of the Third Reich*, but lost interest around the Battle of the Bulge. He nearly finished *The Naked and the Dead*, though it dragged on far too long, like the war itself. Eisenhower's opus, *Crusade in Europe*, presented a more basic problem. For Win, the war had not been a crusade. He likened the war to a highway pileup, a vast wreck of jagged metal and human guts, a cataclysm.

"During the war," Win once wistfully explained after I had reached the age of nine or ten and needed to know, "things were fucked up bad, boy. They were truly fucked up beyond belief."

Guys shot their buddies by mistake; he had seen it happen.

Ships downed their own planes.

Planes bombed their troops.

Besides the blunders, there were the dumb rumors. Soldiers feared they'd be docked a quarter of their pay if they lost any equipment in battle. Sailors believed Tokyo Rose was really Amelia Earhart and the Watts towers in Los Angeles were actually Japanese broadcast stations. Even the officers whispered about allied agents dropped behind the German lines dressed as nuns, about Boston priests with thick Irish brogues working as clandestine Gestapo cell commandos with orders from Himmler to assassinate Harry Hopkins. Berlin was smoldering and Germany was in revolt. Hitler was infected with rabies, insane, foaming at the mouth; he was being treated by a veterinarian. Eva Braun, a secret agent of Eleanor Roosevelt's (and the former lover of Admiral Bull Halsey), had cut the Fuhrer's throat in bed.

The war would be over in a month, a week, by Saturday.

The war had been over for six months already, but the army brass wanted to keep marching until they reached Moscow.

When the news finally came about Japan, the tremendous news that the Americans had dropped a big bomb, a really big beautiful bomb, and the war truly was over, nobody could believe that one at first either. "Thank you, God," prayed my Uncle Win, crying at his ship bunk, "thank you, thank you, thank you, even though I don't believe in you. Thank you for ending this war because it has been truly more fucked up than anybody will ever know."

I listened to every word my uncle told me, and wondered when I would be ready to take my place in the barbarous world.

———

"What do you think the worst torture would be?" asked the Mad Professor.

His real name was Philip Barnes, and he lived down the block in a house slabbered twice over with coats of fire-enginered enamel and a team of three-foot-high ceramic Negro jockeys posted at each corner of his lawn. Phil was a year older than me, small for his age with skin the color of paste, an asthmatic with a propensity for pinkeye and bloody noses. But Phil also possessed a Gilbert chemistry set and microscope—and thus, his nickname. We were best friends.

"I wouldn't want to be covered with honey and staked out in the woods on top of a giant red ant hill," I admitted. I pictured ants with crimson faces like savage Apaches. Their giant pincers would be as sharp as lawn shears. "Or get torn apart by German shepherds."

"German shepherds really aren't that bad," said Benny Chang, an expert on dogs ever since his family had brought home a rat terrier from the pound. "But you wouldn't want the Romans to crucify you, especially if they nail you upsidedown."

The three of us sat Indian-style, feet folded flexibly under our rumps. We plucked longish grass blades from Phil's front lawn.

"I heard about this guy," I offered, "who the Germans, or the Japs, or somebody, tied a wire cage onto his head and inside it they put three starving rats."

"So what happened?" Benny asked. His eyes bulged like a toad.

"They ate his brain."

"Cool."

"When his platoon found him, two of the rats had their heads peeking out of his empty eye sockets. Like a Halloween pumpkin."

"What happened to the third rat?" Benny wondered.

I shrugged. I hadn't considered the third rat.

"Where'd you ever hear that?" demanded Phil, squinting hard.

"From you," I said. "Remember? At least, most of it."

He thought it over. "I don't think it was the Germans. It was probably the Russians. Or the Belgians. I'd have to ask my Dad."

"Maybe it was the Americans."

"What kind of American would tie a starving rat on somebody's head, Benny?"

"I wish I could." Benny Chang lathered his hands together, one over the other over the other, a miniature ghoul.

"It was the Chinese," Phil definitely concluded.

"Oh, I don't think—"

"Yeah, Benny, Chinese water torture. What about Chinese water torture, Benny?"

Phil and I plugged Benny persistently on either shoulder, demanding the truth. "I don't know," he cried out, "my family never did any of that stuff!"

In matters of water torture, etcetera, Phil was the expert. He had earned his reputation as the Mad Professor through the evil works involving his Gilbert chemistry set, manipulating test tubes, Petri dishes, and fatbellied beakers to conduct various experiments of the demented variety. Phil boiled worms in Pyrex bowls atop his Bunsen burner. He speculated whether a house fly could still fly with sewing pins stuck through one eye (it could not) and where a moth would land once it had been soaked in alcohol and set aflame (it landed directly on the garage cement floor, below his father's workbench, a butcher's block of stinking chemicals and tiny gore). It was all for science, he declared. Mad science.

Our long summer afternoons of dismemberment and murder were inspired in part by a lavish black-and-white photo book owned by Phil's father entitled *The Horrors of War: Europe and the Pacific, 1939-1945.* "The gory book," as we called it, showed the human damage the newspapers of the era would have never allowed: torsos opened sternum to belly, like wet valises; soldiers holding up for the camera their souvenirs—an ear, fingers, a foot. The image that excited Phil most depicted Japanese infantry standing over ditches with shovels, burying old men alive in Manchuria. One afternoon, he suggested that we bury Benny alive in our backyard. I reminded him that if we buried Benny, we would just be acting like the enemy.

Some confusion frequently arose regarding Benny's identity: friend or foe? But then our entire neighborhood had been founded upon the complex shifting allegiances of international enmity. Washington Manor owed its existence to Okinawa, El Alamein, Cassino, Normandy. We acknowledged this complicated debt through the games we played, aiming a straightened arm like a standard issue M1 rifle, sounding the boom, and expecting from the other side the cooperation of immediate, artful death. For hours we practiced dying, conferring presence upon the battle tales we had heard all our lives from our fathers and uncles.

Most deadly marksmanship involved the upper body; the heart was a magnet for mortal injury. I made a study of grabbing my chest at its misplaced center, shrieking and falling backward, allowing my head to hit and bounce several times upon the spongy dichondra. I practiced writhing on the cement sidewalk like bacon. We all draped our corpses like strings of Christmas popcorn over the bright young juniper and honeysuckle bushes planted by our mothers, across the new red-brick flower beds erected by our fathers, until watchful parents stormed out of the house to order us back to life and into somebody else's yard for a change. We died all day and into the early evening after dinner. Yet the nationality of the lifeless young bodies scattered across the lawns and sidewalks remained vague and troubling.

Which war, exactly, were we playing? There had been two big wars, we knew; then over time, we heard about quite a few more. The Chestnut brothers, Vincent and Daniel, came from Tennessee, and they always wanted to wage a civil war in which the Confederacy improbably won. It was safer to be a dead German. At play in suburbia, a dead German was as common as a dead Indian. When somebody dragged in the Russians or the Chinese or the Greeks because of a grandmother or weird aunt with troubling stories to tell about firing squads, famine, or even more incomprehensible civil wars in foreign places where nobody even spoke English, the results were complicated and unsatisfying, and soon peace was proclaimed. We all returned home for dinner and the war that still raged in tract home suburbia settled back down until another day.

————

My Uncle Win despised our most righteous warrior, General Douglas MacArthur.

"Dugout Doug!"

He was shouting over a sirloin steak in our small dining room. My father had just informed Win that MacArthur would have made an excellent president, a proposition Dad believed no more than he expected Win to suddenly sprout wings and flap out the bay window.

"President MacArthur!" objected Win. "It turns my stomach to even think about it."

Mom splattered a dollop of instant mashed potatoes on Win's plate, hoping there would not be a fight. I glanced at my father as he frowned to himself and schemed. My uncle believed all the stories about MacArthur drowning his wife's lover in a Philippines swimming pool and evacuating Corregidor with a refrigerator full of wild pheasant and a mattress stuffed with gold coins. A battle, I knew, could not be avoided.

"MacArthur saved you swabbies," said Dad, striking first.

Win stared at the instant mashed potatoes in horror as though their rising white mounds might contain the General himself. "Like hell, Slick!"

"Don't you swear in my house!" Dad hammered the edge of his plate with the blade of his knife. It chimed raggedly. "Profanity," he explained, slicing off a jagged strip of sirloin steak and waving it in the air like a head on a pike, "is the sign of a crude person that can't express himself."

"That son of a bitch bastard," Win said calmly, "can burn forever in fucking hell."

Mom turned in my direction. "If you're done eating," she said, "you can go outside now and play."

I shook my head and studied Dad, who was studying the situation. He was a keen strategist of the household skirmish, a Rommel of contrariness.

"Slick," pleaded Win, "you think about how he fired on the bonus marchers back in Washington in 1932. Veterans themselves. You remember that? The bastard."

"Don't you use that word in my house!"

"I didn't mean nothing."

"What is a bastard?" I wondered.

"Shut up," explained Dad.

"Can't we just have a nice dinner?" asked my mother, really pleading to herself.

"You don't remember it," argued my father. "You weren't there."

"You saying it didn't happen?"

"Yes, of course it happened. Sweet Jesus, didn't you ever read a newspaper in all those years? Or were you too busy getting yourself in trouble?"

Win gathered his wits; he contemplated retreat.

"Anyway, what do you have against him?" My father set down his fork and knife on either side of the plate, framing the meat and the mounds of instant mashed potatoes, a portrait of postwar dinner perfection. "What personal harm did the man ever do you?" He sensed his brother's weakness and prodded. "Well?"

Win took a bite of sirloin and chewed. He swallowed. He turned to me and smiled sadly. "In New Guinea," he began, rousing himself to the effort of recalling the worst time of his life, "everybody I ever talked to—and I swear to God this is true, Little Slick—they all said MacArthur kept a private cow all to himself so he could drink cold, fresh milk when the ordinary soldiers didn't have nothing."

There it was. My father grinned in triumph. "He never had a cow."

"How do you know that?"

"MacArthur had no cow." Dad pushed his plate away, and wiped his mouth with a paper napkin. He drew a deep breath, and exhaled his satisfaction; in effect, declaring victory. "And even if he did, how could he keep the milk cold?"

"You admit it!"

"Having a cow in New Guinea or not having a cow in New Guinea, cows being neither here nor there," my father reasoned, "is a big fat NOTHING! I wouldn't have ever voted for MacArthur for better reasons than a cow."

"Name one." His appetite ruined, Win still clung valiantly to the cow.

"Like the man can't obey an order. Like the crazy sonofabitch wanted to run our army over the border into Red China during Korea, despite what Truman told him. Maybe blow up the whole damn world. Win, livestock just doesn't enter into the picture."

My uncle silently regarded my father, this monument of opposition.

"God damn it, Slick, sometimes I don't even know where you stand."

"Good," replied Dad. "That's the way I like it."

———

One afternoon, we met in Washington Manor Park directly around the corner from my house to examine the gory book for the hundredth time. We sprawled across the grass beneath a budding elm tree, poring for a full hour over the volume's illustrated atrocities.

The carnage was thrilling: splinters of leg bones erupting through skin like a cracked baseball bat, a head held by its hair—all the body parts Win said they always left out. Then we got distracted when a Basset Hound dashed past with his owner in pursuit, the dog chasing a squirrel up a branch of the elm. I settled back on the lawn, hands locked behind my head, and stared at the clouds scattered across the blue sky like pieces of a puzzle. The ancient world of our fathers receded from interest.

Finally, Benny rose from the grass to affirm his boredom. He produced a jackknife from his jeans front pocket, admitting that he had pirated it from his dad's toolbox. Benny flung the knife into the elm. Cursing under his breath, pretending to have in his clutches Hirohito himself, he attacked the tree repeatedly. He completely stripped the bark off one side, and then I joined him for the remainder. A small, pleasant lifetime passed. Eventually, the Mad Professor located a two-page spread showing the American troops liberating Dachau. He flagged it above his head, attempting to revive our enthusiasm. Phil passed me the book, and I stared in silent disbelief at its pages, the starving, hollow-eyed men and women with arms and legs like broomsticks staring back at me. Bodies were stacked up in the distance, as Win had described, like firewood. My mouth fell open with guilty wonder.

"My uncle was a war hero," I blurted out in response to this horror beyond comprehension, this impossibility. "His ship was bombed at Pearl Harbor."

My declaration seemed to clear the air, the stench of cruelty dissipated amid some vague condition of valor.

Benny leaned into Phil's lap, reached for the book, and flipped wildly through its pages until he found a section titled, "Blood-and-Guts Soaked Sand: The Battle for the Pacific." The chapter opened with a two-page spread picturing the flamboyant devastation of Pearl Harbor.

"There's my uncle's ship," I stated, pointing impulsively to the largest vessel in the photograph. Flames licked its deck, and terrific columns of water thrust up from either side like cyclones plunged from the depths of the sea. On the shore, marines ineffectually pinged their rifles at the Japanese Zeroes, the circles under the aircrafts' wings radiating a nauseating red glow. The skies seemed streaked with paint, buckets of black, white, and gray poured down from the heavens. A brilliant puff of smoke rose to cover the flat, orange disc illuminating the Pacific, and all around the harbor, the water was burning.

"Did everybody on his ship drown?" asked Benny.

I took a stab at how catastrophe actually unfolds. "About half."

Phil studied the photograph, searching for flaws. "Getting sunk," he finally decided, "doesn't necessarily mean you're a hero. My dad was a war hero and he was never sunk."

Benny pried his eyes away from the photographs.

"Does your dad have a bunch of tattoos? Was he captain of a ship?"

"No, but he was once secretary to a guy who worked for an admiral."

Benny's lips puckered into a puzzle of disappointment: "Secretary?"

"My uncle was sunk twice. After Pearl Harbor, they fixed up his ship, sailed out into the Pacific to chase the Japs, and he got sunk again. The second time, his ship went straight to the bottom of the ocean."

This ideal phrase hung in the air: straight to the bottom. I shifted my eyes toward Phil and saw him silently calculating: Did getting sunk twice unavoidably equal a hero?

"So how did your uncle get out of there alive?" asked Benny, still poised for admiration.

The night of the battle, Win had told me, was starless and cold. Twenty months after Pearl Harbor, in the Solomon Islands between Kolombangara and New Georgia, at the Battle of Kula Gulf, a Japanese destroyer hit his ship shortly past two in the morning, firing three consecutive twenty-four-inch torpedoes, tearing off the bow. After the explosion and the sudden jolt, the screech of metal folding in upon itself, Win could see only smoke, gray over black. Then the sky lit up with returning volleys of fire and in the suffocating haze, he heard feet tripping upon the deck. Orders to haul down the lifeboats. The wrenching whine of metal, the disintegration of the superstructure. Orders to abandon ship.

In the water, the blackness was relieved only by the light of burning cargo, the percussive eruption of munitions. Win clung to a hot shard of the bow. Pools of oil boiled frantically around him. In another instant, he was swept by the current into the astonishing chill of the ocean. Within twenty-five minutes, the ship tipped, pointed its stern to the cloudy night sky, and sank straight to the bottom of the ocean. Win passed the night in the water, paddling slowly towards distant shore.

Throughout his life, my uncle was prepared to relate these events in hungry detail. But what happened on the island constituted another matter.

One-hundred-sixty men struggled to ground, riding buoyant slivers of wreckage or swimming two full miles to the island of Vella Lavella, north of Kolombangara. They hid in the jungle from Japanese scouts, sheltered by Australian coast watchers who had been protected themselves for two years by the native islanders who despised the invaders. The islanders instructed the sailors how to catch, cook, and eat snakes and lizards. How to identify the venomous species. How to bury your dead at sea during the night undetected. The skies shone pink and purple, the sea smelled of rosewater. The squawk of cockatoos made sunrise roil with music.

In the late afternoons, Win recalled, there were butterflies the size of both his hands—thumbs met, fingers spread wide. Queen Victoria birdwings, they were called; splotches of yellow, black, and seaweed-green flitting down from the trees. They looked like rainbows peeled from the azure sky, their paisley patterns melting in the sun. The butterflies' wing spans measured two-hundred-fifty millimeters. Win had looked them up after returning home to make certain they were real.

A few days before a half-dozen U.S. destroyers dashed up the Solomon slot from Tulagi to rescue the ship's survivors, the sailors at last encountered the enemy. The Aussies had shared their rifles and knives; the sailors killed three Japanese scouts close to camp and wounded another, an officer they took prisoner who chattered day and night in chirpy, agonized English. After two days, the guards drew straws to take the prisoner into the jungle and kill him.

I always imagined that my uncle had been the one to cut the prisoner's throat, though he would never say one way or the other.

I concentrated on the scores of black-and-white images, searching for Win's face amid the legions of young sailors, soldiers, and marines. I almost expected to find Win smiling back to me through the years, bloodied, vengeful, triumphant, gloriously alive.

"Look," said Phil, reading my mind, "there's your uncle!" His eyelashes batted madly.

"Where?"

Phil had flipped to a fullpage photo of four marines, backs turned to the camera, scrambling in formation across a windswept beach. In the near distance, three spindly palm trees bowed in the wind, indicating the cover the men sought under fire.

Phil squealed: "He's running away from the Japs!"

You couldn't see their faces. Just four fleeing bodies, backs bent, their long legs in halfstride, arms swinging a spade or gripped around a rifle stock. Desperate young men in uniform: they could have been anybody's uncle, and in another instant, they might die.

I craned my neck over Phil's lap and stared at the photograph. Four young men doing what they had to do, which was run like hell. If they survived, they might have returned home to build our houses and pave our streets. They were so foreign and so familiar. Maybe they lived next door and worked in a machine shop or warehouse. They were our fathers and uncles, our neighbors, and this photograph contained some part of their story that could never be conveyed: the indisputable terror borne on the other side of the world when they had been preposterously young.

"Let me see," I demanded, reaching for the book.

"No!" shouted the Mad Professor. He gripped his corner and yanked, and I felt the binding tremble before it separated, the paper screeching like a frenzied animal.

The book tore in two, dividing straight down its cheap binding, and we each held half in our hands. Phil gasped, straining to comprehend the mystery of this familiar object now occupying two places at once. Shaking off disbelief, he swept my portion into his own hands, clapped the two halves together, and gingerly set the broken book under the shade of the elm like a wounded bird.

And the next thing I knew, his small, balled-up fist was very quickly and very forcefully driving its knuckles into my face, knocking me flat on the ground.

————

"So tell me, Little Slick." Win grinned at my eye. "Just how big was the kid who gave you the shiner?"

I tried to grin back since I seemed to have something to be proud of.

"I don't know." I shrugged manfully.

My left eye had already swollen shut, surrounded by the immediate blue bruise.

"Here," he coaxed, "like this." Win paced out a defensive stance figuring a three-quarters-moon on his living room carpet. He smelled faintly of Old Times. "Hold your fists in front of your face. Don't worry what you look like."

I raised my fists to guard my chin and checked my stance in the picture window mirror. I looked terrific.

"No, no, this way," said Win. His own fists rose like two big cannons.

I had headed straight to Win's house knowing there would be no sympathy for me at home if I told Dad how I got my black eye. The bruising would have only elicited commentary about the sanctity of other people's property, reflecting finally on my own irresponsibility. Win sized up the world with fewer complications.

"That's right," he instructed, "but higher." My uncle cocked his head, studying my hands.

Then he faked with his right, bobbled his shoulders to either side, thrust his jaw forward with that tricky elastic drop of the head he had perfected as a navy brawler, and plowed his left fist into my midsection.

Stretched out face-up and flattened upon the living room carpet, I could not catch my breath. The world concentrated in my solar plexus. I pleaded for air. I tried to shout that I was okay: I was more than okay. I was happy, I was great, I was just a kid sparring with my uncle, a war hero. But I could only bleat gamely, and gaze up at my uncle.

In my airless bubble, I watched his fat, stinking cigar plugged into his cock-eyed grin, his hardy snowman's face rearranged into a lopsided, crewcut, bourbon-flushed, brokennosed disaster. Win stared down at me with undisguised longing. He must have been forty by then. Still trim, fit, rippling with muscles; still working the line at the cannery, stacking boxes ten hours each night during peach and tomato season. He would have enjoyed a son of his own to jab and dodge and merrily punch in the stomach.

I wriggled across the carpet on my back and propped up my elbows on either side, lifting my chest six inches from the floor.

"Now get up and take a poke at me."

I leapt to my feet and swung wildly.

"That's right, but higher."

I swung, and he brushed my fist away.

"Again."

I laughed and swung deliriously and missed by a mile.

"Again!"

I swung again, the same wobbly trajectory. But harder this time. I nicked his open palm.

"You know Philip Barnes?" I asked Win, easing into the specifics of retaliation. My chest rose and fell with heavy breaths. It rose and fell.

"No."

"Yes," I insisted, "you do. Phil. My friend."

Win stared down at me over his often-broken nose. "You mean that little goofy kid with the glasses?"

"He's a year older than me," I corrected. And then to make certain that Win was still on my side, I unforgivably added: "Mr. Barnes is his Dad."

"Barnes?"

Lloyd Barnes was one of the neighborhood's eternal veterans, a fusty little man with the trim build of a cat and a brown moustache penciled over his upper lip in the exacting manner of Alec Guinness in *The Bridge on the River Kwai*. Win worked with him at the cannery and he loathed him.

"He was secretary to an admiral."

"Sec-re-tary!" Win thrust forward his jaw, instinctively baring his teeth, and I knew I had maneuvered him back into my corner. Win hated officers. To my uncle, an officer was any guy in a uniform or suit who gave orders and liked it, who believed that command was his right and duty. Throughout the war, Win had back-talked, taunted, and spit in the direction of the young junior naval officers who passed their time in the splintering shack barrooms of Olongapo and Honolulu. He had cheerfully spread the rumor among local girls in Pacific port cities that the blue sash on an officer's jacket meant he had contracted syphilis.

I delivered a solid little punch to my uncle's ribs and stepped back, dropping my hands, admiring the damage.

"Now that was a nice tap," he admitted, grinning through a flicker of pain. He eased to the ground in a crouch, gently squaring my shoulders in his two big hands. He looked straight into my eyes. "When I know I'm going to have to fight somebody," he explained solemnly, his breathing a little faster, a little deeper, "I hit him first and square on. Then get the hell out." He caressed my cheek with his fingertips, his calloused thumb brushing too close to the puckered blue fringe of my eye.

I flinched.

"Did I hurt you?" he asked.

I shook my head.

"I know it's hard to stand up right away when somebody's knocked you down. But you got to do it, or they won't never leave you alone. You understand?"

I tried to envision the Mad Professor as a dangerous aggressor, a threat to our suburb's tranquility.

"You understand me?" demanded Win.

I nodded, realizing that on this point at least my father would have readily agreed. At times, you had to take a stand and what happened next didn't really matter. After that, my uncle was speaking entirely for himself.

"Don't wear your Keds. Borrow some work boots, if you can get 'em. Mine are too big for you, so don't give me that look. Now listen. First step you take, you stomp on the little bastard's ankle as hard as you can, maybe you break it."

This prospect made me smile, it made me breathe a little faster.

"It's fair," Win assured me. "Everything's fair, if the son of a bitch thinks he rules the world."

———

The next day, I located Phil in the park, flicking Benny's jackknife into the elm.

"Your eye's really big," he said, turning from the tree's branching shadow to face me. I stood at arm's length while he scrutinized my damaged face as though it were the map of an amazing country.

"I know." I tried to interpret Phil's interest as a formal apology and I thought for a moment that we could forget the whole thing. The sprinklers were twirling fullblast, the scent of damp concrete rising off the ground. Then I wondered if he was making fun of me.

"You deserved it," Phil said flatly. He pivoted and flung the jackknife into the heart of the elm. The blade lodged in the wood and trilled; the handle vibrated. He had probably already told his father about the gory book, blaming Benny and me for everything.

"You want to fight?" I demanded.

He studied the knife in the tree. "No." And then, more obligingly: "Do you?" I didn't answer.

Along the park's perimeter, at the edge of the lawn maybe fifty yards away, stood a row of white and gray stucco houses with the occasional frantic pastel trim, the aggregate riches of Washington Manor. The houses faced either west or south, but otherwise looked exactly the same. A man ambled across the roof of a gray one, a tool belt strapped around his overalls, a hammer dangling from one hand. He stared off into the sky, contemplating the clouds or the setting sun or maybe the flock of gulls sailing overhead toward the landfill shore of the bay. He balanced like a sailor on a great ship's rolling deck, rocked by the waves as he gazed out at the ocean beneath the burning sun. He looked like somebody waiting for the enemy, certain they were coming.

"Look," said the Mad Professor, withdrawing the jackknife from the tree's wound. The blade glistened with sap. "Benny let me take his knife home to sharpen it. It wouldn't cut anything before. Now watch."

He selected from a dangling leaf of the elm a fat, fuzzy black caterpillar with a brown-orange stripe running down its back. He tenderly placed the caterpillar on the trunk of the tree and drew the blade across its middle, dividing the insect cleanly. It wriggled with the madness of pain. Both halves still clung to the bark.

The Mad Professor and I had in the past extinguished a small nation of insects. But what flitted through my mind now were the Queen Victoria birdwings on Vella Lavella, black, yellow, and seaweed green, with wingspans the size of two hands. In our own living room, Win had shown me the butterflies in the pages of the *World Book Encyclopedia*. He had seen them himself, gloriously alive, when he was young.

"You shouldn't hurt them," I told the Mad Professor, pointing to the caterpillar smeared across the flaking bark. "They turn into something beautiful."

"This one won't."

So I stepped hard on Phil's left foot and struck him somewhere in the face, knocking off his glasses. His nose gushed blood, instantly soaking his cotton shirt. Then I swung at him a lot, though I was aiming pretty wildly. He went down waving his arms, slicing the air and missing me entirely. I fell, too, and then more hands slashed at the air, both of us forgetting to clench our fists.

We rolled across the lawn, our legs entangled like trellis vines. When we scraped to a sudden stop, Phil started to cough and wheeze, struggling for breath, and then his face flushed scarlet and he looked terrified.

I threw my weight upon him, pinned him to the ground, my knees upon his shoulders, my hands locating his throat. I could feel the breath of his entire body rasping in my grip, chirping like an insect. I wanted to cry, a rage of tears.

"Give!" I barked into Phil's face. My spittle basted his pink cheeks. I gouged both thumbs into the hard pulp center of his throat.

"Give!" I pleaded.

Phil wagged his head, shut his eyes.

I kept squeezing, harder still, and then with a shriek all the air leaked out from my chest and I knew that I was going to be the one who surrendered. I rolled off Phil, collapsing flat on my back alongside him, arms and legs flapped across the lawn. The scent of wet concrete filled the air like poison gas. I didn't know that Phil was crying until he stopped.

Our chests rose and fell. I listened to Phil breathing and I knew he was listening to me. Later—how many dreamy seconds?—I turned my head toward the row of identical houses, and I spotted the man in the overalls now back on his roof, obliviously inspecting his chimney, not even looking our direction. I felt ashamed, insufficient to the task that circumstance had set before me. Not a killer. Not yet.

Phil whispered, "You're bleeding."

I inspected the small gash across my knuckles.

"I couldn't breathe," he explained. He wiped the damp from around his eyes.

I had wanted to kill him, and although I was glad that I had not, I did not regret the feeling. "You're bleeding, too." I pressed one finger against his cheek, holding it there for more than a moment too long.

The moon was beginning to rise over the elm, although the sky was still light, the blue melting into indigo, a shade of the islands. We were lucky boys, beneficiaries of the remorseless young men who had incinerated the cities of Europe and Japan, conquered the world, constructed the present peace.

"If Benny wants to be one of us," said Phil, "he'll need to slice open one of his veins with his dad's knife. Then we'll see." He tossed one ankle over the other and folded his hands behind his head, cozy and maniacal. "Blood brothers," he explained.

I could see some stars through the blue wooly sky as it began to fade to black. In another hour, there would be a million more stars, Washington

Manor still too small a place to wash away their glow. The heavens were as bright, cold, and untouchable as the sand and plaster sparkles of our living room ceiling. Later in the week, I might ask Win for another boxing lesson, and he would probably knock me to the ground, and I would struggle to stand up, breathless and safe at home.

the snow, the girl
Sharon Solwitz

the snow, the girl

Snow was coming down faster than the Evanston plows could handle, and Allan was the only idiot on the road. But he had a mission. Approaching Whole Foods he pumped the brake. He peered through the passenger seat window, nearly opaque with frost. Lights were on in the store—that, he could see. On the smooth soles of the loafers that he had been wearing when the idea struck, he slid across the sidewalk. The door was locked but people were walking around inside. A guy was sweeping. Allan pounded on the glass. We're closed, the guy mouthed. Allan put his palms together in the universal sign for please, and the sweeper made a pitying face. Can't. Sorry.

Allan saw now the painted sign on the door: they closed at ten. His watch said ten forty-seven. Numbers swirled, snow swirled, the tiny, sharp-edged flakes that come when it's near zero. Forces were propelling him home, but were they the Forces of Good? His ex-wife, fascinated by life's nasty ironies, had once showed him a magazine article about a woman who felt a lump in her breast. Having a long summer trip planned and because the news might be bad, the woman put off seeing the doctor. She signed her own death certificate, said the writer of the article, a line that had filled him with dread even when the problem was hypothetical.

So at five minutes to eleven, snow beating on his windshield like the wrath of God, Allan was driving down to the Whole Foods in the city, where people stayed up late. He needed taro root—which the Jewel wouldn't have—to be ground up along with fresh ginger in the food processor. Logic told him there was a difference between waiting six weeks and waiting until Nate came home from school tomorrow. Logic also had its opinions about the efficacy of a remedy that came from a book called *How to Cure Advanced Cancer*. But in his mind's eye tumor cells fattened, divided, divided again, fast as irrational thought. His current—his preferred, beloved—wife had once said, "With everything there's a time when it's just too late," although she was referring to her chief complaint about him, his reluctance to say what he was thinking, a problem he surely had the power to remedy.

He shook the snow off his jacket, his shoes, out of his hair. He felt impervious to cold—not young but strong, unstoppable. He could drive all night, if that's what it took. East of the sun and west of the moon. He could climb mountains of glass.

Ordinarily Allan wasn't a man who did crazy things. He was—or at least believed other people thought him to be—on the timorous side. Boring, he'd warned Thea when the question of marriage came up, not wanting her to be disappointed. What you see is what you get. He was fifteen years older than Thea, and the riskiest thing he'd ever done in his life (apart from marrying Barbara, though he didn't know it at the time) was ask her out to dinner—Theadora Levinson, a student in his second-year Structures, twenty-five years old and flirting with everybody including him. They didn't sleep together until the class was over, and they didn't get married until she had graduated, but still it was uncharacteristic. He was kidded gently, and thought up worse against himself: *Randy old man, thinks he's a stud.* He was embarrassed for an entire semester, with students, colleagues, anyone who cast a glance at him.

But his shame gradually abated. Thea got a design job, for which she traveled at times, her starting salary barely less than his. She turned out to be surprisingly practical, a good manager of their mutual lives. They had children. Eventually they were accepted as a couple, and now had as many friends as he and Barbara had had, mutual friends who had sided with him, and some of the new hires at his school, who were starting to have their own children. The difference in their ages seemed to attract a range of interesting people. Things were going so well he was nervous as well as pleased. Not that, when disaster struck, he had been ready.

The wind blew harder, snow coming straight off the lake. He turned the wipers on high. He drove slowly, sliding but not too badly, in the middle of the street. He wasn't on top of things but he was nearing the top.

He was turning onto Sheridan when his cell phone rang. His heart folded in half, as it had been doing this past year at such sounds. The phone was in his jacket pocket, but he could hardly take hold of it let alone open it. He pulled toward what he thought was the curb, saw HOME on the little screen, said in a voice he tried ineffectively to lighten, "You caught me."

"What's going on, Allan?"

He told her, without expecting concurrence. Yes, it was crazy. He heard her swallowing over the phone. Her voice strained with patience.

"It's nuts. This weird Holy Grail kind of thing."

"I know," he said, hoping accord would soothe her. He had to get moving.

There were tears in her voice. "You know, I was hoping, Allan, that tonight we could . . ."

"You were asleep."

"You could have woken me."

"I wish I had," he said, not untruthfully. She clucked like a woman twice her age.

"It's for you, not for him."

"I know," he said. "Forgive me?"

As he nosed back onto the road, he asked her to do him a favor. Call the downtown Whole Foods and call him back with the hours. If it were closed he'd turn around. Minutes later she reported, to her dismay and his relief, that the Whole Foods on North Avenue was open until midnight. "Thea," he said, "I don't deserve you."

She didn't respond, but it was okay. Moving swiftly, defroster blasting, he blessed the city snowplows and the tires he'd recently bought, a compromise between economy and traction. Eastward along the drive the frozen crests of Lake Michigan glittered under the streetlamps like the tusked maws of sea animals. He wasn't tired, and soon enough he'd be back in the marital bed. The thought suddenly aroused him. Sex wasn't much on their agenda these days, but it was beckoning now. He accelerated into the flying snow, off to get his son what, if Thea were right—God, let her be right—he didn't need.

It was almost a year to the day, the middle of January, when the book of his life changed from comedy of manners to possible tragedy. He was fifty-four, Nate twelve, Dylan nine (and Thea forty, but who was counting?) when Nate was diagnosed with a variant of Ewing's sarcoma, so rare in the United States that only four hundred children a year came down with it, mostly prepubescent boys. Nate's wasn't in the bone, where it commonly was, but in the belly, which had gotten so large by the end of December that Allan had kidded him about his paunch. Now, of course, Allan hated himself. Hated? Loathed, despised himself. As if he were two people, one of whom would have noticed and acted. But the other, the dolt, was in charge, and in dreamland—until a basketball game when Nate ran out of breath in the second quarter for the first time in his life. To the ER doctor, Allan had said, "Do you think he has asthma?"—still on the comfortable, the mildly anxious side of medical problems. Until the X-ray showed Nate's lungs awash with a fluid that turned out to have come from his abdomen, which housed a tumor the size—it still seemed incredible—of a football.

Now Nate was in remission, that fair-weather friend of a medical word. Promising nothing. Having trusted in his sons' quasi immortality, Allan craved other things to trust. He wished he'd gone to medical instead of architecture school. He read books he used to laugh at: *How to Cure Cancer*, and the sequel, *How to Cure Advanced Cancer*. "As the mixture dries there will be the sensation of heat but do not be alarmed it is the work of the poultice upon the tumor." The word "poultice" reminded him of nineteenth-century remedies for gangrene, and he had to ignore the run-on sentence, but he'd read elsewhere that heat was being used successfully against certain kinds of tumors. And from taro and ginger, applied externally, there would be no side effects. The past year Nate had suffered multitudinous side effects. "Here's our side-effect man!" one of his doctors would say. "The side-effect king!" Allan would laugh, since Nate usually did—when the mouth sores let him. Nate was now four months into his remission, and in two more months a scan would extend or cancel it. But even if it held, Allan would never again relax his vigilance. Allan, who'd razzed his dangerously ill son about a pot belly.

Tonight after dinner, his vigilance had spotted something he hadn't mentioned to Thea yet. In profile, in a tight tee-shirt and low riding jeans Nate's belly had looked . . . not as it had when it was full of fluid, but . . . rounder . . . than right after the surgery. He might be wrong. His lapse had no doubt over-sensitized him. He knew what Thea would have said, had he told her: All his friends are gaining weight; it's what happens before the growth spurt. And, honey, he just finished eating!

Still, tomorrow he'd ask Friedman for an early scan. And tonight, according to instructions, he, beyond logic, would grind up the taro and ginger and apply it to his son's abdomen, his personal weapon against his son's cancer, and probably against his own terror and weakness. So what?

At the back of a large parking lot the downtown Whole Foods looked no more promising than the one in Evanston. The place was lit up, but so had the other been. The lot spread in all directions like a landscape in an anxiety dream—no yellow lines of demarcation, just a vast white flatness marred by an occasional mound. He parked by the entrance, daring the door to be locked.

It was.

He screamed, an exhalation of impotence and unsurprise, loud in his ears and then gone into the blowing snow. Vanished, like a car sliding off a foggy road. He pressed his face to the glass of the door. Inside, there were some people at cash registers. Eschewing the pleading stance, which hadn't worked in Evanston, he beat on the glass with his knuckles and the flat of his hand. And, miracle of miracles, someone unlocked it—a young woman with crayon orange hair and a ring in her lower lip. "You're an angel," he said.

"We closed early. Like, dude, who was going to go out in this?"

She didn't sound critical of him, or impressed either, just matter of fact, like most kids her age. It was the generational effect. His undergrads would compete in mocking things that should have filled them with wonder: The Carson Pirie Scott Building, its proportions (forget the filigree); the long, low repeating windows of the Robey House. They'd seen it all. Allan, who felt he hadn't seen anything, bought a Whole Foods shopping bag made of recycled materials and filled it with what looked like dirty brown turnips. He chose a large prettily branching piece of ginger, and then, in Vitamins, something that promised natural relief for the migraine that was threatening. But on the whole he felt a slight relief from the tension that had been building since after dinner. When he got home, he would make his poultice and apply it while the boy slept (they'd taken out his central line, but Nate still slept on his back). Then he would make love to Thea. Thanking the cashier and everyone he passed in the store, he exited with his purchases and only a tinge of self-castigation for not having brought one of the many shopping bags they saved at home.

Out in the parking lot his car had become another white mound. Luckily he'd parked close to the store and hadn't locked the door. He tossed the bag in back. It was only when he opened the driver's door to retrieve the snow scraper that he saw he wasn't alone. There was someone in the passenger seat.

Jesus, a carjacking! But the thought was so fleeting his heart barely lurched. The intruder was female, and smiling. Since Nate had gotten sick, Allan hadn't passed a homeless person on the street without giving to him, was only glad that in the winter there were fewer of them around. Now he opened his wallet, which held a twenty and three five-dollar bills. "I'm sorry, ma'am. You have to get out. Here, take this." He walked around to the passenger side, opened the door, and held out one of the fives the way you'd lure a squirrel or a dog you were training.

She laughed. "Thanks, but what I really need is a ride. It's not that far. Pretty please?" Her voice was raspy, as if she smoked, but younger than he expected.

"Is that how you ask for favors? You break into somebody's car?"

"The door was open," she said softly. Suddenly he felt bad, as if his negligence had caused her breach. The Torah said something to that effect— about not leaving things out to be stolen, not tempting the weak.

He turned the car on, turned on the wipers, the pale overhead light. He wanted to do the right thing. "Normally I don't turn down money in any form," she said, "but I can't walk far in these." She raised a shapely leg, covered by a knee-length zippered leather boot with skinny high heels. Not the shoes of the homeless. She wore a fur coat and a Dr. Zhivago-style fur hat, warmer than what he had on, and probably expensive. She might be a prostitute. But she sounded too well educated, not her diction but her tone, as if she were used to being catered to. "I need to get to Clark and Belmont. Do you know where it is?"

It was an intersection where runaways hung out in the summer. He wanted to ask her how old she was. Instead he said lightly, "So, what's happening at Clark and Belmont?"

"Could we get going? By now we'd have been there already!"

Allan thought of the night ahead of him. The poultice. Sex. Sleep, too, was required, since tomorrow at nine he had a lecture to give. The girl had her generation's decelerated view of time and space. Moreover, he didn't like her tone of entitlement. A hooker who thought she was doing him a favor. But since Nate's illness Allan went to Temple on Friday night, even when Thea was out of town. He said the prayer for the Jewish sick, he gave to every charity that had his mailing address, he crossed streets to buy Street Wise. Now he pulled out not toward Lake Shore Drive but onto Sheffield, a side street that would take him straight to Clark. He turned the heat on. "Are you cold?" he said. His feet were freezing.

Her name was Maya, and right away she was either baiting him or flirting with him. If flirting, it was a new twenty-first-century type, smart-alecky and challenging. She asked him if he worked for a living, if he were married, if he loved his wife, if he'd ever had a three-way.

He was uncomfortable with silence in any closed space, but this sort of conversation was worse. "I don't think," he said as politely as he could, "that it's any of your business."

He tried asking her questions, but nothing she said rang true. She was at a party, people she didn't know too well. It got rowdy, she took a walk. When she tried to get back in, she was locked out. No purse, keys, phone. Who walks around these days without a phone? Even her name seemed made up. Maya what? He wanted to ask if her mother knew where she was but it seemed rude. Not that rudeness was out of bounds. "Why would they do that to you?" he said, a bit sternly.

"Why does anyone do anything?" She reached into the back seat and hauled his Whole Foods bag onto her lap. "I love their stuff. I feel healthy, just looking at it." Good Lord. Anger and fear, never far from his mind these days, were here again. He regretted how slowly he had to drive in order not to skid, how long it would be before he could let her off. "Put your seatbelt on," he said. She took out a taro root. Sniffed knowingly.

"Good stuff?" she said.

"Put that back! Put it down!"

"Okay. Okay!"

He would have reached over and ripped the bag out of her hands if he could have done it and kept the car on the road. He felt she was contaminating it. He stopped the car and waited until she obeyed. "Do you want to go to the police?" he said, goading her. He was starting to dislike the girl. "To make a complaint? I can drop you off."

She shrugged. "They're not that bad. When my asshole ex-boyfriend splits I'll get back in. Now all I want is to crash in my own little apartment. I hope my roommate's there."

"Is it likely?"

"She's a bookworm. Studies like crazy."

"So, you're in college?" One thing seemed true, at least. "Are you?"

She laughed. "How old do you think I am?"

"Somewhere between fifteen and forty."

"I'll tell you one thing—I'm not jail bait." She took a lipstick out of her pocket and applied it without looking in the mirror. She still hadn't put on her seatbelt. She reached into her own pocket and pulled out a joint, lit up, offered him.

"No, thanks."

"You don't do weed?"

"No."

She laughed. "Better safe than sorry?"

He felt, if possible, even more uncomfortable. She had his number, or so it seemed. His parents were strict but he'd seen no reason to fight them. He'd lived through The Sixties without growing his hair long and received the grace of a high draft number. He hadn't even smoked weed until Thea introduced it. He still preferred alcohol.

He stopped where she directed, in front of an apartment on Clark and Barry, a block south of Belmont. With a last puff, she stubbed out the joint in his ashtray, the first cigarette that to his knowledge had ever been put there. "Thanks. Really," she said. "You're a good guy." She started to open the door, then closed and locked it. "Shit," she said. "Shit, shit, shit."

He closed his eyes while she explained. Her roommate was scared of the dark. She even slept with the light on. No one could possibly be home. "You can go check," she said. He handed her his cell and she made a stab at dialing, then shook her head. "No juice." It was true. "This isn't my night," she went on, with obviously feigned disappointment. "Or yours either, I guess. Will you take me home with you? I'll sleep wherever you put me. I don't snore. I don't want your silverware."

He said roughly, "I'll take you to a hotel. You can call your friend in the morning. I'll even pay for it."

"You're such a good person," she said. "Do you know that?" She reclined the seatback as if the car were home to her now, then just as he got it moving, she opened her coat. She had nothing on, on top. "Do you like me?" Involuntarily, his foot hit the brake. He was safe in his belt but her head struck the windshield. It must have hurt, though she continued to smile. Her breasts were small and round, with coin-sized pubescent areolae.

"Not to worry," she said.

He stared out the window. Not because he was put off but because he wasn't. While kids were going to India and blowing their brains out on pot and having them blown out in Vietnam, he'd gone to college and graduate school and had married a girl from Sholom Singles at the level of prettiness (decent) and intelligence (fairly high) he considered his due, not someone so beautiful and brilliant she would get tired of him. Unfortunately, the girl, Barbara, got tired of him anyway, and it hurt as much as if she'd been stunning. In the three years between Barbara and Thea, he found himself in surprising demand but still he could count the women he'd slept with on the fingers of one hand. And here was possible number six, acting like she came right out of 1968. He felt himself stirring. Then, almost simultaneously, he called to mind what the surgeon had told them before he removed the partially dead remains of Nathan's tumor. It was a tricky operation. There was a chance Nate would be impotent. "So be careful," Allan had said, almost shrilly. "Please!" he said now to Maya, the utterance shamefully ambiguous. His cheeks felt hot.

She had closed her coat. She was looking at him again like she had his number, and a phrase came to his mind from a long ago class in Eastern religion: Piercing the veil of Maya. Is that what she was offering? Maya meant illusion. People wandered aimlessly, dizzily in Maya. "What's your real name?" he said sternly.

She laughed. "What are you talking about?"

He wanted badly to eject this woman from his car and his life. Instead, not like a good person but like a person frightened by superstition, he drove to the nearest decent hotel, a place his parents had once stayed when he lived in the city. He didn't speak, he was in command, and Maya followed him obediently up to the desk.

He was taking out his credit card when he became aware of how he must look to the desk clerk or anyone else in the lobby. A middle-aged man in soggy loafers, a girl in a floor-length fur. He wasn't surprised when the clerk told him in a severely neutral voice that there were no vacancies. And though he was innocent, though there was absolutely no legitimate reason for shame, he scuttled back to the car, his ears flaming. Glad only that he hadn't tried to explain the whole bizarre situation to the desk clerk, not that he was ever going in there again.

The block in residential Evanston was dead asleep when they turned up to the driveway, but their house was lit up as for a party. Dylan in his pajamas was dancing in the foyer, hopping around with excitement that had no other outlet. "We called the police!" he said delightedly. "We called a hospital too. Mom is so worried!"

Thea came in right behind him on quick feet that stopped dead when she saw Maya. She had been about to yell or say something murderous, he was sure. Instead she smiled politely at the girl, ironically in his direction.

"How's Nate?" he said.

Thea raised her eyebrows. "Aren't you going to introduce us?"

Nervously he did so. Dylan hopped from one foot to the other, grinning nonstop at the newcomer. Maya smiled back. "You're a sweet little guy. What sounds do you listen to?"

Dylan hid behind his mother, but he kept peeking out at Maya while Allan tried to explain the situation. "I was thinking she could sleep downstairs? In the rec room? Just tonight?"

"I'll take care of it," Thea said. She put her hands on her hips, then folded them across her chest. "We kept calling. You didn't answer."

"It died. I know. I'll get a car charger. I've been meaning to."

Thea sent Dylan to bed, then took their guest down to make up the fold-out couch. And now Allan was alone in the kitchen with the blender and his Whole Foods bag. Instead of peeling, he washed the roots, then the ginger. He cut them in pieces, put them in the machine. Should he add water? He added a little water. He pressed Puree.

Thea came running. "Are you trying to wake everyone up? What's wrong with you?"

He explained. He was always explaining; that's what he did, what his life, these days, amounted to. She stared in angry amazement. He unfolded a thin kitchen towel and patted the paste onto it, a thin layer to cover Nate's stomach and chest. "How do you like my little mud pie?" he said apologetically.

"Do not go in there. Do not make him anxious."

He explained himself once again.

"I married my teacher," she said, "because I like maturity. Please don't turn adolescent on me."

"What do you mean?"

Her voice shook, which was unusual for her. "Picking up that girl, among other things. And smoking pot with her?" He looked at her, and she said, "Do you think I can't smell it? You hate pot."

"I didn't smoke," he said, feeling like a liar. "Just her." He knew he sounded like a liar or like a twelve-year-old. Both, probably. "Who says I hate pot?"

"It doesn't matter."

He looked at his wife, who was acting now as if she knew more than he. The world knew more than he. It was an occasion he had to rise to, and he did his best. He put his arms around her, kissed her cheek, and she let him. She too was trying. "Go to bed. I'll be there in a little while. You look pretty," he added.

When he heard the door close he tiptoed into Nate's room with the poultice. The boy lay asleep on his back, only half covered by his sheet, breathing deeply, evenly, beautifully. Trying not to wake him, Allan lifted the hem of the extra-large Sex Pistols tee-shirt Nate wore to bed. His stomach looked fairly flat. But prone, Allan's own stomach looked fairly flat. He patted the poultice into place.

Nate stirred, then was wide awake. He tried to sit up. Allan took his arm to keep him still. "It's just for half an hour," he said. "Does it feel hot?"

"It feels cold," Nate said.

He clearly didn't like it, but he bore it, Allan felt him bearing it. Over the past year, a part of Nate had become unusually tolerant. Wise, almost, as if he'd skipped adolescence and gone straight into adulthood. Or sainthood? Cancer had some magical effects, though Allan was reluctant to be grateful to it in any way. "I'll be back in thirty minutes to take it off. Go to sleep." He kissed the side of Nate's face, thinking for once beyond illness of the women in his house. He should be sleepy, but he wasn't yet. The house was charged with sex. Sex, the answer to death. He sat straight up on the edge of Nathan's bed, aroused in a way that he hadn't been for a year and maybe more, since the early days with Thea. There were two women who wanted him. It was funny.

He was about to leave, to deliver himself over to the hallway and the pleasure of temptation to resist, but Nate didn't seem to want him to.

"Where were you, Dad?"

Allan explained, and didn't mind explaining. Nate wanted to know about the girl, Maya, in the basement. "You'll see her in the morning," Allan said. "You might like her. Your brother did." He took his son's hand and kissed the palm. It curled over his mouth.

"Dylan? Wow. Really?"

Nate tried to sit up; Allan held the damp poultice in place. Nate fiddled with the edge of the towel. "It itches."

"So does everything," he replied, absurdly. He stood up, about to pull the quilt over his patient son, when he saw under the stretchy cotton of his PJs, below the edge of the poultice, that the boy had an erection. It seemed vulnerable and intrepid. It had heft.

"Dad," said Nathan, "we thought you were dead."

"A nasty rumor," he said. "I'm alive. Well, more or less."

Nathan giggled, as if Allan had made a funny joke. Allan settled the quilt upon him and backed out of the room as one does from the chambers of royalty, from forces beyond one's control.

everything, clearly
Alexander Yates

everything, clearly

My wife can see again. It used to be she couldn't. About six years ago she got this disease, this disease called Wolfson's. People who get this disease go blind. They also become assholes. Like, chemically. They quit talking, except for cussing, and they start biting and scratching and punching. It's no picnic. Dr. Novak says hers is one of the worst cases he's ever seen. He was reluctant, at first, to even sign her up for the surgical trial—called it a waste of a small fortune. He can hardly believe now that it's actually worked. My wife, still wonky from anesthesia, sits up in bed and tells him how many fingers he's holding up. She reads a newspaper headline from across the room. I wait until she conks out again, and then I rush home. She needs her rest. And I need to clean. Because she can see again.

First thing I do is take Katherine's picture out of the frame on our bed-stand. My fingers shake so bad I almost break the little twisty-knobs on the back as I open it. I shove the 5x7 into my pocket. There's another in the living room, blown up to fit the frame my wedding photo used to be in. And one in the bathroom—a sexy shot from last summer. Katherine holds a threadbare hotel sheet over her naked body, haloed by brittle blonde curls. We'd just done it, and she's all sleepy and smiley. The photo hangs right above the toilet, and guests say leaving it there is the most low-down thing I could do. But that's way off. In six years there were much lower-down things I could've done. And I never did. And I'm proud of that.

I fold all the pictures into tight little squares, take the originals out of the closet and refill the frames. My wife on a narrow dock at Skaneateles Lake, rehearsing for our wedding. My wife chasing me with a fistful of cake and frosting. The two of us grinning like idiots, surrounded by friends at the outdoor ceremony. Friends who've all moved south now, on account of this economy. Friends who couldn't stand to watch their neighbors get foreclosed on. Friends who are either single, or have spouses who can see.

I comb the apartment with a dustbin, trashing Katherine's more conspicuous gifts. She's my boss; a divorcee who calls herself a widow, and I love her. I mean I'm *in* love with her. Thinking about her when she's far away—which is almost always—getting fluttery when we talk on the phone, the whole deal. She's in love with me, too. She's been begging me, for years, to move in with her. She says she needs more of me than she gets. I try to explain that there's no more of me than she's already got. There's only less.

She's not convinced.

Anna—my wife—is awake when I get back to the hospital. She's reading *People Magazine* aloud to her roommate, a man still blind and raging after his fourth trial surgery. Anna notices me standing in the doorway and blinks a bunch, like her eyelashes could move—or fix—me. "Are you really that old?" she says, her fat face pinching a smile.

"Yeah," I say. "Let's just keep *you* away from mirrors."

Anna gets this how-could-I-have-forgotten look and she rushes into the bathroom across the hall. This startles me, because she's not supposed to be able to rush anywhere. Her leather restraints have been left unbuckled. I shoot Dr. Novak a look and he shoots me back a proud thumbs-up. I ask what the hell he's thinking. She could hurt somebody.

"She wouldn't hurt a fly," he says.

"She has hurt flies," I say. "She's hurt rabbits and squirrels and people."

Dr. Novak laughs like a new dad who loves too much to scold. "Not anymore," he says. "I'd describe this success as wild. It's not just her eyes! *All* her symptoms seem to be gone." He makes a *poof* motion with his fingers, and then he says "Poof. No more Wolfson's!"

"Wait . . . " I totter, and then sit on a chair by Anna's empty cot. This is unexpected. I'm having trouble forming sentences, or even sentence-like structures in my head. "Does that mean she'll be . . . "

"See for yourself!" He slaps my back and strolls out of the room, heroically.

I sit there with Anna's roommate, who's chewing his lips and telling me he fucked my mother, which does not faze me. Anna's said worse, in her day. She's done worse. But now she returns looking deflated, and I suddenly feel awful about that mirror crack. It's not her fault she's so damn fat. It's Wolfson's fault; it's *my* fault—I let her let herself go. You don't have to see to use a stationary bike, or an elliptical, and we have both. I bought them with the raise I know I got for sleeping with Katherine. My mind skips here like a record player. Sleeping with Katherine . . . oh God.

Anna takes a big, brave breath. "It's all right," she says. "Everything is fixable." If her luck today is any indication, she's probably right.

Disoriented, almost woozy, I fill out discharge paperwork and lead us through the auxiliary lot. Anna grabs my hand, brings it to her mouth and I flinch. But she doesn't bite it, she kisses it. From the scars on my palm to the scars on my fingertips. Then she holds my hand and stares at it. "Your ring," she says. "You've got a new ring on."

"Oh . . . " I panic. She's right, of course—what an idiot to have swapped out the pictures and forgotten this. I'm wearing Katherine's platinum ring. It's the same size as the ten-karat yellow band I was married in, and when Anna was blind she never felt the difference. Katherine kept the original—wears it around her neck on a magnetic chain like a trophy. I consider telling Anna the truth, only briefly. I consider lesser fibs. I go with playing dumb. "No," I say, "same as always."

"It is?" she cocks her head. "But your ring used to be yellow."

"This is yellow," I say.

Anna takes my hand and turns it in the light. She blinks hard and knuckles her eyes. "It is?"

"Yep." I point at a parked pickup and ask her what color it is. She says green and I say no, it's dark blue, even though it's very, very green. "I'm sure it'll pass," I say, kind of floored by my own incredible pettiness. And the funny thing is, if she were still sick I wouldn't even notice something like this. This would be me on a good day.

"I don't care if it doesn't pass," Anna says. "I'm counting blessings."

"It's a whole new you," I say.

"Not new," she says. "This is the old me. Again."

The old Anna. I hardly remember her. We only knew each other for half a year, or so. We met at a birdwatchers gathering. I took her on a totally non-ironic picnic and we had made out like sophomores. We got married, and she got sick.

The new, old Anna kisses me. But I can't help it. I flinch.

We leave the hospital and get on 81 North, up to our house in Mattydale. On the way we pass the work site I've been at for the last few years—the only place anybody can get a job these days. It doesn't look like much . . . or I guess, more accurately, it doesn't look like anything. Not anything I've ever seen before. It's all scaffolding and fiberglass and these Disney-style artificial mountains. Anna sees it and knuckles her eyes again.

"What. On earth. Did they do to the mall?"

"It's not the mall anymore," I say. "It's an attraction." Two Michaels from St. Petersburg are behind it all, though one is from the less impressive city in Florida, and the other is technically named Mikhail. But still, they call themselves the Michaels. Their idea is to put up a big glass dome over some existing buildings, then heat the dome from the inside. Instant summertime destination. Especially during the wintertime. Ours is one of two; they're building the other one in Russia. It sounds crazy to me, too. But in an economy like this, you never look a gift horse in the mouth. You just take the gift horse and you smile and you say thank you for this horse, Mister. Or Madam.

Hiring local is part of the Michaels' mission statement, which is how I lucked into this job. I'm a glass man. My father was a glass man. And the dome they intend to build is made out of: you guessed it. It was Katherine who hired me, *brought me on board*, as executives like her say, which is accurate, because people who aren't brought on board usually sink. We met at a recruitment booth in the food court and really hit it off at the welcome mixer in Saratoga. She brought me to the track and we bet all our spending cash on a Buckskin Bay named Win-Win, who lost. That kind of delighted us.

Some months later Katherine was permanently transferred to the Russia office. Determined not to mope, we focused on the upside. Katherine got career advancement. I got to focus on Anna wholeheartedly. And Anna got me, focusing on her, wholeheartedly. Win-win. Katherine finds excuses to come back as often as she can, and she always makes sure I'm invited to the two-week technical conference held in St. Petersburg each summer. While I'm there I run seminars for Russian glass men more experienced and intelligent than I. Russian glass men who nonetheless nod thoughtfully at what I have to say because they, too, have been through lean times and they, too, know not to look in gift-horse mouths. When I'm done giving seminars I go back to Katherine's apartment. We stay there together, not like lovers, but like spouses. Spouses who get along exceptionally well.

When we get home, Anna spends near an hour rediscovering our house. She stands on furniture to see what it looks like from up high. She lies down on the carpet to see what it looks like from down low. She touches things, fingering big holes in the drywall with a puzzled expression. One is shaped vaguely like a lamp and another vaguely like a stool, from when she had a fit and threw the lamp, and the stool. I don't even notice the holes, anymore. Or the broken banister or the crack in the back door that doubles our heating bill, or the scar that runs subtly up my cheek. Anna discovers that, too, and touches it. "I'm awful," she says, tearing up. "I'm garbage."

Looking at her, I feel my stomach rusting. I rub her tears away with my thumb. "Wolfson's is garbage," I say. "You are precious, and you are kind." That's how I remember her, at least. And if the last few hours are any indication, that's how she is again. "You should rest," I say, shakily. "I need to check in with the office."

Out in the front yard, I call Katherine on my cell. "Honey . . . it worked . . ." is all I can manage.

"Sweetheart!" Katherine is happy to hear from me. She is always happy to hear from me. "You mean, she can see?"

"She can see."

"So, shapes? Colors?"

"No," I say. "Everything. Everything, clearly. And it's not only that, she's . . ." what is she? "Herself again." Holding it together at this point gets so hard that I just quit trying. "Thank you," I sob. "Thank you so, so much."

"You don't have to thank me," Katherine says, even though she knows I do. She paid for the surgical trial—Anna and I could never have afforded it. "This is wonderful. For her, and for you, and for us. Everybody wins." She laughs. "Have you two had a chance to talk yet?"

By "talk," Katherine means: have I left her? Because she's leavable now. "No," I say, "I'm thinking . . . maybe not yet?" I pause, and an idea hits me. It feels so right that I turn it into words without really thinking. "I'm taking her with me to St. Petersburg next week."

"Excuse me?" she says.

"I think it'd be good," I say. "I think it'd be great for her to come along."

Katherine doesn't take this well and says the word "fuck" a lot. I don't blame her because she's been under so much pressure lately, afraid the Michaels will discover she's skimming off the top. It's not just for Anna and me; she also does it to buy herself cars and condos and rugs. "Does Anna even want to go? Has she even asked you?"

"She hasn't," I say. "I want to take her."

"Tom, Tom, Tom, *Tom*. That's *not* how this was supposed to go," she says.

"Don't panic," I say. "Nothing has changed. Or, better, nothing has changed for the worse. I'm still going to leave her. But I just can't do it right after she's gotten better. Please, let me do this at my pace. Let me take Anna to St. Petersburg and show her a good time. She deserves it."

"Fine."

Katherine sounds like she's trying not to sound reticent. "You do what you need to do. She can have you for another few days, as long as I get you forever."

"You do," I say. "You get me forever. I love you."

"I love you, too," she says.

I hang up with Katherine and take a few minutes to shake the goofy look I get whenever I hear her voice. Then I go back inside and ask Anna what she thinks about a trip to Russia. She squeals and hugs me hard and this time I don't flinch, or wince, or anything.

The days leading up to our trip are super. Anna and I bird watch, like we used to, on the lakeshore. We stargaze off our roof. We sit alone in the IMAX movie theater and see high-definition films about coral reefs and desert lizards. Anna's in a better mood than I've ever seen her in. She's in a better mood than I used to think it possible for a person to be in. She's kind to me, and better yet she's kind to herself. She forgives herself for what she did and felt when she had Wolfson's. She promises never to do or feel those things again. We shop. We pack. We hold hands and even French a little. By the time our departure date rolls around, I'm downright happy she's coming. But part of me is anxiously aware that there's still unpleasant shit to be handed out. There's still Anna's newly fixed heart to be broken again. It's probably that part of me that acts up, all nasty, when, in the airplane, Anna can't quite fit into her economy-class seat. I laugh loud enough for some of the other passengers to turn around and stare. Anna looks down at her lap, hurt.

"I'm sorry," I say. "That's kind of like a nervous reflex. You don't deserve that."

"I used to," she says, running her fingers over my scarred hands. "I would have been mean to me, too." She turns my ring under her thumb, eyeing it now and again. The plane takes off. Anna gazes out the window and plays a game where she says what the clouds look like. They all look like something to her. She sees a mother dog nursing puppies. She sees the Last Supper with just two apostles. She sees my face, big and noble, like it's been carved into the side of Rushmore.

The food arrives, and we eat. Halfway through the meal Anna turns to me. "Sweetheart," she says, all calm, "I don't want to worry you. But I have a problem."

I quit buttering my hard, round roll.

"I can't open my eyes," she says. "I blinked. Or, I started to blink, and now I just can't get them open again."

Anna's eyes are wide open.

"It's all right," she assures me. "Dr. Novak said I might have some light muscle spasms. Will you see if you can open them for me?"

I put down my knife and take Anna's head in my hands. With two fingers I gently close her eyelids. I push on them. "You feel that?"

"Yes, I do." She sounds relieved. "Your hand is on the back of my head."

I push a little harder and open her lids. Her irises roll about like big fish in tiny tanks. I wait and she says nothing. A flight attendant passes and I tap him lightly on the elbow. I ask if there's a doctor on the flight.

"I can't open my eyes," Anna explains, still all peaceful.

The attendant looks her in the face. He scrutinizes her tray table for empty miniature bottles. For a second I think of what I could mouth to him that would keep Anna from knowing. But it's too long a story for gestures or lip-reading, and it's better that she hear it from me, anyway. "My wife's gone blind," I say. I don't look at her, but I hear her breathing change. "We need to see a doctor, right away."

"Your wife is blind?" the attendant asks.

"She's *gone* blind."

Anna's fingernails sink into my forearm. The attendant cocks his head one way, then the other. As if to ask how this problem is his problem.

"It happened . . . recently?"

Anna dissolves into sputtering, weepy panic, and for a moment I feel like I could grab this kid by his mussed hair and beat his head on the drink trolley. But I'm not that kind of a person, and to be fair, Anna's situation is unusual.

"My wife has Wolfson's," I say. "She had surgery a week ago that made her better, but she isn't better any more." I have to speak up to be heard over her—she's started banging her face against the window now. People two and three rows in front of us look back with terrified expressions. A college boy gets halfway out of his seat, ready to die subduing trouble. "Just now, two minutes ago, she went blind again," I say. "I don't know if it's the altitude or the pressure or what. But we need to see a doctor. It could be there's something we can do. It could be there's something we *need* to do. Like, now."

The flight attendant goes to check with the captain, who pours his rich, authoritative voice into the loudspeaker to ask if there's a doctor on board.

Meanwhile, I do what I can to calm Anna down—holding her close, giving her space, rubbing her arms, pinning her hands to her thighs. She's going on and on about how she can't be this way again. "Fuck the fucking world," she hollers. The college boy stands, watching us.

I'm not encouraged when a freckled pediatrician approaches, squats down on her haunches in the aisle, and asks what seems to be the trouble. I explain about Wolfson's. She nods like she gets it, but she obviously doesn't get it because she reaches over and tries to take Anna's pulse. Anna bites the pediatrician, causing her to shriek awfully. She takes about a half-inch of skin off at the knuckle. This puts the other passengers in a flat panic. The college boy steps towards us and I unbuckle, ready to take and give.

But then the captain comes on the loudspeaker again, dripping his thick voice over us, calming us all down. "Many of you may have noticed a disturbance in our economy cabin. Do not be alarmed. One of our passengers is ill—she's lost her eyesight, just now, which I'm sure has to be pretty scary. Let's all have some empathy. Let's all relax. Please return to your seats. For anybody inclined to pray, please put a word in for . . . " he reads the wrong name off the manifest. Angela something. "I know I will."

The college kid looks repentant and sits down. The flight attendant helps the pediatrician bandage her hand. I snatch Anna's phone from her pocket— she tries to claw me, but I'm practiced at this—and turn it back on so I can call Dr. Novak. He answers after two rings and sounds unsurprised. He tells me that all I can do is wait. He says to expect the worst, because pleasant surprises are better than unpleasant ones. Anna wails like she's been stabbed. She wails like all our foreclosed neighbors combined. She wails like someone who lost everything, got it back, and lost it again.

Katherine picks us up at the airport, recklessly wearing my old wedding ring around her neck. The expression on my face, and the fact that I'm leading Anna by the wrist, says it all. Her assistant drives us to a nearby hospital. Anna is catatonic in the back seat, her arms locked around my torso, occasionally muttering words like "asshole" and "rotten." Katherine sits up front, one hand reaching back to hold mine. She does her best to hide the sound of her own crying, because this is so not the trip she's been looking forward to for months. I try to cheer her up by aping Anna's cross-eyed, lippy expression. But that just makes her sob harder.

The hospital visit is useless, something to which I've become accustomed. The Russian specialists just repeat Dr. Novak's advice, to "wait and see," in slightly more comic accents. Then we get back in the van and go to the hotel—a ritzy place right on Nevsky Prospekt. Katherine checks us in with her halting Russian. She explains to the staff about Anna and, like everybody else, they nod as though they get it. Katherine tells me she'll wait at the bar while we get settled in, and I warn her that it might take a while. It does take a while. Anna crawls all around the suite to figure out "where the goddamn booby-traps are." She knocks a room-service tray out of a waiter's hands and throws an ashtray at a window, which, luckily or unluckily, is open. She asks how much does this fucking dump cost, anyway? I tell her half of what it really costs and she goes green and says it's a fucking fortune. She wants to talk fortunes—how about the price tag on her week or so of eyesight? With that much of Katherine's money we could have bought houses. Yeah. Plural.

When Anna settles down, I unpack. I lay her things out in the dresser the same way they're laid out at home so she'll be able to find her Valium and her bottled water and her underwear without too much searching. Then I help her change into her jammies and turn down her bed. I stay with her, dodging the occasional swipe, until she falls asleep.

Hours later Katherine is still waiting for me in the bar with her makeup smeared and a cold absinthe fuming under her chin. "You can't do this," she says.

"You're right," I say, joining her. "Now would be the worst time to tell her."

"No, I mean you're not *equipped*. You can't handle this." She looks at me like she doesn't know me, which is hurtful, because I think she's the only person who does. "It's made you hate her."

"Hate her? I hate Anna, now?" I say.

"I'm not attacking you, Tom."

"No, no, this is good to know. You think I gave up my life because I hate her?"

She puts her hand on my wrist. I try to pull away, but she won't have it; she holds my wrist down the way I sometimes hold Anna down. "I think you hate her because you gave up your life. You don't have to. There are places," she says. "Professionals who specialize in long term—"

"Not a chance," I say. Because I've been to those places. They're nightmares. The nurses have sticks. Every room is a bathroom.

"They're not all terrible," Katherine says. "In fact, I know about one here—"

I wrestle myself out of her grip and put on an expression that I think will end the discussion. "No," I say. "Not ever. That's what I'd do if I really hated her. And I don't."

The next morning, Katherine comes by and takes us both out on the standard tour, because what the hell else are we going to do, mope? Lie in bed and cry all day? Hell, no. Not me, and not Anna, even though she wants to. Towing her by the wrist we stroll along the Prospekt and up the Griboedova canal. We stand in the shadow of an onion-domed cathedral. We visit the Mars Field and the Neva River. We eat ice cream in the Summer Gardens and give each guard some rubles so they'll let us sit on the grass.

"Motherfuckers," Anna says, her face vibrating slightly. "Liars. Are you going to drag me here and not tell me what this bullshit looks like?"

Katherine lights up, a little. "There's lots of big trees," she says. "And that breeze you're feeling, that's coming off the river. The Neva River. We can see it from here, and the bridges."

"And there's a juggler behind us," I say. "There's a bear cub, on a leash."

Anna snorts. "Pah. There's no fucking bear. There's no fucking juggler. We're not even outside." She rips up a handful of grass. "This is cheap fucking carpet."

Katherine actually tries to argue the point, but it's a waste of breath. We finish our ice cream, quietly. A Beatles song starts playing from inside Katherine's purse. *Help! I need somebody. Help! Not just anybody;* her assistant's ring-tone. She answers, happy to have an excuse to get up and walk a few paces away. Anna gropes about while Katherine talks. She finds Katherine's purse in the grass and dunks her hands inside. She pulls out a ledger and opens it, working her thumbs into the inky Cyrillic lettering. I recognize the ledger. It's the real one, the one that Katherine keeps on her always because the Michaels know someone is stealing, and they regularly have the offices searched for evidence. Katherine finishes her call, turns back to us and freezes. I give her a *calm down* motion with my hand.

"Put that book down," Katherine snaps.

Bad idea. Anna rips the ledger at the binding, tearing it in two. "Which one, bitch?" There's no joy in her face as she says this. In fact, it's skewed up like she's trying to have a bowel movement and can't. That's the thing about Wolfson's. The person you used to be is still in there, somewhere. They're always fighting it, and losing.

Katherine goes for the torn ledger and gets an elbow to the face. I snap my fingers by Anna's ear, to distract her, and whip the pages out of her hands. "Be nicer to her," I say. "Katherine has given us a lot of help."

"You're fucking liars," Anna says. "You all haven't helped me with shit."

Katherine takes the torn ledger from me and pinches her nose so blood won't get on her work blouse. *We can't do this*, she mouths. *We have to tell her.*

You do it, and I'll leave you, I mouth back.

Katherine isn't intimidated—she never is. *I dare you*, she mouths. *Just see what I do.* She gives me this long, significant look.

"Assholes," Anna says, kind of sing-songy. "I can hear you whispering."

She falls asleep after her dinner, and that gives Katherine and I our first real privacy. Katherine takes me to an airy flat on Kazanskaya—her newest—and overcooks some pasta. We eat and have awkward sex. It's the kind of sex we usually only have on nights before I'm supposed to fly back home, when we both want it, both enjoy it, but are both still really sad after it's done. We shower together and wrap ourselves in cotton robes. Katherine's assistant calls again—*When I was younger, so much younger than today*—and whatever he says makes her real happy. She plops down on the couch and starts mending her secret ledger with duct tape. I join her, stroke her legs, and peek at the densely scrawled pages. She's made out like a bandit this week.

"You know, I really wish you wouldn't do that," I say.

"Yeah? Well, there's plenty I wish you wouldn't do. And some stuff I wish you'd do, that you don't."

"I'm not kidding," I say. "They're not going to fool around if they find out. Mikhail especially. You'll be lucky if all they do is call the police."

"Don't worry. There's no evidence in here that I ever gave you a dime. You'd be in the clear."

I quit touching her legs. How can she even say that? "Sorry," she says, flatly. "But hey, I'm still mad. About what you said in the park. About leaving me."

"I just wanted to make a point," I say. "I'd never really do it."

Katherine marks her spot in the ledger and closes it. She looks at me like she's making a decision in her head, or weighing one she's already made.

"Wouldn't you?" she says. "Even if you had to choose between us?"

"Katherine, that's silly. There's no choice. You guys are not . . . " I search for the word, "alternatives. You're the one I love. She's the one I take care of, and it's only because she can't survive without me. If she gets better, I'll leave her in a second, but until—"

"Wrong," Katherine says. "Anna got better. And you had a lot of seconds. And you didn't do it."

"Honey, I can't. I can't be the guy who leaves his wife on the day she gets her life back. And now that she's sick again, how can I abandon her?"

"God, you don't even see it, do you?" She shifts her legs so they're no longer in my lap. "You've *already* abandoned her. You loathe her. You should have seen yourself when we came back from the airport, cool as a cucumber, making fun of her. All while her world was ending."

That's just too much. I get up off the couch, drop my robe and start dressing. Katherine stands, also. "It's not a knock on you, Tom. You're a good person. But what you're doing to Anna is not good. You can't keep her around just because you don't want to see yourself leaving her." Dressed, I grab my coat and go for the door.

"It's not about you. She'd be better off with professionals, people who get paid and know what they're doing."

I go out the door, and onto the landing. While the flat is spacious, the landing is narrow and dark. Katherine, still in her robe, follows me. "You won't even get there in time," she says.

I stop, already gripping the handrail above the stairs. "In time for what?" I say.

She bites her lower lip. She tugs the cottony collar of her robe, nervously.

"You're going to thank me," she says. "You're going to give it some time, and you're going to thank me."

"What did you do?"

"My assistant's at the hotel now. He's brought some doctors from the care center I tried to tell you about. They'll explain the situation to Anna, and evaluate her. They won't do anything without—"

My reaction startles Katherine more than it should. I charge back across the landing, push past her and go into the flat. I grab her phone off the table and redial her assistant. I ask him where he is and he says he's in the lobby. He says he really admires the choice I've made. He says he knows it couldn't have been easy.

"You keep away from my room," I say.

"I'm sorry?" he says.

"Motherfucker," I say, "If you, or any doctors, go into my hotel room, I'll kill you. I'll come into the conference tomorrow and I'll find you and I'll hit you on the head until you die."

The assistant doesn't say anything, but he doesn't hang up, either. I imagine him shocked and frightened on the other end. He's known me for a few years, now, and I've always gone out of my way to be friendly.

Katherine comes to the doorway, looking solid. Looking ready for a fight.

"You don't scare me," she says.

"I'd never want to," I say, and it's true. "But, please," I hand over the phone, "tell him to go home. He can't be the one to do it. He can't do it."

I start to cry a little, but Katherine doesn't soften. Her mind is set. There will be zero negotiating.

"I'll do it," I finally say. "It has to be me, though. I have to tell her first. I'll do it tonight. I promise."

"I'm not giving this up," Katherine says. "You do it tonight, or I do it tomorrow. She deserves to know the truth. She deserves caretakers who can handle her."

"I'll do it tonight. I will."

Katherine stares at me for nearly a full minute. Then she tells her assistant to go home. She says she's sure. She says she's fine, and that I didn't mean anything when I threatened him. She hangs up, and holds me to stop my crying. And that's what finally breaks her—it gets her going, too.

We spend another few hours together. I watch Katherine after she falls asleep, touching her back with my fingertips. Then, as quietly as I can, I slip out of bed. I tear a page out of her mended ledger, and write this note on it: "Anna and I are flying out early. I'm keeping the rest of this book. If you bother us, if you say anything to her, I swear to Christ that I'll give this to Mikhail." I debate finishing with "I love you," or "I'll always love you," or "I'm sorry," or something to that effect. They're all true, but somehow an ending like that feels crueler.

I tuck the ledger under my arm and tiptoe out of the airy flat. I take the long route back to the hotel, stop by the Neva River and toss the ledger into the water. Of course I'd never do anything to hurt Katherine, I think to myself. But you just did, I also think. It all feels worse than I thought it could, which is impressive. But life isn't always win-win. There has to be a loser. And while I'm alive, it won't be Anna.

She's in the bathroom when I return to the hotel. She's not like the blind people you read about—or know, if you know blind people, which I didn't, before she became one. She never got that crazy ninja hearing. She spills drinking water over her front and returns to bed without noticing I'm back. Hours later she wakes to look for me. She feels her way across the room, grabs the foot of my bed and runs her hands along it. I silently move my legs. Anna searches and I avoid her, slipping out of bed and doing the limbo to the middle of the room. She calls out my name and I don't answer. She panics. But she's still alive. She's still breathing, I tell myself. Sure, she's sad and scared, but when isn't she? How much worse could an institution really be? I could still go back and trash that note. I could live in the airy flat with the woman I love and am loved by. We could visit Anna on the weekends and take her on supervised, non-ironic picnics. Everything is fixable.

Anna stops breathing. She falls on her butt and has a little panic attack, clawing at her throat. I don't move. She makes a yawning noise. She makes a toilet-flushing noise. She sobs. A gulp of air goes down. She calms a little. She gropes about, looks for her bed, and can't find it. She gets into mine instead and curls up against the wall.

I stand there for minutes without making a sound. I wait for her to drift off, or at least to stop crying. When she does I go to the front door and open it. I close it again, hard. The floor and walls vibrate. Anna sits up in bed and turns her head to the sound. As far as she knows, I've come back.

biographical notes
Editor, Assistant Editors, and Authors

biographical notes

Editor

Kristen J. Tsetsi, author of the novel, *Homefront*, and the fiction collection, *Carol's Aquarium*, is a 2006 Pushcart Prize nominee and a former newspaper reporter, former English professor and creative writing instructor, and former cab driver. She is a recipient of the Storyglossia Fiction Prize and the Robert L. Carothers Distinguished Writers' Award, and her essays and articles can be found in *Women's eNews, Journal Inquirer*, and *Boston Globe*. Tsetsi received her MFA in creative writing from Minnesota State University Moorhead in 2003.

Assistant Editors

Bayard Godsave received his MFA in Creative Writing in 2001 from Minnesota State University Moorhead, where he worked as an editor on *Red Weather*, and his PhD in English from the University of Wisconsin-Milwaukee, where he was a fiction co-editor for the *Cream City Review*. He is currently an assistant professor in the department of English and Foreign Languages at Cameron University.

Bruce Pratt was nominated in 2008 for a Pushcart Prize in fiction, and his poetry collection *Boreal* is available from Antrim House Books (www. antrimhousebooks.com). His fiction, poetry, essays, and plays have appeared in more than forty literary magazines and journals in the United

States, Canada, Ireland, and Wales, and have won several awards. In addition to working with *American Fiction*, Pratt serves on the editorial board of *Hawk and Handsaw*. He also coaches the outdoor track and field team at John Bapst Memorial High School, a small private, non-sectarian college preparatory day school in Bangor, Maine, where his girls' team has won seven of the last eight state championships. A graduate of the Stonecoast MFA at The University of Southern Maine, where he teaches undergraduate creative writing, Pratt lives with his wife, Janet, in Eddington, Maine.

Authors

Sarah Blackman lives in Greenville, South Carolina, where she is the director of creative writing at the Fine Arts Center, a public arts high school, and co-fiction editor for *DIAGRAM*. Her most recent fiction has appeared or is forthcoming in *The Pinch* and *The Fairy Tale Review*, as is her fiction chapbook, *Such A Thing As America*, from Burnside Review Press.

Neil Crabtree lives and works in Miami, Florida. His short fiction has appeared at Verbsap.com, BewilderingStories.com, TuesdayShorts.com, and Denversyntax.com. His first novel, *Rooster*, is complete and at a literary agency. His short story collection, *Believable Lies*, is also complete and ready for market. A second novel, *Rooster: Not Dead Yet*, is in progress. A regular at John Dufresne's workshops, Friday Night Writers, he also attends Sleuthfest, the conference sponsored by the S. Florida Chapter of Mystery Writers of America. He writes the blog "Believable Lies" at www. believablelies.blogspot.com.

H. E. Francis, author of seven collections of stories, two novels, and numerous stories in American and foreign magazines, has won the Iowa School of Letters Award for Short Fiction, the Illinois Series Award, the G. S. Sharat Chandra Prize for Short Fiction, and many other awards. His work has been frequently anthologized, notably in the O. Henry, the Best American, and the Pushcart Prize volumes. He studied under a Fulbright grant at Pembroke College, Oxford, and was three-times Fulbright professor at the Universidad Nacional de Cuyo in Mendoza, Argentina. He has translated works by the Argentines Daniel Moyano, Antonio Di Benedetto, Juan José Hernández, and Norberto Luis Romero. He divides his time between Huntsville, Alabama, and Madrid.

Kate Gale is the managing editor of Red Hen Press, the president of the American Composers Forum Los Angeles and the editor of *The Los Angeles Review*. She is on the boards of the School of Arts and Humanities, Claremont Graduate University, A Room of Her Own Foundation, and Poetry Society of America. She is the author of five books of poetry, editor of four anthologies, and author of four librettos. As a public speaker, she travels widely, speaking on writing, publishing, and editing. She teaches in the humanities graduate program at Mt. St. Mary's in Los Angeles.

Catherine Gentile earned a Masters' degree from St. Joseph College in West Hartford, Connecticut. After a career in special education/mental health, her writing became her focus. Her short fiction has appeared in the *Briar Cliff Review*, *The Chaffin Journal*, *Kaleidoscope*, *The Ledge*, *The Long Story*, and in the anthology, *Hello and Goodbye*. She is the recipient of the 2005 Dana Award in Short Fiction. Her work achieved finalist status in the 2009 Reynolds Price Short Fiction Award and the 2007 Boston Fiction Festival. In addition to her novel, *Sunday's Orphan*, Catherine has completed a short story collection entitled *After the Chrysalis*. She writes for *Portland Trails*, a land conservation newsletter, and for *Maine in Print*, newsletter for the Maine Writers and Publishers Association. A native of Hartford, Catherine lives with her husband on a small island in Maine.

Andrew C. Gottlieb currently lives and writes in Irvine, California. His fiction and poetry have appeared in many journals, including *American Literary Review*, *Beloit Fiction Journal*, *DIAGRAM*, *Ecotone*, *ISLE*, *Provincetown Arts*, *Poets & Writers*, *Portland Review* and Terrain.org. His chapbook of poems, *Halflives*, was published in 2005 by New Michigan Press. He received his MFA from the University of Washington, his MA from Iowa State University, and most recently he's been writer-in-residence at the Kimmel Harding Nelson Center for the Arts. When he's not writing, he enjoys spending time with his wife and her two children.

Cary Groner received his MFA in fiction writing from the University of Arizona in 2009. In the past two years he has won the *Glimmer Train* fiction open, the Hackney Award in both short story and novel categories, and the annual short fiction award at the *Southern California Review*. In 2010 his stories will appear in those publications as well as the *Mississippi Review* an the *Tampa Review*. His first novel will be published by Random House in 2011.

Daniel M. Jaffe is author of the novel, *The Limits of Pleasure* (Haworth Press) and the fiction chapbook *One-Foot Lover* (Seven Kitchens Press); Jaffe is the compiler-editor of *With Signs and Wonders: An International Anthology of Jewish Fabulist Fiction* (Invisible Cities Press); and translator of Dina Rubina's Russian novel, *Here Comes the Messiah!* (Zephyr Press). He teaches creative writing in the UCLA Extension Writers' Program, and his website is http://danieljaffe.tripod.com

Christiana Louisa Langenberg was born in the Netherlands and immigrated to the United States with her Dutch father and Italian mother. Raised trilingually in rural Nebraska, she was naturalized when she was seventeen. She is the author of a bilingual collection of stories, *Half of What I Know*, the winner of the Drunken Boat Panliterary Award for Fiction, Chelsea Award for Short Fiction, and her stories have been published in *Glimmer Train*, *Dogwood*, *Pindeldyboz*, *Storyglossia So to Speak*, *Green Mountains Review*, *American Literary Review*, and others. She teaches in the English and women's studies programs at Iowa State University.

Aimee Loiselle drinks green tea while she writes and eats pizza when she's done. Her novel manuscript, *Being Good About It*, was a finalist for the 2010 Bellwether Prize sponsored by Barbara Kingsolver and shortlisted for finalist in the Faulkner-Wisdom Competition. You can hear her read "Three Women Wishing for a Boy" on *The Drum* website in the May 2010 audio issue. She's had additional stories in *Steam Ticket*, *Blueline*, *Natural Bridge*, *Square Lake*, and *Out of Line*. Loiselle teaches ABE transition-to-college to pay the bills and does yoga to quiet the mind. Grub Street and The Loft have both provided much appreciated feedback and collegiality. Learn more at www.aimeeloiselle.com.

Kristen-Paige Madonia's most recent fiction has been published or is forthcoming in *New Orelans Review*, *Sycamore Review*, *Inkwell*, and *The South Dakota Review*. She received the 2010 Tennessee Williams/New Orleans Literary Festival Prize and has been awarded writing residencies with Hedgebrook, Millay Colony for the Arts, and the Studios of Key West. She is also the recipient of the Marianne Russo Fellowship, the James I. Murashige Jr. Memorial Scholarship for Fiction, and the 2005 Literary Women Festival of Authors Fellowship. Madonia holds an MFA from California State University, Long Beach, and currently teaches creative writing in Charlottesville, Virginia, where she is at work on a novel; "Metal and Glass" is an excerpt from the project.

Loren M. McAuley is a graduate of NYU's creative writing program. She has won fiction awards from New Millenium, The Ledge, and Writers' Workshop, among others. She lives in Park Slope, Brooklyn, New York, where she writes and rescues dogs.

Helen Phillips is the recipient of a 2009 Rona Jaffe Foundation Writers' Award. She won the 2008 Italo Calvino Prize in Fabulist Fiction and the 2009 Meridian Editors' Prize. Her work has appeared in *Meridian, Salt Hill Journal, The Mississippi Review, Small Spiral Notebook, Faultline, The Brooklyn Review, The L Magazine,* and The Hotel St. George Infinitely Expanding Library of New Fabulist Fiction, among others. Her book, *And Yet They Were Happy,* excerpted here, is forthcoming from Leapfrog Press in April 2011. She received her MFA from Brooklyn College, where she now teaches undergraduate creative writing. She lives in Brooklyn with her husband, artist Adam Thompson.

Jendi Reiter's first book, *A Talent for Sadness,* was published in 2003 by Turning Point Books. Her poetry chapbook, *Swallow,* won the 2008 Flip Kelly Poetry Prize and was published in 2009 by Amsterdam Press. Her poetry chapbook, *Barbie at 50,* won the 2010 Cervena Barva Poetry Chapbook Prize and is forthcoming from Cervena Barva Press. In 2010 she received a Massachusetts Cultuial Council Artist's Grant for Poetry. Reiter's work has appeared in *Poetry, The Iowa Review, The New Criterion, Mudfish, Passages North,* and many other publications. "Two Natures" is the first chapter of her novel in progess.

Matt Riordan was born in Detroit and raised in rural Michigan. At various times and at various locations he has been employed as a commercial fisherman, bouncer, digger of crawl spaces, pickle factory dill slices packer, bait shop clerk and worm counter, paper boy, bus boy, small time political hack, short order cook, pizza delivery guy, bartender, and commercial litigator. He lives in Queens with his wife and daughters.

North Carolina native **Terry Roueche** is an award-winning fiction writer and playwright living in Rock Hill, South Carolina. His dramatic works have been produced across the United States, as well as in Canada, England, and Croatia. In addition, Roueche is a documentary film maker and an award-winning photographer. He has taught playwriting and photography at Winthrop University in Rock Hill, and he is the founder and executive director of Rock Hill's Main Street Theater. He has been a newspaper reporter and has published non-fiction articles.

Fred Setterberg's most recent book is *Under the Dragon: California's New Culture*, written with Lonny Shavelson and published by Heyday Books (www.underthedragon.com). He is also the author of *The Roads Taken: Travels Through America's Literary Landscapes*, winner of the AWP prize in creative nonfiction. His essays and stories have appeared in *The Southern Review*, *The Iowa Review*, *The Georgia Review*, and many others. He is a recipient of a NEA fellowship in creative writing, the William Faulkner-William Wisdom essay prize, and numerous journalism awards. This story is excerpted from his novel, *Lunch Bucket Paradise*, to be published by Heyday Books.

Sharon Solwitz's story collection *Blood and Milk* (Sarabande, 1996) received the 1997 Carl Sandberg award and the Midland Authors prize for adult fiction, and was a finalist for the 1997 National Jewish Book Award. Her stories have been published widely; their awards include the Pushcart, the Nelson Algren and the Katherine Ann Porter. Her novel *Bloody Mary* (Sarabande, Inc.) came out in 2003. She teaches at Purdue University in W. Lafayette, and lives in Chicago, where she and her husband, poet Barry Silesky, edit *Another Chicago Magazine*.

Gregory Williams is a retired anesthesiologist. He has published creative non-fiction and poetry in the *Journal of the American Medical Assocciation*. His fiction has appeared in *Blue Mesa Review*, *Elysian Fields Quarterly—The Baseball Review*, and is forthcoming in *Arts & Letters*. Williams is a Pushcart Prize nominee, the recipient of the 2010 Arts & Letters Prize for Fiction, and a 2010 finalist for The Pinch Literary Award in Fiction. He and his wife divide their time between Mesa and Flagstaff in Arizona.

Alexander Yates was born in Port-au-Prince, Haiti, and spent most of his life in Latin America and Southeast Asia. His first novel, *Moondogs*, will be released by Doubleday and Random House Audio in the spring of 2011. He holds an MFA from Syracuse University, where he was a Creative Writer Fellow, co-editor of *Salt Hill*, and winner of Joyce Carol Oates awards in fiction and poetry. Prior to attending graduate school, Yates worked as a traveling contractor and biography writer for the US State Department. Contact Yates at www.alexanderyates.com.